THE PIPELINE PUGILIST

by

D. Wellington Lee

Thanks for your help,

Dwara Lee

Acknowledgments

Thanks to all those who helped me on this novel during its long journey to publication. This includes my grandson Arthur Lee, my son Dennis Lee, my daughter Sandra Neis and her husband Lyle, as well as Jean Benson, Emeline Bradley, and Kathy Salloum.

A special thank you to my Writers Guild of Alberta critiquing group--these five members provided encouragement, valuable suggestions, and in addition to proof reading, kept me on track.

I also appreciate the forbearance of my Revera tablemates, David Lovett and Larry Jewell, who patiently listened to my literary problems during so many dinners.

Grandson, Brian Lee, designed the lovely cover.

Chapter 1

One last outburst before the final reckoning. On the eve of her fiftieth birthday that's all Carrie wanted. Just one more kick at the can. Why was it so difficult?

Alone in the golf club's washroom, she glanced in the mirror. Her eyes snapped closed after an initial assessment, but the image remained: the multiple crow's feet at the edges of her eyes, the creases between her eyebrows and the tiny fissures on her upper lip—like animal tracks in the snow. She remembered being told that she was a glorious sexual companion—eager to give, eager to receive and eager to experiment. All of which should make up for any visible signs of aging in the dark. But would the ghosts of her past demand their blood money?

So, on this early Friday evening Carrie squared her shoulders, raised her chin and marched into the dining room of the exclusive Oilmen's Golf Club. Two years ago, the male-only private club had switched from being a bastion of testosterone to one of heterosexual probity, a so-called mixed club. She had felt perfectly justified in using the accident insurance money for the club's exorbitant initiation fee. For some reason, Cliff, her dead husband, had placed a huge value on his life. When the dust finally settled on the court cases to establish her claims, she knew he would have approved her spending his legacy this way.

Cliff had played golf all his life and his family owned a small golf club in the Caledon Hills north of Hamilton. His mother had initiated her into the game and had been her personal golf coach until Carrie produced Bobby, her only grandson. The family foursome, Carrie with her in-laws and Cliff used to play together every weekend and on holidays. She had loved the game. It had been marred only by her husband's intrinsic need to comment on all her shots. Another life, so long ago.

The Oilmen's 'Business Ladies' had welcomed her and now Carrie was part of a ladies' foursome that had regular tee-offs three times a week. Their raucous laughter and loud voices raised comments from some golfers, but this quartet took their golf seriously. Who could complain when these four women won cups and prizes at golfing events throughout the province? Carrie's team-mates all had husbands to accompany them to the club's popular Friday night 'smorg', but she refused to pass it up just because she was the only single woman in the dining room.

"Good evening, Mrs. March," the uniformed doorman said with a solicitous smile. Carrie was one of the club's biggest tippers.

The head waiter sat her at her favorite table in the upstairs dining room. One chair. Only one place setting. The wide expanse of white tablecloth gleamed in empty anticipation. But it did look over the ninth green, the club's signature hole.

She watched the golfers below putt out before she dug into her purse for her paperback. Gus, the club pro, teased her unmercifully about *reading* in such a posh setting but her golfing friends approved. They accepted her stubbornness when she constantly refused to join them and their husbands for dinner.

The head waiter flourished a carafe and poured a glass of her favorite white wine, a New Zealand sauvignon blanc. She leaned back in her chair to sip and read. Her book and the murmur of conversations in the background were enough in the way of companionship for Carrie. She knew any of her friends would welcome her if she changed her mind about eating alone.

A few minutes later a loud burst of male laughter came from the table next to hers. Her concentration broken, Carrie looked over in annoyance and saw an immense man struggle out of his chair. She went back to her book.

"May I join you?"

She startled at the deep bass voice. The man had moved to stand behind her with the silence and economy of a big fish. She turned and he smiled, a smile that showed his teeth but failed to reach his brittle blue eyes. She did not want his company. She was at the climax of her spy novel. Pulling the paper napkin from under her glass of wine she used it as a bookmark and set the novel down on her side plate. She looked up at him and asked coldly, "Why?"

He ignored her question and hostility as he dragged his chair across the carpeted floor to her table. He held out his hand and announced, "Peter Cummings, president of Cummings Consortium, Inc."

"And that somehow entitles you to interrupt my dinner?" she demanded.

His hand hung in the air between them for a moment before she decided to be civil and extended hers, "Carrie March. I'm an environmental regulator."

His large paw squeezed hers and he smirked at her grimace. His jowls jiggled as he leaned his arms on the table and announced, "In case you weren't aware, Cummings Consortium is a major player in the oil and gas industry of this province. I also donate generously to the local hospital, the school board, and sports events for children. I'm told that Cummings Consortium is one of the best companies in Canada to work for."

A slow blush crept up his neck as if he recognized his bragging was over the top, but she was enjoying his embarrassment. She said nothing for a moment as she ran her eyes over him. Fiftyish, fleshy to the point of being obese, and fighting baldness. He sported green and purple plaid shorts topped with an emerald golf shirt. The chartreuse golf cap perched on the back of his head drew attention to the sun burn on his brow and a strip of scalp.

"We need to talk," he stated as he shuffled his feet.

His accusatory tone felt like a threat and Carrie answered angrily, "No, we don't. I've given my report to the RCMP of your company's truck side-swiping my colleague's."

"This is about golf, not the accident. Can you just listen for a few moments?" He worked his huge body into the chair, "It's very important that my company fields a team in the tournament on Sunday." The flab on his stomach rested on the edge of her table. He signaled the bar, "The guy in the pro shop told me you play golf pretty good."

She winced at his poor grammar. He didn't notice and continued his tirade, "Your game will improve a lot if you play on our team 'cause we're all excellent golfers. You know how playing with good players helps you get better? You're sure to pick up a few tips from our guys. Your handicap will shoot down in just five hours of golfing with us. I can't imagine you witness one perfect shot after another playing with the ladies." He shifted his weight in the seat. "The tournament is on Sunday," he boomed.

She looked at him thoughtfully, "Is that an invitation?"

"Well, yeah." He adjusted his hat.

The tournament was only a day away. Had Gus suggested anyone else? She thought of the long empty Sunday stretching the weekend like pulled taffy and made a snap decision, "You do realize that I work as an environmentalist for the government. I'm in the enemy camp."

Cummings, not amused, huffed, "Yeah, but we can't qualify unless we have a female on the team. Your friend just canceled." He leered at the tanned, leggy teen-ager who placed a foaming beer in front of him.

Carrie gawked at him. Which friend? She started to laugh and couldn't stop. He stared at her until she finally brought herself under control. Tears running down her face, she blurted out, "Besides, I would raise the handicap of the whole team. You'd be sure to win." She wiped the tears off her cheeks and watched him gaze at the waitress' butt, "Why don't you ask her? She just won the Junior Ladies Championship."

His face lit up briefly. "A junior?" he asked, then he shook his head, "I'm pretty sure this tournament has an age limit."

"You could verify that. And check the weather forecast. I'm not interested in playing in the rain." She picked up her book, removed the small napkin and bent her head to read.

Peter Cummings didn't leave. "That's a 'yes' then? Good. Tee off is at nine."

"Wait just a minute," Carrie's voice rose. "I did not say I would play in your damn tournament."

"But you didn't say you wouldn't," he countered. "Come on, it will be fun."

"If it's raining on Sunday I will not be there." She felt as if she had lost a battle. Would it be war on the golf course on Sunday?

Cummings gulped down half his beer, threw a few bills on the table, reached over the table and awkwardly patted her arm. A strip of beer foam framed his upper lip when he gave her a toothy smile, heaved himself up and left.

Carrie's gaze followed him as he squeezed his drum-like girth between the chairs and rejoined his table of male golfers. She knew Cummings Consortium was involved in the lucrative pipeline contract to the British Columbian coast, but it was still at the proposal stage. Would she have to argue her environmental point of view for five hours on the golf course? Did Peter Cummings have an ulterior motive when he issued her the invitation to play on Sunday? She shook her head. To hell with him—she needed food.

As she attacked her over-flowing plate, she thought back to the accident she had witnessed a few weeks ago. She had been following her assistant Troy to a town north of Edmonton where a small, rare-earth producer hoped to build a plant, and who had submitted a request for regulatory approval to the National Energy Board. Carrie knew it was a big job to thoroughly document the plant's processes and she planned to get Troy started, then leave him there for a few days. Shortly after they had turned off the main highway onto a gravel secondary road a dirty half-ton passed her, spraying her car with wet dirt and gravel. The Cummings' black and red logos on both of the truck's side panels were hard to miss. Peering through the streaks left by her windshield wipers she watched the Cummings' truck tailgate Troy's Ford. It pulled out to pass, speeded up and side-swiped Troy sending his car off the road and down a low embankment.

By the time she had run up the road Troy had extricated himself through the passenger door and was bent over the seat rummaging in the glove compartment. When Carrie caught a glimpse of a gold-plated pistol, she had screamed and pushed Troy with both hands causing him to drop the gun. He sprawled against the driver's seat and as he struggled to sit up, she yelled at him,

"Are you crazy? Put that thing away!"

Troy, his face flushed with anger, reached for the gun on the floor and sat up. As he cradled it and checked the mechanism Carrie feared for a moment that he would aim it at her. He put it back in the glove compartment, glowered at her and growled, "My 10-shot Glock 27 can take down a bull. It would have made mincemeat of that truck's engine." The truck that had sped well out of range.

Now in the club's dining room, the incident seemed far away. She wondered if, on Sunday, Cummings would initiate another blow-by-blow description of that deliberate accident. Surely the curtain had closed on it. Does he know, or care, that her job is to ensure companies complied with the environmental laws and regulations of the province and country? It was bound to be another source of conflict between them, especially when he realized she could use her influence to slow down any application he made to either government. But she wanted to play golf on Sunday despite this arrogant s.o.b. She just had to hope the rest of the team was not as obnoxious as this Peter Cummings.

Chapter 2

The Oilmen's was a fabulous golf course in a spectacular setting along the shores of the North Saskatchewan River. Five years ago, a legendary golf architect had worked miracles on the original 50-year-old course. He had narrowed several of the fairways, added ponds and streams, and contoured greens guarded by cleverly placed bunkers. In some of the protected areas he introduced shrubs and plants that did not normally survive this far north. The course was usually reserved for men and couples on Sundays and Carrie didn't have a male companion of any description, much less one who played golf.

Sunday dawned clear and warm and when Gus phoned to make sure she would play, Carrie assured him she'd be there. The rain had stopped during the night and the sun gleamed off the moisture on the practice green's carpet of shorn grass. Carrie watched her ball carve a path in the heavy dew then stop short of the cup by almost two inches.

"You missed!"

The loud voice from the cart path raised the eyebrows of all the golfers in the immediate vicinity. Disturbing putters was a breach of golf etiquette. Carrie, however, recognized the grating voice of Peter Cummings who either ignored, or did not see the frowns and embarrassed looks of his two other partners. He laughed, sounding like a braying mule, and called from his cart,

"We tossed beer caps and I lost! You're my partner. Jump in, we tee off on number two."

"You can't afford real dice?" She asked as she walked across the green to lift her ball out of the cup. The two men in the second cart laughed but she groaned inwardly at the prospect of sharing a cart with this man for the whole round. No hope of getting one of those pleasant looking guys as a partner. They had taken off with wave and a cheery, "See you at the next tee."

Peter frowned and sat drumming his fingers on the steering wheel as Carrie loaded her golf bag onto the back of the cart. Not helping her with her clubs was another faux pas. She started to walk up the cart path.

Peter rode up behind her, "For Christ sake, get in. We tee off in a few minutes."

She climbed in beside him without a word.

He glanced at her stony face, "Hey, I was just kidding back there. Loosen up, will you?"

Carrie sat as far from Peter as she could and even considered jumping out of the cart. Why the hell did she agree to this damn tournament? She had hoped to be paired with anyone but Cummings. How was she going to endure four to five hours of him?

As they approached the tee box the two men from the second cart came forward. The group ahead of them was teeing off and Carrie recognized Edith, the woman who was lining up her ball. Peter ignored the unspoken rule of silence when another golfer is on the tee box as he drove the noisy cart to within three feet of Edith.

The cart coasted another foot before Pete maneuvered his gut from under the steering wheel. He wobbled over and wrapped his arms around the shoulders of his other teammates.

"A pernicious huddle," Carrie thought. When they broke apart in a loud burst of laughter, she suspected they were laughing at her. The handsome one had the grace to look guilty as he half-smiled at Carrie. The other one, tall, lanky and ordinary-looking-- "homely as a mud fence" would have been her mother's judgement--nodded to her with a crooked grin. He glanced at Peter expectantly, shook he head and walked towards her holding out his hand and taking off his sunglasses.

"Hello, I'm Jim Mathews." He gripped her hand in a firm, quick shake. "Welcome to the team. Pete must have forgotten his manners."

"Carrie March." She looked up into warm, grey eyes that blended with his swarthy complexion, "I'm looking forward to the game."

"Here's Dave. Dave Harvey, he's a lawyer and a stickler for detail so make sure your score addition is accurate. Dave, meet Carrie March."

Dave switched his club to his left hand as he walked towards them, his friendly smile making her feel a little more welcome, "You're sure you can deal with we three wokes?" He held her hand in his a few seconds too long.

"I can only try." She released her hand and forced a small laugh. Why am I so antsy? It's only a golf game. She noticed that Edith and her foursome had replaced their drivers and were getting ready to leave.

"We're up. Let's go, guys." Peter pulled a wood out of his bag and walked to the back of the tee box to practice his swing.

Carrie left the cart to speak briefly to Edith. They hugged, wished each other good luck. Her husband called from the cart, "See you at the rally, Carrie!"

Carrie cringed. Just because her best friend, Susan, was organizing an anti-pipeline rally why did everyone assume that she would be involved too? She'd agreed to input the rally's financial data on her personal laptop, but she couldn't jeopardize her position at the National Energy Board by appearing at a public event that was specifically directed against the construction of pipelines. The whole province seemed to be on tenterhooks regarding the problem of getting their land-locked oil to markets.

"Hey Carrie!" Two older men drove up behind their cart. "Hope you're showing these guys how to play the game!"

Carrie laughed and walked to the side of their cart. As she talked to them, she saw Peter offering a mickey to Dave and Jim. Dave took a quick swig, but Jim declined.

"You're up, Carrie," Jim called from the tee box. "They're hitting their second shots." The group ahead was now out of range and it was safe for Carrie's foursome to drive.

The first four holes were uneventful – no lost balls and no eccentric shots. Peter drank non-stop, his voice becoming louder, his language filthier and his speech thicker. Jim and Dave both shook their heads when Peter again and again held out his bottle to them. At their fourth refusal, Peter extended it to Carrie.

"I'm here to play golf," She snapped. "Put the damn bottle away." Holding her driver, she jumped out of the cart, "I'll walk to the next hole."

"Jesus!" Peter exclaimed. "Women!" Loose stones flew up against her bare legs when he sped past her.

At the raised tee box at the seventh, the first water hole, Carrie followed the men up the hill. Because the ladies' tee was located below the men's she would be the last to drive. She pinched her nose to hold back a sneeze when Peter stood over his ball to begin his elaborate pre-drive ritual.

He wiggled his enormous bottom, pushed his golf hat off his forehead and looked at the green. He then studied the ball between his feet and moved his left foot back an inch. He held his arms straight up pointing the club head to the sky as he checked the flag's position on the green again. Giving his bum another wag, he set his club carefully behind the teed ball. Finally, he bent his head in concentration.

Dave, Jim and Carrie waited politely. Carrie recognized that Peter Cummings was an excellent golfer, even when inebriated. She was confident his ball would clear the creek in a perfect two-hundred-yard arc to land and sit unerringly on the small green.

Peter lifted his one-thousand-dollar wood in a smooth backswing, his left arm locked with his wrist cocked and his weight on his right foot. Just as he shifted from right to left to bring the full weight of his 300+ pound body behind the swing, Carrie sneezed. The ball dribbled off the tee, rolled to the edge of the raised tee box and trickled down the incline.

Carrie swallowed the laugh that bubbled up her throat and stammered through pursed lips, "I'm so sorry."

The three men stared at her. Nobody said a word.

Peter glowered at her; his face pinched into an ugly scowl. He dug into his pocket for his spare ball and muttered, "I'll shoot another from the reds."

They finished the first nine holes in an uncomfortable silence.

Peter swung the cart a sharp ninety degrees off the paved path to the tenth hole. He yelled to her over the noise of the complaining engine, "This is a short cut!"

He tortured the cart by forcing the small wheels over rough ground and small rocks. Carrie hung on clutching the metal rim on the front of the seat. Her rigid spine bounced up and down as she tried to direct her tail bone onto the thin seat pillow. At one point she looked back and saw Jim and Dave disappear around a curve in the cart path. She wanted to jump out but was too afraid of breaking an ankle or leg.

They played the next few holes in an atmosphere of forced conviviality. Peter continued his maniacal driving between holes until the 16th, a short par three but the most difficult hole on the course.

Tall pines, spruce and fir trees framed the narrow fairway that crossed a small stream, then curved 90 degrees before fading from view up a steep hill. As Carrie leaned forward to try and locate the hidden green she took deep breaths of the pungent air, hoping the medicinal qualities of the non-deciduous trees would slow her pulse rate. She felt battered, bruised, and somehow used. Only her keen sense of good sportsmanship kept her playing. The team would be disqualified if she quit now, and Cliff, her now deceased husband, would turn over in his grave.

Jim insisted that Carrie tee off first and it was a perfect drive, her ball rolling to a stop in the short fairway grass ten yards before the edge of the water. Peter drove last. His ball lifted off the tee and sailed over the trees on the right. Carrie was sure it would land just in front of the pin even though she couldn't actually see the green. But a gust of wind appeared at the apex of the ball's parabola and on its downward journey the little white ball nicked the top branch of a tall fir tree. It dropped into the creek with a resounding plop.

Carrie forced her lips into a hard line. Laughter following a bad shot was the ultimate in rudeness on the golf course.

"Shit!" Peter exploded as he slammed his driver into the bag, pointed his pudgy finger at Carrie and snarled, "You're bad luck! Just like a woman on a ship!" He yanked a ball retriever out of his bag.

"Really? I caused the wind to blow. Perhaps you're right. I always *have* believed that God is a female."

Dave looked surprised or was he shocked? But the corners of Jim's lips lifted in amusement. When Peter swung his body towards Carrie with his extended retriever half raised above his shoulder she ducked, sure he was going to hit her with it. But he pounded the handle into the ground in frustration and marched to the passenger side of the golf cart.

"You drive the damn cart," Peter ordered as he slumped into the seat, the handle of the ball retriever dangling between his spread knees and its tip extending over his shoulder. He upturned the mickey and downed the last quarter of the bottle in noisy gulps. He reached over to dig out another mickey from the compartment on the driver's side and his fat hairy arm brushed her thighs.

Carrie reined in her anger as she drove carefully down the hill expertly controlling the cart as the back wheels threatened to slide on the slippery grass. She parked the cart along a strip of mud at the edge of the creek and reached to turn the engine off so she could help look for his ball.

"Stay where you are!" Peter ordered her and she obediently left the engine on. He turned and extended his beefy leg out his side.

The weight shift caused the cart to slide sideways towards the creek and Carrie's instinct to gun the engine had disastrous results. Peter shot out of the side of the cart like an oiled seal and slid face down the muddy bank into the murky water. The extended ball retriever snapped in two.

Carrie jammed her foot on the gas pedal hoping the small wheels would get enough traction on the damp ground to prevent the cart ending up in the slough too. She ignored the shouts of 'Wait!' 'Stop!' When she reached the safety of the slope's crest, she looked down at Peter trying to extricate himself from the gumbo. Two pairs of arms extended towards him, but they failed to reach their target.

Peter stared up at her as the slough water dripped down the loose skin of his sagging jawline. His eyes blazed with hatred through the gunk pouring from his eyebrows and plastered hair. He blinked and shook his head to clear it away. His malevolent look challenged her as if to a duel and he snarled, "Bitch, I will get even."

Carrie shuddered. She had never seen such cruel anger in a man's face. She wheeled the cart ninety degrees, so it was pointing to the clubhouse. The wet sucking sound as Dave and Jim pulled Peter out of the goo was almost obscene and she couldn't resist a glance back before she drove on. Jim, a grin transforming his homely face, peered up at her through mud-splattered glasses as he gave her a thumbs up behind Peter's back. She was too surprised to respond and barely noticed the marshal driving up beside her.

"I'll have to let the next team play through if…" the marshal glanced down at her teammate and added, "Correction. The team following you will play through. Think you guys can get your act together by then?" Not waiting for an answer, he pulled away.

Jim called to her, and Carrie waited as he trudged up the slope. He dropped into the passenger seat, "Well, you've got *me* now. Peter not only insisted we change carts, but he is determined to finish the round." His crooked smile was enigmatic as he wiped the muck off his horn-rimmed glasses with a dingy golf towel.

Carrie suddenly realized that Jim, and probably the whole team, thought that she had deliberately dumped Peter into the slough. She wanted to explain but the marshal yelled at them to hurry up, motioning her to the ladies' tee box on the next hole.

She drove slowly even though she was aware that the group behind them had putted out and would be waiting impatiently. As soon as she put on the brakes Jim jumped out of the cart and hurried to her bag.

"He'll get over it," Jim proffered the handle of her driver.

Carrie shook her head, "I'm not so sure."

"One more perfect drive down the middle and I'll buy you a double," Jim smiled, and his face was altered. He looked like a kindly, sympathetic gentleman--like somebody's favorite uncle.

She had to smile in return. In spite of his cleaning a thin film of slough water remained on his glasses. Through the glazed lenses she could see that his eyes were warm, amiable and amused.

The rest of the back nine was uneventful. Jim and Carrie exchanged polite niceties but the tension between the two carts was palpable. Dave and Jim had stopped ribbing each other and Pete maintained his sullen silence. Carrie had never played such a cold, unfriendly game of golf.

At one point, when they were waiting to drive, Dave tried to smooth over the strained silence with a corny joke, "Did you hear about the groom who said to his future wife at the altar, 'Honey, I've got something to confess. I'll be playing golf on Sunday mornings.' 'Well,' she countered, 'since we're being honest, I have to tell you that I'm a hooker.' The groom replied, 'That's okay, honey. You just need to keep your head down and your left arm straight.'"

Jim laughed, Peter huffed a snort, but Carrie simmered at the implied slur on women.

When they had putted out the last hole and started the formality of shaking hands, Peter turned away from Carrie's outstretched hand and stalked off the green. Jim started to object but she waved her hand 'no' and shook her head,

"It's okay. I'll return the cart," She dropped her putter into her bag.

"Not so fast, young lady. I owe you a drink." Jim jumped behind the steering wheel and patted the seat beside him. He dropped her at the clubhouse and said, "See you upstairs in a few minutes." He winked at Carrie, and she laughed when a small clump of dried mud dropped off his left eyebrow.

Carrie practically ran to the club's lady's room. She sat on the toilet, her head in her hands, trying to think of some way out of dinner with these three men.

Susan's voice shook her out of her stupor, "What the hell are you doing in there? Have you fallen in?"

Susan? Here? How can she afford to take time off from organizing the anti-pipeline rally? Carrie emerged from the stall and hissed, "What are you doing here?" She looked around furtively to check for other occupants.

Susan was leaning on the sink smiling benevolently with her arms crossed over her ample bosom. She pointed her finger at Carrie and said in her no-nonsense voice, "Well, Missus Meek and Mild! How the hell did you do it? You certainly gave that oil company CEO his comeuppance! And you've got a hot-blooded sex machine buying you a double!"

"I did not dump that tub of lard on purpose!" She immediately lowered her voice, "Sex machine! Do you know Jim?" She yanked at the tap and jumped back when a full stream of water splashed into the sink and onto her golf shirt. Meek and mild! It was not the first time her emotional control had been mistaken for subservience but surely Susan knew her better than that. She turned to her friend who was bent over laughing, "I bet even you would be a wimp if you had to play golf with three scratch male golfers whose total handicap doesn't add up to ten!"

Susan turned off the tap, "Forget about those jocks. It's your birthday and I bought a bottle of New Zealand sauvignon blanc. Let's go."

Carrie hardly heard her. She could imagine golfers passing on the story of Peter's dump in the slough throughout the golf course--from one group to another on the tee boxes, on the greens and in the clubhouse. It would spread like a grass fire, especially since she suspected Peter Cummings was not the most popular guy in town.

Carrie grabbed Susan's arm and demanded, "Were you, or were you not the one who bowed out?"

Susan shook off Carrie's hand, "Carrie, I've made your apologies to your team. A bottle of your favorite white is cooling in your fridge. It's your birthday tomorrow and..."

But Carrie had seen the guilty look on her friend's face, "Damn you! You cancelled because of that bloody misogynist, Peter Cummings! I bet you've heard about that vulgar, despicable man and knew it would be a hell-on-earth round of golf."

"I cancelled because I've got a shitload of work to do on the rally. You know I've hardly golfed this year, but Gus was so desperate I did initially agree to play," Susan explained patiently.

"To think that I did *you* a favor by employing your kid! Your 'he-who-can-do-no-wrong' Troy!" Carrie yanked at the paper towel roller and lowered her voice, "And you didn't bother telling me Troy packs a gun in his car's glove compartment. I *do* hate you." Carrie looked in the mirror, gave her hair a few pats and brushing against Susan she headed for the door.

"Wait. Carrie! Wait!" Susan grabbed her arm, but Carrie wrenched it away causing her friend to lose her balance. Susan recovered and stammered, "Troy is a gun collector. I thought you knew."

Carrie sniffed derisively and left. The door slammed behind her.

The dining room was buzzing with chatter interspersed with frequent bursts of laughter. Carrie scanned the crowd and could not see her golf team. Thankful for the reprieve she turned away. But someone called her name from the far-right corner of the room, and she finally spotted Jim and Dave waving at her. She sighed in resignation and headed in their direction.

Dave motioned Carrie to the empty place at the table and Jim pulled out the chair. Peter, who had showered and changed into a somber black shirt and shorts did not acknowledge her as she stood with her hand on the back of her chair. He continued to ignore her as he expounded on—wouldn't you know it? --pipelines. He was drunk. His face was red, and spittle showered from his lips. Words spewed from his gums like black Alberta oil, but his voice was clear as he announced, "The Canadian government and their talk of a carbon tax has just given us a carte blanche to build the pipeline. Those tree huggers who are protesting haven't a hope in hell now and..."

"Excuse me," Carrie interrupted. Both her hands tightened on the rim of the empty chair, "Surely you're aware of the court decision to force companies to consult with all the Indigenous peoples whose land the pipeline crosses. That one-time carbon tax does not give the feds social license to by-pass adequate consultations with the First Nations, or to rush environmental planning." She knew she sounded like a 19th-century schoolmarm, but she really didn't give a damn. She wondered how much Cummings Consortium had invested in the pipeline extension to British Columbia.

Jim sat down and Dave said. "Come on, Carrie..."

"Ah!" Peter interrupted, his voice still loud, "the Environment Department speaks!" He held up his hands, palms up, gesturing to his audience the hopelessness of dealing with this woman.

"I'm not with…" Carrie began to say, but Peter carried on.

"Everyone knows a pipeline is the only safe way to get Alberta's oil and gas to tidewater. Thousands of your 'injuns' will be hired for the project. Let me tell you, they are overjoyed to have jobs. Money talks, it always does. The provincial government is firmly behind the pipelines, and that court decision is full of holes. The federal government won't have to consult with the natives." He picked up his knife and fork, "Here's our steak. Finally. Let's eat." His smile to the waitress was forced.

Jim frowned and Dave's face darkened but Carrie persisted, "The feds are legally and *morally* obligated to consult, so they will." She shook her head at Dave who had reached for her arm. She could not face a meal with two disapproving men and this asshole, Peter. She turned to leave.

Peter slammed his knife and fork down and stood up. In an imperious tone he said, "Hold it right there!" Carrie came to a halt in surprise as Peter continued, "Jesus, woman! This country needs my pipeline. Get your head out of the sand." He let out an ugly snort of laughter. "Who knows? Maybe the boost in the Canadian economy will result in some decent winemaking instead that rot-gut we had last night." He held up the bottle of Chateau-Neuf-du-Pape and upended it into his glass. "Now this is wine!" He gulped several mouthfuls, plunked his glass back on the table and sat down satisfied that he'd won the argument.

Carrie opened her mouth to protest, but Dave put his hand on her arm. "Please sit down, Carrie," he said, "What are you drinking?"

"Nothing," she answered and turned to walk away.

As she swung quickly towards the exit, she heard Peter say, "Let her go. Women shouldn't be allowed on the golf course."

"Shut up, Pete," Jim ordered.

Carrie suddenly lost it. She whirled on Peter and at the top of her voice yelled at him, "You asshole! You're the one who should be blackballed!"

The whole dining room went quiet.

Carrie ran between the silent table towards the dining room's exit, oblivious to the downcast eyes and embarrassed faces. She was blind to everything and everyone except getting the hell out of there. When she finally reached the door, the head waiter, shaking his head, held it open and muttered a strangled, "Have a good evening. Mrs. March." She grabbed the railing as she stumbled down the outside steps and wove between the parked cars to get to her vehicle. Yellow convertible, yellow convertible, she repeated to herself. She was parked beside a yellow convertible and through a haze of anger and frustration she found her car.

Her hands shook as she unlocked her car, and she could barely fasten her seat belt. She let her head drop back and closed her eyes trying to regain some equanimity. She never lost her temper. She prided herself on always being in control of her emotions. How could she allow that despicable man to push her over the edge? He hated her. Because of the damn cart sliding in the mud. Why couldn't he see it was an accident?

She rolled down the window to let in the cool evening air, poked the key into the ignition and started the car. Her hand froze when she heard the verandah's door slam and footsteps thumping down the stairs. The engine sputtered and died as she inadvertently turned the key to 'off.' She glanced in the side mirror and through the exhaust still hanging in the air she saw Pete approaching, swaying like an alley drunk between the parked cars. She fumbled for the window button, thought better of it, and with scrambling fingers she searched for the lock. But she was too late.

Peter yanked her car door open, letting it bang against the side of the yellow car, and yelled, "Come here, you horny old maid!"

An alcoholic haze of fumes enveloped Carrie as he thrust his oversize hands into the car, grabbed her knees and started to pull. His eyes gaped at her, angry and hostile.

She slid the key out of the ignition, twisted her body in the seat belt and jabbed the key at his head. When she made contact, she dug the sharp point of the key into his temple and scraped it down through the bristles of his five o'clock shadow. She turned back to reinsert the key, the car door still open.

Peter yelped, staggered back a few steps, and slammed into the convertible. He bent over and still leaning against the yellow car he put one hand briefly on his wounded head. He looked at the blood on his fingers and his mouth worked soundlessly. His eyes rose to hers and bulged with an emotion that Carrie realized was not all hate. It was lust. With outstretched arms he reached for her. He was going to rape her.

She was vaguely conscious of people calling from the club house verandah. Then, in her fury, she became impervious to any distractions. She unsnapped the seat belt, swung the door open and jumped out of the car. Surprised, he bumped against the convertible again and using it for support he walked towards the voices. She followed him between the two cars and as soon as they were in the open, she yelled at him and pulled her muscled leg back.

He turned and muttered, "No!" His hands reached to protect his crotch, but she was faster. Her foot grazed against his leg then dug into the soft genital mass with a force that sent him to his knees. He lifted his face to the heavens, his mouth open in an agonized, silent plea.

She froze on one foot for a second or two, turned and ran the few steps to her open car door and slid in. The engine still chugged, and she was conscious of approaching voices. After shutting the car door with shaking hands, she gripped the steering wheel with white knuckles. She backed out carefully around the crouching mass that was Peter Cummings. Ignoring his loud curse and shaking fist she made it to the exit. Her spikes slipped on the gas pedal, but her mind was centered on getting home, on returning to the safety of her little house. Her clapboard house in a run-down area of north Edmonton was her refuge. She gripped the wheel and steered with the intensity of a beginner driver. 'I kicked him in the crotch.' She was cold with horror. 'I kicked him in the nuts.' She could not think of anything else as the scene replayed in her mind.

She was half-way home when she remembered Susan. Was she still at the club? Surely not—not with a bottle of white wine waiting at home.

As she drove into her garage Carrie whispered to a deity she had not worshipped for years, "Oh, God! Thank you, God!"

The garage door squeaked down behind her, and she was enclosed in the small wooden shed that was attached to the side of her house. Her hands shook as she opened the car door. As he bent to untie her shoelaces, she muttered to herself in horror,

"Oh my God! I've still got my spikes on!" Even though she hated the bastard, knowing he would have raped her, the ramifications of what her spikes could do to his private parts appalled her. Leaning against the car's fender she pulled off her shoes and socks and slipped into her flip-flops. Charlie, her springer-setter cross barked his greeting and scratched on the man-door to the garage. Remembering her thoughts at the beginning of this awful day, she whispered a heartfelt warning to herself into the gas-infused air of the garage,

"Be careful what you wish for."

Chapter 3

She braced herself for her dog's welcome as she turned the doorknob. Charlie pushed through, smashing the old wooden man-door against the inside wall of the garage. Carrie, prepared for the onslaught, caught his paws against her chest letting him lick her face and neck. When he started on her ears she laughed and let him down, "You know my ears are ticklish!"

As she approached the back door of her little house she muttered to Charlie, "Why are the lights on? I'm sure…"

The screen door burst open and with it a chorus of "Happy Birthday!"

Peggy, Mary and Gloria, her golf and bridge partners, spilled out and enveloped her in hugs. Charlie, his excitement raised to a new level, barked, yelped, and circled them trying to join in without getting kicked by a flying foot.

Susan leaned against the door jam, "I kept trying to get you out of …" She stiffened when she saw the look on Carrie's face, and she mouthed, "What's wrong?"

Peggy, ignoring Susan, linked arms with Carrie walking her into the house and up the three stairs to the kitchen. Charlie pushed ahead and sat wagging his tail beside the kitchen table—always a fortuitous spot.

Carrie pulled away, brought her trembling under control, and sniffed, "Mary's broccoli and ham casserole!" She reached for the back of a chair, "I'm starved. Let's eat."

"First things first," Gloria said with a nod to Peggy. The two of them led Carrie into the living room and pushed her into the only armchair. Peggy and Susan settled cross-legged in a haphazard semi-circle around her as Mary handed her a glass,

"You've got some catching up to do, birthday girl."

"Thank you, thank you especially for the 'girl' part. How did you get everything ready?" Carrie tasted the wine, "Mmm. Good. But if I'd had dinner with my team—"

"Yeah, you messed up our timing, but Susan here--" Peggy nodded at Susan.

"Our spy on the scene," Mary interjected.

"I looked for you in the dining room," Susan explained. "I even met your team before I found you on the can. When I couldn't get you to come home with me, I phoned Mary to admit my failure."

"But it all worked out," Gloria put on oven gloves," I'll check the casserole, if that's okay, Mary?"

"Be my guest. My job is over. Drink time!!" Mary waved her half-empty glass. "Let's hear all about the golf game. Did you win?" Not waiting for an answer, she asked, "Somebody pass the lobster tails, please and thank you."

Carrie looked up at Susan, "You were there. Didn't you..."

"I left you in the lady's room pretty upset and I wasn't sure what you'd do." Susan got up to uncover a large tray and offered it to Carrie, "When I got here, I phoned Gus to look for your car in the parking lot. He was laughing so hard he was incomprehensible. What the hell happened?" She took a lobster tail. "How do you eat these things?"

"With a fork." Carrie handed her a miniature fork from the tray. "Okay, here goes."

Carrie recounted the disastrous day as her friends nibbled on lobster, sipped wine, and burst into laughter at Pete sliding into the slough. All except a stern-faced Gloria who admonished her,

"Peter Cummings is a prominent businessman in the province. You can't just dump him in the drink and expect to get away with it." She twirled the oven mitts nervously.

"Oh, come on, Gloria. Have some more wine. I can't wait to tell Jerry; he'll be doubled over." Mary's partner, Jerry, was a successful real estate agent who kept her in the latest fashions which she loved more that she did him.

Carrie waved her hand for silence, "There's more--I hate to tell you." When she got to the 'kick' their indrawn breaths hissed in unison followed by a jumble of comments.

"You didn't! "

"Oh my God, he'll kill you!"

"Oh Carrie, that's too funny!"

Gloria looked aghast, shook her head, "You always did tell a good story, Carrie."

"Gloria, this is the honest to God truth," Susan said impatiently, "or to be more specific, it's the honest to Gus truth." She split the remains of the bottle between herself and Carrie. "You need this. You deserve this whole bottle. I'm so proud of you."

"Poor Carrie, what an awful day," Peggy sighed, "Was he really hurt, or was he faking?"

Mary laughed, "Guys don't fake anything that has to do with that part of their anatomy!"

"What will he do? Will he get even?" Peggy's worry made Carrie sink her head in her hands. Mary came over to hug Carrie's shoulders.

Gloria shook her head, "That would make it even worse. He can't do a thing."

"Well, Carrie should report his assault on her to the RCMP," Mary stated.

Susan snorted, "And if Cummings reports her assault on him?"

Carrie listened wordlessly to her four friends argue her cause. She got up to pour herself a large glass of water and to put kibble into Charlie's bowl. His munching was background to the endless discussion--what Cummings could do, what Carrie should do. Leaning on the kitchen sink she stared non-seeing out the kitchen window and her despondency deepened.

Susan came looking for her, noted her drooping head and shoulders and called out in a loud voice, "Dinner time! Let's eat!"

They all tried to help in Carrie's tiny kitchen but after many bumps and 'sorrys' they managed to set five steaming plates on the table. They dragged the chairs back and Carrie shooed Charlie onto his mat in the corner. Holding up their glasses for refills they quickly realized there was no room for both plates and glasses. Mary had the solution. She dug out an oversized beer stein from the back of the cupboard and had them each pour their wine into it. "A communal mug—isn't that what they used in Chaucer's time?"

They groaned. Another of Mary's incomprehensible literary references.

"Mary, no one, but no one reads Chaucer anymore," Carrie poured her wine into the stein, took an unladylike gulp and passed it to Mary, "But we all saw 'The Knight's Tale.' I think it was based on one of Chaucer's stories."

"Yeah, I remember," Peggy said. "I refused to go at first 'cause Mary said there might not be any sex in it. But she bought my ticket." When the laughter had died down, she went on, "Look gang, we have to help Carrie."

"Of course," Susan put the stein down with a bang, "But how?"

"We can make sure Carrie is never alone," Mary offered, "I can pick her up for work every morning, and someone else can make sure she gets home after work."

"First of all, we should figure out if he will try to get back at her," Susan said.

"And we work out the 'how's'" Gloria added. "Will he, and if so, how will he revenge our girl? Personally, I can't imagine he's the ogre we've painted him to be."

"Well," Mary said, "It depends on what damage Carrie did. I know Jerry wouldn't take an assault from a woman without some recriminations. And, as you say, Cummings is a VIP, a very important person."

Carrie began to eat. With her mouth full of ham and broccoli her voice was muffled, "Tell me everything you know about Peter Cummings." She noticed Susan shaking her head and added, "It's my birthday, after all."

Peggy put down her fork and turned to Gloria, "Do you remember the Hospital Ball I chaired years ago? When Peter Cummings brought his striking-looking girl friend?"

"He had a girl friend?" Carrie asked in disbelief...

"Her name was Jeanie. She had a lovely Modigliani face with high arching eyebrows and the most unusual eyes I have ever seen—large, green irises with dark rims. Her black hair shone like ebony and…" Gloria stopped, "What's the matter, Susan?"

"Nothing," Susan shook her head, but Carrie too had noticed her friend shrinking into herself in thought.

Mary changed the topic, "tell us about the other two golfing hunks, Dave and Jim. Did you let them know you're eligible, Carrie?" Mary punched her lightly on the shoulder.

"I am not eligible. I will never be eligible," Carrie pushed her chair back.

"We know that Carrie," Gloria placed a restraining hand on Carrie and cast a warning look at Mary. They had all tried, at some point, to talk Carrie out of her mourning, tried to get her to date again but Carrie absolutely refused.

"Okay," Carrie relented, "Dave is from Toronto working on a contract, I think, for Cummings. Jim lives in Fort Saskatchewan where he owns a small cobalt plant, Nuovo…"

"Boring! What do they look like? Are they married?" Peggy's dreamy eyes fixed on Carrie, her elbow on the table and her hand cupping her chin.

"I have no idea. We didn't discuss our personal lives while we were putting."

Carrie's sarcasm was lost on Peggy, "Come on, Carrie. Are they good looking?"

"Dave is, but Jim is sort of swarthy and has a crooked smile. Both are fortyish, I would say. Susan, you saw them."

Susan put down her fork, "Dave could be a poster boy for after-shave lotion, all glowering eyes and a sharp chiseled jaw. But Jim is dark with a long nose…" She hesitated and Peggy broke in,

"His eyes, what about Jim's eyes?"

"He's got bedroom eyes." Susan smirked and looked embarrassed.

"For God's sake, Sue, give it a rest," Carrie said.

"I've got to go soon. Jerry is…" Mary saw the exasperated looks on Susan's and Gloria's faces. "Okay, enough about Jerry. Let's hear the birthday cards." She reached up to the top of the fridge for the bundle of cards and passed them to Gloria. "You do the honors, Gloria. You've got the voice for it."

"What's that supposed to mean?" Gloria asked but took the cards stacking them neatly. She opened the top card and read the message, 'The best part of being fifty is that we did our stupid stuff before the internet.'

They all laughed, and Peggy quipped, "Not quite! Carry on, Gloria."

'Just remember when you're over the hill you pick up speed.'

"I wish," Mary put her head in her hands.

"Alright, Mary. Here's yours: 'You're only as old as you remember you are.'

"That's my mother!" Peggy laughed.

Gloria picked up the last card. "This one's the longest. Are you ready?"

Nods across the board.

'Fierce, fabulous and fifty; your naked body should belong only to those who fall in love with your soul.'

"Too true!" Mary said.

"Too late!" Gloria laughed as she drained the stein.

Under cover of their laughter Carrie whispered to Susan, "Stay, I need to talk to you."

Peggy brought in a tall angel food cake, its top aflame with fifty small candles, "Hurry up and blow!"

Carrie took a huge breath and did her best, but two remained sputtering on the frosting.

"Two lovers!"

"Get ready for some action at last," Mary giggled as the others pulled out the candles licking each clean of its icing.

"You look like a bunch of four-year-old's," Susan handed Carrie a serrated knife. Carrie cut the cake into five generous wedges, "Best birthday ever, gang."

Gloria, whose wine consumption had finally caught up to the others, raised her glass, "I'll always remember it as the Tale of Peter the Great Rising from the Slough."

They almost demolished the cake.

Peggy rubbed her stomach, "No action tonight. I'm too full."

"Yeah. Jerry is not going to be happy. Did we finish the wine?" Mary asked.

Gloria stood up to gather up the dessert plates, "Dishes, everyone."

They all chipped in to clean up and restore the kitchen to some semblance of order. With more hugs and birthday wishes Mary, Peggy and Gloria headed for the front door.

"Coming, Susan?" Mary asked.

"I'll just make sure Carrie can make it to bed," Susan said. She closed the door and turned to Carrie, "What's up?"

"Come back and sit down. You can even have my easy chair." She shouldn't be asking but, damnit, she had to know, she needed to find out all she could about Peter Cummings. When they were back in the living room, Carrie leaned forward hoping her need came through to Susan, "tell me everything you know about Pete's girlfriend. I saw your face when Peggy and Gloria were talking about her. What else do you know about Cummings?" She noticed Susan's reticence, "Please, Sue."

"Why? You should forget about Cummings and Jeanie. Get on with your own life."

"I need ammunition—all the information I can get on the guy. I want to be prepared. I have this sinking feeling that he's not the kind of guy who will forget the woman who drove the golf cart that dumped him into a slough, gouged his face and kicked him in the nuts. I will be a good Girl Guide, I will 'be prepared'."

"You can't live your life in fear of this guy." Susan said softly. "You are paranoid."

"Yes, I am. But I saw the look he gave me when Jim and Dave pulled him out of the slough. It was full of hate. He blamed me, he didn't realize it wasn't my fault the cart dumped him. Being the kind of guy he is, he will never admit it was the shifting of his enormous weight that caused his dumping. And started the whole chain of events."

"Carrie," Susan put on her patient tone, "He's had time to simmer down and think things out. He knows that any 'getting back at you' action might backfire. He's not stupid."

"I know that but what happened is not going to fade away into the sunset. Tell me what you know."

After a long pause Susan sighed, "Alright, but it's not much. I was trying to remember the details while we were eating." She took a big breath, "A number of years ago when I was a novice bird watcher I was looking desperately for a female yellow-rumped warbler. They're mostly found in the foothills and mountains."

Carrie blew an impatient sigh through her teeth. How is a damn bird relevant?

"Well," Susan continued, "I was in that area of the park that abuts Cummings' property when I glimpsed one." She grinned at Carrie. "I didn't know it was *his* land. I just had to get a photo, but the damn thing flew into a fir tree just outside the fence. So I climbed it."

"The fence? That's a national park." Carrie huffed a short laugh, "You probably committed a federal offense."

"Whatever," Susan shrugged. "Some of the park fences are electric so I guess I lucked out. This warbler was special, its plumage still had a little bit of yellow. Anyway, I followed it from tree to tree and before I knew it, I was on a wide path and face to face with Jeanie. Peter Cummings' girlfriend."

"Ah!" Carrie picked up interest, "How did you know it was Pete's girl friend?"

"I didn't. She was surprised too, but she introduced herself as Jeanie and was eager to talk. She seemed lonely. So pretty soon we were gabbing away like old pals."

"Where was Cummings? "

"You can be sure that was my first question, and I was ready to skedaddle right back over that fence if he was anywhere nearby. But she said he was in Vancouver for the day." Susan went on, "And wouldn't you know it? The warbler was sitting in clear view on a branch just over her shoulder. I snapped a photo, Jeanie shrieked at me, and my warbler took flight. But I have a great shot of both the bird and Jeanie. Want to see it?""

"Yes, okay, later. Tell me about Jeanie."

"Well, I had to calm her down—she was pretty upset I'd taken her picture. And I sure as hell wasn't going to delete it. I fiddled with the camera and showed her a blank screen to make her think it was no longer there. We sat on an uncomfortable wrought iron bench, and I very subtly quizzed her." Carrie rolled her eyes. Susan ignored her and

23

carried on, "She was born in Bucharest and she and her sister went to a private girl's school in northern England. Very posh and very exclusive. That explained Jeanie's accent which was upper crust British with a mid-European underlay."

"And?"

"That's as far as she got because she clammed up. As if she shouldn't be talking to me. She looked around, very nervous now. She jumped up and headed down the path. I caught up to her and I tried to persuade her to tell me more of her life. Buddy buddy-like, I took her arm, but we were both startled by running feet pounding behind us. I heard Jeanie mutter 'It's him' and I had the presence of mind to slip my little camera down my sweater in between my boobs. I looked back. A big guy with a red face was bearing down on us, hell bent for leather. Jeanie stumbled but I was still holding her arm and she didn't fall. The guy yelled, 'Let go of her!' So I did. She kept walking and I turned to face him. He ranted on about private property, trespassers, police and dykes. I finally shut him up by telling him that there was a six-foot right-of-way on either side of national park fences that was open to the public."

"There is?" Carrie asked in surprise.

"No, but it stopped his verbal diarrhea for a minute. We had a brief shouting match until a couple appeared and asked if they could help. He politely thanked them and pulled out his cell phone--to call in his goons I soon discovered. He caught up to Jeanie and I didn't even have a chance to say 'goodbye' to her. I turned to go back the way I'd come, and I had only gone a little way when two gorillas..."

Sue!"

"I kid you not. They must have been body builders. They didn't say a word, took my arms, one on either side, turned me around and escorted me up the path, the way Jeanie had gone. But both she and Cummings had disappeared. The gorillas led me to a heavy metal gate. One of them unlocked the gate and I pulled free of the other one. Bad move. Their hands were like iron manacles when they grabbed me and pulled me through to another gate, a very ornate one. One goon unlocked this gate while the other pinned me to his chest—no chance of escape, no way to get loose. They deposited me outside this second gate, pointed to the right, and left. After locking all the damn gates behind them. Not a word was spoken, and I wondered later if they were foreigners. Ten minutes later I was on Highway 16, the Yellowhead. I never saw Jeanie again."

There was a heartbeat of silence before Susan stood up, "Now will you get these two out of your system, and deal with all those environmental messes you have to clean up? Cummings is yesterday's story and so is Jeanie." She opened the door, "I'll be back tomorrow to help you finish the cake."

Chapter 4

"I know that regulatory reviews in Canada are long and ponderous," Carrie smiled apologetically at the two oil sands executives. She wasn't hung over after last night thanks to the gallons of water she had downed. Troy sat beside her taking notes on his laptop. The National Energy Board engineer from Calgary had phoned to say he was in the ditch just south of Edmonton. Icey roads after the early morning's freezing rain. So Carrie played the environmental watchdog on her own.

"These out-of-date ecological delays are ballooning our costs," complained the younger of the oil sands team.

"We sympathize and understand, but there are valid reasons for us to move slowly and cautiously on any new fossil fuel development. We must ensure the integrity of the project and protect the environment."

"You must agree, my dear," the older executive directed his watery Bassett hound eyes on Carrie, "that the economies of both Canada and Alberta are still very dependent on oil and natural gas."

His patronizing 'my dear' infuriated Carrie and Troy must have recognized the aggressive flush spreading across her face because he came to her rescue and said,

"Our job as regulators is to is to implement the environmental standards under the Canada Environmental Protection Act. And that is time consuming."

Carrie's annoyance dissipated into amusement at Troy's textbook response, and she added, "Even if our monitoring gets suspended, or gets shut down, for open-pit oil sands mines in Alberta we will still collect data. The Alberta Energy Regulator will perform a thorough investigation on any new project brought forward."

The discussion went back and forth, at times descending into an argument, until five-thirty. She turned down their offer of dinner using Charlie as her excuse, and left Troy free to accept or decline. Driving home she replayed the meeting and regretted thinking of Troy as a 'kid.' He must be at least twenty-five. He was always dependable no matter what job she threw at him, like dumping that obnoxious oil sands duo on him. Troy would undoubtedly accept their dinner invitation.

The evening was coming on in cool shades of grayish purple when she placed her creel and rod case on the grass beside her car. Her day at work had been challenging and tiring, her dinner of leftovers totally unappetizing and to top it all Charlie had dug another hole in the back yard. She had dumped her meal in the trash and said to Charlie, "Let's go fishing." She firmly believed that fishing cleared the mind and perhaps the soul.

Charlie waited patiently beside the car. His tail swished against the cement, his mouth drooled, and his eyes followed her every movement.

She placed the stepladder against the metal shelving that lined the inside wall of her garage and climbed to the top rung. But she was still not at eye level to the upper shelf. She dragged out ski boots, bindings and a box of waxes and dropped them all down to the garage floor. Whiffs of dust rose from both the floor and the shelf as she stretched her arm to reach the back. Charlie barked and she turned her head to yell, "Shut up, Charlie." The ladder slid out from under her feet. She clutched at the top shelf kicking sideways in an attempt to loop her foot around the ladder's struts before it fell to the garage floor.

"Gotcha. You can let go now." Two arms encircled her thighs, and she was slowly lowered until her feet were grounded. Charlie circled suspiciously.

"Jim! What are you doing here?" She wiped her hands on the sides of her jeans.

He picked up the ladder and set it against the shelving. Charlie sniffed the ski boots and Jim bent down to pat the dog. "Hi, Charlie. Am I acceptable now?" He smiled up at Carrie, "Can I get something for you up there?"

She shuffled her feet, "My fishing net should be on that top shelf."

He climbed the ladder, reached to the back of the shelf and pulled out a green fishing net. He stepped down and handed it to her, "Fishing now? It's almost dark."

"Best time to catch trout." She tucked the net under her arm and walked to the car. After picking up the creel and rod case she opened the trunk and packed in all the fishing gear. She was conscious of him watching her—making her feel very uncomfortable. She swung around, "Why are you here? I thought you lived in Fort Saskatchewan." She opened the rear door for Charlie, closed it after him and leaned against the side of the car waiting for his answer.

He handed her a small packet, "Our team came in third, so I selected this prize for you. The pickings were pretty slim by the time it was our turn."

She shook out the contents of the bag and huffed an amused snort, "One hundred colored tees. Just what I need. Thanks."

He shrugged an acknowledgement and asked, "Trout? On the prairies?"

She smiled at his incredulity, "Don't believe me?" She went back to the garage to place the tees on the lowest shelf and to pull down the garage door. It shuddered closed with a loud thud.

The sound reverberated in the quiet street. Jim stood back and as she brushed past him, he said to her back "I do find it hard to believe that any species of trout could survive in these smelly Alberta sloughs."

She did not reply but climbed behind the wheel, closed the car door, rolled down the window and said, "Thanks again for your help. See you."

She felt his eyes on her as she leaned forward to turn the key in the ignition, swivel in the seat and throw her arm over the top of the passenger seat. Why the hell was he still here? She started to back out and heard his voice over the raspy sound of her car's engine.

"Wait a sec!" He walked towards her open window, "May I come? I promise not to talk and scare the fish." He grinned at her sheepishly.

Carrie stopped the car and weighed the pros and cons of his coming. She really didn't want him; she didn't know him very well and he was a friend of Cummings which was two strikes against him right away. Besides, she liked to fish alone or with Charlie. When his grin faded and he turned to his truck she called, "Okay, but the bugs will be bad."

He hurried behind her car to get in the passenger seat. As he fastened his seat belt, she told herself to lighten up. He had seemed embarrassed asking her if he could come and besides, this fishing trip would be short. As he had pointed out It would be dark soon.

Charlie was sitting on the back seat with his head stretched forward to rest on Carrie's shoulder. "Charlie, you're blocking my view," she pushed his head towards Jim and backed out.

Jim scratched Charlie's ears, "Hi again, big guy." He turned to her, "What breed is he?"

"The 'S' breed – springer, setter and something else." She glanced at him and saw him smile. Is he surprised I have a sense of humor?

"You're a handsome dog, Charlie, whatever you are." Jim settled back and Charlie's tail thumped against the back seat.

"Why are you buttering up my dog? It can't be his magnificent conformation or bearing. You know he looks cock-eyed with that black patch over one eye. Whatever it is, it won't work."

"I'm wondering how Charlie would get along with my dog, Tess." He scratched Charlie's ears, "I know she'll love you, but Tess is pretty big."

"You have a dog!" Carrie smiled in spite of herself. That's why he was so good with Charlie. She turned east on the highway, set the cruise control and glanced at Jim. "So. What *are* you really doing here? Does Mr. Asshole Cummings know?"

"I do *not* report to Peter Cummings," he replied sharply staring out the front window. She knew he was annoyed by the edge to his tone and before she could reply he added, "I hardly need his approval to go fishing on a lovely evening with a...."

"Don't you dare say it!" Carrie could feel the blush spreading up her neck.

He laughed. "Okay, I'll rephrase my sentence, 'to spend a lovely evening on a questionable fishing trip in the middle of the Canadian prairies'."

"Better." She glanced in the rear-view mirror before passing a truck loaded with squawking pigs. Charlie's ears perked up and he peered out the side window. "In addition to being his golfing buddy what is your relationship with Peter Cummings?" She knew she was being too inquisitive, but what the hell?

He pulled out his cell phone, "I've known him for several years through the oil and gas business. The unfortunate fact is I want to get out of a contract that I made with one of Pete's business associates." He paused, "Why do you want to know?" He punched at his cell phone. "Look, this is not a good idea. Can you let me out somewhere? I can hitch hike back." He turned to look at her, "I apologize for forcing myself on you and Charlie."

"Whoa!" Her hands came off the wheel to motion 'no' and her shoulders tensed. Yes, she had been too inquisitive, "Don't get mad. I'm a little sensitive where that guy is concerned, and I need to know where you stand. Why did you really come to my place? You could have left my fabulous prize at the clubhouse. I'm a member."

He fiddled with his phone, "Okay, I think you are a decent person who doesn't deserve whatever Pete is planning on dishing out to you in revenge." He turned to look at her, "You should know that Pete is a vindictive guy and he's very powerful."

"As if I'm not scared enough already." She wanted to trust Jim, both he and Dave had treated her with respect during the golf game. But she had learned from her years of widowhood that no matter how polite they were men wanted only one thing. Casual sex had changed the world in the eighties and nineties, but it wasn't for her. She glanced at him. His concern seemed genuine, and she continued, "I know Cummings hates me, and he's probably litigious. He could get me fired." She paused, "Are you going to phone someone or are you coming fishing? Do you want to get out?" Carrie turned off the highway onto a gravel road, put the car in park and sat back to wait for his answer. Charlie dug his nose into her neck and whined.

"Carrie, in spite of what I just said Pete is not all bad..."

"Yeah?" She interrupted him. "Convince me." Her head dropped onto the padded seat and she closed her eyes.

"He's compassionate to the people working for him. He's fair and takes into consideration their personal problems when they're not performing up to snuff. He supports their union and…"

She interrupted him, "I don't believe that guy has it in his genes to be compassionate but carry on."

"He took a number of fledgling companies that were going under and restructured them as Cummings Consortium. Now this company is competitive with most of the bigger oil and gas companies in Canada and the U.S."

"I concede he's a smart businessman." Carrie sighed, "Okay, maybe I should try and get over his ugly behavior on the golf course, but I have this relentless belief that he is an evil person." She paused and asked, "How does Dave figure in all this? Is he a good buddy of Cummings?"

"He's one of Pete's lawyers. Beyond that, I have no idea." He brushed Charlie's drool off his shirt. "But I have played a few rounds of golf with him in the past."

"Has he gone back to Toronto?"

"Again, I presume so, but I don't know," He looked at her curiously as if to ask 'why do you want to know?'

"To hell with them." She said as she pulled the gear shift. "Let's go fishing."

Carrie steered the car into the middle of the bumpy, rutty dirt road and explained, "We're going to a large slough on a local farmer's property and here's the story." She paused as she maneuvered the car around a man-sized hole. "A bunch of local fly fishing addicts tried putting trout fingerlings into a few sloughs near the park. The one we're going to was the only one in which the little wrigglers seemed to flourish. The fishermen negotiated with the farmer and, lo and behold, the first batch grew into reasonably sized fish. I only got to be a member because I blackmailed my friend's husband to get me into the so-called fishing club."

"And I bet you won't tell me how you blackmailed him," Jim said with a grin.

"How right you are! Hold tight. This road is pretty rough." She shook Charlie off her shoulder and he yelped in excitement. His drool dripped on the consul between their seats.

"Hold your horses, Charlie," Carrie said as she drove slowly and carefully trying to avoid the largest of the potholes without sliding off the road. She glanced at Jim who gazed at the surrounding fields. The bright yellow rapeseed flowers stretched and moved like the sea under the darkening purple of the sky.

He sat up straighter, "That canola gold! What a painting this would make."

"Not much further now." She relaxed a bit. "Charlie, get down!" The road led to a copse of poplar and fir, and they caught glimpses of dark water through their branches. As soon as she parked, she let Charlie out and he raced back to the rows of standing grain.

"Francois, the farmer, hates my dog but Charlie loves to hunt for mice in his field," she commented as they unloaded the fishing gear. She sprayed a healthy dose of mosquito dope on herself before handing the can to Jim. She took the fly rod case, Jim picked up the creel and net and they set out on the short walk to the slough. The bow of a blue boat was just visible through a break in the trees.

"Hope you can row a boat," She grinned at him. The anticipation of fishing had improved her mood.

He chuckled, "I'm sure it's like riding a bike—you never forget."

They dragged the heavy boat to the water's edge where a flimsy dock shuddered in the evening breeze. The muddy shore was punctuated with hoof marks.

"Are those from cattle or deer?" Jim asked as he picked up Carrie's fly rod.

She put out her hand to stop him, then drew it back, "Francois's cows, I think."

"Trust me with this?" He motioned to the rod case, "I promise to treat it with the reverence it deserves."

She was embarrassed. This guy doesn't miss a trick. "Well, now, I dunno. It was my father's, and I haven't got a back-up." She climbed back to the stern with the creel and net as Jim carefully settled the fly rod securely against the ribs on the inside of the boat. He got out to lift the bow and push the boat into the slough as Carrie put two fingers to her mouth and blew. She laughed when her shrill whistle made him drop the bow, but Charlie came on the run. Not breaking his stride, he sailed into the rowboat and scampered to the stern to sit at Carrie's feet.

Jim rowed a little way out and stopped to get his bearings. She watched him examine his surroundings. Through the waning light the dimensions of the slough were just discernible. It was a good size, as sloughs go, with several fields running down to its edge. Gnarled willow bushes leaned over the water with stands of poplar and ash and the odd pine tree behind them.

"Which way, ma'am?" He asked.

Carrie squinted at the sun sinking into the western horizon and pointed, "See that big fir tree leaning out over the water? The deep pool underneath the lowest branch is a trout hang-out."

Chapter 5

As Jim rowed, Carrie put together her bamboo fly rod. She rested it carefully on the seat and rummaged in the tackle box. After attaching the leader, she looked up and said, "This should be good. The anchor is under the bow." Charlie inched slowly forward and hung his head over the gunnels. His long ears disturbed the active insect life hovering over the surface of the water.

"Got it," Jim gently lowered the anchor and tied the remaining rope to the bow.

She felt his eyes watching her as she secured a black fly, its touches of magenta and yellow flashing in the dusky light.

"What's that fly called? I've never seen one quite like it." He leaned forward to get a better look.

She hesitated and replied sheepishly, "It's called a 'Carolyn'."

She felt a warm blush spread across her cheeks and hoped he would think it was just the reflection from the setting sun.

"You tie your own flies?" He asked as he gave up the middle seat and moved to the stern. She stood and they inched together, taking care not to touch.

"Well, you know, these long Alberta winters…" She ordered Charlie under the stern seat and waited for him to slowly make his way back. Jim patted Charlie's head when it appeared between his legs.

"He feels safer there with you!" Carrie threw back her head and laughed remembering the time she had caught Charlie's ear in one of her casts.

The unabashed sound filled the space between them and rippled over the water. She should be embarrassed at her loud, boisterous laugh, but what the hell? She had a fishing pole in her hand and her fishing companion was smiling at her. "What?" she asked, wondering about his quizzical look.

He shook his head, "I was just trying to think of a joke to tell you so you would laugh again."

So she did, and its echo made Charlie lift his head in bewilderment.

Carrie whipped the long supple rod back and forth in smooth graceful arcs, the swish as regular as the beat of a Bach chorale. She let the fly settle briefly on the surface of the water before reeling in steadily, not too fast and not too slow, keeping the tip well above the surface of the water. As with most fishing enthusiasts around the world she became oblivious to everything else in her life when she had a fly rod in her hand. Her father had taught her the patience that was required to spend hours casting and retrieving for one truculent fish—one that might not even be in the mood to investigate her bright fly.

In the silence between them the only sounds were the light hiss of Carrie's fly rod and the occasional melody from a red-winged blackbird. In the distance, the ubiquitous quacking of ducks and the occasional honking of geese formed the bass line. Jim sat quietly checking her line and scratching Charlie's ears.

Suddenly, her body tensed. There was a flurry of movement in the water, a thick writhing splash and the line went tight. Their eyes met briefly, and they shared that mystical moment when a fish takes the lure. Carrie kept up a slow steady reel with the end of the rod bent almost ninety degrees. She yanked gently to set the hook and the fish took off in a long fast run. The battle was on.

"Let's hope he doesn't go for the root!" She yelled as she braced her feet.

Jim inched forward and put his arm and hand over hers to help, "It's a big one! Are you sure it's not a pike or a log?"

"Oh ye of little faith," Carrie grinned up at him and he smiled back. He took his hand away but knelt on the uncomfortable slats lining the bottom of the boat, ready to help if needs be.

"Give him lots of line!" Jim said unnecessarily. "Let him tire himself out!"

"I wasn't born yesterday, you know," Carrie said dryly keeping the line taut, confirming that she knew that a loose line means the hook can slip out of the trout's mouth and goodbye to your fish dinner.

His embarrassment was evident as he retreated to the stern. Strangely, she was not uncomfortable with his eyes following her movements. She had the confidence to know that a trout can do unexpected things. Her father had always praised her sixth sense-- when to release the line and when to reel in.

Finally he asked, "Are you okay? Need some help?"

Carrie nodded, "Just to land him. I think he's tiring. Can you reach the net?"

Once again Jim replied, "Got it" as he crouched down near her and held the net over the gunwales.

When she brought the curling fish alongside the boat Jim slid the net underneath it. He grabbed the line close to the fish and held the net with the squirming trout over the boat keeping the line taut.

"Well done!" He exclaimed in genuine admiration as he gathered the net around the fish and banged its head on the gunnels. He removed the hook from the net and the trout's mouth, held the fish up by the gills and said, "I would never have believed you could take a trout this size out of an Alberta pond!" He dropped it into the creel and secured the lid. When Charlie came over to sniff Carrie pushed him away and she corrected Jim,

"'Slough'. Now it's your turn. I'm bushed. Help yourself to any of the other flies. You're not committed to the Carolyn."

"It worked well for you, but I doubt I can live up to your performance."

"Oh, for God's sake, it's not a competition," she retorted and immediately regretted her words and tone. "Sorry. Guess I've spent too much time working with aggressive men." She grinned.

He nodded, accepting her apology and said, "I wish my grandfather had been here to see you land this gorgeous trout. Even he would have been impressed."

Her voice softened, "Do you think he felt the way I do? That fishing is a chance to feel small in the face of the wilderness? Or was it a matter of feeding the family for him?"

He laughed, "He was a pretty taciturn guy, but he did show me rather than teach me that fly fishing is a highly individual experience."

She agreed, "It clears the mind and perhaps the soul." Embarrassed at her weighty pronouncement she held out the handle to him. He tested the feel of the rod in his hands as he looked up and smiled at her.

"It's very old." He released the hook from the cork handle. "They don't make fly rods like this anymore. No wonder you treasure it."

She watched him cast and reel in and asked, "Where were you when you learned to fly fish?"

"In northern Quebec many years ago by two very different grandfathers. It was in the days of private fish and game clubs, before the provincial government took them over and made them public." He gathered the line in his left hand as he reeled in, "I should fill you in on the dichotomy of my ancestry. My mother's Anglo family were rich Montrealers, and my father was French Canadian. He grew up just outside of Kahnawake, the reserve south of Montreal, and played and fought with the native kids. He was even a sky walker with the Mohawks who work the high steel constructing skyscrapers. Dangerous work and although he got fed up catching hot rivets, he made a lifelong friend there. But it was my mother's father who was the avid sports fisherman. I think he belonged to three private fishing clubs at one time."

"So you had the best of two worlds in learning how to fish." She looked at him with new respect and asked, "Have you fished at St. Marguerite's, that expensive fishing camp on the north shore of the St. Lawrence?"

"Well, yes, as a matter of fact I have." Jim played the rod back and forth, enjoying the feel of it in his hands. As he reeled in his cast, he looked at her, "But believe me, watching you land that nice big trout was an experience all on its own." He cast again then asked her, "How do you know about St. Marguerite's? Have you been there?"

She let the question hang in the air before she said curtly, "No, but I used to live in the east." She realized he probably had not heard any gossip about her. Why would he? She had not even confided her tragic past in Susan—only that her husband and son had died in a car accident. She knew her friends speculated on her past life, but they respected her privacy for which Carrie was forever grateful. Changing the subject before Jim could quiz her again, she said, "You know, I did not deliberately dump that bloated mass of self-importance into the brink."

Jim chuckled, "Yes, I'll acknowledge that, but you certainly kicked him in the balls on purpose. Not to mention gouging his face."

"Oh God!" Carrie hid her face in her hands for a few seconds. "Did you see me kick him? Is that an indictable offense?"

"Well, it certainly *should* be." He grinned at her before he threw the line out in a perfect cast, fifty feet further than any of hers had been. "And yes, I was on the top step of the club house porch and I saw everything, including Pete trying to pull you out of the car. Now *that* could be indictable. That's attempted assault. However, he has a shitload of money, and an army of lawyers he can draw on for his defense. Which, I'm guessing, you don't have."

She stared out over the water. Of course, he would know that her government salary would barely cover any litigation fees. She sighed and turned back to him but before she could speak, he yelled,

"I got one!"

Jim played the trout as skillfully as Carrie had, but when they examined his catch in the landing net, they both wondered if it was legal. She found a measuring tape in her tackle box, and announced,

"It's a keeper."

"I'll toss him back and let him grow," Jim responded and looked up at the sky. It was dark; the night had swept the dusk away. "I hope you can find the way back because I can't see a damn thing now."

"Yeah, you're right. Too bad. I wanted you to go home with a catch you could brag to asshole Pete about. Let's change places. I'll call out directions." She looked up, "It's really not *that* dark." The dome of sky was lit by the stars and the moon.

He settled the oars in the oar locks, "We got lost on a prairie slough. Would anyone believe us?" The old boat took off with a jerk, but Jim eased up on the oars and soon the bow was nodding quietly back and forth in the still water.

She took apart her rod as Jim rowed. Setting the packed case down she pointed to the shore behind Jim's back, "See that light over there? That's the farmer's house. Do you remember the little dock just to the west of it?"

She slid the rod case and tackle box under the seat, and sat back with her arm around Charlie, "Can you tell me how you ever got yourself involved with Peter Cummings?"

"Well, I used to be a 'pipeline specialist'." He glanced back at her. "I'm sure you know what that is. I started out with U.S. Steel and ended my piping career working for a Regina company that makes most of the steel pipes in Canada." He hesitated, "I became bored with the job and my bank account was growing so I, maybe foolishly, bought a company as an investment. It's in Fort Saskatchewan and it produces cobalt. When I found myself travelling between Alberta and Manitoba every other week, working days and nights and all my weekends, I quit my job as a pipe specialist to work full time on trying to make the cobalt plant profitable. My investment company."

"Oh, yes. Nuovo Cobalt, Inc. I was involved in some of the regulatory work for the government."

He smiled. "Then I guess I should thank you." Before she could object, he continued. "You may or may not know that the metal composite used in making steel tubing contains small amounts of cobalt. Cobalt is a hardening agent. When I was desperate for business, Pete helped me out."

She shook her head, "I just can't imagine him *helping* anyone. "

"Well, I've known of him for quite a while because of his oil and gas business. Steel pipes and pipelines and the oil business go hand in hand. Anyway, although I'd worked for that Regina company for several years, my position was that of a junior engineer. Pete had much better connections with the right people. Now have a contract to supply cobalt to the major steel pipe company in Canada, thanks to Pete. How's my direction?"

Carrie peered into the distance and replied, "You're headed too far north again. Pull harder to the left. So you're a pipe specialist involved in producing cobalt. Is there a problem?"

"My left or yours?" Jim asked

"Oh God, mine, I guess. You need to go to your right."

Jim laughed, stopped rowing, and looked over his shoulder to try and find the light Carrie had spoken of. "I see it now. Let's switch to 'north' and 'south' for clarification. To continue my litany of woes, yes, I want out of my contract with Pete's pal because there's a much more lucrative use for cobalt now. The engines in the new self-driving cars like Tesla use lithium-ion batteries, and these batteries also contain cobalt."

The moon went behind a cloud and the gloom seemed impenetrable, but she was able to direct him, "A little to the right, to the north. Aren't cobalt and lithium beside each other in the periodic table?"

Jim shook his head, "No, but you do remember some of your high school chemistry."

"Cobalt makes things blue, right?" Carrie joked. "Now to your left. South. You'll have to tell me about the battery business in the car. We're here." She stood up to guide him as he maneuvered the boat gently against the dock. Jim took the oars out and looked back at Carrie as she struggled to hold her exuberant dog.

"Wait, Charlie, wait!" She cried.

Jim laughed when Charlie broke free, dived over the gunnels and swam for shore. "I don't think he knows the word 'wait'." Holding the bow rope, he jumped up onto the dock and guided the boat towards the end the wobbly platform. He wound the rope around the last pier and held out his hand to Carrie. She hesitated before she put her left hand in his and her other hand on his shoulder for support as she stepped up onto the tired boards of the dock.

They carried the fishing gear up to the car and stacked it neatly into the trunk. Carrie whistled for Charlie and laughed when Charlie shook his wet fur in front of Jim. He shrugged as if to say 'I'm wet anyway' but stood well back as he held the back door open for the muddy dog.

As soon as the three of them were in the car and on their way home, Carrie said, "Okay, let's have it—cobalt and Pete."

Jim paused, wondering how much he should tell her. "You know more about cobalt than most people. Lithium-ion batteries are the future, and not just for car engines. Cobalt is one of the essential elements in these batteries. And therein lies my problem. To make Nuovo really successful, to make buckets of money, I need to expand my plant so I can increase my sales of cobalt to the battery manufacturers. There is also another potentially lucrative market—cobalt can be combined with the rare earth element, samarium, to produce magnets that work at high temperatures. Pete could make or break me. I want him to help me abrogate my contract with the Regina company. I've tried on my own, with no success, but I know just a word from Pete to the pipe company's CEO would do the trick. Pete was the one who got me the contract in the first place and he's not going to be enthusiastic about helping me break it. How I do that and still maintain his support and friendship is going to be tricky."

"Well, going fishing with me isn't going to help your cause," Carrie said ruefully and added, "You make it sound so easy – making buckets of money."

Jim chuckled, "Just the false optimism of an entrepreneur." He fiddled with her CDs in the open console and pulled one out, "Schubert's 'Trout Quintet'! Can we play it?"

She smiled, "Yes of course. Very appropriate, I'd say. It's one of my favorites. And you obviously know it."

"Yes, I do." He removed it from the case and slid it into the slot. "My mother has season's tickets to the Toronto Symphony. She miraculously finds one for me so I can join her when I'm in town." He adjusted the volume, "It was several years ago that I heard it with her, but I remember being pleasantly surprised."

Carrie was impressed. She knew few men who were interested in classical music. The bright, lively music filled the car and they drove home listening to Schubert.

"Who was the pianist, do you remember?"

He shook his head, "An Israeli with an unpronounceable name." He turned the volume down. "Where were we?"

"Your cobalt plant in Fort Saskatchewan. I thought most of the big metal refineries were in Hamilton."

"Yes, you're right. The nickel refinery in Fort Saskatchewan was built there because of the abundance of natural gas in Alberta. Pete, who knows everything that goes on in this province, told me about the refinery's hostile takeover by one of his buddies."

"And I bet the bastard was involved in *that* too!" Carrie interjected.

"He may be an investor, I don't know. As I've said I was pretty bored with my job, and I'd socked away a good percentage of my salary. When Pete told me a new CEO had put the cobalt separation plant of the nickel refinery up for sale I was interested. He negotiated for me, and I became the owner of a cobalt refinery."

"Bit of a switch," Carrie commented. "From pipes for oil and gas to cobalt." She swung the car into a roundabout and the lights of the city twinkled in the dark night.

"Yes, but it sure made my life more interesting. I graduated in metallurgical engineering, so I wasn't completely unfamiliar with the metals and processes involved. But I didn't have enough cash or credit to buy the plant. Pete not only provided some of the initial capital himself, he got his influential, rich pals to chip in. I couldn't have done it without him."

"Ah, now I understand. To expand, you're between the devil and the deep blue sea."

Jim chuckled, "I haven't heard that expression for years. It was one of my grandmother's favourites. But enough about me. Tell me about you. I know you work for the government. To use another old-fashioned expression, what do you do to earn your keep?"

"I'm sort of an anomaly and I don't work for the provincial government. I'm officially employed as an environmental regulator for the National Energy Board. I'm the NEB's northern watchdog and lately I've been helping prepare environmental assessment reports. When and if all the proposed pipelines in the province get approved, we'll have months of regulatory hearings before construction begins before the shovels hit the dirt."

"Looks like we're almost home, but I'd like to hear more about your regulatory work sometime."

Carrie parked in her driveway and turned to him, "Would you like to come in for a beer, or a glass of wine? I never buy the hard stuff."

"Thanks, but I'll take a rain check. It's after midnight and we both have to work tomorrow. I'll get the garage door." Before he closed the car door he leaned in and asked, "On second thought, do you want me to clean that big sucker for you?"

"How did you ever guess that cleaning the catch is at the bottom of my priorities?" She grinned up at him and did not add that she detested the word 'sucker.'

They unloaded the trunk and he helped her rearrange the lowest shelf in her garage to make room for her fishing gear. "No more ladders," he said with a smile.

He pointed at Charlie sniffing out the smells in the backyard, "Does he let you know if there are any new smells?"

She opened the back door and asked, "Why would I want him to do that?"

"Don't you lock your doors?"

"No. I know I should, but this is a safe neighborhood, and Charlie is…"

"Charlie may give you a good warning, but he is not much protection if someone did break in." He glanced down at the lock.

She flicked on the kitchen light and Jim stood in the doorway for a few seconds. She tried to see her kitchen as he saw it for the first time. Red and white checkered cotton curtains blew in the breeze from the crack of the open window that was framed with white wooden cupboards. The white porcelain double sink held a stack of washed dishes. ('Thank God I washed her dishes this morning.') A 1950's beige chrome table and chairs nestled against the opposite corner and next to them stood an equally dated gold-coloured stove and fridge. A folded laptop sat on the nearest chair.

"Vintage stuff, I know," she said, embarrassed at her old furniture.

"Don't apologize…"

"Remind you of your grandmother again?" Carrie teased as she dug out three knives. "Take your pick. I'll just take Charlie for his last pee of the day."

"Wait a sec. Newspapers, paper towels, garbage?"

"Right." After pulling Jim's requests out of cupboards and from under the sink, Carrie grabbed Charlie's lead off the hook. Jim rolled up his sleeves and examined the knives. As she headed out the door she called,

"Thank you! Thank you! Thank you!" The screen door slammed shut behind her.

In fifteen minutes Carrie was back, Jim was washing his hands and arms, and two gleaming pink fillets sat on the cutting board.

"Wow, beautiful! Suddenly I'm famished!" She exclaimed. "I know filleting a trout is difficult. I didn't know how I could fit that fish into my frying pan, so you've solved the problem." She knelt down and pulled a frying pan out of the bottom shelf.

"Carrie, we can't eat it now. That trout deserves the best white wine I can buy in this burg." He dried his hands on a strip of paper toweling, "May I invite myself to dinner tomorrow? I'll bring the wine and pick up a salad somewhere."

Carrie hesitated, "Okay, but you know trout is best when it's cooked right off the hook—when it curls in the pan." She sighed, "I'll make a salad."

"Just keep it simple. You need to concentrate on work—getting all that regulatory work done so the oil will flow out of Alberta." He laughed at his own joke and she smiled as he continued, "See you tomorrow about six? Do you want to make it later?" He hovered at the door, waiting for her answer.

She paused, "Six is fine." What the hell is happening? She just agreed to make dinner for this guy. All her promises to herself down the drain but she looked at him and smiled, "Good night, Jim."

"Thanks for a great evening."

She thought he looked worried. About what? Surely he wasn't thinking about kissing her. She backed away.

He grinned, "Lock the doors, okay?" He held his hand up in a make-do wave, patted Charlie's head, and without another word he opened the door and left.

Chapter 6

The empty library beckoned Carrie when she propped open the door thirty minutes before the government's official starting time. The sun streamed in from the high windows and dust motes swirled softly in the air conditioners' light breeze. She relished the unusual peace and quiet of her work environment. Had it really been eight years?

Her office was tucked into the far corner of the library. When she was hired space was at a premium in the engineering department and management decided the next best fit was the library. Carrie loved her little nook--it even had a window and had rejected offers to move back into engineering. She had installed Troy in that department instead and she occasionally wondered if that had been a good idea. The library was usually bustling with staff coming and going, paper churning out of printers, and conversations buzzing at the long tables in the middle of the open room. She dumped her lunch bag on her desk, hung up her coat and ignoring her over-flowing in-basket, sat down in front of her computer.

While she waited for it to boot up, she planned her day and hoped she could accomplish all the items on her mental list in time to get home and prepare dinner. In spite of it all she was anticipating the evening and her lips turned up in a soft smile. When she accessed her email account, she noticed that Troy had answered all her messages late yesterday, even her personal ones.

"Damn that kid. This is going too far," she muttered. Troy was young, but he was far from being a 'kid.' Was he undermining her? Was he trying to prove he could do her job? She knew Troy coveted it even though he only had a chemical technician's diploma. The federal government was cutting back everywhere, and her classification was nebulous and poorly defined. Jobs like hers were the first to be cut in hard times, when budget reductions were needed. Would it be her or Troy? Was she being paranoid?

Carrie scrolled down the screen and thought of her old piano teacher who used to harp at her incessantly, 'Don't scroll—get practicing!' She grimaced knowing that she was letting her insecurities take over. Her nerves were frayed at the prospect of cooking dinner for a guy she had met on the golf course. She bent her head to her tasks and was surprised when the staff began to filter into the library. Where had the time gone?

Two hours later the phone beside the computer rang, Carrie hesitated before she reached for the receiver. Sure enough, it was Alice, her Edmonton boss's no-nonsense secretary.

"Mr. Brown would like to see you right away. He has a meeting with the Deputy Minister at eleven and is squeezing you in." Alice paused, "Chop, chop. See you in a minute."

A quiver of apprehension shot through Carrie as she stared at the receiver. She made a quick pit stop and hurried down the hall. She knocked at the open door and entered. Her boss, Ian Brown, took one look at her worried face and smiled,

"Relax, Carrie. This isn't about your... ah, weekend golf game. I'm sure some version of your encounter with Mr. Cummings has permeated throughout the whole building by now. Susan told me in the parking lot. Please, sit down."

As she pulled the chair closer to Ian's desk, she envisaged Susan's colourful rendition of the disastrous 'Peter' event to everyone from the office pool to the Assistant Deputy Minister's staff. Carrie stifled a groan.

"As you probably know when the Supreme Court granted the Alberta government leave to intervene on the pipeline's extension, Bob Finney from the Research Council became Environment's rep on Alberta's committee. Unfortunately, he is having surgery for pancreatic cancer next week. The powers-that-be at the National Energy Board have agreed that you're a good fit to take over his job as representative, if you agree to it that is." Ian looked at her expectantly.

"Me? I'm not qualified," Carrie stammered. "I've never done anything like that."

"No?" Ian responded. "What about all the regulatory work you've been doing in the last eight years? All those regulations that have been enforced because of you and your work, not to mention the many environmental assessment reports you've co-authored. Even though it's been for the feds, you have a broader knowledge of what goes on in this department, indeed in the province, than just about anyone I know. And you can write. That's a big bonus for any committee."

"But that's different," Carrie objected. She wondered if there was a conspiracy afoot to yank her regulatory job out from underneath her. Conspiracies? She *was* paranoid.

"Look, Carrie, I talked to your *real* boss at the National Energy Board, and he's agreed to release you as long as he gets you back. He insists that you be available for consultation and that you maintain your legal position on the NEB. It will be tricky, but Troy doesn't have the experience to take over completely. Finney's job is not such a big deal. I know you can do it and you won't need me as a morale booster." Ian sounded exasperated so Carrie mentally adjusted her attitude as he went on, "You'll be working with a couple of lawyers to prepare oral presentations. The Court will allow all intervenors' written submissions but not all of their oral submissions. Think how much you will learn from these legal minds! Besides, we need more scientists on the front line."

Carrie looked at him dubiously but had to admit it was an opportunity to enhance her job and broaden her experience. "Do I have to move to Calgary?"

Ian handed her a file. "Not right away. Think about it. Here's what I have on intervening and a list of the current committee members. But in order for you to get up to speed you'll have to tour some of the proposed pipeline routes. Then meet with the other committee members most of whom live in Calgary. Can you give me your answer tomorrow?" He smiled broadly. "By the way, your position reclassification will affect your salary which will go up considerably."

"Since when does the government make decisions so quickly?" Carrie asked.

"Since somebody in the Liberal government woke up and realized they need the extra billions in revenue from our land-locked oil." Ian stood up, came around the desk and placed a hand on Carrie's shoulder. "We've worked together well for a long time, and you will be hard to replace. But it's time for you to move on to other and bigger challenges." He paused at the door, "I do apologize for springing this on you like this, Carrie. But I know you can do the job. We've had a good relationship and I hope we'll remain good friends. I'll always be here for moral support if you need it."

Carrie shook her head, "It's 'when' not 'if.' You'll have your answer tomorrow. Can Troy come with me?" Charlie! What was she going to do with him?

Ian hesitated before answering, "Why don't I get one of the engineers instead? Troy doesn't have the background or education that would help you. Besides, wouldn't it make sense for him to hold the fort here while you're gone?"

Carrie bowed her head searching for an argument. Troy was friendly and had a vast range of contacts in the department. But she had heard Ian's secretary call him 'an arrogant young know-it-all' and mumbled something about LGBTQ.

"Troy has helped me with some of the straightforward regulatory work, and..." Carrie sighed, "But you're the boss." Ian was right, there was no need for Troy to join her on this job, but she didn't like to leave him to make further inroads into her job. What if Pete approached Troy while she was gone? God forbid, but it could happen.

Ian gathered the papers from his desk, a clear indication the meeting was over. "Okay, your decision. I'll try to get one of the engineers you've worked with to cover for you. Troy will have to stay here until the engineer is up to speed and catch up with you later. You'll have to leave on Thursday."

"This Thursday?"

"Didn't I mention we were in a hurry?" Ian had the grace to drop his eyes.

As he went out the door Ian turned and said, "Please be at the meeting in the board room at two this afternoon. Does that give you enough time to read the files?"

Carrie gazed at his receding back and burst out laughing. "What meeting?" she asked the air in the empty office.

Alice appeared at the office door, "I apologize for Mr. Brown. You know how rattled he gets when he has to deal with the federal government." She joined Carrie in a knowing chuckle. "Here's the agenda. I'll put a chair in the corner of the boardroom for you. You won't be expected to contribute. Mr. Brown thought the meeting might help bring you up to speed. And I found a few Alberta government reports that might interest you."

Back in her own office Carrie gazed out the window trying to come to terms with Ian's proposition. She opened Ian's thin file and read about how the government created an intervenor group, the list of members in the group, but nothing on how to actually do the job--how to define the objectives and attain the anticipated results. She googled and was overwhelmed with the number of 'hits.' After narrowing the search and printing out a few of the most promising reports, she searched the in-house databases and discovered even the Alberta government had produced a few gems. How was she going to decide in a few days?

When Susan came to pick her up at coffee break Carrie slammed the report on her desk in frustration and grabbed her mug.

As they left the library Susan read the frustration on Carrie's face, "What the hell is wrong? Come on, wonder woman. You just got an interesting new job and a big raise."

"Jesus, is there anything that goes on in this government that you don't know about?"

"Not much," Susan conceded. "But I'm more concerned about the rally. I'll fill you in on the latest plans for it. We need your help big time."

Carrie groaned, "Sue, I told you, I just don't have time to…"

Susan's face flushed with sudden anger, but she replied calmly, "Just a little inputting on your laptop. It won't…"

"Encroach on my valuable time?" Carrie interrupted, immediately regretting her words and tone. The disparity between hers and Susan's job was sometimes a contentious issue.

"Well, I figure if you can go fishing with that macho guy you could work in a few hours on the rail." Susan grinned and carried on, "By the way, why does an executive type like Jim drive a pick-up truck? Like a roughneck heading out to work on a rig."

"I have no idea. The truck does have a bashed in door on the driver's side." She looked sideways at her friend, "You've had your network of spies out and about, I see." Susan volunteered at the Hope Mission every noon hour and surreptitiously paid a few of the homeless to perform small jobs for her.

They joined the short line-up for coffee and as Carrie poured coffee into her mug a chorus of female voices burst forth in song,

"Carolyn,"

Susan grabbed the coffee carafe before Carrie dropped it and added her boisterous contralto to 'Marian the Librarian,' the familiar tune from 'The Music Man.'

"Car—o—olyn,

Reg—u—la—tar—ian,

What did you do to dump the schmoo?

Reg-u-la-tar-ian!"

As the last three syllables of the song were drawn out laughter and cat calls resounded in the small cafeteria.

Carrie abandoned her coffee mug and ran to the raucous table. Trying to keep her voice at a normal level she said, "I did *not* dump him! The cart tilted on the hill!" First Ian's obvious disapproval and now this!

Laughter erupted again, and when Carrie turned in angry frustration she literally ran into Jim and Ian. Jim winked at her, but Ian marched over to the table of merry women. His face was beet red, and a frown and downturned mouth marred his normally amiable face.

"Oh my God! I've never seen him like this!" Carrie whispered to Jim.

"Enough already!" Ian said sternly to the table of singers. "Mr. Cummings, the chief executive officer of Cummings Oil and Gas Consortium and his staff will be here shortly. We can't have this uncontrolled hilarity at his expense. You sounded like a bunch of teenagers."

The whole cafeteria was stunned. This was Ian Brown who never, ever, raised his voice. Carrie decided against correcting her boss—it was just 'Consortium,' no 'Oil and Gas.'

The women at the table picked up their mugs and silently exited the cafeteria. No one in the room uttered a word.

Carrie turned and followed them muttering, "Shit! Shit! Shit!"

Jim caught up to her at the end of the hall. He handed Carrie her filled mug and said quietly, "Hope you take it black." She stopped to stare at him and he continued, "About tonight. Can we make it seven, not six?"

She took the mug and looked up at him in surprise, "What are you doing here? Surely you didn't come all the way from the Fort to ask me that?" She blushed. Why did she jump to the conclusion that he came specifically to see her? In her embarrassment she stammered an apology, but he broke in,

"Yes and no. I tried to phone you, but I was put on hold and since I was running late I hung up. Anyway, I play squash with Ian and he owes me. He's been promising me lunch for weeks." Jim grinned, "But my winning streak ran out and he beat me last week, so we compromised on coffee."

"I don't believe this. You're a friend of Ian's?" She sighed. "Seven is fine. See you then." As she turned down the hall that led to the library she heard Peter's ugly voice call, "Jim, old boy. Good to see you."

Carrie wondered what Jim's response would be, but she did not wait around to find out. Lengthening her stride to break into her cross-country lope and ignoring her coffee sloshing over the rim onto her shoes, she made for the security of her office. She knew she would have to confront asshole Peter in a few hours but right now she needed time to calm down and prepare for the meeting. She couldn't wait to sink into her desk chair behind a closed door. The settled secure life she had craved and finally achieved was in danger of dissolving into chaos.

At five to two she was sitting in the corner of the boardroom, two pens and her writing pad perched on her knees. Her egg salad sandwich sat in a ball at the top of her esophagus. She watched Alice and five men file into the room and groaned inaudibly when Peter marched in, threw his briefcase on top of the long mahogany table and sat down with his back to her. He hadn't seen her, but she, and everyone else, tried not to stare at the long white bandage on the left side of his face.

Ian entered, saw Carrie in the corner and motioned her to sit beside him.

Peter turned, stared at Carrie and growled, "What...?" He looked down at his papers before finishing the sentence.

Ian held the chair for Carrie as he announced. "Let me introduce Mrs. Carrie March, the Department of Environment's representative on Alberta's intervenor committee on all pipelines originating in Alberta. The National Energy Board has agreed to second her for an indefinite period."

"All?" Peter said. He fixed his gimlet eyes on her with a cold, feral look that sent a shiver of fear through her chest.

"All." responded Ian firmly as Alice passed out the meeting's agenda. Carrie's heart sank as she mentally counted the pipelines that were in the loop. What kind of miracle worker did Ian think she was?

Although Ian officially chaired the meeting, Peter immediately tried to take over. Ignoring the agenda, he asked Alice to project the statistics he had accumulated on the beneficial effects of the new pipeline extensions – the downward spiral of unemployment, the cost reductions to households and Alberta businesses, and finally, the extensive experience and superior expertise of his company's staff in the oil and gas business.

'You idiot! You're preaching to the converted,' Carrie thought but she said nothing. She sensed that everyone at the table recognized the inappropriateness of Peter Cummings' short speech.

The Assistant Deputy Minister of the Alberta Natural Resources Department pointed to the agenda and suggested they get back to it. Peter started to interject, thought better of it and sat back, sullen and annoyed.

Ian called the meeting to order and following Robert's Rules of Order to the "T," and conducted the rest of the meeting with little dissension or interruption from Cummings.

The discussions on each agenda item were interminable. As usual, every man had to state and restate his point of view for fear of being seen as an inconsequential member of the group.

By the time Ian adjourned the meeting it was four thirty. Everyone stood to begin the ritual hand shaking and Carrie smiled tightly as Cummings turned away, refusing to shake her hand. Glancing at the now frayed bandage on his face she wondered how he explained his damaged face. She swallowed her laughter, but she could not hide her triumphant smile.

"How will I ever be ready to serve dinner by seven?" Carrie mused as she backed out of her parking stall. But she did it—Charlie fed and walked; her kitchen table dragged into her small living room and set with her good China, her stainless steel 'silver' and two tall white candles; pan and utensils ready for the fish; small new potatoes waiting in a pot of cold water; showered and dressed in her best skirt and blouse—all in an hour and half.

She started her cd player and made the mistake of collapsing in her old stuffed armchair. In five minutes, Carrie was sound asleep with Charlie curled at her feet and Rachmaninoff's piano concerto tinkling softly in the background.

Chapter 7

Charlie barked, Carrie jerked awake, and the knocking persisted.

She apologized when she opened the front door, "Sorry, I fell asleep on the job."

"You must have needed forty winks, and we've got all the time in the world." Jim thrust a bundle of flowers into her hands with his right arm. The necks of two bottles peeked out from a paper bag cradled in his left arm, "I hope you don't grow these in your garden. Hold it, Charlie." He grabbed Charlie's collar as the dog started to jump down the cement steps.

"Well, I did, but that early frost finished them. Thank you so much. I love glads. Come in, come in." Then to Charlie, "You too, you escape artist." Jim closed the door quickly before releasing the dog.

Carrie bent to let the soft flower petals caress her cheek as she backed out of the small foyer. "I'll just put these in some water. I can't even remember the last time I received flowers. Thank you so much."

"Hope you have a corkscrew," He followed her to the kitchen, took the two bottles out of their bags and set them on the counter.

"Yes, of course. Wine is a staple, isn't it?" She grinned at him and glanced at the labels as she dug in the drawer. "A Pouilly—Fuisse white and Smoking Gun's Cabernet Sauvignon! What a treat! Thanks. I can't seem to stop saying 'thanks'." She handed him a corkscrew, "Can you operate this cheapie version?"

"I can manage. I didn't know whether you liked red or white, but I think I mentioned that this trout deserves good wine. Glasses?"

Carrie climbed up on a step stool and pulled out a large cut glass vase from the cupboard over the fridge. She placed it carefully on the counter, climbed to the top rung and stood on tip toes to reach the back of the shelf.

He grabbed the stool to steady it, "This is almost déjà vu." He grinned as she stepped down with two crystal wine glasses.

"Thanks. I would have been 'desole' if I'd broken my last two wine glasses, not to mention a leg or arm," She set them beside the vase.

He picked up one and ran his thumb down the delicate pattern, "We don't need to use your best glasses. I've been known to drink wine from the bottle."

"They're the last of a set of twelve, would you believe? But wine tastes so much better in good crystal, don't you think?" Why was she so nervous?

He chuckled and poured the wine while she arranged the flowers. She motioned to the living room, "Can you bring the wine?"

Holding the vase on her hip she shuffled sheet music to clear a space on the top of a mahogany upright piano. After pulling at a few branches to perfect the flower arrangement, she pointed to the two easy chairs in front of the casement window.

"I peeked in this window and Charlie saw me. Sorry about waking you up," He waited for her to sit then handed her one of the of the glasses as Charlie spread out at Carrie's feet with a heavy sigh.

Jim raised his glass and said, "Cheers, and may your life be like your golfing –it's the follow-through that makes the difference."

Carrie laughed, "Did you make that up?"

"No, I read it somewhere. How long have you been playing golf?" He settled back in his chair to sip the red wine.

"Off and on, for more years than I'd like to count. Why do you ask?" She twirled her glass gently, admiring the deep red of the expensive wine.

"You've got a natural swing. But I'm sure you've been told that before."

"Yes," She nodded. "Gus remarks on it every time I manage a lesson with him. But I don't know exactly what that means. What part of my swing? Are my feet positioned correctly, are my shoulders and arms okay for each part of the swing? What should I change to get more distance?"

"Well," He smiled at her, "I'm no pro, but I would say don't change a thing. It looks completely effortless. I guess that's what 'a natural swing' means to me. If you think too much about it, you'll mess it up."

Carrie shook her head. "Why can't I get the ball to go where I want it to? And why doesn't it go 200 yards straight down the middle of the fairway every time?"

Jim laughed, "If you were that perfect, the game wouldn't be challenging at all." He dipped his glass towards the piano, "Will you play for me after dinner?"

"That sounds so eighteenth century," She smiled and noticed his eyes lingering on her face before he took a gulp of wine and swallowed noisily. Time to change the subject.

"You haven't really talked about you. Where were you born and raised?"

He shook his head, "Well now. That is a pretty boring topic. In Montreal, then Toronto where my mother still lives. I mentioned that my parents came from different

Canadian worlds. My father died in a completely preventable canoeing accident—he liked to take chances and..."

She waited, unsure of what to say, but he continued, "My father was Quebecois-- my mother still calls him 'my French lumberjack.' Are you sure you want to hear this?"

"Absolutely," she said firmly.

"He was on a fishing trip in northern Quebec when the accident occurred. I think I told you he grew up just outside the Kahnawake Reserve, south of Montreal and he played with the Indigenous kids. He maintained his friendships with two of them over the years and they went on a canoeing/fishing trip every summer. Anyway, this time they hadn't scouted the river, which every canoeist should do. They had portaged the first two sets of rapids they encountered, and I suppose my dad was fed up lugging the canoe and gear through underbrush. The third stretch of rapids they came to were 'iffy.' But Dad insisted they were navigable, he even pointed out a doable route. But river water is changeable and I'm sure they all knew that. My father rode the rapids solo and was swept onto a big rock that jutted out—one that they hadn't seen from above. The canoe split in two and he was swept downstream. He was dead when his two friends finally found him. The coroner ruled that he had not drowned but died of a concussion."

"Oh, Jim! I'm so sorry to have made you revisit..."

"Hey!" He interrupted, "Don't be. It was a long time ago, and probably needs remembering now and then."

"Have you written it down? For your descendants?"

"No," He shook his head, "But you could do it. You're the writer." He grinned and Carrie realized she was beginning to find that crooked grin somewhat irresistible.

She smiled, "And your mother? What's her name?"

"Alvena." He got up to pour more wine into both their glasses and asked, "Wanna hear about her too?"

"Of course," Carrie settled back into the soft cushions.

"She was upper crust Montreal. Both her parents were rich in their own right and one of my grandfathers owned a dry goods business. She went to a private girls' school of course, every girl in her social class did. But she loved to fish. Her father was a member of a private fish and game club near Joliette, and it was on a week's holiday there that she met my father. He was the club's guide, a French Canadian with some Anishinaabe blood and my mother fell in love with him. And guess what?" He raised his glass, "I appeared on the scene."

Carrie looked at his dark skin and nodded, "And? Did they marry?"

"Yes, and I don't think she's ever gotten over him, or really accepted his death. We moved to Toronto after his accident, his death—her parents had never hidden their disapproval of him, and her marriage and Mother wanted to get me away from all that. So she sent me to Upper Canada College, a private school in Port Hope."

Carrie nodded and he continued, "Anyway, one of the men who was with my father felt so guilty—he thought they should have prevented Dad from running those rapids--that he took me fishing every summer. Mostly in the Eastern Townships, sometimes on the reserve, and always with his son, Barry. We have always kept up over the years even though I think he's been stationed in every province in Canada with the RCMP."

In the break that followed Carrie asked, "And your mother? Did she like Toronto?"

"She loves Toronto. She was an aspiring actress in high school and was in McGill's 'Red & White Revue' while she was there. I may have that title wrong. She played some bit parts in professional theatres in Toronto and that seemed to satisfy her theatrical ambitions. Kept her busy and happy while I was away at school. She still has her little finger in that world, and she keeps up with her old theatre friends. She lives in a condo on Harbour Square overlooking Lake Ontario. She's happy. That's all that matters." He looked over and smiled, "Now it's your turn."

"No, no! Let's eat." She stood up and collected their empty glasses.

He put out his hand and touched her arm, "Carrie, I know about your accident."

She stopped, backed away and looked down at him, "Pete, I suppose?"

He nodded. "That's why I changed your dinner from six to seven. It's hard to say no to a guy you're indebted to, but I do apologize. I just wanted you to know…"

"That you knew. Well, no surprise, I suppose, but I'm sorry you had to hear it from him. Was it very colorful?" She bit her tongue.

"It was brutal. He even printed out the old newspaper articles."

"Does he still have them?" Fear crept into her being. She had begun to doubt Susan's accusation of paranoia, but here it was again—how was Pete going to avenge her ruining his face and the humiliation of being kicked in the groin by a woman? She cleared her throat, "Would you like to throw a few for Charlie while I get the dinner organized? I should warn you, he's insatiable when it comes to playing catch."

He opened the second bottle while she dug out Charlie's ball from under the sink. She stood up and faced him, "Do you have the articles?"

"Yes." His response was wary.

"May I have them?"

He paused. "Yes, of course." He stepped down to the landing where his jacket was hanging and pulled a legal envelope out of the breast pocket. When he handed it to her, he said, "I wish I'd burned them. Come on, Charlie. Let's see what you can do."

After they left Carrie pulled out the newspaper photocopies and spread them out on the table. 'No, not now,' she said to herself, gathered them up and stuffed them back in the envelope which she placed on top of the fridge. She turned on the stove and glanced out the window. She watched Jim walking towards the back of the yard, Charlie dancing at his heels. As she put the vegetables on and seared the fillets, she tried to see her garden through his eyes. Raised beds bordered the green strip of lawn that ran straight back to a functional chain-link fence. Potato plants in need of harvesting took up the left section. On the right was a row of carrots, one of beets and a poor excuse for asparagus filled the third. He threw a few balls for Charlie to retrieve and was walking back when Carrie rapped on the window to call him in.

Both he and Charlie galloped up the back stairs into the kitchen. Charlie was panting and Jim took off his jacket and folded up his sleeves. Very neatly, she noticed.

"Smells delicious. My mouth is watering. What can I do? Pour the wine." He reached for the two bottles, but Carrie said,

"I think maybe I've had enough," She poured kibble into Charlie's bowl.

"Nonsense. Working over a hot stove deserves at least one more glass," He washed his hands at the sink, and she motioned him to the head of the kitchen table.

He poured the wine into the clean glasses she had put out while she filled the plates and Charlie munched on his dinner. When she placed the filled plate in in front of him, he smiled up at her, nodding his thanks and approval. Pan-fried trout with lemon quarters on the side, new boiled potatoes in their jackets, green salad, and thick slices of fresh bread.

She sat down at the side of the table, held up her glass and rubbed her stomach, "My turn to toast: rub-a-dub-dub, thanks for the grub, Yeah God!"

They laughed and clinked glasses.

"How long have you lived here, in this house?" Jim asked.

"Ten years. I moved out west twelve years ago, but it took me a while to get used to the climate, the space, just Alberta, I guess. As soon as I realized the job was perfect for me, I started looking for a house. After a few years, I decided the big yard needed a dog."

"You could put a putting green in that yard," he suggested.

Carrie laughed, "Yeah, for a few thousand grand. Dessert?" Carrie asked. "It's just ice cream and cookies…"

The jangling phone interrupted her, and Jim got up to clear away the dishes. She was conscious he would be able to hear her side of the telephone conversation, but she picked up, listened, then spoke as softly as she could into it,

"I won't be able to make it tonight—I have to leave for Jasper to meet my colleagues on Wednesday morning. Work, work, work, you know." She held out the phone and Jim heard the loud expletive at the other end. "Sorry, but I'll be back for the big day. Call Susan—she's the rally's main coordinator, not me." Carrie listened for a few minutes longer, "I know she's hard to get hold of, but she's the one you need to talk to. Gotta go now. Good luck." She hung up to a string of complaints coming over the line.

"Carrie, you should have told me you have plans for the evening," Jim said when she put back the receiver. "I'll clean up. You probably have a million things to do to get ready for your trip tomorrow. Please. Do your thing." He started stacking the dishes.

"Let's finish. Dessert's the best part of the meal. Anyway, the meeting is just an informal get-together with the PEC president and he's already supporting the rally. I'm really just on the fringe of all Susan's environmental activities, and sometimes I wonder why I let myself get roped in. I enter data into the programs she uses, financial and scheduling. Stuff like that. But the more I do, the harder it is to stay uninvolved."

"PEC?"

"Protecting the Environment Council."

Jim groaned, "I didn't realize you were an environmental activist."

"Activist? I know your whack-job friend calls us 'environmental crazies'." Carrie grinned, thinking of Pete's probable reaction to the PPC, Susan's Prevent Pipelines Society. "Sorry, I forgot momentarily that your livelihood was dependent on pipes and pipelines. Good thing you can't take back that expensive wine now that I've guzzled most of it. I'll put on the coffee."

Jim, suddenly sober, said. "So you admit you're against pipelines. And all these anti-pipeline groups that are funded by dark foreign money." He folded his napkin. "I never eat dessert and I don't drink coffee in the evening. But you go ahead."

"I don't *need* either, so I'll forego them too," She upended her glass and burped. "Susan is involved in an advocacy group whose focus is to support renewables as an alternative to fossil fuels. She's on board with the Alberta government with that one. Notley is really pushing for green energy and diversifying, in other words, renewables."

She played with her glass and looked at him quizzically. "As to 'foreign funding' I'm certain none of Sue's organizations receive it. I would know."

Jim regarded her thoughtfully before he responded, "This is 2015 and no one as yet has put forward a solid case on how planes, ships and northern populations are going to function without fossil fuels. Your friend's goal of land-locking Alberta oil would be disastrous to the province. Dismantle a three billion dollar industry!" His face was flushed and she watched him bring his incredulity and emotion under control. His voice, however, was strained, "Do you know where the money comes from to fund the rally and all the expenses associated with your, with her environmental activities?" Not waiting for a response, he carried on, "Forget it—that's a whole different ball of wax. Apples and oranges. I think I mentioned earlier that hopefully, my cobalt business does not forever depend on steel pipes, but right now Pete's business is a lifeline."

"He's more than a business partner." Carrie made it a statement, not a question.

"Yes, even I have trouble defining my relationship with Pete, but you need to be wary of him. I stay out of his way as much as possible because I have witnessed the lengths he will go to inflict misery on an adversary just for his own amusement."

She shifted in her chair, "And now I'm his adversary." She tried to smile, "Back to oil and gas, I know of several research agencies that are working on alternatives. It will happen someday."

"Perhaps your optimism will be justified." He shook his head, "But you know and I know how long research and development projects take." His smile looked like a peace offering and when he stood, he held out his hand to help her up. "I'll do the dishes if you have other things to do."

She refused his hand and said abruptly, "Do you want to wash or dry?"

"Wash, please."

They cleared the table in an uncomfortable silence.

He started to fill the sink as she stacked the dishes beside him. She looked at him coldly, "I need to get the dish detergent from under the sink."

He stood back, "Carrie, let's not end the evening like this."

In a sudden flash of anger, Carrie swung on him, "How long are you and your pipeline cohorts going to ignore all the oil spills that are never reported and never cleaned up? Oil will be seeping into the watersheds across the province for decades. Children and old people will get sick and die. That's the heritage people like your friend Peter Cummings is leaving us."

He looked surprised at her outburst and let it hang in the air for a minute before he responded, "Surely, as a regulator, oil spills are within your jurisdiction. The government should insist the companies involved do the clean-ups, but I know that means legislation which will take forever. In the meantime…"

Carrie shook her head, "Keeping Alberta's oil underground is as crucial as keeping the Amazon rain forest standing tall. And it seems the politicians are on our side. Look at all the pipeline projects that are stuck in regulatory mud."

"Yes, but at what cost?" Jim rinsed a plate, wondering how many years she had mucked around in that 'regulatory mud' and continued, "Investment in Alberta is drying up. Middle-class families vote with their pocket-books – they need steady incomes, dollars to pay for all their household expenses, and they are not going to sacrifice their jobs for expensive renewable energy policies. Policies that mean it will cost more to heat their homes, drive their kids to hockey practices, or go to the cabin on the weekends." He watched her vigorously wiping the wine glass. "You're wiping that glass so hard you'll break the last of your good crystal."

"Oh! Well, if I do it's your fault for getting me all riled up." She recognized that he was trying to inject some levity into their conversation, but she was a little drunk and on a roll. She placed the glass carefully at the back of the counter. "Petroleum will never again play the same role in the world's resource mix that it did twelve or fifteen years ago. The sun is setting on that industry."

Jim shook his head, "Oil is still the most heavily traded commodity on the stock exchange. The problem with your anti-pipeline organizations, you 'keep-it-in-the-grounders,' is that you don't want cleaner, safer oil pipelines. You want *no* pipelines. You are blind to the fact that not only does Alberta rely on one major export, but there's too much oil and gas in the world. The province's increase in bitumen is leading to brimming storage tanks and insufficient pipe capacity to get it to either refineries or markets. The result will exacerbate last year's collapse in oil prices." He paused, "You environmental fear mongers and pugilists have failed to bring forward a practical economical replacement for oil." He turned back to the dishes.

"Fear mongers? Pugilists?" Carrie almost shouted. "When the World Health Organization is predicting an end to our world as we know it in twelve to fifteen years? Preparing for the worst is a global necessity. Get real. And you've avoided the most sensitive aspect of the pipelines—the Indigenous people whose lives will be affected by the pipelines on their land. You can't build a project like this without the First Nations onside."

"Come on, Carrie. Of all the Indigenous groups consulted in the Federal Court of Appeal, only four objected to the pipeline expansion. A pipeline that will stretch over a thousand kilometers from *your* Alberta oil sands to the B.C. coast where oil products can be loaded onto oil tankers bound for the lucrative Asian market. But no, you're happy to keep selling *your* oil at reduced prices to the U.S. and eastern Canada markets."

"*My* oil sands?" Carrie asked.

He looked sheepish, "Well, Alberta's oil. Surely, like most affluent Albertans, you have invested in the companies mining the oil sands."

"I'll ignore the fact that your question is an invasion of my privacy. But no, what funds I have I would never trust to one of those money-hungry traders who scramble to make a buck by promoting their own version of the truth." She paused, "and there's the whole question of the effect of the pipelines on Indigenous land."

Jim shook his head, "The burning question is how Indigenous people exercise their rights over their lands as they have done for thousands of years."

"Surely the most important point is how they exercise these rights for the benefit of Canada." Carrie tossed her head, "This argument is going nowhere. I thought we were discussing the pipeline."

"We were," Jim agreed. "I was trying to say that not all Indigenous people are against the pipeline expansion."

"What do you mean? The majority…"

"Most of the Indigenous tribes are for the pipeline." Jim repeated.

Both he and Carrie had turned their attention away from the dishes and were facing each other like two boxers in the ring.

Carrie took a step back and said, "Well, I agree that not all have been consulted, but the ones that have…"

"The B.C. First Nations see it as an economic safety factor," Jim contradicted her.

"Like, which ones?" Carrie almost sneered. "Not the Salish, nor the ones in the B.C. interior."

"Carrie, let's not add the Indigenous question to this argument. You know of the oil and gas projects that have been proposed…"

"Yes, and some of them seem like pipe-dreams for pipeline companies," She snickered at her own joke and realized she'd had too much wine.

"I'm sure John A. Macdonald was accused of pipe-dreaming when he proposed a railway across this huge country." Jim countered.

Carrie shook her head and hung the dish towel on the stove handle. She clung to the handle for a few seconds. Then she turned to face Jim and said, "But some Indigenous people in B.C. are opposed…"

"Yes," Jim agreed. "The urban First Nations in Vancouver and other cities are vocal in their opposition to pipelines, but they are affluent by Indigenous standards. They're into real estate which is very lucrative in B.C. at the moment."

"The federal government and the courts will…"

"Carrie, sorry to interrupt again but this issue is close to my heart. The First Nations' right to be consulted has been developed in the context of individual proposals, such as mines and oil wells and ski resorts. But the pipeline is a linear project—it's of no value unless it can be completed from beginning to end. The courts have yet to face the complexity of corridor projects involving dozens of Indigenous communities."

"Well, as you mentioned, John A. Macdonald did it." Then Carrie sighed, "But I'm pretty sure Sir John A. would have run rough-shod over any native opposition."

He nodded, "Yes, but this is now. Susan, her green friends, her foreign funders and shady politicians in concert with a very small group of First Nations will continue to frustrate the hopes of many more Indigenous people for a better life,"

But Carrie persisted, "The government has to obtain from the Indigenous communities informed consent prior to the approval of any project affecting their lands. These are their real legal rights."

"Yes, you're right there," Jim conceded. "But it does not give them the right to veto a project."

Carrie was thoughtful for a moment then said, "But one Indigenous community along the many pipeline routes could block one project, even if other Indigenous communities are on board."

"I doubt that" he said. "How did we get side-tracked here? The future of Indigenous Canadians is much more than the pros and cons of pipelines."

"And of Canada," She agreed. "You know what they said during the Mackenzie Valley Pipeline debate--that one hundred and fifty years of Canadian nationhood could be dismantled over a pipeline."

He shook his head, "God forbid."

In a tired voice she said, "I think you should leave now. But before you do, can we just agree that the world will need a mix of energy sources in the decades to come?"

They stared at each other.

With one hand Jim let the water out of the sink and said, "Agreed. To both your suggestions." He wrung out the dish cloth and turned to her. "I couldn't help overhearing you say you're going to follow the route of one of the pipelines. Be very careful. Pete will know of your every movement--he won't need me to tell him. He's out for revenge, and he has access to people who will do what he wants. Watch your back." He hung the dish cloth neatly on the faucet and turned to her. He must have seen her frightened look because he stammered, "Carrie, I'm sorry…"

She knew her fear was written all over her face, "Just go. Leave. Please."

She avoided his eyes. After a long pause he went to the door, gave Charlie a quick pat and with an abrupt "Thanks for the dinner" he let himself out the front door.

Chapter 8

"Okay, okay, I hear you," Carrie said to Charlie a few weeks later as she poured the remains of her morning coffee down the drain. She looked out the window at the heavy clouds in the overcast sky, "The weather is lousy, you know."

Charlie's tail thumped against the floor, and she said, "Ok, we'll go, but your girlfriend probably won't be there." All dogs needed socializing with other canines, and Charlie had fallen in love with a pure-bred Springer who was often at the dog park on the weekends. She dressed warmly, grabbed the leash and a few dog biscuits and they were on their way.

The off-leash parking lot was practically empty as Carrie searched for a parking spot between the murky ice-covered puddles. The October day was bleak, Indian summer well gone. Charlie could hardly contain himself, but Carrie obeyed the rules and kept her dog on his leash until they reached the path that skirted a recently harvested field. As soon as she released him, he bounded ahead barking and scrabbling over a gopher hole.

She tied the leash around her waist and walked carefully along the path that was slick with either ice or wet mud. Head down, her mind was in turmoil. She had alienated Jim, possibly her only ally in her conflict with Peter Cummings, and all because of the damn pipeline debate. How the hell had she gotten into all this? She realized that her grieving for Bobby, and to a lesser extent, Cliff, had subsided to a dull ache. Almost as if it had taken second place to her worry about that pipeline CEO. Before the golf game, she had been content with her life. She had an interesting job with a decent pension plan to see her into a comfortable old age.

She stopped abruptly, flinging out her arms to maintain her balance as she slid in the goo. A sleek, grey-brown animal streaked in front of her. She thought at first it was a small German shepherd, but when it turned its head briefly to look at her its hostile yellow eyes and over-sized pointed ears made her change her mind.

"A coyote?" She knew they were normally shy of humans, but when the animal took a flying leap towards the field, she glimpsed a row of nipples hanging from its belly. She was suddenly afraid for Charlie. But surely the coyote didn't have pups this late in the year. Pups were born in the spring but perhaps there were some hangers-on.

The coyote lunged for the wriggling gopher in Charlie's jaws. Charlie dropped his half-dead prey to growl at the coyote. The gopher lay still for a few seconds, got up wobbling a bit, and scuttled off between the sheared stalks of wheat.

Carrie screamed, "No, Charlie! No!" She ran through the muck to the edge of the field her boots sinking through the thin layer of ice into the soft loam. She stopped and watched the two animals thrash in the stiff stubble. Stepping gingerly forward she jumped sideways, back and forth, desperate to interfere but not knowing how. Instead, she yelled at the top of her voice, "Get out! Get out!"

The coyote and dog were at each other's throats, and both ignored her shrieks. Their rumps performed a primordial dance as they circled in their efforts to tear out each other's throats. Round and round they went, in and out of the stubble. Carrie had witnessed dog fights before but this one was especially horrifying. The only sounds were the occasional muffled growl, and the scuffing of their back paws on the dirt or against the dry wheat stalks. Each animal was determined to kill the other in a quiet duel. The contest seemed to go on forever and when Charlie yelped Carrie suspected her dog would be the one to weaken first.

She couldn't stand it any longer. The damn coyote was going to kill Charlie. She moved closer and waited for her opportunity. She moved in concert with the two animals until the coyote's side was facing her. Her right leg was bent and ready. She rammed the toe of her boot into the soft mass under the coyote's spine and felt a moment's disgust and dismay when one of the coyote's nipples swung up to point in her direction.

In one swift wrench the coyote released its hold on Charlie, turned its head and sunk its teeth into the calf of Carrie's leg. She screamed and fell backward. Charlie, taking advantage of the coyote's brief distraction, jumped on its back and bit into the tender areas beneath the coyote's ears.

Carrie leaned back on her elbows and stared at the wriggling mass of fur. Her dog's white and black short curls intermingled with the coyote's long gold-streaked brown hair. The beauty of the coyote's coat was marred with patches of encrusted hairless skin. There was the crunch of bone and the coyote whimpered as Charlie shook his victim's head. Carrie screamed again, much weaker this time. Charlie gave the coyote's neck another sharp tug before turning towards Carrie. He was triumphant, proud, blood and saliva dripping from his jaws, a wild, feral look in his deep brown eyes. Carrie shuddered. Her dog had become a killing machine.

"Oh shit!" She tore her eyes from Charlie to focus on the burning pain in her leg. She used her other leg to push herself up on her elbows.

Charlie limped over and started to lick the blood that was oozing through her jeans. Carrie pushed feebly at her dog. The coyote struggled to its feet. Fear cursed through her body again, but the limping coyote disappeared into the wheat field. She let her head and body drop back into the prickly stubble and heard, through the vibrations in the ground, the thump of three-footed steps behind her. A three-legged monster? She closed her eyes to pray as Charlie snarled and barked beside her.

"What an unholy sight! Are you alright?" The booming voice was the most welcome sound Carrie had ever heard. She gazed up at a Santa Claus without the red costume. The lower half of the man's ruddy bespectacled face was covered with a neatly trimmed white beard. His thick russet eyebrows met in a frown as he bent over her leg. His cap fell off revealing a ring of white and auburn hair circling a tanned bald spot on the top of his head.

"Who bit you, the dog or the coyote?" He asked as he took off his jacket and shirt. He tore his shirt into strips and folded his jacket. "Which one?" he repeated.

"The god-damned coyote. Charlie would never bite me." She sat up on her elbows and asked him, "Do you think she was rabid?"

"I have no idea," he answered grimly as he examined her leg. "I heard your yells and got to the top of that rise just in time to see you interfering in what looked like a dog fight. It could have been either animal who bit you." He wound the strips just below her knee and tied them off. Dabbing gently at the blood still seeping through her jeans, he looked at her, "What's your name?"

"Carrie. Carrie March."

"Okay Carrie, hold still. There's dirt everywhere. It's mixed in with your blood and I don't want to get any more into that wound. I think the tourniquet worked, the bleeding seems to have stopped. Lay back, and don't try to talk." He gently lifted her head and slid his folded jacket under her tangled hair. "Here's a pillow."

"I thought you were Santa Claus." Carrie held out her hand to Charlie. "Charlie, Charlie, you crazy, brave dog."

The man snorted, pulled out his cell phone and punched it three times and knelt beside her as he waited for a response.

"She listened to Santa Claus give detailed directions into the phone. The pain had lessened, and she wondered if she was going into shock.

Although Charlie's eyes followed every movement the man made, he no longer snarled. He laid his head on Carrie's stomach and she patted his head and said softly, "Good boy, Charlie."

Despite the wet ground, her rescuer sat on Carrie's other side and took her hand in both of his, "Help will be here soon, Carrie" He apologized when he used the tail end of his undershirt as a handkerchief and tucked it back in under his belt. "Has Charlie had a rabies' shot recently?" He patted Charlie's rump, keeping his fingers well away from the blood and saliva on the dog's neck. "I'm surprised the coyote could get his teeth around that thick neck, Charlie. No bleeding now, anyway."

"Yes, he's up-to-date, but I'm not," Carrie said ruefully.

"The coyote definitely has mange, but he, or she, may not be rabid."

"Oh shit. I didn't think of that." Carrie stared at his bare arms and shoulders that were covered with a mass of white hair. His undershirt looked grey against his hairy chest, and she shivered, more for him than herself. "You must be cold."

"No talking now, my dear. Let me do it." He took her hand in both of his. She was surprised to find it a comfort: a hand holding hers. She knew he was patronizing her with easy endearments, but his presence was so welcome she smiled up at him.

"I'll tell you about my life and that should put you to sleep, even in these conditions," he said.

Carrie closed her eyes and wondered why she was so exhausted. All she'd done was kick the damn beast. But the man's sonorous voice resonated in the quiet field as he started on his life story.

"I'm a retired musician," he said, "or I should say a semi-retired musician."

She started to tell him that musicians never retired, but he squeezed her hand and shushed her.

"I was born in Rhodesia, which is now Zimbabwe, as you undoubtedly know. My parents were missionaries, and in addition to relieving the natives of their ancient beliefs, they also took away many of their carved artifacts—ivory sculptures that are now subject to restitution. But that's another issue." He paused and patted her hand again.

Carrie examined the wrinkles around his eyes and mouth. A sad smile had appeared on his furry lantern jaw. "Your accent?" she asked.

"You had trouble placing it? Most people think I'm South African. I, however, am rather proud of the way I speak. At least it's not British, but I'm afraid I'm losing it to your unique Canadian English." He turned to look at her leg, frowned slightly, and looked up and around for his 911 responders. "Close your eyes, Carrie March, and try and concentrate on my life story and not your leg. My parents feared I was turning native, so they sent me away to an English public school." He paused, smiled, and then continued, "Good, you're lying down, but scowling. At my schooling? Yes, it was quite terrible, and I hated every minute of it. The only redeeming feature was learning how to play football and tennis. And I was introduced to the classical guitar and the basics of harmony."

In spite of the burning pain in her leg, Carrie found his deep voice and regular cadence comforting. But she was cold, the ground was hard and unyielding, and her leg throbbed. But worst of all, the fight and the savage look in Charlie's eyes kept buzzing around in the recesses of her mind.

A shout from the rise beyond the field interrupted Santa Claus' monologue and her brooding thoughts.

"Finally," Santa Claus said as he struggled up, waved his arms and helloed back. Charlie raised his head in alarm, but Carrie sighed in relief. The pain in her leg pulsed with every heartbeat, but she managed to ask her rescuer,

"Do you have a name, Santa Claus?"

He chuckled, "I do. I'm Don. And here they are." Don smiled down at her and took a few steps to meet the two men who were hurrying down the slope with a stretcher. Carrie heard Don tell them her name and give them a brief explanation of her encounter with the coyote.

Charlie stood on guard at Carrie's side with his ears perked and his eyes focused on the newcomers. When he let out a low snarl, Carrie told him 'no,' then closed her eyes.

"Hello, Carrie. We're here to help you," a voice behind her said.

His hands gripped her shoulders and other hands slid under her thighs as she was lifted onto the stretcher. A cry of pain escaped from her lips, she cursed under her breath and said through gritted teeth, "Sorry."

"Be gentle with her," Don snapped as he grabbed Charlie's collar.

"Are you coming with her?" the voice holding her shoulders asked.

"No, I'll look after her dog. When you get her into the ambulance, can you untie that leash around her waist and pass it to me? And send someone for that dead coyote before the wolves get at it."

The men talked to her as they walked, but every step sent a jolt of pain up Carrie's leg, she made no effort to decipher their words. They slid her into the back of the ambulance, and Carrie let out a sigh of relief, but she could hear Charlie barking and whining to follow her in. Then Don called in the door,

"Carrie, I'll take care of Charlie. Do you have a car in the parking lot?"

Carrie rolled over and tried to reach her car keys in her back pocket, but one of the attendants placed his hand on her arm and said, "Here, let me get them."

She swore at him when she felt his hand on her hip as he retrieved her keys and fumbled with the leash around her waist. He finally slid it out from under her and handed it to Don through the back door. He held a pill and a water bottle to her lips and said,

"This should help until we get you to the hospital."

The back door of the ambulance clicked shut as the attendant tucked a blanket around her. The engine started, and she tensed every muscle in her body as the vehicle bumped over the field and the rutty road. It seemed interminable. The fog rolled through her brain, and Carrie sank into a drugged sleep.

Chapter 9

"Wakey, wakey,' Gloria's soft voice pulled Carrie out of a restless sleep.

"Gloria?" Carrie rolled over on her side and struggled to a partial sit-up.

"'Tis me, sleepy head," Gloria bent down to kiss her cheek. Carrie breathed in her familiar perfume and watched her carry a large plant to the windowsill. "I know your favorite is azalea, but I couldn't find one, so this hydrangea will have to do," Gloria said. "What a gorgeous bouquet, who's it from?" She read the card, "To Alberta's star punter. Get well soon, Jim,'" Gloria read, "Who's Jim? Oh yes, from the golf game." Without waiting for Carrie to answer, she said, "Look, I can't stay, but I'll be back tomorrow when you're more awake." Gloria was at the door, "Mary and Peg are coming sometime today. See you. Go back to sleep."

So Carrie did. Until a nurse gently shook her shoulder, helped her sit up and held out a pill and a glass of water. "No," Carrie shook her head.

"Doctor's orders," the nurse waited patiently.

"What are these for?" Carrie asked suspiciously, and heard Susan's voice,

"Stop fighting with the staff and take your pills with these," Susan walked in tearing the purple and gold paper off a box. She held the open box under Carrie's nose, "Have a chocolate."

"Thanks, but right now I couldn't face a chocolate. Maybe tomorrow." Carrie let her head fall back again. She could hear Susan and the nurse whispering, and it annoyed her. She extended her hand, "Okay, where are the damn pills?"

The nurse smiled and as soon as Carrie had swallowed the four pills, she left. Carrie turned wearily towards Susan, "Where's Charlie?"

"Charlie is fine—being spoiled and pampered by an old British gentleman." Susan examined the chocolates and finally selected one, "Ah, I found it, a chocolate cherry." She licked her lips, "Yummy. Since when did you turn down Purdy's chocolates?"

"Since they put me on all these damn pills – pain killers, antibiotics, and a rabies vaccine. I've been a basket case while they worked out the dosages." She let her head fall back and smiled wanly, "I still am. Don't worry. I would never let those chocolates get stale." She paused. Why was talking such an effort? "Anyway, Don is not British, he's Rhodesian, and a musician. A classical guitarist." Carrie sagged against her pillows relieved Charlie was being cared for. After all, Santa Claus Don did come to her rescue. Surely he would be good to her dog. Her memory was vague. "He had a melodious voice and, said something about artifacts."

She saw the concern in Susan's face, so she took a few deep breaths before continuing, "What about the rally? Shouldn't you be down there getting ready for the big day? Is someone doing my inputting?" She closed her eyes for a few seconds and for some reason she remembered her father saying that her mind was like a grasshopper, it moved abruptly in unexpected directions. Why was she thinking of Dad? "Sue, please, you have to get me out of here. It's the least you can do for an old friend," Carrie whined, but Susan turned her back to Carrie and put on her coat,

"I have to go and you need to sleep." At the door she called, "Ciao," and bumped into Peggy and Mary.

"Time's up. Our turn," Peggy said.

"Just going. Hi, you two," Susan turned her back, but Carrie heard her low voice say to Peggy and Mary, "Just in case the question comes up, I do not have room in my small apartment for a guest, healthy or crippled." She glanced back at Carrie over her shoulder, did a Hi-Five and left.

"Well," Mary closed the door. "That was abrupt. How are you doing, Carrie?"

Carrie bent her good leg and lifted her heavily bandaged leg to the edge of the bed, grimacing in pain. "Help me get dressed." She clung to the mattress when the room started to tilt. Taking several deep breaths, she looked up at Mary and said, "I feel like shit. But I'm out of here."

"Why? You'll get better far faster staying right here," Mary put her hand on Carrie's shoulder.

"Why?" Carrie's voice rose to a dim screech as she repeated Mary's question, "Because I want to be back in my own little house with my own big dog."

"Hold it right there. You need a doctor's discharge slip. Don't you know anything about hospitals?" Peggy held out her arms to prevent Carrie from getting her good leg onto the floor. "And where will you go? The renovators are tearing my house apart so you can't move in with me, and Mary…"

"Oh, God!" Mary literally wrung her hands, "You know if it was just me I'd have you in a minute. But you can't recuperate in our house. You know Jerry loves you dearly, Carrie, but he won't even let my mother stay with us overnight." She put her arm around Carrie's shoulders, "Why don't you want to stay here in the hospital?"

"Because all these doctors and nurses are turning me into a drug addict. I'm leaving. Charlie needs me—I'm not sure if Don, you know, the man who rescued me. I'm not convinced he can look after my dog." She took a deep breath, "Besides, Susan needs me for the rally."

"And just how do you think you can help with the rally now?" Peggy asked.

"I'm getting out of here before they give me any more of those damn pills that make me ga-ga." Carrie shimmied out of Mary's hands, gritted her teeth, clutched the mattress and shuffled until both her feet touched the floor.

"No. Carrie, behave," Peggy grabbed her waist, "I don't want to hurt your leg. Mary, hold her!" Mary put a tentative hand on Carrie's shoulder as Peggy carried on, "Be reasonable. Susan said the coyote's teeth hit a bone in your leg, nicked your bone and that's the infection the doctor is worried about."

There was a knock on the partially open door and a hesitant male voice called, "May I come in?" The three women looked up as Troy pushed opened the door, glanced in, and hastily retreated.

Carrie looked down at her tanned thighs splayed across the white sheet. She tugged at the hem of the hospital gown, "Shit-a-god-damn!"

Peggy laughed and collapsed in the visitor chair. Even Carrie had to smile as Peggy's loud guffaws pierced the quiet ward.

Another knock on the door and Jim walked in with Troy in tow, "What's the joke?" He strode boldly over to Carrie and gently lifted her good leg, then her bandaged leg back on the bed.

"You're not planning on leaving, are you?" Jim asked, "We just got here."

Carrie stared at him in surprise until she realized her gown was now almost up to her crotch. She grabbed the top sheet, pulled it up to her chin and glared at Jim, "Damn you!"

Peggy laughed again.

A nurse appeared at the door, "I'm sorry, but some of you will have to leave. Only two visitors are allowed at one time." She held the door open and waited.

Peggy and Mary stood up. They kissed Carrie's cheek in turn and Peggy said, "Do we get to meet these two gentlemen before we leave?"

Jim led the self-introductions and when it was all done Mary called from the door,

"I'll be back tomorrow. Make sure you're still here!"

Everyone, except Carrie, laughed at Mary's parting shot. She laid her head back against the pillow and smiled thinly at Jim, "Thanks for the flowers, Jim. They're lovely." A dull ache had started in her right temple, and she swallowed hard to try and control the nausea that crept up her throat. "Sorry I swore at you."

Jim shook his head, "No problem. You're allowed."

She managed to ask Troy in a weak voice, "Troy, what's happening at work?"

"Everything's great!" Troy replied as he moved to her bedside. "I'm still helping that engineer do some of your regulatory job. He's kind of slow and methodical so I have some time for my own programming. And I'm working on another great idea."

"What great idea?" Carrie asked. Suspiciously. Troy sounded mysterious.

"Well, I talked to some of the regulatory guys in Calgary and a few others in the department, and I, I mean 'we' have come up with a plan..."

Jim pulled out his cell phone and went to the door, "I'll leave you two to talk shop while I make a few phone calls."

"What plan?" Carrie was alert. She couldn't imagine what scheme Troy had up his sleeve. Troy had almost as many contacts in the government as she did, just different ones.

"Well," Troy seemed reluctant to divulge his idea. "The plan is to delay Cummings in expanding his pipeline."

Carrie was fully awake now, "Troy, how the hell can you do that? It's been approved!"

Troy looked smug as he replied, "You know my aunt is pretty influential in the Alberta government and we're building a case to have his, Cummings' pipeline project sent back to the Alberta Energy Regulator. That's one reason I'm still there."

"On what grounds?" Carrie was skeptical.

"Number one--we're going to prove that the company has failed to develop basic safety requirements, and number two--it encroaches on the land of one of the First Nations'—land they want set aside for traditional use."

"And you've got this Indigenous group on board?" Carrie asked.

"Oh yeah! The chief is wild about the idea," Troy held up his fist in a 'win' signal.

"And all this will be from the regulatory office I just left, and so I will be held responsible." Carrie put her hands over her mouth as Jim returned. She grabbed the basin and heaved in loud gasping spasms. Troy shot out the door, but Jim quickly moved to hold her shoulders with one arm and the basin with his other hand until she was just gagging air. He helped her resettle, then put the basin in the hall. He came back, went to the sink, wrung out a face cloth and wiped her face. She closed her eyes and tried not to think about Troy's 'plan.'

She opened her eyes, saw Jim swallow a few times and knew he was fighting nausea too. The smell of her vomit permeated the room.

He recovered, "You should rest now. I'll put the bed down." Jim started to wind the lever at the foot of the bed, but Carrie shook her head,

"I actually feel better now. Don't go. Tell me about Charlie."

An older nurse marched in and asked, "Is everything under control here? I'm the head nurse and I need to know about that basin in the hall. It's yours, I presume?" She glared at them, and Jim answered for Carrie, "Yes, I thought you might need to analyze…"

"Good thinking," the nurse said and without another word she left.

Jim cleared his throat, "Charlie is fine. I talked to the vet yesterday. It's you we're worried about. Just close your eyes and rest, Carrie. I'll wait until you're asleep."

Carrie sank back into the pillows but knew she couldn't sleep. All she could think of was the havoc Troy was wielding. Jim, sitting on the step stool beside her bed, dangled his hands between his legs as he stared off into space. From the hall came the sound of urgent voices and a cart being wheeled past Carrie's door. Then all was quiet.

"Do you think Troy will be back?" Carrie asked.

Jim shook his head, "He looked pretty peaked."

Carrie lifted her hands in frustration. "I'm supposed to play the Beethoven duet with our choir director in a few weeks. I'll never be able to use the pedals."

"That's the least of your…" Jim started to say. But Santa Claus Don's booming voice from the partially open door startled them and brought a small smile to Carrie's lips.

"Room for another visitor?" He put a brown-paper wrapped bundle of flowers on Carrie's tray, stood back and asked, "How's the coyote kicker? You do know there's a bounty on coyotes in this province? I'll make inquiries on how you can collect it."

Jim stood up chuckling and he and Don shook hands.

An intern stuck his head around the door and said, "We have an injured patient in this bed. Please keep your voices down."

Carrie could see the poor young man was just doing his job, "Wait! Can you write me out a discharge slip, please?"

"Well, ma'am, I'm afraid I can't do that. Dr. Wyatt is your doctor."

"Where is he? Can you get him for me?"

The intern looked puzzled, but answered, "He's in the hospital – in the children's ward, I think."

"Will he come to see me soon? Can you get him for me?" Carrie asked again.

Don and Jim looked on in amusement as the intern backed out saying, "I'll see if I can locate Dr. Wyatt."

"What are we going to do with this recalcitrant patient?" Don asked.

"Tie her down?" Jim suggested.

Don placed his large hand on Carrie's shoulder. "Carrie, you would not be here if your doctor didn't think you needed to be. What good are you to anyone with a puffed up leg and a possible rabies infection? Charlie is or was fine with me. I may be a septuagenarian, well almost, but I still know how to look after dogs, even your Charlie." He paused and seemed uncertain before he continued, "Your car is safely in my garage. I'm sure the federal or the provincial governments can manage without your services for a while. Sit back and enjoy your stay. Hospitals are notorious for getting rid of patients too soon. You'll get out in good time."

Carrie glared at him. He was treating her like a child and how did he know about her jobs? She sipped at her ice water and felt somewhat revived.

"But Charlie..." Carrie started to object, then looked at Don suspiciously, "What do you mean--is or was fine? What's happened to him?"

Don hesitated a few seconds. "He's in quarantine for two weeks although he's apparently up-to-date on his shots. Some kind soul gave the RCMP the name of your vet." His bushy white eyebrows rose in a question mark, and Carrie suspected the 'kind soul' had been Susan. She dipped her chin in a nod and Don continued, "One of my poker club friends is a doctor in this hospital so I know that they have started you on rabies immune globulin." Don glanced at Jim, "It's a human rabies vaccine and Carrie will have five doses over the next four weeks."

"So much for professional confidentiality," Carrie muttered. "So, the damn coyote was rabid. Charlie?" She looked at Don, but he quickly tried to ally her fears,

"The RCMP insisted that Charlie be put in quarantine, and your vet will treat and monitor him. You do know that rabies is fatal for both humans and animals if not treated immediately?"

"Yeah," Carrie said dully. "I know. I went to a lecture on rabies. And I also know the vaccine costs a bloody fortune." The bottom line on her last bank statement flashed before her eyes. "But all they have to do is dissect the head of the coyote to determine if it was rabid."

Don cleared his throat, "Unfortunately, the coyote may not be dead. The government people and RCMP searched for its remains but didn't find a dead body. Lots of blood on the ground, but no coyote. So both the vets and doctors are operating under the assumption that it was rabid. The only way they can verify rabies in Charlie is to euthanize him and test the fluid in his brain."

"No!" Carrie said as she sat up straight, then winced. The ties her hospital gown came undone, and the gown slipped off her shoulders. Both men looked away as she grabbed the ends and pulled at them. Jim came over and retied them. She tried not to flinch when his fingers brushed her skin.

Don said, "Sorry, Carrie. I shouldn't have been so abrupt. Charlie is being well-cared for. It's you everyone is worried about."

"Maybe they should euthanize me," Carrie slouched down in the bed. "I could have sworn Charlie killed that coyote." A vision of Charlie's final shake filled her mind, and she could hear the crunch of bone. She shuddered, "But I suppose it's possible she survived."

"She?" Jim asked.

"Yes, it was a lactating female, I'm fairly sure of that."

"Then she must have a den nearby," Don said. "But wait a minute. It's October, and coyotes have their pups in the spring. It's doubtful they would still be nursing. But I'll let the wildlife people know. And Carrie, I'll take care of Charlie's expenses. Money is the least of your worries."

Carrie looked at him in apprehension, wondering why the hell he would pay Charlie's bills. When she glanced at Jim she could see surprise on his face too, but Don wasn't finished,

"You're going to be feeling pretty miserable as long as you're on that vaccine, and your leg is badly infected. You won't be able to look after yourself for a while. I have known your friend Mary for some time. When I called her a short time ago, she told me you don't have any place to recuperate except perhaps the Glenrose Hospital. And I found out they have a waiting list."

Jim cleared his throat. Don ignored him and went on,

"A month ago, my long-time housekeeper retired, and I have hired a wonderful woman, Helen, to replace her. Helen not only performs household chores, she advises me on my art acquisitions. I think between the two of us we could look after you until your leg heals sufficiently for you to return home." He smiled at her stupor of disbelief, "Please give my offer some thought. You've got a few days to decide."

Carrie gazed up at him suspiciously and asked, "Why would you do that for me? You've already done so much, and you don't know me." She could feel the tears starting in the back of her throat. What the hell is the matter with me? I never cry.

"Well," Don responded. "One reason is that I enjoy entertaining notoriety."

Carrie was confused so Jim said, "You've been fresh meat for the media, as well as Twitter fodder. The Edmonton Sun is calling you 'the woman who attacks coyotes'."

Carrie groaned. She doubted Don's sincerity and resented his attempts at humor. She trusted *no* man and made it part of her modus operandi both at her job and on the golf course. She banged her head back against the pillow. "Oh, God!" She grimaced at Jim, "Asshole Peter probably cheered when he heard about all this."

"You don't want to know," Jim winked at her.

Carrie did a double take, but the head nurse walked in and announced in an officious tone, "The doctor is on his way. You all have to leave now."

"Me too?" Carrie asked hopefully.

Her two visitors laughed. Don pointed a finger at Carrie and said, "Please, try to rest and sleep." He paused then added, "I know you were probably in shock back there in the field, but your language was atrocious." He cocked his head, smiled at her and left.

Jim chuckled and pressed her arm, "See you on the golf course." He ducked out leaving Carrie staring at his retreating figure. Suddenly she called him, "Jim, may I borrow your cell phone for a minute?"

"Sure thing." He came back in and pulled it out of his pocket, "Can I dial a number for you?"

She rhymed off Mary's number, he punched it in and handed it back to her, "I'll wait outside."

"Wait, please. She may not be at home." When there was no answer, she bypassed the voice mail, handed the phone back to Jim and asked him to dial Peggy's number. He punched at the keys, handed the phone to her, waited until he heard a faint 'hello' on the other end and left.

As soon as the door closed behind Jim Carrie blurted out, "What do you know about this Don?"

"Nothing, except that he lives in a castle and is probably rolling in dough, like your friend Peter," Peggy replied.

"Friend? Not even a friendly enemy," Carrie snorted. "How did Don make his millions? And why on earth is he helping me?"

"I have no idea." She paused. "Look Carrie, we are not deserting you. We'll be visiting you every day, well, one of us will be. Jerry knows Don, so we can get his address. You'll be fine. What could possibly happen?"

Chapter 10

The head nurse appeared at the door and apologized for Dr. Wyatt who had been called out to an emergency. Jim came back to recover his phone and say goodbye.

"Can you stay for a few minutes?" Carrie bent her knee to push herself up as the nausea and dizziness swept over her again.

Jim sank down in the visitor's chair and glanced at his watch. "I have a plane to catch in a few hours. I didn't get a chance to tell you that I'm leaving for a board meeting in Toronto tonight. A crisis that somebody thinks I can fix," A loud sigh whistled out between his teeth.

"Why isn't your head office in Edmonton? Why Toronto?"

His laugh was short and sharp, "Because Toronto is the epicenter of the Canadian investment world. Dave likes to say that everything you could ever want is in Toronto and you can use your laptop to experience the rest."

Carrie did not laugh, "Dave from the golf game?"

"Yes. I was surprised to get an email from him. He's coming out to ski Jasper sometime and asked if I would join him. I'll phone him when I'm in Toronto." He leaned his head back and closed his eyes, "I'd much rather stay right here. Do you think they would serve me dinner?" He pushed his elbows into the arm rests and sat up. "How can I help you?"

Carrie hesitated. "Don. Why do *you* think he's offering his home for my recuperation?"

"I would say he must like you," Jim said.

When he would not meet her eyes Carrie resorted to pleading, "Please, Jim. Be honest. He really doesn't know me at all. Not one of my best friends can take me in, everyone has an excuse. My other option, the Glenrose, has a waiting list, so Don's offer seems too good to be true. Why is he being this altruistic? Helping me after the coyote attack was something anyone would do, but he's been visiting me here at the hospital. Even though we've had some wonderful discussions on politics, American history, classical music. But I think offering to look after me at his house is above and beyond." She was exhausted and hoped he didn't notice.

"Sounds as if he might be looking for some good conversation," said Jim. "Are you okay?"

She gave him a weak smile. "Fine, but Don must have an ulterior motive and I can't imagine what it might be." Although old, Don looked pretty healthy and he could still be virile, or quirky. "How old is Don, do you know?"

"I would guess in his late sixties or early seventies." He looked down at his hands, "If you're worried about your safety..."

"Should I be? I just feel helpless with a nonfunctional leg and dozy with antibiotics and the anti-vaccine serum. I know I can't look after myself. Lying here in this damn hospital...well, Don's offer is irresistible." Carrie sighed, remembering Don's tonsure of auburn and white hair when he bent over her leg and his deep bass voice comforting her. "Sorry, sorry! I don't mean to put you in an untenable position. Forget my moaning and groaning." Why the hell was she unburdening herself to this man? Get a grip.

"I remember Pete teasing Don about his big house and multiple servants during one of our golf games. So you won't be alone with him. Besides, Don is a respected and successful businessman. He undoubtedly admires your bravery, as we all do, and as a dog owner myself I can understand your trying to rescue Charlie in his fight with the coyote. I'll be back in two or three days, and I'll visit you at Don's." He thought for a few seconds, and with a twinkle in his eye he said, "Can you wink? Surely those lovely eyes can do that. One wink says you're OK, two winks things are bad. How about it?"

Carrie surprised herself by laughing, "I will work on the art of winking."

His teasing relaxed her, and she asked the question that had been tweaking her curiosity, "Cummings' face, how bad does it look?"

Jim hesitated, "I saw him last night at dinner. A scab is starting to form so it's quite prominent." He grinned, "It looks as if an angry woman scratched her pointed fingernails down the side of his face. He doesn't tolerate any kidding about it."

"Oh, oh," Carrie winced.

"Yeah, it's not pretty. But it probably won't leave a scar. Don tried to talk him into going to his vacation home in Arizona for a few weeks to let the sun hasten the healing." He took a big breath, "I suspect Don is trying to get him away from this conflict between the two of you. Hoping he will simmer down if he goes on a holiday."

"And?" Carrie asked hopefully.

"No dice," Jim shook his head. "He's obsessed with your old accident. That's all he talked about." He paused, "He showed us the newspaper clippings. He couldn't wait for us to finish reading them before he extrapolated his theories on what happened and why you weren't charged. As you can imagine, his ideas were pretty wild. But I trust the accuracy of the reporters, and I can certainly understand why you moved from Toronto to Alberta."

"Yes, but it's followed me thanks to Peter Cummings." Her voice was bitter. "My husband and son died in a car accident from which I walked away almost unscathed. And somehow this guy is going to benefit from it by crucifying me."

"No, I will do my best to prevent that from happening," Jim was adamant. "I doubt if he'll listen to me because he seems to think you and I are in some kind of relationship. He keeps calling you my 'girlfriend'." His wry smile confused Carrie as he continued, "I'll keep bugging Don to talk reason into Pete—he's probably the only one who can."

"Jim, let it be," Carrie pleaded. "You will jeopardize your relationships with Don and Pete, all because of an old accident." She wiped her nose and threw the used tissue in the wastepaper basket. "Look Jim, don't worry about me. My friends have promised that one of them will visit me every day. Even Pete isn't brave enough to face the ire of five coordinated women." She had hoped for a laugh, but the edges of his mouth barely lifted. She coughed. "Uhm, I have another question." She was relieved when he dipped his head and waited for her to go on so she asked, "How well do you know Don?"

"Not well at all, although I've been acquainted with him for quite a while." He leaned back." For a few years Don was a sales agent for a Regina company that makes most of the steel pipe in Canada and I was a piping specialist working for the same company. But I told you that earlier. He worked out of the management offices and I, of course, was in the plant. But our paths did cross a few times. Cummings Consortium bought pipe from us to move their oil, so Don would have known Pete then."

Carrie shifted her position on the pillow and winced. Jim stood asking, "Are you okay? Should I leave?"

"I'm wide awake now and fascinated. I think the pills' effects are wearing off." She realized her pain must register on her face. She'd have to be more careful.

He nodded putting his hands in his pockets. "I've played golf with Don occasionally over the years but I'm not in his league either socially or in golf. I did get the impression when I talked to him here at the hospital that he too is wary of Pete. My guess it has something to do with money and possibly investments."

"Interesting." Carrie mused. "Pete and Don, both rich men, living in a fairly small city and golf buddies. Have you been in Don's house?"

"No, but I remember Pete giving Don a bad time about his servants and his big house on the hill." Jim paused. "He supports several charities, and you know he and Pete sponsored that golf tournament we played in."

"Yes, but I still could be alone in a house with a man I don't really know." Was she repeating herself? Was she letting herself be swayed by the prospect of living in opulent surroundings for a few days? Did the servants stay overnight? Would the nurse Don promised be with her twenty-four/seven? Why was she worrying about 'safety'?

"Look, Carrie, don't look a gift horse in the mouth." He held up his hand and started counting on his fingers, "Between the rabies vaccine, the patched-up gash in your leg, the chip in your bone and all your other meds, you need nursing care. All of which Don is providing and you won't be alone with him. When you're able to walk, you can come to my home in the Fort. My Alsatian, Tess, will guard you during the day. She'll stick to you like glue. I'll be home for lunch—will you make it for me?" He smiled.

"Guess I could slap together a peanut butter and jam sandwich," she replied. "But in a few days I should be fine on my own." Why the hell would she camp in with another man she hardly knew? Imagine Peggy's reaction if she went to Jim's house after Don's!

"Carrie, just go to Don's. I'll phone tomorrow night and the night after. I wish I could get out of this trip." He turned to get his jacket, 'When are they discharging you?"

"Tomorrow or the next day. Depends on what my leg looks like." Carrie lifted her bandaged leg an inch or so.

He didn't see her wince as he shrugged on his jacket, "Is Don driving you to his place? If not, I'd be happy to arrange a ride for you if it's before I get back."

"Don has offered, and so has Susan. I'm covered, thanks."

"You still look worried." He stood by the bed, his jacket open.

"Yes. I'm worried about what Troy will do now. He wants my old job and if I stay in this damn hospital much longer he'll probably get it." She was feeling overwhelmed.

He looked at her in disbelief as he attached the bottom of the zipper. "That young man worships the ground you walk on. He will never undermine you."

Carrie laughed softly. "Sounds like another one of your grandmother's clichés. Come on, Jim. I'm almost old enough to be his mother."

Jim zipped up his jacket. "Since when is age a barrier to love, or lust?"

"You can't be serious. Troy and I have always worked well together, and I have never, ever, gotten those kinds of vibes from him." Jim's suggestion was over the top. What the hell was he thinking?

"Okay." He glanced at the book on her tray. "Are you reading the classics by choice?"

"No, Susan brought it." Carrie picked up the book. "She prides herself on reading only classical literature." She noticed Jim's raised eyebrow and she added, "Under that ditzy demeanor, Susan is a very intelligent woman."

Jim bowed his head, "If you say so."

Carrie fought back a smart-ass retort to his condescension. He doesn't approve of, or like, Susan and he seems suspicious of Troy. So I should care? They're my friends, and loyal.

He pulled a worn paperback out of his pocket and put it on the tray. "I finished this while I was waiting. Do you like sci/fi?"

"Anything beats revisiting Miss Havisham." Carrie dropped "Great Expectations" onto the bed. She reached for Jim's book, "Will I have trouble understanding it?"

"You? No, just keep an open mind. It's not fantasy—it's all within the realm of possibility." He turned to leave. "See you soon," he gently squeezed the toes of her good foot that poked up under the covers. He was out the door before Carrie could thank him.

The next morning was a flurry of activity. The harried doctor gave her leg one last look and declared her dischargeable. He wrote out prescriptions for pain killers, antibiotics and sleeping pills and placed three vials on her table, "Here's a few samples to tide you over until you get the prescriptions filled. I'd like to see you in two weeks. Please phone my clinic for an appointment or if you have questions. Let the pain dictate your walking, moving about. Just be sensible. Good luck, Carrie."

By midafternoon Carrie was in a wheelchair at the hospital's front door, waiting for her ride. They had given her the usual array of pills with her lunch, and she was eager to get going, to get out of the damn hospital. She greeted Troy and Don with a big smile.

"Hello there, coyote kicker!" Don laughed as he took over the wheelchair.

She groaned but said 'Hi' to Don, "Good to see you, Troy." She looked back at him as Don whisked her out the door. "You look worried, Troy. What's wrong?"

Don answered for Troy, "Can you believe he brought a document for you to sign? I tried to throw it into that waste bin." He snickered and Troy, his face a beat red, held open the rear door of Don's hatch back.

"I can walk." Carrie swung her feet off the rest.

"No, you cannot." Don turned the wheelchair and he and Troy lifted her onto the seat. "This is why I needed Troy. Here, I'll help you get your feet up on the seat. All set now?" He pulled the door down and shoved the wheelchair in Troy's direction, "Fold this up and put it in the back seat, Troy." He climbed into the driver's seat and called back to Carrie, "The hospital is letting us use the wheelchair for a few days."

Carrie nodded and Troy climbed into the passenger seat. He had still not said a word. So rather than trying to draw him out she made intermittent conversation with Don. She had to yell over the noise of the traffic—asking about Charlie, the weather, his job, any trivia she could think of until they were at his house on the banks of the North Saskatchewan River.

While Don waited for the garage door to open, Troy quickly got out to follow the car into the garage. He opened the hatch back, handed her a file folder and whispered, "Can you sign it before he gets back here?"

But Don rushed towards Troy, his eyes glued on the folder that Carrie held to her chest.

"You must have a fantastic view here," she commented as they entered the front door.

"Yes, on three sides." Don handed their coats to Troy. "Hang these up, will you? I need you to help me get Carrie upstairs to her bedroom."

"No, please," Carrie looked up at the long circular staircase knowing once she was up there it would be hard to get down again. "I'd like to visit with you for a while. I am thoroughly fed up with beds and anything resembling a ward, like a bedroom."

"Okay, your call. How's the living room?" Don asked as he turned the wheelchair and stopped abruptly when Carrie grabbed the hand brakes.

"What the hell, Carrie?" She laughed when his face appeared over her shoulder. He said angrily, "It's not funny. I almost ended up on top of you and your bad leg."

Carrie pointed to the marks on the parquet. "Look at the tracks the wheelchair is leaving. I'm walking."

"No, you are not! Troy?" Don put a restraining hand on her shoulder.

She clutched the folder as they lifted her out and carried her into the spacious living room and deposited her in a huge armchair in front of the fireplace. Troy gave her a pen and she opened the file folder.

Don hovered over her shoulder. "Couldn't it wait for a few days, Troy?" He tried to read the document she was perusing.

"No, it's..." Troy stammered.

"I see what it is," Don's voice was tight with rage. "It's another review of Cummings Consortium's pipeline extension. You're trying to delay it."

Carrie slapped the folder shut, and before she could say a word Troy shouted, "Yeah, and we're going to shut down the oil sands too."

"Sit down, young man." Don seethed and Carrie watched as he tried to bring his anger under control. "Canada's oil and gas industry remains a major employer in this country and that includes the thousands who make the oil move in our steel pipes."

"Maybe, but that has to change before it's too late for humanity," Troy declared.

Don scoffed and Carrie jumped into the fray. "Don, what if massive investment portfolios, like those mega pension funds, what if they phase out their fossil fuel investments?" She looked at the red, angry faces of the two men. "I know how tedious regulatory reviews can be. They sometimes take as long as five years. But I'm sure this is just a small glitch." She read the document, signed it and handed the file back to Troy. "How are you involved, Don?"

Don ignored her question. "You anti-pipeline activists are ganging up on us. But it's Pete you should be arguing with. I'm just a bit player…Carrie, what's wrong?"

She had closed her eyes. "I've had it, guys. I need that bed now." She knew she was in no condition for another pipeline debate.

They hefted her upstairs and left her sitting on the bed refusing any further assistance. She started peeling off her clothes and the effort was exhausting. She gritted her teeth and pulled on the flannel nightgown that was on the bed. Swiping her clothes onto the floor she climbed between the sheets.

She fell asleep to the sound of Troy and Don's heated exchanges drifting up the stairwell.

Chapter 11

Carrie opened one eye and realized it was day light. She watched a piece of sunlight dance on the carpet for a few minutes before she rolled over onto her back and groaned. Something was not right. Her brain felt like cotton wool, her tongue was coated with fur, and her eyes kept wanting to close.

She lay still trying to orient herself and listened to the melody of the chickadees. Were they harmonizing? She remembered all her friends—Mary, Peggy, Gloria and Sue abandoning her. Well, not really, but each of them had a valid reason for not taking her in. Don had offered *his* home. It had been her only option, and he and Troy had brought her here in the late afternoon, helped her up the stairs. She had collapsed on the bed. "Just 'til I get my breath," she had said to them. But now she was in a nightgown. She shuddered. Did Troy and Don undress her? No, she remembered the struggle to put it on.

Pulling herself up on her elbows she surveyed the small room. A green pull-down blind covered the small dormer window at the side of her bed. It was set into a steeply sloped ceiling, so she must be in an attic. On the third floor? How large was the window facing the bed, the one with the heavy drapes? Carrie decided she had to get moving.

She sat up, lifted her good leg then the bandaged one over the edge of the bed and stood, her hand on the bedside table for support. She felt like a dragon-fly skimming over the surface of her troubles. How long had she been here in Don's house? He had been at the hospital, and she now cringed at how she had jumped at his offer to recuperate at his house. But how long ago was that? Susan needed her at the rally. Where was Charlie? Did he have rabies? Where was her cell phone? Why couldn't she think straight? Taking a few tentative steps in the direction of the bedroom door she was surprised that her wounded leg gave her much less grief than it had the last time she put her weight on it.

A surge of relief flowed through her when she found the door was unlocked, but why would it be otherwise? She slowly made her way to the open bathroom, grabbed the plastic glass over the sink and filled it with tap water.

"I've been drugged. Surely Don wouldn't dope me. But who else?" she muttered, strangely satisfied to hear her own voice. She gulped down the water, then another full glass, hoping it would dilute the foreign chemical in her body. But all that it did was make her use the toilet. However, she forced part of another glass of water down, burped, and looked into the mirror, "God, I look awful!" At least her voice was clear.

She splashed water on her face, finger combed her hair, glanced at herself, and muttered, "Not much better." Time to explore.

She listened at the open door, but the house was deathly quiet. She shuffled into the hall, silently cursing the long, unfamiliar nightgown.

The door to the only other room was locked. Not expecting success, she stretched on the toes of her good leg and ran her fingers along the top molding. Layers of dust filtered down on her head and shoulders, but she dislodged a brass skeleton key and managed to catch it in her other hand. The door opened easily, and Carrie pawed both sides of the door frame feeling for a light switch. Giving up, she peered through the gloom of the room and noticed a long pull cord attached to a single light bulb in the ceiling.

She stubbed her good toe on the edge of something hard as she moved cautiously inside the room. "Ouch, ouch," she whispered as the pain spread throughout her foot. She yanked the cord, flooding the small room with bright light, and she was able to identify the offending source of her now aching toe. The corner of a large wooden frame poked out from an off-white cotton sheet. She set the key on the floor, pulled the sheet off and sucked in her breath. The ornate frame almost tripled the square footage of a painting of a lady in red. Everything she wore was red, a red cloche hat, a red and white striped scarf tucked into a red fitted jacket. Her expression was stern with an accusing look in her dark eyes, and her gloved fingers held a tall parfait glass of red wine. She was quite young, and quite lovely, but Carrie thought she looked familiar. *Where have I seen her before? I must be delirious, or delusional. I've never seen any woman that gorgeous. And why would anyone store a painting flat on the floor?*

She was intrigued. When she started to lift the portrait to set it against the wall, she heard the door below open, then footsteps on the stairs. She grabbed the key in her left hand, hobbled back to her room using her right hand on the wall for speed and support. Fisting the key securely she knew she should try to return it to the door ledge sometime. She lifted her bandaged leg onto the bed, slid under the covers and turned her back to the room. And remembered with a jolt that she had not pulled the string to turn off the single light bulb. Had she closed the door of that curious room? She leaned over and slid the big brass key under the mattress as far as she could reach.

A few seconds later the bedroom door opened, and a sultry female voice said, "Carolyn? You must be awake. We heard you moving around up here."

Carrie grunted but did not turn over. She hadn't been called 'Carolyn' since her mother died. A tray slid onto her bedside table, and the delicious aroma of coffee filled her nostrils. There was a gentle hand on her thigh, and the low voice was now in her ear, "We had a terrible storm last night. Did you hear the wind? It blew that old poplar over the driveway, and all the deliveries were late this morning. Even your nurse couldn't get through. Don was quite upset, and he asked me to play nursemaid. Carolyn? Open your eyes, dear, and turn over. I'm Helen, Don's artistic director. And here's something to make you feel better."

Those words, 'make you feel better' were locked in the amber of Carrie's memory. Now she associated the phrase with lethargy and grogginess. Drugs in her food, she was sure of it. She rolled over and stared at the woman. When her eyes focused on the glass of orange juice under her nose her befuddled mind cleared. She took a deep breath, sat up on one elbow and held out her open hand.

"No! No! You know I have to put the pill in your mouth first." Helen sat on the edge of the bed, a picture of patience. She smiled again and said, "Tongue, please. Then you can have the juice."

Carrie pushed herself up on both her elbows, opened her mouth and stuck out her tongue. Helen placed the damn pill as far back on Carrie's tongue as she could, but Carrie turned, bowed her head and frantically worked her tongue, cheek muscles and front teeth until the pill was under her tongue. She twisted back to look up at Helen and swallowed.

"Did it go down? Let me see," the woman ordered.

Carrie clenched the pill on the underside of her tongue and opened her mouth an inch or so.

"How can I see in with your mouth like that?" Helen grabbed Carrie's chin with her left hand and forced Carrie's mouth open with her right. She peered in, but the pill stayed put. Carrie jerked her head free.

"Now, don't be like that," Helen's voice was honey sweet again. "If I have to call Don up here, he's not going to be happy." She got off the side of the bed, turned quickly and brought her fist down on Carrie's bandaged leg just above the knee.

Carrie yelped in pain, and Helen's hand was in Carrie's mouth again, her long painted nails scraping the delicate skin between Carrie's inner cheek and back molars. Carrie snapped her teeth down on Helen's index and middle fingers and ground them back and forth hoping she could break one of those damn claws.

"Agh!" Helen pulled her hand out and yelled, "You bitch! You'll pay for that!" She was just about to smack Carrie's leg again when the door swung open.

"What on earth is going on up here?" Don triple-stepped briskly to Carrie's bedside followed by a huge scowling man. Don pressed her hand and asked, his deep baritone dripping solicitude, "How are you, my dear? We've all been so worried about you." He motioned with his chin for Helen to leave, and she scampered out nursing her bitten hand to her chest.

Carrie leaned over the side of the bed and spit out the pill. Her back rigid against the pillows, she glared at him, "Why?"

Don slowly ground the saliva-covered pill on the floor under the toe of his shoe, "To heal your wound and let you sleep. The doctor recommended complete rest and giving you sleeping pills was the only sure way of keeping you off your feet. Don't you agree there is much less pain in your leg now?"

His confident smile and condescension irked her.

"Until your girlfriend punched it." Carrie's eyes closed as two images, superimposed on each other flashed through her mind—Helen's furious, blazing eyes and the dark, accusing eyes of the lady in the portrait.

"What? Helen? I can't believe that. She looked in pain when she left. Did you hurt her? Were you two *fighting?*"

Carrie forced back a triumphant grin, "I was, I am, protesting her damn pills. Come on, Don. I'm a big girl and I can judge how much pain I can handle and how much action my leg can sustain. It's only a dog bite. Where's my dog?"

"You know the coyote's teeth grazed your shin bone, and the tear from its bite is ragged and was hard to stitch. God knows how long all this will take to heal."

Carrie gave in and nodded, mainly because she knew he was right. "Charlie? Is he okay?" Fear rose up from her gut, "Is he alive?"

"Charlie is being treated for a possible rabies infection, by a reputable vet. He'll be fine."

"OK. Thank you." She leaned back in relief and asked, "Who's the lady in red?"

Don frowned, "You've been snooping. We left your bedroom door unlocked so you could use the bathroom when you woke up." He studied her for a moment, then pointing to the man at the door, he said, "This is Oscar by the way. He has been helping Helen look after you. Now that you have alienated her, I will have Helen bring you some clothes. Why don't you have a shower, or get freshened up? Then we'll get you downstairs for dinner." He turned, but as he put his hand on the doorknob, he looked back at her with a grim expression, "I look forward to your company at dinner." As soon as the door closed, Oscar grinned and started towards her.

"Get out! Don't you dare touch me!" Carrie shouted.

Oscar stopped dead in his tracks. With a disappointed, angry look he turned, and not looking back at her, yanked open the bedroom door and slammed it behind him.

Carrie took a deep breath, refusing to submit to the tears that were welling up. She was alone in this house of strangers, none of whom she trusted now. Why had she taken up Don's offer in the hospital? But she knew why. She hadn't had a choice and the stream of visitors had exhausted her. She remembered thinking of Don as a father figure. But now? She slumped on the edge of the bed, oblivious to the strap on her diaphanous nightgown sliding down her arm. Was Don her friend or foe? Was he helping her, or was he holding her captive? She shook her head at the breakfast tray and coffee. No, she couldn't take a chance. Those gaga pills were probably in the food.

Five minutes later Don and Oscar were in the room again. She held the covers up to her chin as Oscar thrust a shopping bag into her lap. She looked up and watched Don hang a black dress on the back of the closet door.

"Can you manage on your own? Helen refuses to come anywhere near you, but Oscar can help."

Oscar snickered, and his salacious eyes roamed hungrily over her bare shoulders.

Carrie shuddered, crushed the bag against her chest and glared at the two men. She told herself to calm down. She would gain nothing by losing her temper. Stay cool. Something strange was going down, and she was determined to get the hell out any way she could. She wiped the frown off her face, "I'm fine. Please leave."

Don looked hurt, "We're just trying to help you, Carrie. We'll be back in thirty minutes to help you downstairs."

Carrie wondered how Don would help her since she suspected he could barely navigate any stairs himself. His condescension grated on her nerves again, but she was a fighter. She could do this. As soon as the door closed behind the two men, she examined the contents of the bag—two sets of bra and panties, one black, the other pink; panty hose; low-heeled black pumps; creams, powder, mascara and eyeliners, a manicure set and lipsticks. What else does a girl need? Maybe shoes. But having either of those men buy clothing for her was creepy. She carried all the clothes and accoutrements into the bathroom and managed to have a shower without getting her bandaged leg wet. It was good to be clean again, but now what? If only she had her cell phone. Asking Don for it could be a test. If he refused, she would know he was keeping her here for some ulterior purpose.

When Don and Oscar entered again without knocking, she was waiting in the soft armchair, make-up applied, and dressed all in black except for one bandaged leg and a bare foot.

Don smiled, "You look stunning, in spite of those unseemly toes."

"How long have I been here?" she asked. "How long have I been comatose?"

"Not long. A few days. But you haven't eaten much. How about a roast beef dinner?" He motioned to Oscar.

"I need my phone, Don." She said in a cold voice. "I do have a job, you know. I'm usually in contact with my colleagues daily, and they're going to wonder where I am." A blatant lie, but what the hell.

He looked at her dubiously, and without answering he said to Oscar, "Help her."

Carrie jumped up, wobbling on one leg, "I don't need help."

Don ignored her, "I will go down first then Oscar will descend backwards immediately in front of you."

"Good," Carrie responded. "If I fall, I'll wipe out the both of you."

She stomped to the top of the landing, but Oscar was there before her.

"I can manage, damn you," she said as he planted himself on the first step.

"Carrie, be reasonable." Don's voice came from above her. "There are three sets of stairs and one of them curves."

Carrie yelled, "Move!" She swung her bandaged leg at Oscar's face, but he grinned and ducked. She almost lost her balance, and Oscar reached forward to grab her elbows.

Humiliated, Carrie gave in, gritted her teeth and let Oscar support her down the long staircases. When they finally reached ground level, she was exhausted. But at least Oscar finally let go of her and drifted away. She rested a hand on the pommel of the balustrade, tried to breathe normally, and looked in awe at the huge foyer.

Framed photographs of sour old men lined the sage-green walls. Antique mirrors were angled just-so at convenient heights, the better to reflect their ancestral glory to all who entered. Small towers of fresh flowers stood on shining mahogany side tables along the walls.

"Impressive," she nodded at Don, determined to control her fear at being alone in this big house with strangers who had drugged her. *Focus on escape!* She remembered Jim talking about Don's mansion on the hill. He must have meant the banks of the river. But which bank, north or south? Probably the south, but she should be able to tell by looking out the windows.

"My forebearers," His tight, insincere smile was brief. 'Are you interested in art, Carrie? We *are* going to have so many topics to discuss over dinner. Right this way." He held out his hand to usher her into a formal dining room. An ornate chandelier with white candles hung over the long table that was covered in a white damask tablecloth. Set for only two, much to Carrie's relief. No Helen for dinner. The warm glow reflected from the gold-leaf covered ceiling made the whole room seem surrealistic.

Chapter 12

Don stood waiting at the head of the table; his expression unreadable. Oscar held her chair and managed to slide his hand over her waist as Carrie sat down. She spun around and elbowed him in the gut, but he just stepped back and grinned. His abdomen was like a steel plate, and she knew he barely felt her sharp elbow. Not nearly hard enough. She sat down, glared at her host, and asked,

"Where exactly is my dog? I'll take him to my own vet."

Don ignored her and nodded to Oscar who appeared with a carafe of white wine. She put her hand over the crystal wine glass, shook her head, and asked again, "Charlie?"

"Your dog is fine. Have some wine. It's your favorite," said Don.

"How do you know…?" Carrie started to say, and Don smiled indulgently.

She turned her eyes away from the brilliant carmine wine that Oscar poured into Don's glass. She had one mission—to get out of here and wine was the last thing she needed. But she had to play along until she knew Charlie's whereabouts.

Carrie nodded at the bottle and said, "I'll have what you're having, please."

Don raised his eyebrows but flicked his fingers for Oscar to fill Carrie's glass.

Helen came in from the kitchen pushing a tea cart laden with bowls and a steaming soup tureen, complete with a silver soup ladle. She managed to arrange it all in front of Don's place setting despite her bandaged right hand. What the hell? Don's artistic director was now the serving girl?

"You will have soup? It's homemade beef bouillon." He waved the long handled engraved utensil. Pure silver, Carrie thought, as the light danced on its deep bowl.

Carrie nodded and watched Don ladle the steaming dark brown consommé into the bowls. Her mouth watered, but she waited until Don took his first sip before she picked up her spoon. She noted his delicate, almost feminine manner of eating soup, and she resisted the urge to indulge in ugly slurping. Too childish and would achieve nothing to her advantage. The only sounds were the munching of crackers and the occasional 'ding' of a spoon against the delicate china. She had to find out where Charlie was before she attempted an escape.

"You're famished. We're not going to poison you. You are quite safe," Don said when she put her spoon down.

"Yeah?" Carrie sneered. "Just drug me into oblivion."

"Carrie, be reasonable. The sedatives were for your own good. You must agree that your leg has healed most admirably under our care. Does it hurt to walk?"

"Not much, despite your artistic director's punch. Fortunately, she had a lousy aim."

"You mentioned that before. I don't believe Helen would actually hit you." He didn't sound convinced.

"Believe it, buster." She examined her bandage, "I don't see any blood, but she may have gotten it bleeding again."

"Oh, Carrie, I'm sorry," His head dropped into his hands. He was either a great actor or a wimp. Probably both.

"How long have I been comatose?" She waited. And waited.

Finally, he answered, "Your rally was yesterday."

"Oh, no!" Her heart sank. "They needed me, and you kept me drugged so I missed it. Why? Why?" She threw her napkin down and stood up, resting her hands on the table for balance. "I want to leave. Right now! Call a cab and give me back my cell. And write out the name and address of whoever has Charlie."

"Please sit down, Carrie. There's nothing you can do now for the anti-pipeline rally. Finish your dinner, and we will talk about getting you home."

Carrie stared at him. She needed food. In spite of the soup and crackers, she felt weak from hunger and knew from experience she was useless in this state. The smells from the kitchen were irresistible so she sat down and waited for the next course.

Don feigned sympathy as he continued, "The anti-pipeline rally was quite a disaster for your friend. Not only was the weather uncooperative with heavy, wet snow, but the organization of the event left a lot to be desired. The public address system kept kicking out, there was a shortage of chairs and people had to sit on the wet ground. Yes, quite an unsuccessful event." Don sat back and began folding and unfolding his napkin.

Why was he so nervous? Was the rally really that disastrous? No matter. "Where's my dog?" Her voice was strident.

He ignored her question again, "But the sun came out from behind the clouds when the native leaders spoke towards the end before people started drifting away. It was somewhat gratifying that First Nations' leaders were able to speak to hundreds of Canadians directly, because by that time the TV cameras were set up. They spoke passionately about the urgent need to redress not only the pipeline issues, but also the inequalities in Canadian society. Those men and women, adorned in their ceremonial clothes were heard, applauded, and cheered. Something I never imagined I would see."

Carrie shook her head at his condescension but said, "You were there?"

"Yes. But here's our salad. My favorite course," Don said as Oscar placed a large glass salad bowl and two smaller ones on the table.

Carrie ducked when Helen's hand appeared over her left shoulder to remove the soup bowl and plate. Helen's face was grim as she performed her job with one hand, avoiding Carrie's eyes. Don served the salad, and Oscar and Helen left.

"The salad dressing is in front of you, three kinds. Please help yourself."

"After you," Carrie said. She passed the divided glass dish to him.

"I don't use salad dressing. Too much fat. It eliminates the beneficial aspects of the salad," Don said.

"I believe you, so I won't either," Carrie speared one green leaf.

The meal progressed with Carrie insisting Don help himself first to vegetables, meat and gravy, even the salt and pepper. Don chattered about current events to bring Carrie up-to-date, and she tried not to guzzle her food as if it was her last meal she would ever have.

"I know you're a news freak," he commented.

But she kept thinking, "And Charlie? Why didn't he mention Charlie? Why did she have to keep asking?"

As they were waiting for dessert, Don approached the subject of pipelines. "I may be bucking a dead horse, Carrie, but you must realize that only a small percentage of the Alberta population thinks as you do. Oil and gas pipelines are the lifeline for this province. Canada is the world's fourth largest oil producer, and its heavy crude is in high demand in the United States. The refineries there are facing a shortage of crude owing to sanctions on Venezuela, and lower production from Mexico."

"Surely you know that the United States will be overflowing with oil once the shale in Montana is exploited," Carrie responded. She reached for the bowl of tiramisu that Helen had left. "Dessert?"

He regarded her thoughtfully and said, "I do apologize for the sleeping pills, but the food at this table is perfectly safe…no more sedatives."

"I trusted you—you rescued me and my dog. But it's my own fault. I don't trust many people. For some reason I let my guard down with you. Probably because you seemed like a nice, older gentleman. But I was always told to beware of strange men."

Don winced, "Ouch, it was…"

"It was for my own good?" Carrie mimicked. "But it certainly wasn't for the good of the rally. How on earth did you benefit by keeping me away from it?"

Don flushed a dark pink and reached for his wine.

Carrie sat back waiting for his response.

He put down his fork and glared at her, "I have a reputation to uphold in this community. If you think for one minute that I put you up in my house, paid a nurse to look after your leg and personal needs, paid the vet fees for your dog…"

"Charlie. You still haven't told me where he is. What have you done with my dog?" Carrie was getting desperate, "Is he responding to the rabies vaccine?"

"Yes. He was quite miserable for few days, but the vet is pleased with his progress."

Carrie sighed, "Thank God. But I'm still completely in the dark as to why you locked me up on that third floor."

Don shook his head, "Your bedroom door was open, as was the bathroom's."

"What about the door at the bottom of the third-floor stairs? It was locked." Carrie was just guessing.

Don paused, "How do you know? You didn't go down those stairs to try out that door." But he sounded unsure of himself.

So she was right. "I want to leave right now. Give me the vet's address and my cell and handbag." She flushed in anger, "Where *are* my clothes?"

"Thrown out." Disgust in his voice. "They were encrusted with mud and blood. You're quite welcome to keep the clothes you have on, and I told Helen to replace your old clothes. But why not stay until tomorrow? We could have a game of crib, or…"

"You threw out my clothes just because they were dirty? You had no right…"

A loud knock at the door startled them both, and Don's face became grim again. "Probably your female friends," he said. "They've been here in twos and threes every evening asking about you, and they have gotten quite aggressive."

They heard the click of Helen's heels on the parquet, then Jim's voice, loud and clear from the foyer, "We need to see her." Followed by Susan's shrill soprano, "You can't keep her imprisoned forever."

Carrie jumped up from the table and ignoring the jolt of pain in her leg she hobbled to the entryway. Swaying on one leg she held out her arms, "I'm so glad to see you both. Jim, when did you get back?"

Jim wrapped his arms around her and hugged her, "A few hours ago. Are you alright? Why didn't you answer your cell? How's your leg?"

Carrie nuzzled his neck and whispered into his ear, "Something really strange is going down here. Play along with Don." She broke away as his arms started to tighten.

"You don't even look like you." Susan eyed her outfit, "Nice dress. I've never seen you in black."

Don joined them, "Come in! Have some dessert and wine. I presume you are here to visit Carrie."

"We're here to take her home," Jim replied coldly. "We'll wait."

"I'd love some dessert and wine, thank you," Susan smiled sweetly at Jim, and took off her shoes.

"Right this way," Don gestured to the dining room, and called down the hall, "Helen, set two more places, please."

Carrie was so grateful to see both of them she grinned at Jim's sour expression. She understood too well his frustration with Susan. Taking his arm, she leaned on him as they moved into the dining room.

By the time Don served the tiramisu, Jim had thawed. He even made the effort to be pleasant by commenting, "Beautiful house, Don. Very unusual to see a three-story stone house in the middle of the prairies. Is there a history to it?"

"Well, Edmonton *is* on the prairies, but it is also a respectably sized city now. My mother's grandfather made his fortune by investing in Alberta's coal at the turn of the last century. He built this house for his British bride who unfortunately did not survive when the *Lusitania* went down."

"It's been in the family for how many generations?" Carrie counted on her fingers. "He must have gotten over her and married another."

"Yes, and it's a good thing he's not here to see his line end with me." Don said. "I have never married or sired an heir."

"So what will happen to the house?" Jim asked.

"I had thought I would convert it into a senior's residence, but the stairs are a problem and putting in an elevator isn't an option." Don replied. "The Historical Society came to my rescue. It will be a heritage house."

Jim and Carrie sat in rapt attention as Don outlined his plans for the house, the garden, the five acre lot. Susan half-listened as she twisted her head to examine every detail of the dining room, its furnishings and the art on the walls.

Don entwined his fingers on the table, smiled and said, "And that's it."

Carrie rose from the table, "I'll just get my things together. Wonderful meal, Don. Thank you."

"Yes," agreed Susan. "Thank you, Don. May I use the washroom?"

"Of course," Don said, and called for Helen. "Helen will show you how to find it."

Carrie leaned over the table to hide her laugh. She knew her friend well enough that this was Susan's excuse to snoop. Well, good luck to her.

Don and Jim followed Carrie into the hall.

Jim watched Carrie navigate the first steps and moved to help her, but Oscar appeared out of nowhere. He bounded up the two stairs and slid his arm around Carrie's waist.

She jerked away from Oscar and swayed on the edge of the step, but Jim was right there to steady her. She put her hand on Jim's shoulder and said, "Thanks. Will you help me get packed?" She was suddenly embarrassed at the intimacy implied in her request.

Jim took her arm, "Of course, let's go." He glanced at Oscar and said, "Thanks anyway, old chap."

As Oscar turned to go back down the stairs Jim's right foot shot out and hooked the big man's ankle. Oscar swore as he lost his balance and grabbed the old oak banister for support. The creak of wood, Oscar's loud curses and the thumps of his tumbling down the stairs filled the quiet house. Carrie stopped in surprise. But Jim's grip on her arm tightened as he pulled her up to the landing. She turned to look back at Oscar. He cradled his limp right hand in his left and glared up at them, his face a mask of pain, frustration and fury.

Carrie gasped and started to speak, but Jim shook his head and said, "Not now" as he helped her up the next flight of stairs. She pointed to the open door.

Helen was folding clothes into a large suitcase. Her movements were awkward, obviously hampered by her bandaged hand.

They heard Oscar cursing two stories below them and Helen looked up at Jim, "What on earth did you do to him?" She resumed her packing, "Don is insisting you take everything you're wearing now and then some." Her voice was cold as she handed Carrie a camel hair overcoat, "Even this brand new coat."

Carrie stared at the coat and at the pile of neatly folded clothes in the suitcase. "I'd rather have my old clothes back."

"Is this ready?" Jim reached for the suitcase.

"I can't take all that stuff," Carrie said but Helen grabbed the lid of the suitcase and slammed it shut, narrowly missing Jim's hand.

"Don's orders. Put the coat on. It's cold out, snow flurries tonight," Helen turned and left.

Carrie slipped on the coat, "Ready when you are. But first…" Her voice was soft and low, "Do you have a cell phone? Can you take a photo for me?"

Jim nodded. She pulled the key out from under the mattress and whispered instructions to him. Looking bewildered, he quietly left the bedroom.

Carrie stood at the open door listening for footsteps on the stairs, but Jim was back in a few minutes. With a nod he picked up the suitcase, steered her to the landing, and paused,

"Put your arm around my waist and I'll help you down."

His arm felt like an iron bar across her back and his fingers dug into her side as he practically lifted her down the stairs.

"I'm not helpless, you know," she panted but the feel of his firm chest and arm did something to her libido.

Susan was waiting and motioned them to hurry as she held the front door open. Neither Helen nor Oscar was in the vicinity, but Carrie heard them arguing with Don in the kitchen. Jim linked his arm with hers and they hurried out the front door.

She balked at the height of Jim's truck, but Susan and Jim hoisted her into the back seat. Susan pulled herself in lifting Carrie's bandaged leg gingerly onto her lap. As Jim backed out Carrie saw Don watching the truck from the picture window. He looked so forlorn that Carrie waved to him through the truck's side window. And Jim noticed,

"What the hell?" He swiveled back to steer the truck down the street, shook his head, and asked, "OK, Carrie, what do I do with the key?" Jim asked.

Carrie burst out laughing. The relief of being swept out of that house by Susan and Jim was overwhelming, and she swiped at the tears that had appeared at the corners of her eyes.

"What key?" Susan asked. "What are you two up to?" But her question went unanswered as Carrie stared out the car's side window, and Jim bent his head forward, concentrating on his driving.

He steered the truck around the sharp turn out of the cul-de-sac and a large object slid out from under Susan's coat. Carrie recognized Don's white damask napkin and she asked Susan in disbelief, "You stole a *napkin?*"

"I've always wanted a sterling silver soup ladle." With a satisfied smile Susan unwrapped the napkin and held up her gleaming treasure. Carrie shook her head.

Jim looked over his shoulder again and winced, "Jesus, Susan, that is theft. And stealing is still a crime in this country." Then he grinned, "That's one way to start a silver collection. Where to, ladies? Your place or mine?"

"Mine. I can hardly wait to…" Carrie replied quickly, but Susan interrupted her,

"Carrie, you should go to Jim's. He and his big dog can protect you—you are very vulnerable now especially since you can barely put any weight on that leg."

"But…" Carrie just wanted to go home, her own home.

"No buts, Carrie. Susan is right. Fort Saskatchewan, here we come," Jim swung the big half-ton onto the approach to the high-level bridge.

Chapter 13

Children, their voices bird-like and overlapping, woke Carrie the next morning. The sound was carried on the cool breeze from the open window. Kids at the playground across the street, or on their way to school or recess? She heard a soft bump against her closed bedroom door and fear snaked through her body. But the heavy sigh that followed the thump reassured her. It must be Tess, Jim's shepherd, and he was telling her it was time to get up just the way Charlie used to. She rolled over on her back, opened her eyes and remembered where she was. Jim's place. Both Jim and Susan had been insistent that she not go home, that she stay where she could be protected by Jim, his dog, and even the RCMP in Fort Saskatchewan. Susan's exaggerated fears of Cummings' revenge had convinced Jim in the end.

She sat on the edge of the bed. "Okay, Tess old girl, I'm coming," Carrie called to Jim's shepherd as her bare feet slapped on the cold floor.

As soon as she pushed against the dog's weight to open the door Tess stood up, her long tail swishing on the hardwood and her mouth open in a wide, welcoming grin. Sunlight flooded onto the hallway from the skylight and Carrie groaned, "What time *is* it?" She absently scratched Tess's ears. "It must be lunchtime. Kids go to and from school in the dark at this time of the year. I never sleep this late." She bent down to rub the dog's shoulders, "Oh, Tess, I didn't realize you were so big. You're going to gobble up my Charlie in one mouthful." She straightened up, "Where's the bathroom?"

Tess wagged her tail and followed Carrie into the main bathroom at the end of the hall. A large old fashioned white clawed tub with matching toilet and urinal dominated the room. It faced a corner shower and his-and-hers basins. Carrie opened the door at the end of the tub and the warm cedar aroma of a small sauna escaped into the cold bathroom. Fluffy blue towels hung everywhere. She closed the door reluctantly, and watched Tess pull and scratch at the scatter rug. The big shepherd lay down with her head between her paws, prepared to wait for however long this human took.

Carrie sighed in resignation, "No privacy allowed. You are some guard dog." She talked to Charlie all the time, so why wouldn't she talk to Jim's dog?

She showered and wrapped herself in the flannel bathrobe that hung on a hook beside the shower stall. Breathing in Jim's scent on the robe she rubbed her hair dry and finger combed it back off her face. She pulled the sash tight and tried to remember the details of the previous night. The most prominent memory was Susan ranting about the danger of Carrie staying alone in her little house in north Edmonton. Next was Jim with his arm around her waist, helping her up wide stairs to a small bedroom. And Tess waiting on the landing, wagging her long tail.

Susan had rejected Carrie's pleas to come to Fort Saskatchewan with her even though Jim insisted there was room in his house for them both. She had tried to belay

Carrie's worries by telling her Jim was the most honorable man she had ever met. Jim's laugh had not reassured Carrie. She had not wanted to spend another night alone in a strange man's home. But Jim was not a stranger, he was her golf partner. Her leg had ached, she had felt nauseous and tired. Too tired to argue.

In the clear light of day, Carrie wondered why Susan had sloughed her off on Jim. Was it only because Sue's place was so small? There had not been many choices at that time of night. Jim's offer had not only been expedient, his was the only one. In any case, here she was talking to a dog in the home of her one-time golfing and fishing mate.

"Come on, Tess, you gorgeous animal. Let's find some coffee."

Jim's house was a 1960's split level. It reminded Carrie of one of the houses she'd lived in with her family. The first time her aunt visited she had said it was like being in an Eaton's department store because of the four flights of stairs. Carrie peeked into the master bedroom, the only other room on this top level, but she was reluctant to invade Jim's private space. She hobbled down the stairs to an L-shaped living-dining room whose wide expanse of picture windows looked out over bush and far below, the river. A door opened up to a small kitchen and she almost ducked in to search for coffee. But she carried on to the ground level and rested on the top step. To the left of the stairs was an office and bathroom. On the right she could see a billiard table backed by rows of partially filled liquor bottles sitting on glass shelves. The room was way too small for a pool table. "How does anyone take a corner shot?" she asked Tess who sat patiently beside her. She leaned on the dog as she stood up, "Let's carry on."

But the next level was the basement, and it was dark, reminding Carrie of the drive here on the Fort Trail. Away from the city lights, the black of the dark sky had shrouded the car. The stars and the new moon had stayed well hidden behind the clouds, and the only light had come from Jim's headlights and those of the occasional oncoming car.

"Enough with dark, Tess. We'll give this one a pass."

Carrie's breath was coming in short gasps when she finally sank down into a kitchen chair. From pain, from the damn vaccine, or was she just out of condition? Her leg pounded and the exercise of the stairs had winded her. She noticed a sheet of paper on the Formica surface of the counter that was held in place by a set of cut-glass salt and pepper shakers. Its edges flapped gently in the slight breeze from the open window.

"No wonder it's so cold in here. Is your master a fresh air freak?"

Tess looked at her expectantly, and Carrie wondered if Jim fed her from the table. Probably, and she pictured his lazy, laid-back crooked smile. He had set the table for one—a plaid placemat with a matching cloth napkin, stainless steel cutlery, a juice glass, bowl, plate and a coffee mug. The morning paper lay folded in the middle of the table.

She reached over for the note and read aloud to Tess, *Good morning, Carrie. Help yourself to whatever you can find—juice, milk and eggs in the fridge. The coffee pot on the stove is ready to perc (sorry, no fancy electric one). Please, please stay inside and keep Tess with you. She's like a camel and she won't need to go out. I'll be home around 12:10. Call if you need anything. 780-998-5500.*

Carrie turned on the heat under the battered aluminum coffee pot, poured a glass of juice and downed it. Feeling refreshed, she opened the cereal box and commented to Tess, "Organic granola. What a treat!" She filled it to the brim, found the milk, and picking up her breakfast she wandered into the dining room.

She browsed the books on the shelves above the credenza and moved to stand in front of the floor-to-ceiling picture window in the living room. The dark ribbon of the North Saskatchewan River curved in the valley below. The dining room window was adjacent to the picture window, and its door led to a small porch with four steps leading down to a long, deep patio. Opening the door, she was about to go outside when she noticed a black pick-up truck parked at the curb. Did Jim have two trucks? She knew the one from last night was blue. But then again, this was Alberta, the land of pick-up trucks.

A low rumble from the back of Tess's throat startled her. The hackles on the dog's back had risen to a stiff bristle and her upper lip was pulled back. Carrie stepped back inside and closed the door. The growl erupted into a loud bark.

Carrie startled instinctively, spilling the milk from her cereal and knocking her hip against the edge of the table. She set the bowl down as she followed Tess's long nose. It pointed to the tall trees and thick bush that framed the end of the patio's concrete slab. She thought she saw a movement in the low wild rose bushes that fronted the thick mass of Manitoba maple saplings and mountain ash bushes. A row of Lombardy poplars interspersed with fir trees soared up behind the shrubbery.

Tess jumped up on the window of the dining room door, growling and barking.

Her hands shaking, Carrie grasped the door molding as she backed up into the kitchen from the dining room. Was she being paranoid, or should she trust Tess's instincts and phone Jim? Who would be crazy enough to hide in those scratchy wild roses? Glancing at the kitchen clock she knew she couldn't wait an hour until 12:10.

"Tess! Here Tess!"

But Tess ran to the living room picture window and scrabbled at the glass. Drool slid out of her open mouth to form viscous drops on the wide window ledge as she barked excitedly.

Carrie snatched Jim's note and hurried to the phone that was set in a small alcove in the hall. Fumbling for the receiver, she forced herself to punch in the numbers slowly and carefully.

A female voice answered on the second ring, "James Mathew's office."

"May I speak to him, to Jim?" Even in her panic, she realized she didn't even know, or remember, Jim's last name.

"I can barely hear you," said the woman on the phone. "Speak up!" She paused, "Is that Tess barking? Stay on the line."

The receiver banged down on a hard surface, and Carrie heard her calling, "Sir! Mr. Mathews! Something's very wrong at your house!"

Keeping the phone jammed between her shoulder and ear Carrie put her hand out to restrain Tess but it was hopeless. The big dog was beyond control.

"Carrie?" Jim had picked up. "What's Tess barking at?" He was yelling to be overheard above his dog's fracas. "What the hell is happening? What's wrong with Tess?"

Carrie shouted too, "I think there's someone in the rose bushes. Should I let Tess out to scare them away?"

"No! No! Keep her with you. I'm phoning the police. I'll be there in five minutes. Hang tight."

The line went dead. Carrie slunk back down the hall, as far away from the windows as she could get.

Tess ran between the picture window and the glass door of the dining room jumping up on both, barking, growling and whining. Back and forth the dog went, her bark now high-pitched and frantic.

"Oh God! Is the back door locked?" Carrie whispered.

To ensure no one could see her through the windows Carrie got down on her hands and knees and crawled painfully to the top of the stairs leading to the back door. Tess pushed past her, jumped down the three stairs, and scratched at the door leaving deep gouges in the wooden panel. From the front of the house she could hear receding footsteps running to the school. Late kids. The school bell had rung several minutes ago. If she screamed would the kids come back? And put them in danger? Would they get someone from the school to help her?

Whoever was outside kicked the door three times to no avail. She heard a few steps before he threw his weight against it; with a loud thud. But the door stood, staid and solid. She knew this guy's next move would be to take the hinges off the damn door.

Instead, he shattered the lock with two shots.

She screamed. A true blood-curdling scream. Even Tess paused briefly in her barking to look back, her foul panting breath engulfing Carrie in the constricted space.

The approaching police sirens and Tess's barking drowned out Carrie's voice as she gawked to Tess. Whoever was on the other side of the door must have heard the ear-splitting sirens because the outer door swung shut. She half-stood and glimpsed a baseball-capped head run by the kitchen window.

"Tess! Come! Please come," Carrie's voice had dropped several decibels and Tess stopped barking but whined as she reluctantly came to her. "Oh, Tess, are you okay?" She ran her hands over the dog's body and head and, not finding any blood, she sank back and pulled a squirming Tess into her arms. She murmured meaningless words onto the dog's head and Tess gradually relaxed against Carrie's body.

A few minutes later Jim unlocked the front door to let himself and two RCMP officers into the house. They found Carrie sitting on the landing hugging her protector, her nose buried into the dog's neck. Tess broke away from Carrie's clutches and bounded down the stairs to greet her master.

Carrie sat back in relief, and said in a quavering voice, "You should know by now that I'm just trouble with a capital 'T'".

"Are you alright?" Jim's face was next to hers as he knelt beside her. She gazed at the wrinkles fanning out from his worried eyes as she gulped and nodded.

The two officers ran past them to the back door, the heavy one almost tripping on Tess's tail as he spoke to Jim, "Problems in paradise, Jim?"

Accepting Jim's helping hand she noticed his face was beet red. At the gendarme's implication that she and Jim were an item? "I'm fine. Thanks so much." She reached down to pat Tess who stood against Jim's legs. "He, whoever he is, almost shot Tess! Oh Jim, I'm so sorry. You shouldn't be involved in the mess my life has become."

"I thought you would be safe here," He squeezed her hand.

"Pete." Her voice was bitter, "It's taken him this long to execute his revenge." She needed to sit; her legs felt as if they couldn't hold her up.

Jim gently took her shoulders, "Pete would never be this crazy. What else are you...?" He stopped abruptly as the back door was pushed open. "You got him!" Jim released her, "Well done. This is Carrie, my house guest. Carrie, meet my old friend, Barry."

The big, swarthy First Nations officer kept a firm grip on a wiry man who struggled valiantly, but uselessly. "When I have a free hand," Barry nodded at Carrie, "we'll shake." He snapped handcuffs on his prisoner.

The second officer squeezed into the crowded foyer and gripped the captive's arm, "Anyone here know this man?"

Jim shook his head, "Carrie?"

"No," Carrie answered as she pressed herself against Jim, hating herself for being the helpless female.

Barry grabbed the captive's hair, pulling back his head so the man's hostile eyes glared at Carrie.

"What's your name?" The officer in charge demanded.

A stream of cusses in both English and French filled the air but when the officer twisted the prisoner's arm into an impossible position he yelled, "Hey, don't do dat! Me, I'm Gascon. Gascon Tremblay. What you want to know?"

His French-Canadian accent surprised Carrie, and a new wave of apprehension coursed through her body. Tess growled and sniffed the captive's legs.

"I have to read him his rights…"

"To hell with that!" Jim said and turned to the surly captive, "Who's paying you?"

"You do not know them. Far away," His French accent was thicker now.

"How far away?"

Gascon hesitated, looked down and said, "La Tuque." He shrunk from Tess, "Keep dat damn chien away!"

"Where the hell is La Tuque?" Barry gave Gascon's head another tug,

Carrie quickly answered, "It's in northern Quebec. I agree with you, Jim. This is not Pete's work. "Jim looked at her, question marks in his eyes, but he said nothing.

The two police pulled Gascon up and Barry said, "You are coming with us. Illegal use of a firearm plus breaking and entering." Barry read Gascon his rights and the two officers pushed Gascon out the front door saying, "We'll be back." Barry said over his shoulder to Carrie, "Be ready to answer questions." He closed the front door and the outside aluminum door whispered shut.

Jim pulled her hand to make her look at him, "Barry will be relentless when he questions you. I need to know everything, Carrie, before they come back."

"I KNOW! I KNOW!" Her face was red, but she brought her voice down, "But I can't tell you because..., because I would just be speculating. Let me deal with the police. I'll go with them and leave you out of it. There's no need for you to be involved. You don't *want* to be involved in my crazy life." She pulled her hand free and stepped up the three stairs to the next level, "I have to use the washroom. Can you make more coffee?"

Chapter 14

"Smells divine," Carrie said as she sank down at the kitchen table "and it isn't just the coffee." She lifted her throbbing leg to rest it on an empty chair and tried not to wince.

"Here you go," Jim said as he slid a grilled cheese sandwich onto her plate, then poured coffee into her mug. He brought the lazy Susan closer to her and twirled it. "Help yourself to milk and sugar. Sorry, no cream."

She waited for him to sit down with his sandwich and coffee before she took a tentative bite. Her stomach heaved and she resisted pushing the plate away. She swallowed and asked, "Is this your specialty?"

He grinned, "It's the extent of my culinary expertise."

She watched him eat as she took small sips of coffee. He ate quickly and when he started on the other half of his sandwich he looked up,

"Not hungry?" He asked nonchalantly but his face was concerned. He set down his mug. "Are you still taking antibiotics?"

"Finished the last of them this morning."

"But you're feeling shitty." It was a statement, not a question. "Perhaps you should see someone here. Even emergency could give you something for the nausea."

She shook her head, "I'm sure it's just the vaccine. They warned me it could take weeks before the effects wore off." She smiled weakly, "Guess it's better than being dead." But she was tired of the ache in her leg and the churning in her stomach.

He looked at the frayed bandages on her leg. "Well, at the very least they could re-bandage your wound."

She bent forward to regard them and agreed, "They do look pretty disreputable. But you have a job to go to. I can get a taxi..."

"I'm not going to get fired if that's what's worrying you." He finished his lunch quickly and got up to put his dishes in the sink, ignoring hers. "I did a little reading about rabies, so I know that it's fatal in humans if it's not treated. But should your leg still hurt? It should be starting to heal by now."

She looked at him dubiously and he added, "But it's not, is it?"

"I don't know...."

He crossed his arms, his back against the sink. "One of the doctors here is my badminton partner. I could try to get him to have a look. Or we could go to emergency."

"How many well-positioned sporting partners do you have?" She tried to smile.

"That's a 'yes' then. I'll get our coats."

"But you need to get back...."

"The hospital here is one of Lougheed's legacies. It's small and I must admit I've never had to visit it." He was back in a few minutes with their coats, holding hers open for her.

"How can I ever repay you for everything you're doing, and have done, for me?" She heaved herself up and looked over her shoulder at him as she slipped her arms into the sleeves.

"You can tell me what the hell is going on, for starters. But not now. Let's go." He put Tess in the back yard as she hobbled down the stairs to the front door.

In spite of Jim's contacts at the medical clinic, Carrie's appointment took most of the afternoon. Jim told the desk staff that she was on rabies vaccine because of a coyote bite, and they placed her at the front of the line. After producing her Alberta health card, she was ushered into a small room with a high examining table. Jim followed.

"Are you this lady's husband?" the nurse asked. When he hesitated, she added, "If you're not, you can't come in."

He shook his head, "I was afraid you'd ask that." He pressed Carrie's shoulder and went back to the waiting room.

The nurse helped her take off her jeans and commented on the fact that Carrie had cut off one leg at the knee to accommodate the bandaging. "What a shame to ruin a good pair of jeans," she teased. "Dr. Wilkins will be in to see you shortly." She left but was back in a few minutes with a glass of ice water.

Carrie listened to the muffled conversations and sounds, put her head on the pillow and wished she'd had a chance to brush her teeth. A little while later, there was a knock on the door and a white-haired man entered. He nodded,

"Hello, Ms. March. I'm Dr. Wilkins. Jim left a message about your rabies vaccine. I've read about your entanglement with the coyote in the paper. You are almost a celebrity." He smiled and held out his hand.

Carrie grimaced and shook his hand. The door opened and the same nurse came in.

Dr. Wilkins put on the standard blue stretchy gloves, "Let's have a look." He nodded to the nurse and together they removed the soiled bandage. While they worked, he asked her to tell him about the coyote attack and she repeated it once more. Almost by rote. He described the tell-tale symptoms of rabies in an animal, all of which she knew but she told him she couldn't even tell, or remember, if the coyote was drooling. When the bandage was off, he pressed gently on her swollen leg and foot. He sat at the end of the examining bed and opened his laptop. After a few minutes he grunted,

"Doesn't look as if they took X-rays at the Alec, did they?"

"No, I don't think so, but I was pretty well out of it with all the drugs they pumped into me." Carrie got up on her elbows to look at the wound, which was red, puffy and angry-looking. The stitches were digging into her skin. "It looks infected."

"It **is** infected." Dr. Wilkins agreed. "Let's get those X-rays taken and I'll be back. Jim mentioned that you had the empty vial of the antibiotics you were taking. May I have a look at it?"

"It's in my purse…" She gestured to the chair.

"Here you go," the nurse quickly passed it to Carrie. When she handed the empty bottle to Dr. Wilkins, he grunted again and muttered,

"Wouldn't have been my choice."

He started to leave, and she stopped him with a question, "What do you expect the x-rays will show?"

"We need to see if the coyote's teeth grazed a bone or two. It's not likely, but we need to make sure." He smiled encouragingly and left. The nurse scooped up the dirty bandages and asked if she needed anything. Carrie felt like saying, "Yes, Jim please." But she shook her head and closed her eyes. She was way too dependent on that man now.

The air on her wound was somewhat soothing but the throbbing did not let up. She closed her eyes, but even dozing was out of the question. She sipped at the glass of water the nurse had brought and imagined various scenarios of life without pain and nausea. She was picturing Troy in her office chair, in her job, when they came to take her to be X-rayed. Dr. Wilkins came in while she was still there and after examining the photographs of her bone on the screen, he enlarged them and pointed to faint marks on the image of her shin bone.

"Can you see these lines? They're undoubtedly the coyote's teeth marks. I will consult with my colleagues, but I'm quite sure you have an infection in that bone. That's why there's very little healing taking place, and you are still in pain. At least the bone is not chipped." He went into some medical terminology which she tuned out.

She squinted at the image and could barely make out the marks he had pointed at. She gulped, "Now what? Not another operation, I hope."

He shook his head, "No, but we will have to keep an eye on it. I will give you prescriptions for nausea and the infection. I should warn you that the pills for your tummy might make you more talkative than usual."

"Poor Jim."

He chuckled, "Knowing Jim, I'm sure he can handle that." The nurse came in and bandaged her leg under Dr. Wilkins watchful eyes. He nodded his satisfaction and said, "It's been a pleasure meeting you, Carrie. Here's some information on bone infections. See you in a few days." He gave her a photocopied sheet of paper, which she glanced at and folded. By the time she had put it in her purse, he had left.

Armed with sample antibiotics, two prescriptions, and a follow-up appointment slip, Carrie approached Jim in the waiting room. He was typing furiously into his laptop, but he looked up and smiled,

"All done?" he asked hopefully.

"Finally. Is everything okay back at the plant?"

"Hunky-dory. Who needs the boss? Let's go. You can tell me what the doc said in the car." Jim snapped the lid on his laptop, "Pizza and beer for dinner? How does that sound?" He followed her out and as he closed the door on the sniffy kids and crying babies. She ignored his question and asked,

"How can you concentrate in that bedlam?"

Jim grinned, "Bit of a challenge, I agree." He had a firm grip on her elbow as he steered her through the parking lot. Unlocking the passenger door he asked, "Would the back seat be better?"

She hesitated but shook her head, "I can do this." The seat was still back as far as it would go from their drive to the hospital. She knew he wanted to help but she was determined to go at it alone despite the jolt of pain when she lifted her bandaged leg in.

He closed her door and she watched him pick his way through the ruts in the snow around the front of the car. She was grateful for his help but wondered why he was doing this—taking her here, waiting hours for her.

"What did the doctor say?" He threw his arm across the top of her seat as he backed out. His face inches from hers and he smiled at her almost as if he wanted to kiss her before he turned back to the front.

"Your pal Dr. Wilkins looked after me. He showed me the coyote's teeth marks on my shin bone. I could hardly see them."

"Come clean, Carrie. How bad is it?"

"Well," she pulled out the printed page Dr. Wilkins had given her. "It's called osteomyelitis." She read out loud: "Although once considered incurable, osteomyelitis can now be successfully treated.' Oh, God, listen to this: 'Most people need surgery to remove areas of the bone that have died. After surgery, strong intravenous antibiotics are typically needed. Dr. Wilkins assured me – no more surgery. He promised."

They waited for a break in the traffic, and Jim strummed on the wheel, "Surely he would have ordered it if he thought the bone was infected."

"I reacted pretty violently when he suggested it."

He shook his head, "Nothing is ever simple, is it? Don't worry. I'll get you back to the hospital and doctors whenever you need to go."

"Thanks, but I can get a taxi. I need to go home, and you've got your own life…"

"No arguments please." He swung into a strip mall and parked in the small lot, "Here's the pizza place. Do you want to take your prescriptions here or to your own drugstore? There's a Shoppers across the way that I use all the time. Your choice."

She looked back and saw the large drugstore at the corner. "Let's use this one. I'd like to get started as soon as possible. I can go in…."

"No way, Carrie. Stay put. I'll leave the engine on to keep you warm."

He was back in five minutes, "They can make up the prescriptions right away. Do you want to get out and stretch?"

"No, thanks."

He put a box of DVDs on the console between them, "Why don't you pick out something while you wait?"

While Jim was gone, Carrie had a few moments to reflect on what she should do. No more damn babysitting by strange men, that's for sure. But she didn't think of Jim as a stranger. She felt comfortable in his presence and in his house. She was torn between wanting to get home to her own little house or staying at Jim's with all its creature comforts. Not to mention his protection and that of Tess. What the hell was wrong with her? She had tolerated being pampered by Don, but she had been in a drugged stupor most of the time. Now here she was again. She was an independent woman, so why did she relish being cared for? But Jim might be the only one who could provide answers to her questions: the lady in red, Pete and Don's relationship, Troy's loyalty to her or Pete, and how, or if, Jim was involved in any of it.

He came back, dumped the Shopper's bag on her lap and asked her what kind of pizza she liked. "You choose," she responded hoping the nausea pills would work quickly. She opened the bag, read the labels on the vials, and swallowed one pill out of each.

As they drove up to Jim's house Carrie cursed when she saw the familiar white and black police car parked at the curb. "Shit!"

Jim glanced at her, "Well, I expected them. I'm surprised you didn't."

"What should I tell them?" Carrie asked.

"How about the truth?" He had the grace to laugh.

"You make it sound so easy," Carrie wiggled out of the car. When she stood up on the pavement Barry and his colleague appeared offering their arms.

"Thank you, kind sirs. Have you been waiting long?" Carrie asked sweetly and Jim led the way to his house. He looked back, laughing at her.

"No," the burly police officer responded. "Jim has..." He stopped, as if uncertain.

"Come on in, everyone. But there's only enough pizza for two here," Jim unlocked the front door, "Beware of my exuberant dog."

After an hour's questioning at Jim's kitchen table, the two gendarmes left, but not before Jim and Barry had a brief confab. When Jim came back, he congratulated Carrie, "I'm impressed. You managed to answer all their questions and say absolutely nothing of any value. How do you do it?" He turned on the oven.

"Years of working for the government, I guess" She pushed back from the table.

"Let's go upstairs to more comfortable chairs." He pulled two beer from the fridge. "Here, let me help you."

She declined his assistance on the stairs saying, "It's really easier on my own, now that I've worked out a system."

A few minutes later Carrie was sitting in an easy chair in front of the large picture window. Tess, her nose close to the glass, followed the goings and comings of a myriad of birds at the feeder. "They're gorgeous! They must be hoarding for winter. And so many of them!" She mimicked Tess, her head moving from side to side as she watched the birds.

"My secret is peanut butter and oatmeal sandwiches. They much prefer them to bird seed, even though I can't convince my neighbor. Would you believe she buys organic bird seed?"

Carrie laughed as she lifted her leg onto the footstool Jim had set in front of her chair. "Just look at that gleaming white bandage. I feel like a new woman." She paused to take a long slug of the beer Jim had set on the side table along with a generous slice of pizza. "Seriously, Jim. I can't thank you enough. All I can think of is to let you beat me at golf."

"We might have to wait until next year's golfing season. Should you be drinking alcohol while you're on those pills?"

"Where did you ever hear such old-fashioned nonsense?" Carrie cocked her head and smiled up at him but wondered if perhaps he was right. She swallowed, and swallowed again, trying to keep the nausea at bay.

Jim looked at her, shook his head in defeat and said, "Okay, Carrie. Time to fill me in on what the hell is going on."

"I was going to ask you the same question with regard to Don and Pete."

"Come on, Carrie. I'm in the dark there too. Please, from the beginning."

"Well..." Carrie hesitated. "It's a long story..."

"We've got all night and lots of beer and pizza," Jim carefully lifted a pizza slice. "I'll keep the pizza warm in the oven, but perhaps you should go easy on the beer."

"I think you're right there," She managed a weak grin. "That damn vaccine is making my stomach roll in spite of the nausea pill, so I'll stick to water."

He disappeared down into the kitchen, returning with a glass of ice water for her and another beer for himself, "Okay, all the fortification we'll need."

Carrie took a big breath. "Well, here goes. I was a spoiled only child, and I had everything a girl could want growing up in Montreal. This was after Quebec's Quiet Revolution. The days of the wealthy English minority lording it over a Francophone majority were over. My mother refused to accept the political change, and we continued to live our privileged lives in upper Westmount, which in case you don't know, was the preferred address of all the crème de la crème of the former rulers, we the arrogant Anglophones."

Jim nodded his encouragement and Carrie carried on, "My husband's family and mine had been friends and business partners for generations. They supported the same charities, went to the same church, ran Montreal's annual St. Andrew's Ball, were members of the same golf club, went on European ski holidays together. You name it, they did it together. Cliff was fifteen years older than me, very shy and quite anti-social. But he could relax with me, I was just a kid. You can imagine how thrilled I was when he played board games with me. He even taught me chess. His parents were bridge fiends and the four of us played—well, we played a lot. I spent as much time at their house, Cliff's house, as our own and it was their maid who taught me joual, much to Mother's disgust." She smiled at the memory, "Mother loved to come over and drag me home for dinner, and I didn't suspect a thing. Anyway, it seemed to be understood that I would marry Cliff, the heir to the thriving business. A month after graduating from McGill, I did just that. I was to be the families' brood cow."

Jim shook his head as Carrie continued, "I was naïve and had no idea that my mother and Cliff had been lovers for years. When I look back, I can see how Mother manipulated everyone, especially my father and me, and probably Cliff as well."

"Did your father know he was being cuckolded?"

"What an awful word!" Carrie frowned. "Yes, he must have, but he was so infatuated, so in love with my mother he probably turned a blind eye, or perhaps just refused to believe his friend and wife could..." She took a bite of pizza, chewed slowly, and when it finally slid down her throat, she continued, "You should know that she was beautiful, witty and charming. Everything an ambitious man wants and needs in a wife." Carrie's voice had become bitter as she swirled and contemplated the ice in her glass. Why was she talking so much?

Jim twisted the screw top of another beer for himself, "Go on."

"He was a wonderful father," Carrie's voice was warm again but hesitant. "He more than made up for my mother's lack of attention to me. He often included Cliff in our outings and Cliff became a big brother to me. Cliff had always been a loner and his parents were positive it was me who brought him out of himself. My marriage to Cliff was easy and genial. He was always kind, considerate, and I'm sure he loved me a little bit in a distracted sort of way. He did not want children, but I kind of tricked him into that. However, he did come to love Bobby as much as I did. He had our son's life plotted out like an engineer's critical path." Her voice broke, and when she felt Jim's hand on hers, she looked up at him with a weak smile, shook her head and said, "Cripes, it's been so many years...."

"Years don't count for much in the death of your child," Jim looked embarrassed and muttered, "I'm sorry, Carrie...."

"You're right, of course," Carrie sat up straight. "My mother hates me now and vowed revenge during her only visit to me in the hospital. I killed her only grandson and her lover. So I'm guessing she hired someone, some thug, to shoot Charlie, some degenerate who mistook your dog for mine."

She leaned her hands on the arm rests, starting the process of leaving, "I have to get away from this town before something happens to you or Tess."

"No, you can't leave." Jim was adamant. His hands were on her shoulders again gently pushing her into the chair, "Carry on with your story. How can a mother hate her own child?"

"Well, she didn't always hate me," Carrie sighed and relaxed, "Even though she didn't want me. She tried to abort several times, but my father told me he was able to intercede. And, of course, I was a difficult birth. You wouldn't believe the gory stories… Anyway, when I became the apple of Dad's eye, she was jealous. She was so used to being the center of attention and everyone's darling, and now she had competition. How do you compete with a cute little two-year old who had inherited some of your own best features? Except for the eyes. No one could figure out how a blond, blue-eyed beauty like my mother could produce a brown-eyed brunette." Carrie became wistful. "But we did have some good years when she treated me like a doll—buying me clothes, fussing with my hair. She loved me in dresses. She was always buying me dresses. I remember her loving eyes when she put a new outfit on me." Carrie drank more water, "God, my mouth is running off like a… a. Tell me to shut up, Jim."

"No way." He smiled, "I love this new you. What changed?"

He was flirting with her! Carrie took a deep breath, "I became a teenager and I refused to wear make-up, lipstick, push-up bras—the whole caboodle. I became a tomboy in dirty jeans with an attitude, then the athletic girl who could beat up the boys. The plus side was that I learned to play all the sports I enjoyed, even ice hockey. But our home was a war zone, and I was the main aggressor."

Jim sat back, "I can just see you as a skinny kid with pig tails hammering some supine, pimply boy." He looked at her thoughtfully, "Why did you marry him?"

Carrie paused, then said, "It was partly to do with money. I hate to admit I was so mercenary, but I had no job prospects after McGill. My mother presented me with two options: marry Cliff and have the money to do anything you want with your life or, you're on your own. Completely. No more family, no big house to come home to, and of course, no Cliff. He would marry someone else. There were lots of debutantes to choose from in Montreal. She even threatened to restrict my access to Dad. He had just been diagnosed with cancer, and his prospects were not good. At that point, he was my only real family, the only person I truly loved. I knew I couldn't leave him to face the chemo and all that shit with just my mother as his support."

"Is he…?" Jim asked.

"Yes. He still writes to me, but his handwriting is almost illegible now." Carrie paused. "He was with me the night Bobby was born. He came to the hospital because he knew Cliff and Mother were shacked up in the Laurentian Hotel."

"And you would have been alone." The disgust in his voice was palpable.

Carrie noticed of course, and she set aside her glass, "Look, Jim. I think I'd better go." She started to get up again.

"Not yet. You think your mother was behind the shooting? After all this time?"

"I killed the love of her life and her grandson. She's been hospitalized for a 'mood disorder' several times in the last nine years. They kept her in for two years the last time. But now she's out, with pots of my father's money to pay for whatever she wants to do. She's got power of attorney, in spite of her mental condition. I have to hope that she and Pete never find each other." Carrie coughed a short humorless laugh.

"How old is she?"

"Sixty-one, and still glamourous with a good figure." Carrie picked up their glasses and the empty pizza box. "Can you phone me a taxi?"

"Wait, please," Jim stood up to help her, "Tell me how you became involved with a raving mad tree hugger like Susan."

Carrie bristled. "Raving mad? Isn't that a little strong?" She sat down again, still holding the glasses. "I admit I do help her out but only to input financial and scheduling data. She's a computer Luddite. I met her when I was documenting Canadian environmental groups with American affiliations. Sort of an offshoot of regulatory work that no-one else wanted to do at the time. "Carrie looked up at him, "But I agree that Susan probably does more harm than good now on the anti-pipeline movement. She didn't used to be so radical, so hysterical." Carrie shook her head and said, "I need to go home."

"Look, I'm perfectly capable of driving you home. But why not stay here another night? I have a meeting in Edmonton at nine tomorrow and I can drop you off on the way into downtown. Surely you can trust me now."

"Of course I do. But that will mean how many nights I've been here? Won't your neighbors notice?"

"I don't really give a damn if they do. Leave those few dishes, Carrie. Let me help you on the stairs." He took the glasses out of her hands and laughed when he saw her disdainful look. Before she had a chance for rebuttal, he put his hands on her elbows and lifted her effortlessly out of her chair. "I'll be right behind you in case you falter, you independent cuss."

Chapter 15

It was still pitch dark when Jim's clock alarm trilled through the thin walls of the wartime house. She hurried to the bathroom and dressed. Was she imagining it or had the pain receded?

Jim greeted her cheerily from the stove and she groaned inwardly. Not another morning person.

"Do you like your eggs sunny-side up or over-easy? Will you pop that toast down, please?" Jim switched a knob on the stove and took two plates out of the oven.

"Whatever you're having is good," Carrie maneuvered her bandaged leg under the table, marveling that it was an almost painless exercise. She pressed the toaster bar down.

Their breakfast was quick and easy. He had already read the morning paper and filled her in on the latest world news as they ate. They donned their ski jackets. He insisted on lending her a hat and mitts and they were on their way.

Dawn was a hairline crack of gold on the horizon when Carrie carefully swung her legs out of the front seat of Jim's blue truck. The wind, carrying the icy fingers of the winter to come, whipped at her toque. She leaned against the open car door, and with two gloved hands, edged the knitted hat down over her hairline and ears. She called back to Jim who had his door open, ready to come to her aid. Once again.

"I'm fine! Stay put. I'll return your tuque and mitts first chance I get." She slammed the car door shut before he had a chance to object.

She could feel his eyes on her as she scuffed up the walk. After unlocking the front door, she turned to wave and was relieved to hear his answering short honks before he pulled away from the curb. Once inside she sank down on the bench, waited for the pain to subside and pulled off her boots. Alone, on her own, no helper. At last.

The kitchen was spotless—thanks to Susan, of course, she had a key. Carrie poured a large glass of water, dug in her pockets for the vials and downed several pills from each. She shuffled into the bedroom and lay on the bed. "I'll just close my eyes for a few minutes." And in those "few minutes" she was out like a light.

Twenty hours later she woke up thirsty and hungry, under the covers and in her pajamas. She vaguely remembered being manhandled, whispers, and Peggy's loud voice.

Feeling one hundred percent better after a shower, she found Susan's note on the fridge door, 'Egg McMuffin beyond this door. Coffee ready to go.' Carrie was scraping up the last of her breakfast when the doorbell rang, and Susan's voice yelled,

"Are you awake? Another beautiful day in the land of milk and honey."

They sat in the living room drinking coffee while Susan brought her up-to-date on the rally. Ever the optimist, Susan was not discouraged by its failure, "This was just a warm-up exercise. We'll do better next time."

"Yes, I'm sure *you* will," Carrie said.

Susan snorted, "Yeah, well, there's another little matter you need to be aware of." She waited until Carrie looked at her before she said firmly, "Peter Cummings."

Carrie groaned, "I'm not well enough to do battle with him again."

Susan pulled a cell phone from her pocket, "Jim's super smart phone."

"But why have you got it?"

"Jim lent it to me. He's got another one and he wanted us to hear this. Two nights ago, Cummings took Jim and Don to dinner at his club. Jim got there early, put his smart phone on record and had a server tape it under Cummings' favorite table. He paid that waitress and another one to keep an eye on it for him. Apparently, they do it all the time for wives, and whoever. Here goes if I can find the 'play' again." Susan fumbled with the phone, pushed it closer to Carrie and pressed the 'play' button.

For the first few minutes Susan and Carrie listened to subdued laughter and muffled voices, but suddenly heavy footsteps approached, and a low male voice said, *"What's so important you have to see me tonight?"*

"Don, sit down," Pete's voice was low and suddenly accusing, *"You let her go, you dimwit. She fell into our laps like a gift from the Gods, yet she escaped from right under your nose. You were supposed to keep that meddling bitch under wraps for at least another three days."*

"Hardly a gift from the Gods," Don's voice. *"I spent considerable time, effort and money to get her here."*

"But" Pete said, *"I had plans for her that you botched. What the hell happened?"*

"Helen and I were helpless against the opposition--Jim Mathews and Carrie's friend Susan. Your 'over-the-hill babe' Carrie bit Helen's fingers and somehow Mathews caused the accident that put Oscar out of commission. Carrie's saviors whisked her out of here so fast there was nothing we could do to stop them. Didn't you see the bandage on Helen's hand?"

"What? Why the f…. would I notice a maid's fingers? And where was Oscar?"

"He fractured his wrist when he stumbled on the stairs," Don sounded disheartened.

"Jesus! I don't believe this!" Pete exploded. *"What a bunch of incompetents. Do you know where they took her?"*

Silence, followed by Don's quiet voice, *"No, I…"*

Pete interrupted Don's stammering, *"She's in Fort Saskatchewan, protected by Jim Mathew's huge Alsatian and a detachment of RCMP."*

"You can't be serious," Don sounded surprised. *"Where does Jim get his pull? He's only a two-bit owner of a small metals plant."* Pause. *"What's an Alsatian?"*

"A German shepherd. The Brits didn't like calling their dogs 'German,' so they adopted the word 'Alsatian' for them. Why the hell are we talking about dogs? I want to know what you intend to do now. 'Cause I sure as hell won't bail you out of your debt unless you get that woman back in this mansion of yours. We have to ensure there's no more protests, marches or rallies for this babe."

"What do you expect me to do? Kidnap her?" Don sounded exasperated. *"And she's hardly a 'babe.' She's a government employee with a responsible job. The rally's come and gone. Let her be. She can't do any harm now. Besides, she's way down on the totem pole. She's not the one you should be focusing on."*

Pete's sneer came across, *"No? She's one of the key players in the regulatory arm of this province's government. Her best friend is the main shit disturber against pipelines and the March babe can keep her anti-pipeline buddy informed of every move that's in the works for Alberta. Not only that, she's got relatives in Quebec, another hot bed of pipeline resistance. She's a major threat to my pipeline, even though she's getting paid to support it. How the hell she pulls the wool over her bosses' eyes is a mystery to me."*

Don's voice was incredulous, *"A key player? Carrie? She's…"*

"She's rich," Pete interrupted. *"How does a lowly government employee get the cash to buy an island in the Caribbean?"*

"What?" Don's voice was raised in disbelief.

"I've had my staff do some digging, and that was one of the first surprises. She's got the cash to do me more dirt, and I'm going to stop her," Pete said.

"She's almost a cripple now."

"Not for long," Pete said in a lower tone. *"Mark my words. She's the brains in that duo. Susan, the dyke, and your girlfriend Carrie are like human dynamos."*

A long pause followed by Don's voice over the rustle of a newspaper, *"Have you seen this?"*

More paper rustling and finally Pete said, *"What is this rag?"*

"'Spotlight on Edmonton'. It's a weekly paper that focuses on local events and happenings."

"Well, at least it's not the 'Edmonton Journal'," Pete said.

"Not yet," Don said. *"Do you remember that kid whose Buick one of your truckers side-swiped? His father is the owner and editor of the newspaper you just tossed away."*

"Christ!" Pete, exasperated or angry, or both? He continued in his nasal twang, *"The friends that woman keeps—a dyke and a faggot with a motor-mouth papa."*

"What makes you think Susan is gay? Or that Troy is a homosexual?" Don asked in a quiet voice.

"Well," Pete said, *"that Susan sure looks and acts like a butch to me, and I know for a fact that the kid bends both ways. I've been doing my homework. Give me a moment to read all of this."*

Rustle of newspaper again, and after a few minutes silence Pete said, *"Jesus! It even includes the golf game. What's its circulation?"*

"It's free so everyone and his dog can get a copy," Don said. His voice became persuasive, *"Look Pete, this is old news already. Let's focus on the positive side of things."*

Pete swore again, *"I'm going to get back at that woman if it's the last thing I do. What if I get the paper to write my rebuttal?"*

Don's response was instantaneous, *"Bad idea. Why refresh people's memories? Instead, we should promote your pipeline expansion and stress the jobs it will generate. We could work up pro-pipeline presentations on social media—Instagram, Facebook. Think of the coverage. It will get your buddies, and their wives, everyone talking it up."*

Pause and Don carried on, *"As a follow-up you can make speeches. You're good at that. With your silver tongue and paper handouts we'll bombard the communities—libraries, town councils, wherever people meet and greet. Until the federal government, or the Supreme Court, rules on the pipeline expansion we might as well proceed as though it's a go."*

Pete harrumphed, *"Yeah, but there are still a lot of people who think this country runs on pixie dust."* Another pause and Pete's voice was firmer now, *"I just can't get this woman Carrie out of my mind. Who said 'revenge is sweet'? God damn, whoever said it hit the nail on the head."*

"Pete, come on, leave her be." Don again.

"I told you I've got my people digging into your girlfriend's past - how she got off scot-free on a murder charge over ten years ago. I should hear back in a day or two." Pete sounded self-satisfied.

"She's hardly my girlfriend," Don sounded annoyed. *"I think it's the cobalt supplier who's in there like a dirty shirt. Local gossip has it that not only did they go fishing together, Jim's been at Carrie's house for dinner."*

"Jim" I thought I saw him here earlier," Pete sounded surprised. *"Maybe not. Anyway, he sells his metal to the guys who make pipe, not me. He's not significant. I'm hiring a financial guy to*

check into the dyke. Where did she get the funding for the rally? Probably from foreign environmental groups. We're going to close down these two women one way or another."

(No speaking for a minute. Rattling of cutlery and dishes in the background.)

"Hi, sorry I'm late," Jim sounded rushed. *"I had no idea this club was hidden behind the old Mercantile Bank. Pretty nice, green leather chairs, brass trimmings…"*

"Hey, Jim! What are you drinking? Scotch?" Pete asked, then called, *"A double Glenfiddich here!"* Chairs scraped on the floor and carpet, *"I've got to go but you two enjoy the ambience."*

Pause, and Don stammered, *"Wait. There's another problem."*

"Well?" Pete said, sounding annoyed.

Don's meek voice, *"Carrie has seen the portrait."*

"She what?" Pete yelled. Jim and Don shushed him, and Pete lowered his voice, *"You promised me that room would be locked at all times when I let you keep the painting. What the hell happened?"*

"The maid was cleaning it, and Carrie must have snuck in then. I'm having a bolt installed on it now, but Carrie asked me about 'the lady in red'." There was silence for a few seconds and Don continued, *"You must admit it's a pretty impressive portrait."*

"You stupid…." Pete sputtered. He sounded furious and his words seemed to escape between clenched teeth, *"You let that March woman see the painting of Jeanie!"*

"I just told you - it was a mistake. The cleaning woman…" Don's voice changed - no longer submissive, he demanded, *"Where is she? Jeanie. What did you do with her? Where is Jeanie?"*

"Your lady in red" Pete sneered. *"Christ, haven't you gotten over her yet? I told you, she went back to her own country, Serbia, or one of those shit-hole countries. I should have sold that damn painting years ago. But then again, it must be worth more now. Who's the artist? Archenko? Something like that."*

"That portrait is not yours to sell" Don said emphatically.

"Okay, okay, keep your pants on." Pete snorted, *"With all the money I've loaned you, given to you, over the years I must be a part owner at the very least. Just make sure you get that March woman back in your house, or mine. But for God's sake don't get the hots for her."* Slap of gloves on the table, *"I'm off. And here's Jim's scotch."*

"One Glenfiddich. For you, sir?"

"No." Don said. *"Here you go, Jim."* A glass was plunked on the table as Don thanked the waitress. Receding footsteps were covered up with the sound of the table being cleared. Finally, Jim broke the silence,

"Don, what the hell is going on?"

Don coughed to clear his throat. *"Jeanie was, is, the love of my life. Much too young for me, but what has that got to do with love? Those were the happiest days of my life. I realized I was probably a father figure to her, but it didn't matter. Nothing mattered except being with her."* His sigh was heart rending, *"You know I've always been involved in the arts community. I had one of my Russian artist friends paint her. I thought he would be the best one to catch her exotic beauty. I cashed a few of my mother's bonds for the artist's commission, but I had already started borrowing from Pete— for her clothes, jewels, fine dinners—anything to make her happy and keep her with me. Jeanie, my 'lady in red' as Carrie called her."*

"Where's the painting now?" Jim asked.

"Carrie found it in my attic," Don sounded downcast again. *"I kept the portrait there, away from Pete, and I would go up to gaze at her like a mooning lover. I thought the painting was well enough concealed, but Carrie said she tripped on a corner of the frame."*

"What happened to her, to Jeanie?" Jim sounded sympathetic.

"Pete happened," Don was bitter. *"He won her over, even though she swore she loved me. But his silver tongue, his phony charm, his money and his social position impressed her. But most important, he told her if she even thought of leaving him, he would send her back to Serbia."*

"Jesus." Jim's disgust was palpable. *"I had no idea Pete was such a monster. I presume you've looked for her."*

Don snuffled, *"Of course. It's like looking for the proverbial needle. I hired a translator and the two of us went to Serbia, to Belgrade and to her hometown. What a bloody waste of time and money. I have to hope that wherever Jeanie is, she's not miserable, that she's found some happiness."*

"Can I top you up, sirs?" The server's voice was shrill.

The gurgle of coffee being poured, and Don said, *"You probably don't know Pete as well as I do. Be careful, he demands soul-sucking obedience from his suppliers and anyone he does business with."*

"Well, thank God I don't have to deal directly with him," Jim said, then added, *"I'll get the bill."*

"Too late, my friend." Don's voice. *"Pete's got it covered. It's his club. And here's our coats."*

Chairs moving, then zippers sliding as Don continued,

"You know, Carrie predicted that the energy industry will be affected by a combination of low prices, environmental warnings and court rulings. I added government mismanagement to which she raised an eyebrow. But she could be right about oil. Pete's company may be in trouble someday. The world has hundreds of years' worth of oil energy, and the environmental activists are getting stronger."

"Yes," Jim agreed. *"The challenge is how to transition to carbon-free energy resources without slowing down economies."*

"And, as your girlfriend said, without hurting the worst-off people in society. Smart gal, your Carrie." Don said. *"Let's go."*

"My Carrie?" Jim asked then added, *"I wish. Good luck to you, Don."*

Sound of receding footsteps and low talking.

. . . .

Susan stopped the recording and Carrie breathed, "Wow."

Chapter 16

The sky was leaden, the grey clouds oppressive, and the icy rime on the concrete sidewalk in front of Carrie's house made walking treacherous. When Jim grabbed her elbow for the third time to prevent her feet from sliding under her, he said, "We're almost at the truck."

"You, at least, had the foresight to put on your spikes," Carrie responded with not a little resentment in her voice.

She had only agreed to this walk and talk with Jim because Charlie needed a run, and she could do with a little fresh air. The vet had finally released him a few days ago, but Carrie did not want to drive on the slippery roads to the closest dog park--the one where she and Charlie had had their fateful encounter with the coyote. Earlier in the week Susan had dropped off a printed copy of the conversation between Pete and Don that had been recorded on Jim's phone. The phone Susan promised to get back to Jim, somehow. Carrie had read and reread the transcript. Bad move. She hadn't slept properly for nights, and now she couldn't imagine Jim had any other topic but Pete under his hat. Perhaps he had some answers, but could she formulate the appropriate questions without sounding like a basket case? In any case, here she was, letting Jim lead her to his parked car. She glanced over her shoulder every few seconds as if she expected Pete to pop out from nowhere. Her body shuddered and Jim noticed. Of course.

"Are you okay?" He helped her into the front seat. "Stay, Tess," he pushed his dog's head back, then helped Charlie up onto Carrie's lap. "You're sure your leg is up to a walk?"

"I'm fine, thanks." She turned her head to greet Jim's dog, "Hi Tess, you big lug." She hugged Charlie and he covered her face with wet licks. She laughed and insisted on keeping him there as they drove to Jim's choice of an off-leash area. Tess, from her perch in the back seat, laid her big head on Carrie's shoulder. Much too close to Charlie who was not about to make friends with this monster dog. Carrie leashed him as a precautionary move. She envisioned Charlie jumping over the front seat to get at Tess, even though he wasn't belligerent at the moment. Just curious and apprehensive.

"Actually" Carrie said, "I haven't felt a twinge of pain for days. Kudos to your doctor."

"Good. Susan delivered my cell phone to you. I presume you listened to it?" He asked.

"Yes, of course. I don't know whether to thank you or curse you," she sighed. "Sue made me a printed copy so I practically have it memorized now." She shuddered involuntarily.

"Carrie--"

"What do you think he'll do?"

Jim shook his head, "I have no idea, but I thought you should hear that conversation. Was I wrong?"

"No, Jim," she patted his driving arm lightly. "It's better that I know the extent of his hatred. I just don't know what to do about it."

"Do you really own an island in the Caribbean?" He slowed for a red light.

"Are you kidding?" Carrie snorted. "Dad and I used to vacation on an island south of Trinidad. I guess I would know if Dad bought *an island* for me." She snickered, "Where does Cummings get his misinformation?"

"There is something really weird going down here." He drove slowly through the intersection, "And you and I are going to get to the bottom of it."

Jim parked the car on the street near the entrance to a gated property. The leaves of the dying vines on the fence were painted in scarlet, copper and rust, reminding Carrie of the paintings of one of her favorite colour-field artists.

"We'd better keep the leads on the dogs until we get inside," Jim said as he reached back to grab Tess's collar and snap on her leather leash. He got out, opened the rear door to let Tess jump down as he kept her on a short lead. Before Carrie knew it, he was holding her door open.

"This looks more like a millionaire's property. It's a dog park?" Carrie asked as she tried to exit the high truck gracefully. She searched vainly for the familiar city warning signs for unleashed dogs in recreational areas.

"Well, no," Jim said. "According to last night's weather forecast the sun was supposed to be shining and I expected any ice to have melted. I walked it yesterday to make sure it would be okay. For your leg, I mean." His forehead was creased in a worried frown. "But I don't know. Perhaps we shouldn't chance it. We can drive the long way round." He waited, "Your call, Carrie. I have no idea what condition the path will be now—it's almost mid-afternoon." His dog yelped in excitement. "Easy, Tess."

The two dogs eyed each other warily. Charlie barely came up to Tess's shoulder and Carrie sighed in relief when he decided not to fight. "Come on," she urged Jim. "We can't disappoint the dogs."

The old gate screeched when Jim dragged it open, and an eager Charlie pulled Carrie through it. Instead of the verdant lawn that Carrie had expected, she gazed in apprehension at a vast expanse of shrub and tough woodland beyond a narrow field of hay. She halted abruptly, and poor Charlie yelped as his collar dug into his neck. She asked in horror, "Do we have to go through *there?*"

Jim cursed under his breath and his face registered his chagrin, "Sorry, Carrie, I should have thought—but it's just a short distance through that bush, and the path is broad enough to walk side-by-side. Here, I'll hold onto your arm."

Carrie's two fists were wrapped around the handle of Charlie's leash, "I will never again go into any woods with or without Charlie." Her boots seemed to be frozen in place.

"Fine. We'll go back to the truck." He had a hold on her elbow, and he gently tried to turn her but she didn't budge. His arm fell to his side, and she followed his gaze at her white knuckles. She repeated to herself: "You can do it. The dogs are here. Jim is here. He will hold on to me. The dogs will protect us." She smiled weakly, "No, let's do it." She stepped forward and he walked beside her as he explained in his calm, deep baritone,

"Look, Carrie, this is private property within the city limits. I often walk Tess here. No sign of coyotes, wolves, bears or musk-ox." He looked down at her anxiously but she refused to move forward. So he continued, "And the city police don't come near here."

She tried to smile and failed. She released one hand from the leash and reached for his arm.

"Let me take Charlie," He covered her hand with his and rubbed it gently until she relaxed enough for him to take over the handle of Charlie's chain lead. Holding both leashes in one hand he grabbed her elbow in a firm grip and let the dogs pull them both towards the field. "Stay!" he called in a commanding voice.

Both dogs, and Carrie, halted immediately and waited.

He smiled down at her in amusement and pressed her arm against his body as he let the wiggling dogs free. They ran, nipping necks and bumping rears, towards the bush.

Carrie yelled, "No! Your dog will kill mine!" She pulled away and tried to run after the excited animals. Her run was nothing but a fast hobble and the agony in her leg pulled her up short.

Jim caught up to her, "The dogs are fine with each other. If they were going to fight it would have happened by now. You're the one who will incite them with your worries. Leave them be."

Her wound throbbed relentlessly. *Why the hell did I think I could run?*

Putting all her weight on her good leg she dug into her pocket for her whistle. When she put it to her lips Jim held up his right hand to stop her. He pointed down the field. She followed his gaze and realized he might be right because the dogs were ignoring each other as they raced towards the bush. The frozen stalks of hay remained parted in their wake.

"Your leg is hurting," he said. "Do you want to go back?"

She considered it. Not a bad idea but she hoped the pain might subside, at least to a dull ache. Taking a deep breath she replied, "No, Is there a castle to go with all this?"

"Not quite. A pre-war house set way back in the left corner. For privacy." He linked arms with hers. "There's a stump you can sit on along the path."

They picked their way carefully along the strewn hay mowed down by the dogs. Jim was slightly ahead leading her, chatting amiably, "It's quite glorious in this field when the wildflowers are in bloom. Watch that hump there." He lifted her over a clump of dirt. "We're almost at the path now."

She clung to his arm and repeated to herself, "I'll be fine. I'll be fine…another dark woods, another god damn dark woods." Looking beyond him she saw the dogs waiting patiently at the head of the path.

"It's just amazing," Carrie said keeping her eyes on her feet, "I think Charlie is in love! He's usually so hostile to any other dog, big or small, male or female."

"Well, Tess is pretty laid back." He grinned at Charlie trying to mount his big shepherd and said, "Good thing I had her spayed." He let go of her arm, "Here's the path and it looks partially frozen. There's a little incline a few yards in. Can you ski?" He laughed at his own joke and pulled aside a willow branch that was hanging over the path's entrance. The two dogs ran ahead, Charlie trying valiantly to keep up with Tess's long strides.

Carrie hesitated, took a deep breath and crouched under Jim's arm. They entered the woods.

He took her arm again. Her confidence returned until they came to the top of a small incline. He gave her arm a little squeeze,

"Here we are. We should have skates, not skis." He hesitated, "I don't like the look of this. It wasn't at all slippery yesterday. Sure you're alright? We can still go back."

She shook her head hoping he didn't notice her ersatz self-confidence, "And disappoint the dogs?"

Releasing her arm he squatted and patted his thighs, "Can you sit between my knees? I can hold your bad leg up and we can slide down together."

123

She burst out laughing, in spite of her pain and terror. "I'm fine. Show me how."

He glided down on his heels, turned and held out his arms. It looked like fun and so easy, but it was not for her. Bracing herself the inevitable jolt of pain she grabbed twigs to slow her descent on the small icy hill as she alternately slid and side-stepped down. On reaching the bottom she pretended she didn't see Jim's outstretched arms as she regained her balance a few yards from where he waited.

"Well done," he said, and Carrie averted her face to hide the pain that shot up and down her bad leg. She blinked at the rays of the low sun shining through the poplar trunks.

He gazed at her eyes, his face softened, and he swallowed as he stammered, "You...you have beautiful eyes." He turned quickly towards the path, "Shall we catch up to the dogs?" His cell phone rang. He pulled it out of his pocket, glanced at the caller name, put it back and grasped her arm again.

Carrie regarded him curiously as they started down the gloomy track that was infused with the smell of evergreens and rotting leaves, "This is creepy. I think we need a flashlight." Trying not to grip his arm too tightly she asked, "How did Susan get your cell back to you?"

"I have no idea. The receptionist phoned to tell me it was on her desk. She was busy when I picked it up so I don't know if Susan drove out to the Fort, or what."

The dogs kept pace with them in the bush beside the path. Their yelps, barks, and crashing through the underbrush were reassuring sounds to Carrie, she gripped the whistle in her free hand just in case. She turned to Jim and asked, "How did you find this place?"

"It belongs to an old friend. I've known her for years. She lets me use this piece of her property to walk Tess, provided I pick up the poop. I helped clear this path and I keep it open for her. She loves to walk it, summer and winter."

A twinge of jealousy gripped Carrie. A 'her'? She chastised herself. What right did she have to feel protective towards this guy? She hardly knew him.

The path became more muddy than icy in the sunny stretches, but the black dirt was as slippery as the ice. She was so occupied trying to protect her sore leg and keep her other foot on the ground, she didn't have time to wonder about the 'her' in his life. Charlie kept running back to check on Carrie. Tess waited impatiently for her new pal.

"Good girl, Tess," Jim praised his dog and abruptly switched topics, "Have you talked to Susan lately?"

"Yes and no. We had a long talk a few days ago," Carrie answered. "But it's very strange. She doesn't answer her cell now. It goes to her recording. And when I try her government number, the secretary always tells me Susan is not available. Is something happening I don't know about?"

Jim shook his head, "I'm the last person to know the answer to that question."

"But why are you interested in Susan?"

The discordant trill of Jim's cell phone startled both Charlie and Carrie. Tess veered off into the bush, and Jim swore.

"I thought I turned that thing off." He glanced at the screen, put the cell back in his pocket. Pulling her arm tighter they picked their way carefully down the path. Carrie could feel the phone's vibration through their coats. On the umpteenth ring she suggested,

"Maybe you should answer it?"

"Yeah," Jim muttered as he halted and pulled it out. "Don again." He punched the phone and said into it, "Sorry, Don. I'm in the midst of a forest, fighting brambles, cattails and mud. My apologies for not getting back to you sooner." He shook his head and said to Carrie, "I can barely hear him."

"The reception may be better in that open area," Carrie waved her arm to a sunny spot beyond a pile of rotten logs. "I'll just amble ahead with the dogs." She was ashamed of her false bravado. The last thing she wanted was to be alone on this damn path, even with two dogs. She had only taken a few, cautious steps when Jim called,

"Wait up!"

With a grateful smile, she turned as Jim reached her side again. He whistled for Tess. She knelt down on a fallen log and hugged Tess and Charlie as Jim took his phone out. She fisted Charlie's collar. Tess lay stretched out beside him.

Carrie heard Jim say, "Yes, she's with me..." He turned his back and walked a short distance into the brush, phone against his ear. The rest of his conversation was lost to her. In the quiet that followed, the sounds of the forest returned. Warbling chickadees and raucous blue jays started up, ensuring that there were no humans hiding in the bush. She waited until she heard Jim cursing. Smiling to herself she imagined him tripping over the logs. When she was sure he was on his way back she took a deep breath, gripped Charlie's collar and walking quickly and awkwardly she plunged into the dark bush. Tess loped right behind them. *Was Jim's dog frightened too?*

By the time a grim-faced Jim had caught up to her, Carrie was throwing sticks for the dogs at the edge of a small frozen slough. Typically Albertan, it was bordered by a grey-brown expanse of scrub. She glanced up at his scowl, "Whatever is the matter?"

Tess, her mouth in a wide slobbering grin, bounded up to Jim. After giving his dog an absent-minded pat, he said, "Your first guess was right on. It was Pete who was behind the shooting at my house."

Carrie paused and said dubiously, "According to Don."

"According to Don," he repeated. "I don't understand why you doubt him. Why would he lie about this? He's indebted to Pete, so what does Don gain by accusing him? Especially if the charges are false." Jim shook his head. "It makes no sense to me. Don could lose his company. I know Pete is a bastard. He could retaliate by cutting all funding to Don, and why the hell would Pete pay someone to shoot my dog anyway?"

"You know that shot was for *my* dog. How do--?" Carrie started to ask.

A strange sound, like the clash of symbols, drifted above the tops of the trees.

"The drink signal," Jim seemed relieved, and taking her hand, he led her to an old wooden stairwell. "It's missing a few steps, so be careful." Holding onto the slim pole that served as a railing, he pulled her over the gap. "This is what worried me most, and you're practically jumping over it."

"Only with your help," she said, but with two feet on the next step she gazed around her and asked, "Where are the dogs? Where are we going now?"

"Our pre-dinner cocktails await, and the dogs too are probably waiting for us." He gave her hand a gentle tug and they climbed the wooden boards side by side. At the first landing he paused to let Carrie catch her breath again, "Are you okay? Let me lift--"

"Hey!" Carrie retorted, "What kind of a wimp do you think I am?" Her voice was weak, and pain shot up and down her leg.

Jim switched his hand to her elbow, "Brave and tough. I'm the one who's in the dog house for taking you through that obstacle course. Please believe me, it was nowhere near that state yesterday. You are a tremendous sport, Carrie."

Not answering, Carrie reached for the railing. The stairs zig-zagged up the steep incline, and when they reached the final landing, she was panting, from pain and lack of breath. Leaning back against the rail she gazed down and saw snatches of the grey-black water far below. She closed her eyes and pictured a scene from the eighteen hundreds - a flotilla of Indian war canoes rounding the big curve, paddles dipping in unison, a silent, dangerous menace hurtling down stream. To the west the tall buildings of downtown Edmonton reflected the setting sun. "Where are we?" she asked.

Chapter 17

"We're here. In one of the city's oldest residential areas," Jim pointed behind him to a one and half story house with small windows and a peaked roof. He either did not hear Carrie groan, or he chose to ignore her, as he dashed across the street into the arms of an older woman who had appeared on the porch. She had crinkly bottle-blonde hair, her face and neck were lined with wrinkles, and she wore a flowing ankle-length black dress.

Carrie slid onto the nearest bench at the top of the bank. She clutched her knee, willing the pain in her lower leg to subside. Her eyes streaming with tears, she heard the woman exclaim in a shrill voice,

"James! You old rogue! I've seen you run up those old stairs!"

A wave of anger swept through Carrie as she swiped her face with her coat sleeve. She watched and heard Blondie give him a noisy kiss. Was it disgust or jealousy that swept her consciousness? In any case, at this particular moment Carrie hated Jim and hated this grasping woman. Who the hell was she? Why hadn't he warned her? She bent over to let her nose drip on the path and swiped the excess with the back of her glove. The throbbing gradually lessened.

"And you are Carrie." The woman was directly in front of her, clinging to Jim's arm and holding out her free hand forcing Carrie to stand and greet her. Couldn't they see she was hurting, that it was difficult for her to stand up properly?

"Carrie, meet Aunt Lottie, Aunt Lottie, this is Carrie," Jim released his arm to hug his aunt's shoulders and Carrie seethed, wanting and needing that arm to be around *her*. She was the one in pain, after all. But she straightened her back, smiled (well, sort of) and shook hands with Aunt Lottie who quickly withdrew her gnarled claws and said,

"Come in, come in. Your dogs are two drinks ahead of you." Aunt Lottie turned to grab Jim's arm again. Carrie followed them to the verandah as Charlie appeared around the corner of the house. He immediately rubbed against her legs, demanding attention.

The aunt shrieked, "How did that dog get out? I put them both in the back yard."

Jim laughed as he bent to scratch Charlie's ears, "But this one is an escape artist."

"Well, any friend of yours is a friend of mine," Aunt Lottie said as she opened the door. "Even if he is a canine." Charlie squeezed by her as she led them into a small foyer, and Carrie wondered if she had to be of a different species to be acceptable to Jim's aunt. She chastised herself, told herself to be reasonable. Jim helped her with her boots and muttered, "Were those stairs too much for you? You told me your leg was back to normal." Tears tightened in her throat again. What the hell was the matter with her? Why was she so emotional all of a sudden?

He didn't wait for her response as he stood, motioned her into the living room and called Charlie to his side. They, Jim and Charlie, joined the older woman in the kitchen and Carrie heard him exclaim, "Ah! Guinness! You bought the good stuff. Good girl!" The fridge door clicked shut. Carrie sank onto the arm of the nearest chair.

She imagined another hug and kiss for his favorite relative, who wasn't a real relative, but Aunt Lottie was in the doorway asking, "What would you like to drink, Carrie?"

Jim, standing behind his aunt answered quickly, "She can't drink anything alcoholic because she's on a whole truckload of meds." Carrie glared at him.

"Oh," Aunt Lottie sounded disappointed. "Pour me my usual sherry, James."

"Me too, please." Carrie challenged him, "I'm on *one* pain killer, Jim."

He nodded as if to acknowledge her annoyance and asked his aunt, "Alright if I let Tess in too?" Without waiting for a response, he opened the back door for his grateful dog.

"Sit in this easy chair, dear". Aunt Lottie swiveled a high backed armchair towards Carrie and kicked a stool in front of it, "For that injured leg." She sat down on the sofa, turned to Carrie and closed one eye in a semblance of a wink. "Jim once told me that sherry could not qualify as a proper inebriating liquor." Carrie nodded with a wan smile.

Jim appeared with the drinks on a tray. After the standard cheers and well wishes, Aunt Lottie and Jim embarked on a two-way conversation about old times and relatives.

Feeling excluded, Carrie sank down into the oversized armchair and looked around the small room. The furniture was genuine maple, the lamps Colonial-style, and the two oil paintings hanging over the fireplace looked very much like Kurelek's. A round purple shag rug drew the room together. The smells of the cedar paneling lining the walls combined with the burning wood in the fireplace produced a heady, but pleasant odour. The pain kept its metronome pulse as it gradually subsided, and her eyes threatened to close, but she made the supreme effort to stay awake by asking at the first break, "How are you two related?"

"We're not, in the true sense of the word," Aunt Lottie's shrill laugh startled the dogs in the kitchen and they both barked. "Quiet, you two." She clapped her hands to emphasize her command and her chicken arms shot out of the wide sleeves. The dogs obeyed and settled down again. Jim finished his beer and started on the scotch while his so-called aunt continued, "James is my nephew-in-law, my favorite relative, still and always." She picked up a photograph on the side table and handed it to Carrie, "These are my four lovely nieces. James ignored my advice and married the youngest and most beautiful of the lot. I warned him she would bring him nothing but pain and misery. And, of course, she did."

"Look," Jim said in exasperation, "Let's discuss something else…the weather, or even, God forbid, the environmental effects of the oil sands."

Carrie laughed, and Jim had the grace to smile.

Aunt Lottie said, somewhat haughtily, "An inside joke, obviously. How unlike you, James."

Carrie's cheeks burned knowing the reprimand was directed at her, but Aunt Lottie continued, "I know nothing about the environment, and I find it all quite boring. The life of my nephew is much more interesting." She turned to Carrie, "Did you know that James won the gold medal in his engineering class, and he got another--"

"Enough already. What's for dinner?" Jim interjected.

Carrie went along with his attempt to change subjects and swiveled her chair to face Aunt Lottie, "Tell me about *your* life, please."

Jim nodded his thanks to Carrie and settled back twirling his glass. Carrie sipped her sherry as Aunt Lottie, obviously pleased at Carrie's request, obliged, "Well, my dear, I married money, prestige and power but not, unfortunately, looks and personality. What else can I say? It's been a life of privilege, and I don't regret one minute of it. Shall I go on?"

"Yes, of course." Carrie was warming to the old gal. Jim's cell phone beeped again.

"Take it here, dear, "Aunt Lottie ordered, "I'll refill our sherries."

"Don again," Jim said to Carrie as he stood and went to the window presenting his back to the room.

Carrie tried vainly to eavesdrop until Aunt Lottie reappeared with two fresh glasses of sherry and whispered, "You're the woman who kicks coyotes and wounds odious men like Peter Cummings. Are you brave or just foolish?"

"Mostly foolish, I guess," Carrie admitted. She leaned forward and asked her hostess, "Do you know…did you know Peter Cummings?"

Aunt Lottie hesitated and looked away before she answered, "Yes and no, but I did know Don socially. And Jeanie. James told me you played golf with Don."

"Jeanie?" Carrie asked as she wondered about Aunt Lottie's reluctant response.

The older woman gave her a curious look as she continued, "She was a lovely girl, and everyone liked her." She gazed out the window lost in thought for a moment. "There were all sorts of rumors when she disappeared. My bridge club became the investigative authority on the case." She cackled with a gleam in her eyes, "We even wrote a report."

Carrie was astounded, "Your bridge club? Why?"

"One of our members - she died a few months ago," Aunt Lottie paused, and Carrie was afraid the older woman was going to digress, but she just sighed and went on. "Phyllis and her husband sponsored Jeanie, you know how the immigration path is smoother for people who are sponsored by Canadians. Jeanie lived with them for a while and they, Phyllis and her husband helped her rent an apartment. Jeanie put her mind to learning Canadian English, you know, our accent. She took all sorts of courses - accounting, Canadian history, you name it, she took it. She met Don at the one on ballroom dancing. And Jeanie became our favorite bridge spare after she took the bridge course. Smart young lady, she played quite well for a beginner."

Jim was pacing near the window not saying very much, and Carrie suspected he was half-listening to his aunt. She leaned towards Aunt Lottie, "Go on, please."

"Well, all of a sudden Jeanie was no longer Don's, ah, what can I say, Don's special friend. She was with Peter Cummings and unavailable for bridge. She stopped phoning Phyllis or answering her calls - they had always kept in touch. And Cummings, well, he was much too important to talk to a member of his wife's bridge club."

Carrie gasped, "They married?"

Aunt Lottie nodded, "Yes, apparently on a trip to one of the Caribbean islands. She married the rich, old fool and divorced her friends. And after a while, I've forgotten how long, she disappeared. Phyllis, who really liked the girl, was obsessed with finding her, or at least finding out what happened to her, and she persuaded us, to help her." She sipped her sherry, her mind far away until Carrie reached over to press her hand,

"What did you find out?"

"Oh!" Aunt Lottie came to life. "I forgot to mention that Jeanie became pregnant, and Cummings was ecstatic. He bragged about his "son-to-be" everywhere he went. When they were here in Alberta, that is. You have to read our report. I know I seem very disjointed-my memory, you know. It's as if there are holes in my brain. But I will do whatever I can to help you."

Carrie didn't know what to believe but she wanted to hear more, "You're doing a fine job. Tell me about your report."

Aunt Lottie seemed to get her second wind, "We applied our bridge skills to the search for Jeanie - analysis of a problem, formulating plans, knowing when "to fold 'em and when to hold 'em," and executing the solution. It was the last one that stumped us, actually finding her, but we did write that report, incomplete though it was."

Jim was listening to his aunt from the window, "I didn't known the whole story."

"No," Aunt Lottie said, "You were too busy working two jobs and travelling between Alberta and Manitoba."

"Do you still have your report?" Carrie couldn't contain her excitement, and Jim, with his phone under his chin, came back to sit with them. Carrie could hear the voice on the other line. Don's, she supposed. Jim responded to him in monosyllables.

"Yes, somewhere here," Aunt Lottie's laugh was cut short by the rise in Jim's voice as he stood up, his eyebrows arched in surprise, "No way! On what charge?" Jim listened, clapped his phone shut and replaced it in his pocket. He looked down at Carrie and announced, "Your friend, Susan, has been arrested."

Carrie stared at him in incomprehension, "How can they do that?"

"It seems," Jim answered, "that she refused to be subpoenaed for your premier's preliminary inquiry into the foreign funding of provincial environmental groups." He sat down, picked up his scotch and drained it.

"What can we do? Where is she? Will they let me see her?" All thoughts of Jeanie had been replaced by concern for Susan.

"I don't see why not. She's at the Remand Centre." He turned to his aunt, "Did you tell Carrie everything on Pete and Jeanie?"

"Yes, what little I know and remember." Aunt Lottie turned to her, "Carrie, I'm sorry about your friend. Would you like more sherry?"

Jim raised his eyebrows, "We should go and see what we can do about Susan." Carrie glanced at him suspiciously. He did not like Susan so why was he so eager to help her now?

"Please stay for dinner," Aunt Lottie said. It's just pot roast and I can have it on the table in two shakes of a lamb's tail."

So this is where Jim gets his unique expressions, Carrie thought but said, "How can we not stay? It sounds delicious and they probably won't let us see Susan at this hour." She felt guilty about dismissing her friend, but she was a little drunk and very hungry. Besides, she might be able to quiz Aunt Lottie a little more.

"I'll get the address." Jim walked to the window, talked briefly into his cell, wrote in his notebook and joined them in the dining room.

Aunt Lottie had everything prepared - the table set, a salad ready to be dressed, and pot roast and vegetables in the oven. Jim uncorked the wine bottle and sliced the beef, Carrie dished out the vegetables, and Aunt Lottie put the salad on side plates. To Carrie's surprise, she asked her to talk about herself during dinner, so she expounded on the importance of environmental regulation in Alberta.

All three of them had lived in Montreal at some point in their lives and they discussed the city and how Quebec had changed since the Quiet Revolution. Jim smothered a yawn, "Dishes?"

"You are not doing dishes at my house, James. You know better than to even suggest it. My cleaning lady will do them tomorrow." Aunt Lottie stood up, "Coffee?"

They retired to the living room to drink coffee and pick at an assortment of squares and cookies for dessert. Aunt Lottie asked Jim about his job. He was suddenly alert as he dived into his favorite topic, the cobalt plant.

"We're hoping to boost production of battery grade cobalt by 30.5 MT ..."

"MTs?" chorused Carrie and Aunt Lottie.

"Metric tons. We're hoping to tap into the demand for rechargeable batteries as the world weans itself off fossil fuel. And—"

"Peter Cummings will hate you too!" Carrie commented.

"Yeah, maybe. I have to restructure our debt and I foresee that as the major problem I'll have to deal with Pete. Hopefully, I'll be able to pay him off and keep him out of the picture. I'm embarking on a joint venture with a major Canadian nickel producer in Moa, Cuba to mine the laterite deposits. The tension between the U.S. and Cuba is a worry."

"Wow!" Carrie breathed. "And I thought I had problems!" She noticed Aunt Lottie's eyes drooping and she gave Jim the high sign that they should leave.

He stood up and grasped his aunt's hands, "We're on our way now, Aunt Lottie, before you fall asleep."

"Bring your car to the front door, James. Don't make Carrie walk down those decaying stairs in the dark. "Aunt Lottie might be sleepy, but she was still sharp.

Carrie stared at Jim as he put on his coat, "You could have driven me to the front door? You b...."

"And miss that gorgeous view of the river?" He teased as he went out the door.

Carrie fumed and muttered, "Even though I might have split the stitches open?"

Aunt Lottie stood up, "Don't be too hard on him, please. He means well."

Carrie went to the dining room and began stacking the dishes thinking what a vapid expression that was--'he means well' – but she told herself to shut up. By the time they had piled the dirty dishes in the sink, Jim was back.

He helped Carrie on with her coat and boots then hugged his aunt, "See you soon. Try to stay out of trouble."

"Thanks very much for everything, especially the sherry," Carrie held out her hand with a sideways smile at Jim.

"I'm always here and I will get you that report. Come see me any time but be wary of that awful Cummings." Aunt Lottie held Carrie's hand in both of hers in a gesture that seemed sincere. "Just remember, my dear, I have a bountiful fund of resources I can draw on."

In the car Jim said, "You've made a conquest. Did you learn anything of value?"

"The more I learn the more confused I get," Carrie sighed. "Is she very rich? Is that what she meant by a 'bountiful fund of resources'?"

He hesitated, "Probably more than money - contacts, influential friends. I wish I'd paid more attention at the time of the bridge club investigation."

"It was only a ladies bridge club," Carrie waited for his reaction to her sarcasm.

"Yeah, that too," he agreed. "But I've always known Aunt Lottie is no light weight."

After a few moments she asked, "What's the story between she and Cummings?"

"Story?" Jim's foot hit the brake in his surprise. "There's no 'story' as far as I know. What makes you think that?"

"Don't know. Just a feeling, just a sense that there may be a history there." She let her head drop back as she mused, "Aunt Lottie and Peter Cummings - who knows?"

Jim shook his head, "You've got that guy on your brain. She must be at least ten years older than Pete. I can't imagine -".

She interrupted, "You're right. I'm probably all wet again." And immediately regretted her wording, "I mean…"

"I know what you meant," He grinned as he turned off Ada Boulevard, "But Carrie, please be careful. Keep me informed and I'll help if I can."

"As I said before, your association with me can only be detrimental to you." She put her head back, "tell me about her youth. I bet she was beautiful."

"Yes, I've seen her wedding photo, but she hardly ever talks about her marriage. I think the decision not to have kids was hers. Her husband died before I was born." As he related a few family reunions, his voice softened. And Carrie was envious.

By the time they got to the Remand Centre, visiting hours were over. It was very dark when Jim parked in front of Carrie's house.

"Phone me any time," he said as he helped her out of the car, "Even if it's just for moral support."

"Bye now, and thanks for Aunt Lottie. She's a gem," She smiled up at him, all her former acrimonious thoughts having faded away into the black night.

Chapter 18

The guard at the Remand Centre was inflexible, "If I've told you once, I've told you a million times: you cannot see or talk to Ms. Susan Heard." The vein on his neck bulged and his heavy sigh ended in a wheeze. His eyes never once lifted to Carrie's as he sputtered on, "That's final. If I see you come through those doors one more time, I'll have you escorted off these premises." He motioned to the RCMP behind him.

Carrie retreated to her car and banged her fists against the steering wheel. The sun was striving valiantly to peek through the smog as she arrived back at her house. Driving was hard on her leg, and she wasn't adept enough to use her left foot on the pedals. Charlie had been cooped up in the house all morning and demanded his walk, but it was so damn cold. After a short rest with her foot up she relented, and Charlie was satisfied with a crisp walk around the block. He was not fond of below zero weather.

With a mug of hot coffee cradled in her hands, she sat in her living room staring out the window. She was determined to find Jeanie. Somehow this girl (woman?) would be the ammunition she needed against Cummings. The hate in his voice as he swore to get back at Carrie reverberated in her mind. Just as she was certain that Pete would exact his vengeance eventually, she was equally certain that Jeanie was a key to preventing him—to stopping him. Why else would there be so much secrecy, furtiveness, about her? As if her whereabouts were of a classified nature. But Carrie wasn't Jeanie's relative, not even a close friend. What would her legal position be if she did find her? None, she suspected. Should she contact one of her lawyer colleagues? How could she explain the situation without letting him read the transcription of Cummings' purloined conversation? It was not admissible evidence. How far did Peter Cummings' long arm extend? Into the RCMP?

She had to get her hands on Aunt Lottie's report. The thought of driving again made her cringe. Her breakfast pills sat on the kitchen counter and there they would stay. The rabies vaccine was still unsettling her stomach but the anti-nausea pills on top of the pain killers made her too dozy to function effectively. She needed advice, or at least moral support.

It was almost noon, but she caught Peggy on her cell before her lunch break. After listening attentively to Carrie's tale, Peggy haughtily called Susan 'a political prisoner' and advised Carrie to report Susan's plight to the Edmonton Journal and the Sun. "Gotta run, now. You know who is waiting for me."

Over a lunch of milk and cheese and crackers, Carrie rejected her friend's advice. Peggy disliked Susan ('she's not one of *us*') so why the hell did I phone her? After putting Charlie in the back yard, she phoned a taxi, and at two o'clock she was on Aunt

Lottie's doorstep. She paused before lifting the heavy knocker as Jim's words echoed in her ears. "Be careful."

The clang of the metal against metal as she let the knocker drop brought Carrie back to the present, and she waited patiently as the slow footsteps on the other side of the door got louder, then stopped.

"Carrie! I hoped you would come back," Aunt Lottie said with a broad welcoming smile. "Come in! Come in! My neighbor just brought me fresh muffins."

Carrie sniffed recognizing the spicy aroma of pumpkin muffins, "I've been told I have an unerring sense of arrival when it comes to food." Pulling the door closed she added, "Thanks again for last evening."

"Take off your coat. I'll make a pot of tea." Aunt Lottie led her into the kitchen and had Carrie set out the plates and mugs while she put the kettle on.

"How did things go at the Remand Centre?" Aunt Lottie asked as the two of them bustled about the kitchen.

"They won't let me see her or talk to her," Carrie blurted out, sitting with a thud, "And my friend Peggy is calling her a 'political prisoner.' Would you label a rally organizer a 'political prisoner'?"

"Well, no." Aunt Lottie poured the tea and pointed to the milk and sugar. "But everything is 'political' in an election year, even if it's just the year for choosing a new library board." She placed a crocheted tea cozy around the pot and joined Carrie at the table. "Are you aware that the Journal columnist called your friend an 'environmental activist,' and you a 'pipeline pugilist'?" She laughed. "In any case, jail is the safest place for Susan to be right now. What did you really come to see me about, our so-called 'investigation', Mr. Cummings, or Helen?" She pushed the plate of warm muffins towards Carrie.

"Your report, Peter Cummings definitely, Jeanie. But why Helen?"

"Ah, Helen." Aunt Lottie looked pensive, and Carrie worried about her digression. "Yes, the lovely Jeanie most definitely fits into the mix." She paused and took a big breath, "Back to Helen…perhaps my old brain is getting addled, but yes, I'm curious. Why does this Helen appear on the scene at this particular moment? What's her relationship with Don, not to mention Cummings and Jeanie? I met Helen at an ecumenical meeting at the Catholic church one morning. Did you notice her accent?"

"Helen? Slightly British?" Carrie replied. "She's Don's new girl Friday. Are you intimating she's more than that?" She paused wondering how much Jim had told his aunt, "You know I bit her fingers."

Aunt Lottie chortled, "Yes, of course. The civil servant who attacks coyotes also bites the maid's fingers and kicks the president of an oil consortium in his vitals. I hear the scab on his face is finally peeling off." Her eyes crinkled, "I haven't had a high-voltage person in my life for a long time. Why don't you come live with me?"

"I'd just get you into trouble too." Carrie shook her head and munched on a muffin. "Mm, good." She licked the crumbs off her fingers, "hope that Journal writer doesn't find out about Helen's fingers."

Aunt Lottie settled back in her chair, "Let's get down to brass tacks. What can I tell you that you don't already know?"

Carrie drank the last of her now lukewarm tea. "Okay, first things first, what did your investigation into Cummings turn up?"

"Quite a bit, but not enough because Peter the Great stopped us in our tracks—he and his influential cronies." Aunt Lottie grimaced, "You undoubtedly know that he's a self-made man. He's the product of a broken marriage and he brought himself up by the bootstraps. His silver tongue and shady dealings have got him where he is now. But he's left a trail of failed court cases and disgruntled partners in his wake." She patted the thick brown legal-size envelope on the chair beside her, "Here's our report. You can judge for yourself."

"Thank you, thank you. It will be a start." Carrie slid the large package into her shoulder bag and gathered up the plates and mugs. "Thanks for the refreshments. I can't wait to read what you and your bridge club came up with."

"Leave those dishes. I need something to keep me occupied this afternoon." Aunt Lottie placed her hands flat on the table and heaved out of her chair. She retrieved Carrie's coat from the closet, "You are most welcome. But you must promise to be careful. If Cummings suspects you're delving into his past, you will be in serious trouble. Trust an old woman's intuition and talk to Helen first. She goes to eight o'clock mass on Sundays at the basilica." She extended her hand, "Good luck."

Carrie took Aunt Lottie's frail hand in hers and sat down again, "Why is Helen so important?"

"She's new on the job," Aunt Lottie eased herself down again but held onto Carrie's hand, "It would be natural for her to ask the other staff about her boss and even his friends. Don has a driver, a cleaning lady who cooks for him, and now Helen. He's always inviting Cummings to dinner, and you can bet they talk about their businesses. What else, besides women, do men talk about? You can also be sure that the staff gossip amongst themselves. Gossip can carry valuable smidgens of truth."

Carrie wished Jim could see her now, holding hands with his favorite aunt. She smiled ruefully, "Helen probably hates me. She's as dangerous to me as Cummings."

She remembered the other question she had for Aunt Lottie, "Is Jeanie the focus of your report?"

Aunt Lottie nodded, "She's the *reason* for the report. The mysterious Jeanie. Where is she? She did not make it back to Serbia, no matter what Peter Cummings claims. Our committee paid good money to verify that. Another problem in this complicated affair." Aunt Lottie paused, "But Carrie, my dear, you must promise me to be very, very careful. Cummings is a vengeful, spiteful man."

"I know, believe me." Carrie smiled grimly, "How could it get any worse?"

"It could, and it will, if Cummings finds out about your research into his past. Hopefully, our report will answer some of your questions." Aunt Lottie smiled, "Remember my untold resources. They're yours for the asking. I like to quote my British friend: 'Everything that is good in the world owes its origin to privileged persons'. "She laughed and immediately became serious, "James would never forgive me if something happened to you. I suspect he might be very angry when he finds out that I'm encouraging you."

"Jim? He's as bad as you with his warnings. I'm sure he knows I'll ask you for your report sometime." She stood to put her coat on and bent to kiss the old lady's wrinkled cheek.

"Good luck to you, and take care of that leg," Aunt Lottie walked her to the door and watched Carrie carefully sidestep down the porch steps and added, "Be careful and watch your back."

Carrie smiled up at her trying to remember who else had recently used that same expression, 'watch your back.' Counting the number of times Aunt Lottie had said 'be careful' she noticed a silver car, a Mercedes, just like her dad's. It was parked across the narrow street and looked ominous and out of place in the old neighborhood.

She punched in the taxi's number on her cell phone and looked up when she heard a familiar honk. Jim's blue truck pulled up to the curb and he reached over to open the passenger door for her. As she hopped on her left foot onto the front seat, she noticed the Mercedes had disappeared. I'm getting paranoid again, she thought.

Jim stood up inside the car door, waved to his aunt who was still on the porch, then slid back behind the wheel. "Hi there. Can I drive you somewhere?"

His infectious grin made the corners of her lips turn up, "Back to work before Troy makes me redundant." She snapped the seat belt, "How are the roads? Are you following me?"

Jim shrugged, "No, it was just a hunch. Your first question--the main streets are okay--guess the plows have been out. I had an early afternoon meeting here in the city and I usually pop in for a quick visit with Aunt Lottie before heading back to the Fort." He looked embarrassed, "I was hoping--I knew you were dying to drill her."

"How does she know so much about *everything*?" Carrie asked.

"This town is her life," Jim said with a chuckle. "She has an intel network--her bridge pals, whose tentacles spread far and wide, her book club, her volunteer library job. She even talked herself into an investment group--the only female member, I might add."

"Wow," Carrie shook her head in amazement. "Hope I have that energy when I reach her age."

He glanced over at her. "I'm sure my aunt warned that you haven't a hope in hell of doing that if you don't give up on Cummings and company."

Carrie sighed, "Not quite, but close."

On the way to the Federal Building Carrie related her conversation with Aunt Lottie, adding her fruitless visit to the Remand Centre. "Have you met Helen?"

"Helen?"

"She works for Don…"

"Right, I know who you mean now. The foreign gal who makes a maid's black uniform look sexy. The one who packed your bag at Don's." He grinned, "The one you bit."

"She had her damn fingers in my mouth!" Carrie cried. "It was an automatic reaction. What would you have done?"

"I refuse to answer that. Do you really expect Helen to talk to you?"

Carrie closed her eyes and shook her head, "That probably depends on how badly I damaged her fingers. I was thinking of approaching her at church--she goes to mass every Sunday morning, according to your aunt. But that has the potential of creating an awful scene. Any suggestions?"

Jim hesitated, "Yes, drop this whole business. You now have two people who…"

"Who I have physically harmed."

"Carrie, please tell me you won't start spying on Helen, too."

"I kind of like the idea. Might get me some leads to Asshole Pete."

"If you get caught, you're in even bigger shit." He glanced in the rear view mirror. "That Mercedes again! I saw it pull away from Aunt Lottie's as soon as I arrived there."

Carrie's head shot around, but the Mercedes driver quickly brought his visor down over the top half of his face. Bulbous lips leered at her in triumph. She shivered, and Jim noticed, "Are you cold? I'll turn up the heat."

"No, I'm fine. I just got a glimpse of that sleazy looking driver behind us."

"Do you know him?"

"No," Carrie glanced back again. "But this whole scene is scary." She leaned forward to face him, "Jim, you have to distance yourself from me. You might be in jeopardy because of the mess I seem to be in. Just drop me off at my office and get back to your job in the Fort. Return to whatever your normal life is."

"But 'normal' is so boring. Just a sec." With one hand he pulled out his cell phone and pressed it against his ear, listened, and spoke into it, "Okay, on our way."

He leaned forward, jammed on the brakes, and did a U-turn onto two lonely tire tracks in the median. The car bumped and swerved, and Carrie clutched the dashboard with both hands. Jim wrestled the wheel until he was able to merge into the traffic going in the opposite direction. Carrie looked back, but she couldn't see the Mercedes behind them. Or in front. And no cops either. Jim drove carefully into a suburb.

"Where now?" she grabbed the safety strap as Jim turned quickly down one street, peered at the street sign, continued straight and turned at the next intersection. "Do you know where you're going? This is the wrong direction for the Federal Building, and I have a ton of work to get at this afternoon." Her voice sharp and annoyed.

"Sorry, Carrie. Change of plan. We're going to meet Dave at Uncle Ed's. Hold on and keep an eye out for that Mercedes!" He started down one street, changed his mind, swung the car around and gunned the engine to the next cross street. "Hope there's no kids around," he muttered as he continued in a mad sequence of streets and avenues until Carrie was completely lost. And this was *her* city!

"Not Handsome Dave from the golf game?" she managed to ask.

"The very same. He came out hoping to ski in the high country, but the freezing rain early this week, followed by this sudden drop in temperature, put the kibosh on that plan. They're not letting anyone in the mountains for recreational skiing. Too dangerous. Ice everywhere, shifting glaciers. Here we go again." He did another U-turn when he saw kids playing street hockey then ducked down an alley. The back end of the truck veered wildly, narrowly missing a corner fence. "Why aren't those kids in school?" he muttered. "Don't they know it's thirty degrees below zero?"

"Probably let out early because of the weather," she answered. "They're taking advantage of the Alberta clipper that made them an instant outdoor rink."

He glanced at her, "Alberta clipper. Is that what this abrupt change in weather is called?" Not waiting for an answer, he swung the wheel into another lane, "These back lanes are a God send." The truck skidded on the ice. "If only they weren't so damn icy. I convinced Dave to find out what he could about Troy and..." He paused, "He's one of the best lawyers in Toronto, and he's intrigued with you and your 'mess,' as you call it. Can you see the Mercedes?"

Carrie twisted in her seat, looking out all the windows, peering down the streets they passed, but there was no sign of the big, black car. "Nope. You must have out-witted that sinister..." She shuddered involuntarily. "What do you mean, 'intrigued with me'? As 'attracted to,' I hope," she snickered. He did not respond and when they passed the oil refineries, she commented, "We're a long way from 108th Street. And my workload." Her face reddened as her anxiety grew. "Jim, I need to get back to work."

"Don't get mad. Please. We need you here and I apologize if I've been mysterious. I dropped Dave off at this seedy bar earlier, so yes, I know where I am. I just stay away from the "A" streets and avenues, and I can tell the difference between north and south and east and west. "He smiled and added, "Reminds me of our rowing expedition. How about you?"

"No, not at all." But she remembered. It seemed a hundred years ago.

"Here we are." He pulled into a small run-down mall, drove around to the back, and parked so that his side of the truck was against a green dumpster. The truck's back fender put a small 'wow' in a chain link fence, and its nose pointed towards the alley.

He pushed back his seat, "Best I can do to hide this blue truck." Leaning across her to open her door his nose brushed her cheek, "I'll climb out your side."

Carrie eased her bandaged leg out and twisted her body so she could touch her left toes on the frozen dirt. Having to hide their presence here worried her but she didn't question him as he shimmied across the seat.

Taking her gloved hand in his, he pulled her forward, "Let's go!"

They hurried to the line of heavy doors, and Jim banged on one near the middle of the row. Carrie did not have time to formulate the obvious question, 'how do you know which one?' before the door was opened by a heavy set, bearded man who yelled above the cacophony of canned music and loud voices coming from the smoke-filled room behind him.

"Hey Jim, old boy! How's it hanging?"

"Okay, Slim. Meet Carrie. Is Dave still here?" Jim pulled Carrie around Slim's rotund belly. The heat from the crowded bar enveloped them when Slim closed the outside door. Jim peered through the haze looking for Dave, and Carrie surveyed the room. The bar definitely lacked the elegance of a world class hotel bar, but it had its own character. Brightly lit, sawdust was sprinkled on the wood floors, and the few empty tables gleamed in the light from the large windows stretching across the west wall. A long padded bench lined the east wall and matching stools sat in front of the bar itself, behind which were the usual array of bottles mirrored to the rowdy clientele. Welcoming and comfortable was Carrie's assessment.

Slim pushed his belly against Carrie, and pointed, "Over there in the far corner. Still pounding away." He put his hand on Carrie's shoulder and propelled himself behind the bar.

Carrie recoiled and bumped against Jim's chest, regained her balance and swore. She swiveled and glared at Jim, "What the hell?"

Jim put his arm around her waist and spoke into her ear, "Dave and Slim are old football buddies. Can you believe it?" Not waiting for an answer, he pushed through the crowd towards Dave with Carrie in tow.

Chapter 19

Dave jumped up, his chair scrunched Jim's legs and Carrie winced in sympathy.

"Carrie, my favorite golf partner!" He wrapped Carrie in a smothering bear hug, then held her shoulders, "You look like a million bucks. Country life must agree with you. Sorry to hear about your kicking leg. How is it now? Come, sit, sit." He pulled out a chair.

"Country life?" Carrie asked. Why was he so hyper?

Jim held her coat, slung it over her chair and explained, "Any place outside of metro Toronto is 'country' to this guy."

Carrie smiled and nodded her thanks to Jim as Dave motioned to Slim for drinks.

After gathering up his papers to make room at the table, Dave organized them into three neat piles, removed the top page of the first pile and set it aside, paper-clipped each pile and placed them carefully into his open briefcase. He snapped it closed, folded his laptop and set them both on the chair beside him, "There. Everything safely tucked away from any prying eyes in this place." He turned his attention to Carrie, "I thought you would need something to warm your shackles after being out in this god-awful weather."

Slim appeared and set a bottle of sherry and three glasses on the table, "Anything else, folks?"

Jim looked askance at the sherry, "Yeah, a Guinness please."

Slim nodded his approval, removed one of the glasses and went back to the bar.

"Does Slim always serve you personally?" Carrie asked as she watched a middle-aged woman carry a tray of bottles and glasses to another table.

"Yeah, that waitress is as slow as molasses in January," Dave pointed his chin in the woman's direction. He poured two sherries and handed one to Carrie. "Cheers, dear. Let's not wait for Jim's beer." He clinked his glass against hers, "Jim has brought me up to date on your exciting life, and since my hopes for an early season ski have been dashed, I am trying to figure out what the hell you have gotten yourself into, Carrie March."

She sighed, "Not by choice. My descent into chaos seems to have started with being bitten by a coyote."

"Who you had kicked," Dave chuckled. "Is that bite still bothering you? I noticed you limping."

Jim answered before she had a chance to, "The wound is infected, and every step is painful for her. Carrie is on rabies vaccine and antibiotics and should not be drinking." He put his arm around her shoulders and squeezed lightly in a protective gesture.

Why was Jim suddenly so controlling? Carrie drew away from him, "Sherry doesn't count. Anyway, I'll just sip." She turned her shoulder to Jim and addressed Dave, "Thanks for asking, Dave. Despite what Jim says, my wound is getting better every day." She patted her thigh, "Forget my damn leg. What did your searching turn up?"

Dave paused, picked up his sherry, and peering over the rim of the glass at her he asked, "How well do you know Susan Wright?"

Both Jim and Carrie looked at him in surprise, and Carrie answered in a hesitant voice, "Well, she works for an engineering consulting firm to whom the government contracts a lot of environmental work, so I have known her through work for a few years. But it's only since I got involved in her anti-pipeline rally that I've spent a lot of time with her. Why?"

"I think--" Dave started to speak but was interrupted by Slim who slammed down a bottle of dark ale in front of Jim and announced,

"We're gonna get a doozy of a storm."

"How can it storm when it's so cold?" Carrie asked.

"Temperature's been shooting up in the last few hours." Slim looked up as three men with ice-encrusted beards came through the front door. "Good ol' Alberta weather keeps bringing in more customers."

"Bring another Guinness and leave the bottle of sherry please," Dave said putting on his Eton and Harrow accent.

"I s'pose," answered Slim as he topped up Carrie's sherry. He winked at her, "Enjoy, young lady." He positioned the bottle over Dave's glass and let it overflow.

Dave jumped back in his chair, "Jesus, Slim, watch what you're doing."

Carrie stifled a laugh and took a few sips looking at the windows, "It's getting dark already."

"God, you're right," Dave shuddered. "How far north are we here?"

She hiccupped in excitement, "A dark night makes me think of 'Hamlet' and 'pathetic fallacy' linking nature to human behavior. Perfect! An ideal night to bump off Peter Cummings!" She drained the small glass and pushed it towards Dave and the open bottle.

Jim watched her drain the second glass and shot a warning glance at Dave.

She laughed in delight, "As the storm raged, somebody murdered the CEO of Cummings Consortium, Inc." She burped, gulped from her water glass and looked around the room, "Where's the ladies'?" She stood, and the room spun.

"Behind the bar. You'll have to get by Slim's corporation again." Jim warned.

"Corporation?" Carrie asked.

"His belly." Jim held her chair, took her elbow and led her through the filling tables. Several men were shooting pool in the corner and Garth Brooks blasted from an adjacent juke box. The aroma of barbecued chicken wings wafted out, presumably from a kitchen behind the bar. He pointed to the sign painted in red, 'Girls' Loo', "Want me to wait?"

"No." Using her hand against the wall for support she pushed the door open. Swearing silently, she stumbled into the first open stall and locked its door. She knelt in front of the toilet, closed her eyes, and tried to remember how Peggy described making yourself throw up. Her eyes felt gritty and swollen as she shoved two fingers down her throat. Not far enough. She rammed them as far as she could, gagged, and vomited. After washing her hands, she splashed water onto her face then drank from her cupped hands. Pulling the last sheet of paper toweling from the white metal holder, she rubbed her face dry and glanced into the cracked mirror. And grimaced.

Both men started to get up as Carrie approached the table, but she waved them down. "I don't deserve such respect. I apologize profusely for getting drunk."

"Carrie," Jim said, "you are *not* drunk by any stretch of the imagination. Let's order something to eat so we're out of here before the storm hits." He slid a spattered menu in her direction.

As the two men argued the merits of Ukrainian borscht versus Polish cabbage soup Carrie thought how different Jim and Dave were to each other. Dave, intense dark eyes, barrel-chested, broad-shouldered, and about five-ten or eleven, he was a perfect foil to tall, lanky, laid-back Jim with his sleepy smile and warm brown eyes.

"They make the best red borscht in the world here. How about it? It's fast and we can talk while we slurp." Jim gathered up the menus.

"Okay, how about you take our orders up to Slim? While I schmooze alone with Carrie," Dave worked his chair closer to hers. When he smiled, his dark eyes softened to a warm grey.

Carrie and Dave talked about skiing until Jim came back, trailing the waitress who carried a tray containing three huge steaming bowls and a platter of buttered black bread.

"Thanks, old boy." Dave said as he made room on the table for their food. "Carrie filled me in on the best runs at Jasper, if I ever get there." Jim pulled his chair closer to Carrie's and as soon as they were alone again, he nodded to Dave,

"We're all ears. What did you discover anything interesting?"

Dave stirred his soup thoughtfully, "I went to the Provincial Archives, and they steered me to this gal, a librarian I guess, who really knew her stuff."

"Probably a records manager, but she could be both," Carrie interjected.

"Well, she was a cute young thing and we got along famously."

Jim and Carrie exchanged knowing smiles which Dave noticed. Glowering at them he said,

"Come on, you two. Pay attention. Here's what I found out. There is no existing death certificate for a woman named Jean Marie Stuart Cummings anywhere in Canada, but we found the marriage certificate."

"He *did* marry her!" Carrie exclaimed.

"Yes. She, the librarian, asked me for keywords: Cummings of course, Jeanie, North Saskatchewan River, and your name Carrie. She combined these keywords in all sorts of ways and I had trouble keeping up with her, but I know she added 'tailings pond' at some point." He paused his eyes shifted, "I hate to tell you, Carrie, but she found the articles on *your* old accident in the east."

"Oh," Carrie said, presuming the librarian had searched the Toronto papers too.

"Back to the present: when she combined 'march' and 'cummings' she got a hit in the "Letter to the Editor" section of the Edmonton Journal that related to the *Ides of March*. The Journal had asked for true stories that verified March 15 as a "bad luck day". I hadn't been aware of that superstition, but to make a long story shorter, a C. Padoroski submitted an account of an event that happened to her husband on that day nine years ago. Curiously, it was the same day that Cummings claims he put Jeanie on a flight to eastern Europe."

Even Jim had put down his spoon to listen to the story unfold.

Chapter 20

Dave tipped up his glass, waved to Slim for a refill and continued, "Padoroski was the night watchman at a chemical plant adjacent to one of Cummings' properties. On his last round of the night, he thought he heard the sound of loose chains near the plant's tailings pond. By the time he got to the pond and shone his flashlight around, all he saw was a bulky figure disappearing on the other side. When Padoroski called out, the figure looked back, slipped, recovered, and then ran. Padoroski got to the approximate place he'd seen the man--he assumed the figure was male--but he saw nothing." Dave finally ate some borsch and rubbed his little protruding pouch in satisfaction.

"Shone his flashlight around what? Just the tailings pond?" Carrie asked.

Dave shrugged. "Anybody's guess. And your next question, did they drag the tailings pond? Apparently, a private citizen, no name, requested it, because he or she had just reported a missing teen. But a scientist explained it would be difficult to retrieve a body if there was one there. The bottom of the pond is Alberta mud covered with debris, pieces of metal and discarded equipment. The company is obviously breaking some environmental law there. Whatever Padoroski's guy threw in would probably slide under the heavy material, sink down in the slime God knows how far. It would have to be drained. Before the paperwork for drainage was done the teenager turned up, drugged and happy. A little later Cummings bought the chemical plant, including the tailings pond." Dave wiped his mouth with his usual fastidiousness.

"Really? I wonder why," Carrie's lips turned down in sarcasm, "Can we get someone to drain it now?"

Jim shook his head and said, "It's private property and Pete would never give his permission unless it benefitted him." He frowned and seemed lost in thought for a few minutes. Carrie wondered if he suspected Aunt Lottie to be the 'private person, but, partly to himself he mused, "Why the hell would Pete buy a tailings pond?"

He shook his head and continued, "The land it's on was undoubtedly worth quite a bit. It slopes down to the river and as I said, it's adjacent to his." Dave swirled his sherry. "Carrie, we will need a reason, and a lot more evidence of malfeasance to get a court order to drain and excavate." He sipped. No slurps. "I don't want you to do any more snooping, Carrie," he said firmly. "I can't protect you if Peter Cummings decides you're becoming a menace to him."

"But…" Carrie objected, and Jim cheered,

"Atta boy, lay down the law."

"No buts. I'm committed, Carrie, pro bono for you. Until I can get skiing, anyway." He smiled at her, "Great borscht, eat up while it's warm. We've been talking too much."

She relented and the three of them quaffed the thick soup and black bread.

Dave pushed his bowl away and leaned back, "The curious thing is that the librarian at the archives mentioned that I was the second person in so many days to ask for these particular records. Even though we found the newspaper article there, we cannot assume the two events are related."

"Really?" Jim remarked. "Why not?"

"Who?" Carrie asked. "Who was the other one asking at the archives?"

"No one at the archives would tell me, of course," Dave replied. "To get back to the newspaper article, I'm going to try and talk to the Padoroski's."

"May I come too?" Carrie asked, wondering how she could justify the time off.

"It would be my pleasure," Dave actually bowed, "I'll work it into my schedule and let you know." He got up to leave.

"Wait!" Carrie cried. "What about Aunt Lottie's report?"

"Who?" Dave struggled to get his overcoat over his suit jacket.

"Jim's aunt and her bridge club," Carrie answered. "They wrote a report on Jeanie's disappearance years ago and…"

"I don't believe this." Dave dropped back down in his chair and his heavy overcoat gaped open, "An old ladies' bridge club?"

"Better not let Aunt Lottie hear you," Jim said with a smile.

"Okay, I give up. Let's see it." Dave glanced at Jim, "Is your aunt's surname 'Mathews' also?"

"I read it last night and I brought it with me to get you or Jim to clarify some of the legalese. Jim's driving and I can finish it in his truck on the way back. I'll let you have it tomorrow."

"Let me have it now, Carrie. Please." Dave held out his hand.

"Maybe Slim can make a copy," Carrie pulled the report out of her shoulder bag and called, "Slim! Do you have a photocopier?"

Slim appeared from behind the bar. "Yeah, but it's an old one." He threw the dish cloth he was holding into the sink and held open the swinging gate, "Come on, it's back here. I even have an unopened bottle of toner." He led them to a small office near the back entrance, and shuffled an assortment of junk, hardware, and papers, off the dirty white machine. "It don't work too good but here's the stuff for it." He pointed to a bottle on the floor. "If you guys can get it working, I'll give you free beer next time you're in."

Carrie stared at it, "It's an old bubble jet."

"Can you work it?" Dave asked. "If not, just give me the damn report."

Carrie threw her shoulder bag and coat on a dusty chair, "We'll see."

She found the cord, handed it to Jim and said, "Can you find an outlet somewhere?"

Carrie called out instructions to the two men. "Pull it out from the wall, pry open the back, now remove those screws." After removing a jammed piece of paper, she asked the men to find her a rag of some sort while she poked at the mechanism. Jim handed her a greasy rag and she made a face, "Is that all you could find?" But she used it to remove some of the grime from the copier's moving parts. She filled the toner receptacle and ten minutes later they were in business, but not before Carrie warned them, "The copies will still be a little damp. Can you two executives figure out a way to dry them without smudging the ink?"

Jim and Dave worked out an assembly line production. Jim picked up each sheet by its edges as it emerged from the copier and handed it to Dave who took it into the bar and found a reasonably clean surface on which it could dry. The place was starting to empty--customers going home for dinner, so they wiped down the tables, and soon the back end of the bar resembled a messy office.

Slim came in as the copier chugged out the last pages. His eyes were wide in amazement when he saw papers on every flat surface in the room. Ignoring Dave and Jim, he hugged her, and she was encased in his round, soft stomach, "You got it working! Free sherry for you, ma'am! Anytime!" He released her and picked something out of her hair.

"Thanks for the use of your old machine." Dave noticed Carrie's face, "Jesus, Carrie. Look at you. A little more ink and you'll be 'Little Black Sa ..., correction, our 'Black Beauty."

Dave grinned at her derisive look as Slim came back wringing out a napkin.

"Will this do?" Slim asked and added, "Lots more where that came from!"

Jim pulled a wooden stool across the floor and helped Carrie sit on it. She yawned, "Why am I so tired? I could sleep on my feet."

"It's the air in here," Jim took the damp cloth from Slim and wiped the smudges of ink off her cheek and forehead. Standing back, he smiled, "You're almost presentable. I was afraid the fumes from that old machine would asphyxiate us all. We should get out into the fresh air."

"May I use it now?" Dave found a clean corner on the napkin and wiped his hands, "Can't say it hasn't been fun. See you at the Mac tomorrow, six o'clock sharp." He put his hand on Slim's shoulder as he went out the front door and said, "Now *you* owe *me*."

Slim walked to the back door and held it open for Carrie and Jim, "Come on you two. Fresh air." He grinned at them as they ducked under his arm, "I'll lock this door now. See you."

Carrie started to ask Dave what he wanted to know about Susan, but he was unlocking his car and two minutes later he was gone.

As they walked to Jim's truck Carrie promised herself she would climb in on her own. But Jim opened the passenger door, put his hands under her arms and lifted her onto the seat. He left her to work her legs in on her own.

He wound the truck windows down as far as they would go and they basked in the freezing breeze while the engine warmed up. He reached into the back seat and lifted a dark green blanket onto Carrie's lap, "Here, even if it's smelly it should help a bit. The heater in this truck takes forever to generate any warmth."

"Thanks. Tell me about Slim." She spread the blanket up to her waist.

"Not much to tell." He glanced in the rear-view mirror, "Shit! The Mercedes again. I can see its nose poking out." He pulled the truck carefully away from the dumpster.

"Oh no!" She slunk down pulling the blanket up to her shoulders, folded her good knee up to the seat and rolled herself into a ball, "Is it following us? Can they see me?"

"They must know you're here but suit yourself. I don't see him but he's probably waiting to see which way we go." Jim exited the alley, looked both ways and turned towards 97th Street. Peeling off 97th, he wove between two commercial blocks, "I hoped to end up behind them. I can't see the Mercedes so we might be home free, but you'd better stay like that for a while longer."

"Okay. Dave and Slim? They seem to be good friends." She leaned her head on the seat and bent her legs so her toes were under the heater.

"What I know isn't much." He sped up and pulled in front of a transport truck. "Our friends in the Mercedes won't be able to tail us now." He set the cruise control, "Dave had recommended Slim's bar when we were here for the golf game. A week later, after a particularly grueling day, I stopped in for a beer on my way home. I sampled Slim's soup—well, his mother's soup-- and I was hooked."

"Hmm, I can understand that."

"How's your leg? It must be cramped in that position." He looked down at her, "You can sit up now." He glanced in all the car mirrors, "Slim and Dave met in their last year of high school when they played football on an all-Canadian team that toured…I've forgotten where. Dave from Toronto and Slim from Edmonton."

"I can just see them as high school football jocks," Carrie said.

Jim nodded in agreement, "Dave stops in at Slim's bar every time he's in town. Has done for years. Slim is remarkably well-informed, and he loves to talk politics. You know Dave, he's a born debater. Dave helped him with his income tax one year, and since then he's been doing Slim's books. Soup in exchange for financial services. How good a deal is that?"

"What a great story. Those were probably Slim's papers he tucked away as soon as we arrived." She yawned and stretched.

"Think you can sleep in this rattle-trap of a truck?"

"I could sleep anywhere but I won't." She sat up straight, "Why are you and Dave helping me?"

He took a few seconds to answer. "I know why I'm somewhat involved in your crusade against Pete, and Dave is a lawyer. He's always on the side of justice."

"But…"

"Do you know a back route to your house?" He interrupted her as he cast worrying looks in his rear-view mirror, "The Mercedes; it's back."

"Oh, damnit to hell!" She peered out the side window, "Why the hell don't they just park at my front door?"

She kept watching for the Mercedes as she gave directions. Jim was completely disoriented but he trusted her. He slowed down for every turn and corner and when they pulled into the back alley behind her house he muttered, "Good thing this old truck has a good turning radius."

"No Mercedes," Carrie said. They high fived and grinned at each other. "You and Dave will both have to watch your backs now--fugitives from Pete."

Jim looked surprised, "I can't believe Pete is in that Mercedes. Not his style. And I think Dave and I are both capable of looking after ourselves. Are you going to do as Dave says and stick to your knitting?"

Carrie smiled, "Your grandmother's expression again."

"You didn't answer my question." After a moment he gave up and sighed, "I'll pick you up for dinner tomorrow about five-thirty. Okay?"

"Perfect." She turned to open the door, "I haven't been to the Mac in years."

"Good," he replied as he got out, "Hopefully it will be a treat for you rather than another disaster." He slid around the truck and held out his arms to help her.

"You pessimist!" She laughed as she braced her hand against the open door and jumped down on her good leg avoiding his arms. He caught her as she wobbled on one leg and said in all seriousness,

"The inability to see the worst-case scenario ahead of time can lead to dangerous predicaments."

Laughing she pulled her arm free and limped up the walk. The wind was brutal and she was anxious to get inside. But she paused, her gloved hand on the doorknob and turned to wave. He pulled away from the curb and acknowledged her 'Salut' with a few short honks.

It was getting to be a ritual. She let herself in and remembered with a jolt that Jim had not told her why he was helping her. And Dave had given no inkling to why he was interested in Susan. Two unanswered questions.

Chapter 21

Carrie gazed out the kitchen window as she washed her breakfast dishes. The storm had left a carpet of glistening snow and she could picture Charlie and Bobby rolling and playing in it. Bobby had loved dogs, and she and Cliff had even decided on the breed that would be best for a toddler. A boy and his dog. The water gurgled out of the sink as she absently pulled the plug. God, she was getting maudlin. Although she realized her grief had lost some of its sharpness, it seemed her memory only tightened as past moments replayed.

The engine whine of a ski-do in the alley startled her. Talk about dogs! All the dogs in the neighborhood were barking at the noisy vehicle. Carrie empathized with them. She hated snow mobiles. A few minutes later a substantial figure in a black ski jacket appeared at the corner of the garage and approached the back porch.

Carrie sucked in her breath wondering if it was a homeless person. She couldn't imagine losing her little house, having to live on her own without a home, especially in this frigid weather. Susan had told her that some criminal types had joined the ranks of the homeless and were wandering north, out of the downtown core. But a homeless person on a ski-do?

She opened the back door and stood shivering on the small porch. Arms crossed against her chest she waited for "it" to approach. She tentatively reached for the steel handle of the shovel that rested against the porch railing. But she knew her fingers would freeze to the metal, so she let her hand slide down the shovel's wooden shaft-- her only weapon. Some defense! If 'it' got too close, what should she do? Whack it over the head with the shovel? She could hardly hold the damn thing; her fingers were almost immobile now.

"Who are you?" Carrie called. "What do you want? If you stay where you are, I'll bring you a sandwich and coffee."

The figure stopped and unwound a thick scarf from around its head, neck and face, and called in a clear voice, "Carrie, it's Helen. We need to talk."

"Helen! What...?" She paused. Helen had come to her. Why? Retribution? In any case Carrie decided she wasn't going to freeze her butt off any longer or let more cold air into the house. With a great deal of trepidation, she opened the door wide, "Come in, Helen." She gestured to the bench and boot rack.

With her cold hands under her armpits Carrie watched Helen remove her boots. Helen had still not said a word, but she held the dripping boots in the air letting the melting snow spatter onto the kitchen floor.

Keeping her annoyance in check Carrie asked, "Why are you here?"

Not answering Helen removed her jacket, stuffed her mitts and hat into one sleeve and threw it onto the bench. With a sly smirk on her face, she turned to face Carrie.

Carrie blocked her, "What do you want?"

They stood eyeing each other and Carrie became increasingly uncomfortable. Should she fear this woman? She wished Charlie was with her as she hesitated. She wanted Helen gone. Was Helen seeking revenge for her bitten fingers? She pushed her hands into her pockets, fingered her cell phone and found the dial pad. She could dial 911 surreptitiously but Helen finally spoke,

"Any coffee?"

Sighing heavily, Carrie emptied out the leftovers of her breakfast coffee from the pot and put on a fresh one. In the meantime, Helen had made herself comfortable at the kitchen table, her socked feet resting on the chair that Carrie usually sat on.

As she put mugs, milk, and sugar on the table she glared at Helen, "Are you going to tell me why you're here? I don't have time for this nonsense."

"Cool it, girl. We need to talk." Helen grabbed one of the mugs and held it out, "Coffee smells as if its's ready."

Carrie obliged, filling Helen's mug, and one for herself, then sat at the end of the table and studied her uninvited guest. This is the woman who kept her drugged at Don's house and fed her lies. Where would Carrie be now if Jim and Dave hadn't rescued her? Still in a comatose state from which she might never recover? She shuddered.

"Any cookies?" Helen's blunt question broke into Carrie's thoughts, and she got up to put cookies on a plate. A Pavlovian response? What in God's name was wrong with her? Get a grip. Shove Helen out of her kitchen and house, or ask her if she knew Jeanie.

Helen crunched with her mouth slightly open, "Homemade. Chocolate chip. My favorite."

"Are you still working for Don?" Carrie pushed the plate closer.

Helen lifted her hand and wiggled her fingers in Carrie's face, "Look, no broken bones, no teeth marks." She cackled a witchy laugh and helped herself to another cookie.

"How did you find out where I live? And why?"

"God, woman, get real. Phone book, Facebook, Twitter. And I've been following you. Surely you've noticed." Helen wrapped both her hands around the coffee mug and shook her head, "In this freezing cold weather." She held up her splayed right hand again and grinned, "All is forgiven."

Carrie stared at her for a moment before the light bulb went on, "Ah, the Mercedes. Not very subtle. But why?" Carrie was truly angry now. What right did this woman have to follow her? In a sports car that could easily overtake her small Honda? Was tailing another car against the law? She became more determined to phone the police. However, when Helen looked up her hazel eyes held the cold, single-mindedness that Carrie remembered.

Helen leaned forward and snagged her sweater on the metal around its edges. "Jesus, can't you afford a modern kitchen table? This one must have been your grandmother's." She tied the edges of the yarn while Carrie smiled, thinking Helen sounded just like Jim.

Helen's eyes shone as she answered Carrie's question, "Peter Cummings. I think we both want the same thing."

"Oh? And what is that?" Carrie had a sinking feeling that she knew what was coming.

"To bring him down." Helen set down her mug. "No more coffee for me. Where's the john?"

Carrie waited, elbows on the table, her chin cupped in her hand. A whole plethora of emotions cascaded through her mind--fear of Pete but anticipation at the thought of Cummings suffering, shame and guilt for cheering a human being's death. She wondered how to respond to Helen's suggestion. What on earth did Helen have in mind? In spite of herself, Carrie felt a jolt of excitement at the thought of harming Pete in some way. Maybe just deter him. Helen came back and Carrie said,

"Just like that--bring down Peter Cummings. One of the province's most powerful men."

"Yeah," Helen blew on her coffee, "You have influence and contacts in the Alberta government. Plus, two able-bodied hunks at your beck and call." The furrows between her dark, penciled eyebrows deepened. "Who are also friends or business associates of Cummings. Do you trust Dave and Jim? Where do you think their loyalties lie, you or him?"

Carrie hesitated. She had never considered that Jim or Dave might have to choose between herself and Pete, and she should have. She knew Cummings used Dave's legal services for his Toronto affairs. But Jim?

Helen grabbed another cookie and her question hung in the air. Her loud chewing reminded Carrie of Charlie guzzling at his supper bowl.

"Together we can do this," Helen picked up her mug. "Together we can bring this man to trial."

Carrie's hand, reaching for a cookie, halted in mid-air, "Are you crazy? He's a millionaire, he has pull, he's…"

"Yes, he has a shitload of money," Helen conceded. "Even though he has always been a shady businessman, Cummings seems to be on the up-and-up right now. But you and I, we can destroy this evil creature." With the back of her hand, she wiped the cookie crumbs from her upper lip. "I know that you and your friend, Susan Wright, are trying to stop his pipeline. Is she still in custody? At least *you* don't have a police record now."

"A police record? Why would I? I was only inputting data. I didn't do any marching." Carrie stood, cookie forgotten, snatched a dish cloth from the sink and began to wipe the counters. Anything to avoid Helen's intense, cold eyes. Staring blankly at the countertop she asked Helen, "What has Cummings done to you?"

"Just know that I have a personal vendetta against the man, and I need your help to exercise it." The edges of Helen's lips turned up, "There's an old Polish proverb that says, 'where the devil can't manage, he'll send in a woman'." Her grin was malicious.

Carrie hung the dish cloth on the edge of the sink and turned, "I need to know why you want to bring down Peter Cummings."

"Why I'm doing this is personal and irrelevant at the moment," Helen replied. "With careful planning, and using your resources, I feel confident that we can accomplish our goal."

"*Our* goal? Resources?" Carrie's voice was shrill.

"Dave and Jim, and maybe Don, your colleagues in the government, your father's wealth." Helen smirked, "My contribution may seem small, but I still work for Don. He doesn't do much that I don't know about."

Carrie stared at her and whispered, "Jesus Christ."

Helen barked out a laugh, "Yeah, maybe even Him." She played with her empty mug, twirling it back and forth, "You encourage Dave to dig up as much dirt about the big man as he can, and share it with you of course," Helen sat back. "We combine it with what I know, what we've gleaned from other sources, and make a plan. You're having dinner with those two guys tonight so you're the coordinator."

"How do you know--" Carrie paused, "You should come too." Leaning her back against the counter she tried to figure out how this woman knew so much from following her in a Mercedes. Helen must be tapping her phone, spying on her emails, what else? Carrie thanked God she never posted online. She tried to imagine Dave and Jim's reaction to Helen and couldn't.

"No," Helen said to Carrie's suggestion. "None of these men should know that we have met," She blew her nose loudly, looked at the tissue, crushed it in her hand and placed the wet wad on Carrie's table.

"Why not?"

"Just the two of us for now," Helen did not smile, "Let me tell you what I know about Peter Cummings."

Carrie was amazed at the details Helen spouted. "Peter Butler Cummings. Only son born to Judith Alma and Rodney Francis Cummings in Swift Current, Saskatchewan, June 2, 1955. Predeceased by his mother in 1958 and father in 1960. Graduated with a BCom from the University of Western Ontario in..."

"Enough already!" Carrie looked at her in astonishment, "You have all this memorized?"

"Yeah, well, I have one of those crazy minds that retains everything."

"You're eidetic! Dave will love you! You *must* join us for dinner." Carrie went to the phone, "I'll call...."

"No!" Helen shouted, and immediately lowered her voice, "I have to maintain my persona as Don's assistant. You know that's essential. Find out what you can tonight without mentioning me. But for God's sake, only one glass of wine."

"You haven't even given me a hint as to why you're so much against Peter Cummings," Carrie's voice was cold. Dictating how many glasses of wine she should drink? She was fifty years old; first it was Jim and Dave, and now Helen was treating her like a six-year old. "Before I commit to anything with you, I need to know more."

Helen hesitated, "I will tell you; I promise. But not today. I've been hoping for Cummings' demise for a long time, and I apologize for being mysterious." She got up to put on her ski jacket, "That coffee will help against the biting wind out there." She sat down to pull on her boots.

"Do you know Jeanie?" Carrie blurted out even though she had planned on approaching the subject of Jeanie tactfully.

Her innocent question caused Helen to crumple—her whole body sagged and her face blanched. She leaned on her knees with her head hanging down between them and murmured, "Jeanie. Yes, I knew Jeanie." She jumped up, started for the door, seemed to think better of it and collapsed in the chair again. "Jeanie used to read Emily Dickinson to me. She tried to make me appreciate poetry the way she did. We plagiarized one of her poems about sisters. Do you know it? 'You do not sing as I do, it is a different tune...' If Jeanie is alive, she will remember that poem."

Helen opened the door and left without another word, letting the aluminum-framed storm door click shut.

Carrie waited until she heard the ski-do start up before she slowly closed the inside door. So Helen knew Jeanie well enough to read poetry with her. Were they related? Could they be sisters? Why did bringing down Pete seem to be a life and death issue to Helen? How in God's name could she cooperate with Helen and maintain her relationships with Jim and Dave? Is the fact that Helen is working for Don significant? How were all these disparate things connected? At the very least, she would look up the Dickinson poem on Facebook.

Chapter 22

As soon as Jim pulled up in front of Carrie's house, she was out her front door, sliding down the walk in her black pumps. Jim could see what was going to happen. He hurried around the Toyota, plowed through a snowbank at the curb and grabbed her elbows just as her feet slid out from under her. For a brief second, she clutched his ski jacket as she scrabbled for purchase on the slippery surface. He lifted her up effortlessly and put her down on the snow-covered grass. Her elbow tucked securely under his arm, he led her to the car, opened the door and leaned forward to help her.

"I can do it, thanks." She lifted her bandaged leg. "I'm fine, really."

"Just an infected coyote bite." He muttered. With his hand on the hood for support he slid around the car to the driver's side.

She snapped in the seat belt buckle as he settled behind the wheel, "Sorry if I appeared too independent." When she saw his face soften and the corners of his lips turn up, she asked, "You own a car too?"

"No, it's a company car." He glanced at her feet and asked, "Why aren't you wearing boots?" He slowed for a red light and shook his head, "A seasoned Westerner like you without boots in this weather."

"I can't get my snow boots up past my ankles now, and there is blood on my hiking boots. Don't know whether it's mine or the coyotes but it turns me off. Anyway, they don't go with my fancy-dancy dress."

Jim laughed. "You sure the blood isn't Pete's?" She gave him a horrified look, the light changed, and he asked, "Are the malls open tonight?"

"I guess so. It's Friday. Why?" Before he could answer she said, "No, Jim. We haven't got time to stop for boots. Besides, the mall is north and we're headed south."

"I can do a U-turn up ahead." His eyes scanned the neighborhood.

"That's illegal in this province. Let's not be late for Dave's dinner."

"Okay." He sighed, "You win. This time."

He dropped her off at the front door of the Macdonald Hotel and drove down the ramp to park the car. The liveried attendant rushed to open the side door for her, obviously glad of something to do but the door was stuck in muddy ice. He threw up his hands in a 'watcha-gonna-do' gesture and went back to standing guard, stamping his feet to get them warm. Carrie smiled at his grumpy face then pushed through the revolving doors to an equally grumpy Dave pacing the deck.

But he grinned when he spotted her and embraced her, "Carrie, I don't think I've ever seen you with make-up. You look ravishing!!"

She reflected on his exquisite manners as they settled in the lounge's tub chairs. He had helped her off with her coat, held her elbows as she eased into the low seat and rolled a stool over for her foot. And he was still the handsomest man she knew.

"How's the leg? Still sore?"

"Getting a little better every day, thanks." She smiled.

"Jim has told me a little about your coyote bite, but I'd like to hear all the details from the horse's mouth, so to speak."

"Ever the lawyer!" Carrie laughed.

"What'll you have to drink? I've found that sometimes an alcohol-infused memory reveals surprising details," Dave perused the drinks menu.

"White wine please. But we came to hear *you*."

"Let's wait until Jim gets here. Come on, Carrie. From the beginning."

By the time Jim joined them, Carrie had related the coyote attack to Dave, hoping this was the last time she'd have to retell that experience. Dave looked at her in admiration, "You are a most unusual woman, Carrie. You can kick a coyote, put up with an infected leg, listen to Peter Cummings rant against you, and still laugh. Cheers to you."

Forty-five minutes later, Carrie, Jim and Dave were waiting for their menus in the Harvest Room. They discussed the menu, sipped the Pouilly Fuisse and Dave leaned across to Carrie, "Okay, old girl, what else have you been up to lately?"

"Not much." She ignored Jim's snort, "I'm pretty busy at work, learning a new job and getting to know the team I've been assigned to. I still have a somewhat nebulous supervisory responsibility of my former regulatory work at the NEB. Much to Troy's disappointment. But Jim and I want to hear what you've unearthed, Dave."

Dave glanced up at the hovering waitress. "Shall we order? The best feature here is the beef."

"Of course," Jim agreed. "We're in Alberta. I'll have roast beef, medium rare with mushrooms and asparagus."

"Sounds great. Make that two, please." Carrie handed her menu to the waitress with a smile.

"Okay, three, but mashed potatoes and lots of gravy," Dave said, winking at her.

Jim glanced at Carrie, "Dave, Carrie is on pins and needles waiting to hear what you've found out about Cummings. And so am I."

Dave speared a slice of the red meat, "You know I'm Pete's attorney in Toronto, but I've never had any need or desire to delve into his past business dealings here in Alberta. Initially I thought combining the odd visit out here with skiing in Jasper or Banff was good management on my part. But it is past unbelievable what Cummings has gotten away with." He popped the loaded fork into his mouth and chewed contentedly.

Jim looked surprised, "Gets away with what?"

Dave ignored Jim, "Tell me about your life, Carrie, while I chew on this prime rib."

"Look Dave, leave Carrie's personal life out of this…"

Carrie shook her head, "I'm perfectly fine with my life, Jim, thank you very much. I like my job, I love my little house, my kooky dog. It's comfortable and I hope it stays that way until my retirement."

Dave swallowed and asked, "And then?"

"Golf, tennis, skiing hopefully. Can you tell us now, or do you want dessert?"

Dave stretched, "Let's go whole hog and have apple pie with ice cream followed by liqueurs and coffee." He motioned to the waitress.

"Just coffee for me." Carrie patted her stomach. "Gotta keep the middle aged spread under control."

Both men smiled and Dave muttered, "I'll get back to Pete when we get rid of the serving staff."

They finished the meal in silence and Dave explained, "I don't trust anyone except you two." He gazed around the empty restaurant and settled back, "Make yourselves comfortable folks, because this is a long story with lots of question marks. You will understand why I've done a 180 on Peter Cummings. I obviously should have researched Pete more before I signed a contract with him, small as it was. Peter Cummings tried to make a fortune in northern Alberta by duping the natives and a whole lot of other people. I've been investigating a pulp and paper company that he bought years ago."

"How far north? I'm surprised there's any lumber up there." Jim said.

"There was, poplar and spruce, but by the time he bought in the stands, things were getting thin. He constructed a paper trail to hide all his former company's nefarious dealings, fabricated paperwork, and phony audits. He had managed to force kickbacks that became too top-heavy to sustain."

"I'm not sure I follow this," Carrie said and added, "They're called 'the Indigenous Peoples' now, Dave."

"Noted." Dave smiled at her, "All this may be somewhat incomprehensible to Jim too, so I'll try to leave out the details. Besides insider trading, Cummings has done things so outrageous and beyond the scope of monitored business that it seems like a video game. You wouldn't believe it Jim, even though you probably never play video games."

"My nephew has introduced me to a few," Jim said.

"Well, maybe you can get him to explain how Cummings got away with what he did. We found empty figures from non-existent partners of Cummings' rolling into their accounts like pin ball machines."

Carrie looked confused, "Pin ball machines, video games, this is modern business parlance?"

"If it weren't so close to reality, it would be amusing," Dave replied.

"How long ago was all this?" Jim asked Dave.

"He began nineteen years ago." Dave answered. "I was lucky to find a few people with long memories. Some quite bitter. Partners had sold stock options and cashed them out of the general pension fund. Finance officials had created over a hundred special purpose entities in order to legally launder money. They had used any accounting trick they knew to book profits that didn't exist, or wouldn't exist, for at least thirty years."

"But Pete built his reputation on that company," Jim interjected.

"The company on which he built his reputation was nothing but a fake. It hadn't turned an honest profit in over a decade, hadn't made a legit deal in as long as anyone could remember. Even when he'd been reporting profits in the thousands, almost a million, he'd actually been losing money."

After a long silence in which Jim and Carrie digested these facts, Carrie spoke up, "I just don't understand how he could have developed Cummings Consortium. How did he get investors? Where were the regulatory bodies? Surely someone in this province remembered his old company and its failings."

"His current investors are all offshore, numbered companies, impossible to track. In twenty years, many players have died, moved on, whatever. And who would be interested until it was too late? He got his dollars, yuans, yens, and he made damn sure

Cummings Consortium was legitimate in every way. Now Peter Cummings is sitting on influential boards, a member of the right clubs, and hauling in cash by the fistful. Anyone who dared bring up his past is silenced."

"How?" Carrie asked.

"Bribed undoubtedly, threatened maybe. It doesn't matter. Now everyone wants to be a friend of Peter Cummings."

"But it does matter!" Carrie was on her feet. "It's unethical, it's dishonest, and he should be in jail." The first tingles of fear gripped her chest.

"Yes," Dave nodded, noncommittal.

Carrie shuddered and sat down as Jim said, "Be careful, Dave. Is all this worth it? You are a Toronto lawyer trying to operate in this underpopulated Canadian province. Against a tycoon like Cummings with all his connections. Back off before it's too late, before you lose everything."

"Hey, come on," Dave said soothingly. "This is Canada, not some third-world country. This is the most interesting case I've seen in years. So, tell me, Carrie, what do *you* know of Peter Cummings?"

Carrie swallowed, "Well, Dave, you were there--the infamous golf game."

"Yes, although I missed his attempted assault and your well-aimed kick. Have there been any repercussions since then?"

Carrie told him about the Quebecois incident, but Dave said, "It doesn't fit in with our guy Pete's style, but who knows?"

"Carrie?" Jim prodded her.

She cleared her throat. "Initially, I suspected my mother of engineering that event, but after listening to Jim's smart phone recording I think it was Pete's doing."

"Your mother? What's her name?" Dave took out a small black book and scrawled in it, "I came across references to Don. What's your take on him?"

Carrie shook her head, "I just don't know. He was very kind to me..."

"He's in cahoots with Pete. You know that Carrie." Jim continued, "I found out that Don is indebted to Pete--he bailed him out of a failing company. I just can't help thinking that your recuperating in Don's house was one of Pete's ideas."

"Jesus, you guys!" Dave exclaimed. "Things haven't exactly been dull around here, have they? I agree with Jim. Why didn't Pete come after you at Don's?"

"We think he tried, but it backfired," Jim postulated. "I think the Quebecois event was Pete-inspired. He thought Tess was Carrie's dog, not mine."

"You know, this would make a great dog story for kids," Dave commented. "So now, Jim, you're part of the revenge scenario. What else?"

"The lady in red portrait." A light bulb went on in Carrie's head. "She looks like Helen!"

"Who?" Dave was baffled.

"The lady all in red in the portrait that is in Don's house! Not hanging, mind you, but laying covered on the floor. She resembles Helen, Don's girl Friday." Carrie sat back, thoughtful.

"Well, maybe the lady in the portrait *is* Helen," Dave sounded confused.

"Do you remember the portrait, Jim?" Carrie asked. Why hadn't she noticed the resemblance before? It was the smile, and Helen certainly hadn't done much smiling. Was it possible? "Could it be a portrait of Helen? You know how some portrait artists take a lot of poetic license with their subject."

"Yes, I suppose. I didn't see any resemblance at the time to Helen, but I didn't really look that carefully. Too much red for me." He pulled out his cell phone and started scrolling. "Here it is. A wonder I didn't delete it." Jim passed his phone to Carrie, who examined it intently before giving it to Dave.

"Gorgeous gal, whoever it is." Said Dave, the skirt chaser.

She took the phone back and stared at the image again. "No, I don't really think it's Helen but then I've never seen her all dolled up, with make-up and her hair...No, there is a resemblance, but I think Helen's features are coarser, not as delicate as this woman's."

Jim raised his bushy eyebrows, "Have you seen Helen recently? You didn't go to her church, did you?"

Carrie was at a loss for words. She had promised Helen not to mention her. Shit! Shit! Shit! "No, I did not go to her church but..." Carrie put her head in her hands.

The two men waited quietly. Finally, Dave said gently, "Come clean, Carrie. I can only help if I have all the facts."

"I spoke to Helen yesterday," Carrie said in a dull voice. "She came to my house, on a ski-do. She's the one in the Mercedes who's been trailing me."

Jim leaned towards Carrie, "Did she tell you why she had the gall to follow you so openly?"

"I promised her I wouldn't tell you that we had met, and here I am blurting it out." Carrie banged her fists on the table in frustration.

"So? Did she tell you anything new or different?" Dave's tone indicated he had switched back into lawyer mode.

Carrie shook her head, "Nothing you don't already know,"

Jim spoke into the chilled atmosphere, "I think you should know about Troy, Dave. He works for Carrie." Jim told Dave about his suspicions when he saw Troy in Pete's office.

Relieved to be off the subject of Helen, Carrie related the 'gun' incident. Then she added that she had hired Troy a few years ago as a favor to her friend Susan, Troy's mother.

Dave rose. "I'm going upstairs to work on a critical path for all this. Come with me. I need your input. Perhaps that will make everything a little clearer. It's a method for analyzing time allocations on a project going forward, but it might help us here, going backwards."

Once they were in Dave's hotel room, he produced a small roll of paper from his closet. Jim was not surprised, but Carrie asked, "You brought this with you?"

"No," Dave rolled out several widths on the small desk, "But every city in North America has a Staples, or equivalent. Hope this is enough, but there's always scotch tape."

Two hours later, Carrie gazed at her life on paper.

"The big question marks are Troy, Helen, Susan and maybe Don. I'll get at that later." Dave looked at his watch. "It's getting late, and I have an early morning flight. Ciao, guys. I'll be in touch." He grinned at Carrie, "But first, a hug." He held out his arms and Carrie walked into them. Jim watched, unsmiling.

During the drive north to Carrie's house, Jim needled her, hoping to jolt her memory for a few more details. As he pulled into her driveway, he said, "You've been a trooper, Carrie. I know you must be fed up with all these questions."

"I just feel frustrated that I can't seem to remember more."

Jim leaned across to open her door, "Perhaps there's no more to remember." He squeezed her gloved hand, "Sleep well. I've got a packed day tomorrow, but I'll get Charlie back to you even if it's after dinner. Is that good?"

"Yes, fine," Carrie closed the car door and started up the still slippery walk to her porch. At the door she dug in her purse for her keys, turned and did a thumbs-up at Jim who was idling, plumes of white exhaust twirling up into the black night. He honked a response and as she watched his taillights recede, a warm glow warmed the inside of her body as the outside shivered. Hurrying upstairs to her bedroom she stripped and snuggled down into the cozy flannel sheets. She kicked the electric bed warmer to her feet and closed her eyes. Images of a lazy grin and warm grey eyes flashed through her consciousness before she fell asleep.

Chapter 23

The next week went by quickly, the major highlight being Susan's release from custody. Carrie held a celebratory pizza dinner that was marred by Susan's exhaustion, Troy's sullen behavior, and worst of all--Jim's absence. His flight from Toronto had been delayed. She was glad to close the door on her two guests and was giving the table a last swab when the doorbell rang. Charlie's excited bark and the low rumble on the other side of the door left no doubt. Tess and Jim.

"Any pizza left?" Jim asked as he enveloped her in his arms. The dogs whirled around their legs barking their greetings to each other.

"No, but I can make…" Carrie backed away reluctantly.

"Just kidding! I ate on the plane. How was the big celebration?"

"Pretty god-awful." Taking his hand, she led him to the sofa. "I'll fix the drinks."

He reached up and pulled her down into his lap, "Tell me."

She snuggled into the hollow of his shoulder, "Well, Troy had told me about his meeting with Cummings this morning. It was a rant and rave session because Pete thinks that Troy and I are conspiring against him. I think the bastard is trying to distance Troy from me at work."

"How can he do that?" Jim stroked her cheek, and she reflected on how comforting his rough finger felt on her skin.

"Cummings knows a lot of people in the Alberta government's senior management. He could easily spread misleading rumors about my association with Susan and her damn anti-pipeline rally. The more Pete wines and dines Troy, the more aloof Troy becomes to me. Not only that, Troy is spending a lot of time at Human Resources."

"What does that mean?"

She shook her head, "Not sure. Either he's looking for another job or he's building a case against me. Formulating an official complaint--the government has a special procedure for just that."

"All this doesn't make too much sense." He sat up straighter, pulling her with him.

"Well, it does in a way. Troy expected to walk right into my NEB position when I went over to the Environment Department. It must be especially galling to have me still supervising him." She sunk back down onto his chest. "You probably think I'm paranoid. Susan does."

"No." He was thoughtful for a moment. "I've always been able to avoid office politics, but I know they exist in most companies."

"Especially in the government." Carrie shifted to look directly into his eyes. "Why hasn't Cummings made another move against me? I like to think I'm prepared for anything now." She heaved a big sigh, "I can never forget the hate in his eyes when he stood up in the slough--dirty water pouring down his forehead, his shirt stuck with goo to his fat belly. I have made a few enemies in my lifetime, but no one has ever looked at me like he did."

Jim frowned, "Peter Cummings is a smart guy. That's why he's achieved what he has. I suspect, however, that he has no scruples. I also suspect he's biding his time-- unless he was responsible for the Quebecois at my house. I only hope…"

"What?"

"Let's phone Dave. He may have some inkling as to what the big man is up to."

"But…"

"I know, Carrie. Dave is under contract to Pete. But contracts can be abrogated, at least temporarily. We need Dave for both his legal expertise and his inside knowledge of Cummings."

"Dave would do that for me?" She was doubtful.

"Yeah," He said grimly, "I'm quite sure he would." He glanced at his watch. "It's well after midnight in the east. He's a night owl and he may have company."

"Like a woman in his bed?" Carrie had always hoped that all his hugging of her meant she was special. But her logical mind told her that Dave merely liked women in general.

He chuckled, "You know Dave better than I thought."

Charlie whined and tugged gently at her feet. "Wait. We can't ask Dave to jeopardize his reputation as a lawyer. He could be disbarred if he reveals inside information about a client. No, no, Jim…"

"Hmm. You're right, of course, but Dave would know where to draw the line." Charlie whined again. "Your dog needs to go out for a pee. And so does mine." He lifted her off his lap. "Let's go. The moon is out, the stars are shining."

"And it's going down to twenty below tonight," Carrie complained.

"Come on. A quick walk and then Tess and I will get out of your hair."

They bundled up, slipped down the path and glimpsed the river sliding by, slate-grey and viscous from the cold. The dogs raced down the river road nipping each other's necks.

He tucked her arm in his and they walked in unison, Jim shortening his stride to hers. She looked up into the sky and murmured, "The shifting glory of the aurora borealis."

He hugged her arm, "That's pretty poetic for an environmental regulator."

"You don't think I could make up something so lovely about the northern lights?" She slid her hand down into his. "One of the few redeeming features of this northern climate is the colorful winter sky." She noticed his eyes on her, not the sky.

He gazed down at her, "In this strange light the blues and greens in your eyes are as bright as the stars."

"Oh, for God's sake, Jim. Now who's being poetic?" She turned her face away to hide her pleasure. "That quote was probably from a library book." The wind was colder close to the river, and she shivered.

"When you do find it…" He stopped. "We should turn back. You're cold and so am I."

But the excited barking of their dogs, overlaid with the sharp yips of coyotes, brought them up short. Carrie thought immediately of the coyote biting her leg and she turned to run. Jim tightened his grip on her arm and pulled her back. He lifted her slightly as he ran towards the animals. Her feet seemed to dance on the ground as they went up a light rise. They stopped to look down on a ring of coyotes circling their furious, bewildered dogs.

Jim let out a roaring bellow that startled Carrie and probably every living thing in the vicinity. The pack broke apart and loped towards the trees. Tess and Charlie barked at the receding coyotes until Jim whistled, a short, high-pitched trill through his teeth. Tess turned and ran into Jim's arms almost knocking them both over. Charlie mewed against Carrie's legs, so she knelt, patted him, and rubbed his ears comforting him with endearments as one would a child. She laughed when Jim got down on his knees and stretched his arms around Carrie and the two dogs.

Tess and Charlie broke free to bark at the woods into which the furry rumps with the long bushy tails had disappeared. But the dogs did not budge from their owners' legs.

"Look at our brave dogs now," Jim commented.

"Well, I do admit to being pretty scared for them, and me," Carrie said as she accepted his helping hand. She stood putting all her weight on her good leg. The dull pain in her other leg suggested that it had been taxed a little too much. She clapped her gloved hands together, "It must be fifty below down here."

Charlie took her clapping as a signal, and he led the way up the hill. They stopped on the patio and their clouds of white breaths dissipated in the wind that blew towards the river, towards the piercing cries of the coyotes.

"The yodel dogs," Carrie said quietly. "Shouting their half-keening, half-laughter to their goddess moon. I can imagine them sitting on their haunches, their heads raised, their snouts pointing up." She gestured to the icy sliver of the moon.

Jim glanced up, "That's a great image, Carrie, but I think those damn jackals are mocking us." He opened the back door and asked, "Are you okay? Want me to come in for a bit?"

She nodded with a guilty, but grateful, smile.

He banked up the fireplace and got a blaze going while she settled the dogs on Charlie's mat and made the drinks--his, scotch neat and hers with lots of ice and water.

"Are you out of white wine?" he asked, accepting his glass.

"No but scotch always reminds me of Dad. This acquired taste every scotch drinker talks about. How long does it take?"

"Carrie, you don't have to do this. I'll send you a case of *good* white wine."

The fire crackled and popped, and they rearranged the furniture so they could face the fireplace.

"We need the bear rug to sit on." She pointed to the white bear hide hanging above the sofa. He held her waist as she stood on the sofa's arm to reach up to unhook it and he said,

"This is 'déjà vu.' Remember when you almost broke your last two wine glasses?"

"They're living on borrowed time with me." She felt his eyes on her as she smoothed out the white fur rug in front of the fire. The dogs came over to investigate but after sniffing, they went back to their own mat, leaving their masters to snuggle on the bear rug with their backs against the sofa.

Jim picked up an edge of the hide and held it to his nose, "Why does it have a pine smell?"

She paused, "Promise you won't laugh?" Not waiting for an answer, she explained, "I treat his hair with a special pine-scented lotion. It makes it soft and I can even run a wide-toothed comb through it. My bear comes from a pine forest. Do you know that the lodge pole pine is Alberta's arboreal symbol? Anyway, after all my loving care I feel the bear is truly mine now. My main problem is keeping Charlie off it. That's why it's on the wall."

"Was the bear quite old when…"

"No, but he was hurt. My husband told me the only reason he and his hunting buddies were able to track and shoot the bear was because he had a wounded back paw. They just followed the drops of blood. Real sportsman, my husband." She made a face. "Apparently up to that point the bear had been quite elusive."

She sipped her scotch and continued. "It was really my husband's trophy. They had caught a glimpse of him limping at the edge of the forest and they let the dogs loose." She shook her head, "My poor bear. Anyway, Cliff killed it with one shot, and they butchered it on the spot. Which, would you believe, was in a stand of lodge pole pine?"

"I believe." He hugged her. "Go on."

"Cliff was furious with me for making his prize headless--it cost me a fortune, by the way. But I think of the bear as mine because of all the hours I've spent cleaning and curing his hide and treating his long white hair. I have gotten quite fond of my anthropomorphic bear. You know, there are some lovely myths about…" She leaned back and examined her glass. "I must be getting drunk because I'm talking too much."

"You are not talking too much. Carry on."

"Well, in Inuit mythology, Nanuk, which means polar bear in Inuktitut, was the master of the bears. Inuk hunters worshipped Nanuk believing that he decided which hunters deserved success. Legend has it that if the hunter properly treated a dead polar bear, the bear would share the news with other bears who would then be willing to be killed by him. A hunter was meant to pay respect to the bear's soul by hanging his hide in a special place in his house. There's more but that's the gist of it."

"Is yours a polar bear?"

"No. We're too far south, as you probably know. It was a brown bear with white fur. An albino. That's why my bear is so unique. If you look closely, you can see a few dark brown hairs."

"Later perhaps." He reached up to place their empty glasses on the side table then he gently pulled her head to his shoulder, "That's a beautiful, unbelievable story. Thank you for sharing it." She turned to stare at the fire, and he repositioned his arms around her. When he stood up disappointment twitched though her consciousness. But he whispered, "Be right back."

She heard him put water in the dogs' dishes, give them each a treat and settle them on the mat. He came back and folded her in his arms again. And she lost herself in the pine forest of the white bear. She lost herself to Jim.

Chapter 24

They dawdled over breakfast the next norming then took the dogs for a long walk at the Belgravia off-leash dog park. It was a crisp autumn day with a light sprinkling of fresh snow on the pine, fir, and spruce trees.

"Another great view of the river," Carrie said as they sat on a bench and watched the dark waters curve languidly to the northwest. "Let's drop the dogs off in my back yard and catch the end of the downtown farmers' market."

"Do you need anything?" Jim asked.

"No, but I'm sure something will catch my eye if we go."

He chuckled and pulled her up. The market was jam-packed but they found a spot to nibble on perogies and listen to the upbeat music of a four-piece band. They got back to Carrie's in time to feed the dogs and they were discussing timing, showering, and what to wear when Dave phoned.

"Sorry guys. Can't make it. I'm back in Toronto on another rush-rush case."

"Do you know how many times you have stood me up, Mr. David--?" Carrie asked.

"I'll make it up to you. Promise. Ciao." And Dave hung up.

Jim shrugged, "Who needs the guy? But we do need to change for the Mac."

"But we don't if we stay here and have my lamb stew." Carrie's eyes twinkled expecting a polite rejection from him.

"Great!" was his response. "I love homemade stew. What can I do to help?" And they got pleasantly inebriated on wine and beer while the stew defrosted. She found a partial loaf of French bread and after slavering it with garlic and butter one would never guess it was days old.

They were soaking up the last of the stew's gravy with the tail ends of the bread when Susan phoned.

"Hey, Carrie," she boomed into the phone. "Just to let you know that Helen and I are having a lovely dinner at Don's. He's taking us to West Ed tomorrow and—"

Carrie interrupted her, "You *hate* West Edmonton Mall."

"Yeah. Well, all in the line of duty." Susan's loud horse laugh made Carrie extend the phone and Jim grimaced.

"Sue, be careful." Carrie was not comfortable with the idea of these two women together. What the hell was Susan up to? But her friend had hung up without signing-off which was not unusual for Susan.

Carrie went back to the kitchen to help Jim with the dishes and complained, "The fact that the last two people I talked to on the phone hung up on me must demonstrate a serious defect in my character."

Jim shook the water from his hands and bent to kiss her cheek, "No defects that I can see." The dishwater gurgled down the drain and he asked, "May I invite myself for another sleepover tonight?"

....

The sound of the jangling phone woke them early the next morning. Carrie untangled her legs from Jim's and fumbled for the phone on the bedside table. "Jackie! What's wrong?" She asked as she got out of bed.

Jim sat up straining to hear the voice at the other end of the phone. She gave him a bleak look and her voice broke as she responded to Jackie,

"I'll try to get on the earliest flight. What hospital is he in?" She grabbed a pen and scribbled the hospital information on the back of bill. "Thanks, Jackie. I owe you big time."

She gave Jackie her cell phone number and promised to call back with her flight information. She hung up and slowly turned to Jim, "It's my dad. He's had a stroke. A bad one, according to Jackie, and he's in intensive care." She stared into space for a moment, then sank back down on the bed with a tremulous sob.

Jim held her and stroked her hair. "Get packed. I'll use my VIP card to get you on a plane. What hotel is closest to the hospital?" He released her, swung his legs off the bed and pulled her up.

"I don't know," Carrie said from the bathroom door. "But try the Sutton, Sutton Place--that's where I usually stay in Toronto."

Thirty minutes later they were on their way. He backed his car quickly down her driveway and asked, "Which is faster, 99th Street or Calgary Trail?"

"Probably 99th at this hour." She put her coffee mug in the holder, "At least there won't be as many accidents." Dry-eyed, she was still too stunned to react, so she thanked Jim repeatedly until he stopped her,

"Carrie, one thank you is enough. Don't worry about anything here. I'll look after Charlie and check your house periodically. Who is Jackie?"

"She's my cousin. We've been good friends since we were little, and she knew Mother would delay letting me know."

"Really? Why?"

"It's the way she is--unstable and unpredictable, but she does love Dad."

Jim dropped the subject and concentrated on his driving. The desultory conversation that followed hardly filled the silence in the car.

Carrie sat straight up and stared unseeing out the window, mesmerized by the swiping of the windshield wipers as they brushed away the erratic snow. She closed her eyes and thought of the love in her father's eyes when he looked at her, of his sonorous voice that was always so gentle when he spoke to her. Her throat tightened and she had to swallow several times to force back the tears. Why couldn't she be more positive? Why was she so afraid? Lots of people ended up in the ICU and survived.

Jim turned into the airport and cursed the slow drivers ahead of them. When they finally reached the departures entrance, he gently punched the brake pedal to control the truck on the icy ramp. He parked and was out the door in a second holding on to the sides and back of his vehicle as he skidded around it to retrieve her bag from the back seat.

"You'll have to run. Careful, it's slippery. Phone me." He helped her down off the high seat, squeezed her shoulder, put her bag in her hands and gently turned her towards the door. "I'll wait in the parking lot in case you don't make it."

She was the last person to get a boarding pass and she phoned Jim as she waited in the line-up onto the plane. He picked up on the first ring and she said in a calm voice, "Made it. Just boarding now, th--"

"No more 'thanks'. Phone me--any time of the day or night."

"Gotta go."

The plane sat on the tarmac for over an hour before it took off. Carrie had a window seat and she drifted between dozing and thoughts of her father. The last time they had been together was at Jackie's wedding, her third. The event was spoiled for Carrie by her mother's criticisms—of Carrie's dress, of her make-up, and why on earth was Carrie staying at the YWCA? Carrie and her dad were able to snatch a few five-minute conversations here and there and she worried about him. His eyes drooped, his skin was sallow and febrile, but he had bragged about getting through his last medical with flying colors. And that was only a year ago.

It was after nine o'clock when she registered at Sutton Place and the clerk surprised her by handing her a message from Jim. Who else would welcome her to Toronto? She tipped the porter and waited until he had closed the door before she picked up the phone. She was finally connected to the hospital's intensive care unit and a tired voice answered her question,

"Your father is resting peacefully now, and the hospital visiting hours are over."

"May I come and sit with him?" Carrie asked.

After a slight pause the nurse said, "I know you've just arrived from the west. By the time you get here and prove who you are…" She cut herself off and after a few seconds resumed, "Why don't you get a good night's sleep instead? I will phone you if there is any change in his condition."

After repeating her room number and hotel's phone number twice, she collapsed on the hard desk chair. She rifled her purse for the sleeping pill that Susan had forced on her months ago. She made her way to the bathroom to scrub her face and arms. After brushing her teeth, she gulped down one half of the pill with a mouthful of watered toothpaste.

She was at the hospital at ten the next morning, prepared to wait for however long it took to see her dad. However, after proving she was indeed A.V. March's daughter, the ICU staff were efficient and kind. There was no sign of her mother and Carrie's calls to her had all gone to voicemail. A nurse appeared, who led her down the hall and spoke quietly to her,

"Your father's stroke was quite severe, and he is very ill. You must be careful not to distress him or tire him. He is very restless and keeps asking for you. Here we are."

The nurse pushed open the heavy door and another nurse stood up from the chair beside the head of the bed. She motioned Carrie forward. *Was she a private nurse? Hired by Jackie?*

His breathing was horrible, rasping with periods where he did not seem to take a breath. She bent down and her father turned his face towards her. It was almost completely masked by tubes in his mouth and nose and a bandage around his forehead. His eyes misted when he saw her, and his forehead contorted as he tried to speak.

"Don't be afraid," the nurse said. "It's the Cheyne-Stokes reaction. Very common and he's not in any discomfort."

Carrie stared at her in disbelief. *Not in any discomfort?* She leaned over to kiss the only visible strip of her father's cheek. She wiped his tears with her thumbs then gently stroked his high cheek bones and said, "Hi, Dad."

With a trembling hand he slowly pulled the tube from his mouth. He crooked his finger to bring her closer. The hoarse bubbling with his every breath broke her heart, but she leaned forward, her cheek against his and whispered, "I love you, Dad. Please don't go."

He coughed and she caught the phlegm he brought up in the corner of the sheet. He swallowed and she could see his throat spasm as he tried to speak. "Your mother..." He gasped in one final effort and his agonizing breathing stopped.

She stared at his still form, not comprehending the immensity of the moment. When she realized he wasn't breathing she cried, "Dad! Dad!" And pushed the call button over and over again until the nurse rushed in and caught her hand. They both turned towards the bed when a long breath escaped from his body.

"He's alive!" Carrie grabbed his arm.

"No, no, dear." The nurse put her hand on Carrie's shoulder, "It's just the reflexive action of his lungs expelling the air that was trapped there."

A male dark-skinned doctor came into the room and he checked, and rechecked, her father for vital signs as Carrie looked on helplessly. The doctor pulled up the sheet and pronounced the patient dead. His accent was heavy and his words ran together as he expressed his condolences to Carrie. With a slight nod he left the room.

Shaking her head, the nurse gently pressed Carrie's arm and said, "He's gone, dear. Be thankful he had a peaceful death. We'll give you a few moments alone with him. I'm very sorry."

Both nurses left and Carrie stood by the side of bed. She tucked the sheet around his still warm shoulders and stared down at her father's stricken face. Surely he wasn't dead. She put her fingers on his face, traced his nose and cheeks, and when she came to his open, tranquil mouth the stark truth hit home. He was really gone from her world. The only person who had truly loved her.

"Goodbye, Dad. I will miss you so, so much..." Her throat was tight and aching as she pulled the sheet up as far as it would go over his head.

Then her mother was there. When she saw the sheet drawn over her husband's face, she let out a long, eerie, high-pitched wail that must have been heard in the parking lot. Two nurses rushed in as Carrie's mother tore the sheet away and clawed at her husband's face. The nurses pulled her back, but she wriggled in their restraining arms and screamed at Carrie, "You killed him! You killed him!" She kicked backwards, made contact with one of the nurse's shins and almost got free.

The three of them managed to get the screaming woman into the chair. Carrie moved back out of her mother's vision and watched the two nurses pacify her with soothing words in calm, benign tones. One stroked her hair and the other held and rubbed her wrinkled hands. Carrie stared. *When did Mother's skin start to age?* Before she knew it her mother had sunk back in the chair, her screams reduced to moans, her head drooped and her limbs relaxed.

Carrie backed up just as the door opened. The same incomprehensible doctor came in, apologized for bumping her with the door then suggested that Carrie might consider letting her mother stay in this hospital overnight.

"Will you be giving her drugs?" Carrie asked.

"No, not without checking with her regular doctor."

"How long will you keep her?" Carrie asked knowing that she could not handle a distraught woman in her hotel room.

"Until tomorrow, or until you make other arrangements for her. We will have your father's body moved to the funeral home he set forth in his personal directive. Unless, of course, you have--"

"No, no." Carrie felt as if she was on auto pilot. "Do it, please."

She retrieved her mother's purse and two hours later her Mrs. A.V March was admitted to the geriatric ward, surprisingly docile and amenable to whatever her nurses suggested.

She somehow got back to the hotel. She sat on the bed, pushed off her shoes and relived the awful scene. But no tears came. She closed her eyes and leaned her head against the headboard, still no tears. Heaving a long shaky sigh, she reached for the phone and dialed room service and ordered a double scotch and water.

The young boy in the hotel's uniform who delivered her drinks looked at her curiously as she tipped him, "Are you alright, ma'am?"

"Yes," she responded dully. "Thanks for asking." She waved him out, sat at the table, poured the scotch over the ice ignoring the small pitcher of water. She took a big mouthful, swirled it around her mouth and choked when she swallowed it. Another small sip to help her cough, and she reached for the phone.

"Carrie?" Jim's bass voice seemed to fill the room with warmth.

"Where are you?" She could hear static and a thrum in the background.

"Just driving home. How goes it?'

"He just died."

There was a pause before he responded in a low, sympathetic voice, "Oh, Carrie. I'm so sorry." He turned the radio off, "Do you want me to come?"

"No," she gulped down a sob. "You don't want to be here. I don't want you to be here. I don't want to be here." She knew she was slurring her words and hoped he didn't notice. But it was so good to hear his voice. She closed her eyes to see his face.

"Carrie, where are you?"

"At…in…the hotel…room." Her words did not want to form a sentence.

"Good. Finish your drink and go to bed. Everything will make more sense after a sleep, even if you are hung over."

"Okay," she paused, "I'm hang--" Her hiccup was a combination of a strangle sob and a loud burp. "I…Jim? Your voice, it's…it's…" She swallowed, "My mother…my mother…"

"Yes, your mother?"

"She went berserk. She said I killed him. She … I'm hanging up." As she reached over to set the phone in its cradle, she heard him say,

"I'm coming east. Good night, my darling."

When she managed to get the receiver back, she lay back on the pillows and the tears finally came in great gushing, gasping sobs.

....

She woke up in the middle of the night to the sound of sirens. The room was pitch dark, her mouth was dry, and she had to pee in the worst way.

The face in the mirror was a witch—running mascara, smeared lipstick, bloodshot eyes behind red lids, and eyebrows that seemed to have a life of their own. The room swirled as she clung to the basin and tried to count to twenty. At fifteen, she took off her crushed skirt and ruined blouse and threw them in a corner. She knew she would never wear them again.

Ten minutes later she stepped out of the shower feeling a little better and wondered if the sirens ever stopped in this damn city. After brushing her teeth, she took the other half of the sleeping pill, managed to get her nightgown over her head, and zigzagged to the bed holding onto the door jamb, a chair--whatever she could reach.

She drifted off to sleep with the image of her father's ragged face behind her eyes.

Chapter 25

Carrie was up and dressed with only a slight headache when the hospital phoned the next morning. After confirming her identity, she waited to be connected to Dr. Spalding. Holding the receiver and the god-awful music away from her face, she focused on the practical aspects of her father's death--the mortuary, the funeral, the burial--all the details her father had helped her through following Cliff and Bobby's death so many years ago. She shuddered at the prospect.

The music stopped abruptly, "Good morning, Carrie." Without waiting for a response, the confident baritone voice continued, "Dr, Spalding here. We have met on several occasions, and I would like to express my condolences for your loss. Your father was a sterling man. I feel fortunate to have known him and we have had many interesting discussions over the years." He cleared his throat. "Your mother is my concern now. She spent a comfortable night at the hospital, but she is being discharged today. We are reducing her sedatives, but she needs 24/7 care for a week or so. If you are in agreement, we will transfer her to the Nightingale Respite Centre where she will get the psychiatric care she needs right now."

"I…" Carrie searched for the right words. "Are you afraid she might hurt herself?"

"No." He answered quickly, "But she needs to get over the shock of your father's death. I understand he made arrangements before his demise for this very situation. There are several long-term care facilities in the Hamilton/Burlington area--"

"That will kill her," Carrie said abruptly remembering her mother's rants against nursing homes.

"That is a little extreme," he chastised her in a gentle tone and said, "As you know, she is a highly strung, intelligent woman who became very dependent on her husband. We will watch her closely and keep you advised. I don't see any point in you disrupting your life--you live in Edmonton or its environs. It would be very unwise to move your mother away from her familiar surroundings in Burlington. However, she may never be capable of living in that house by herself."

Relief flowed off Carrie's shoulders. Having to actually live with her mother again was inconceivable, and her mother's Burlington friends were certainly more important to her than her own daughter. Guilt replaced the relief, but she managed to say, "Thank you for all you've done for both my parents. I know it has been above the call of duty."

He sighed heavily, "I miss your dad. Good friends are irreplaceable, especially at my age." Silence then a light cough, "Carrie, I think it would be better if you do not see your mother for a few days. At least until the funeral is over."

"Yes. Yes, of course you're right." She realized he must know of her strained relationship with her mother.

"Goodbye, Carrie, and good luck."

The click of the phone disconnecting seemed to signal another ending. Would she ever speak to this kind man again? She found her purse and dug into it to make sure the key to her parent's house in Burlington was still on her key chain. Glancing at her watch, she decided to have the hotel's complimentary breakfast. It was fast and she could write out her to-do list as she ate.

In the hotel foyer she helped herself to juice, a sweet roll and coffee. Seated alone at a corner table she started writing in the little notebook that was always with her. Stephen Sumpka, her parent's lawyer, was at the top of her list. But her mother's hostility still bothered her. What was Dad trying to say about her? Surely as the only child of Mr. and Mrs. A.V. March, she was the only person able to make the decisions that had to be made and sign the documents that had to be signed.

She stared into space as she sipped her coffee and tried to remember the good times she had had with her parents: the trips to Europe, the Middle East, the Pacific islands. Her mother loved the Italian art galleries best of all. In Venice, Florence and Rome she passed on some of her extensive knowledge of Renaissance art to Carrie. Christmas and birthday gifts had invariably been heavy books on art. Her father had sought Carrie's advice before he bought a small Botticelli for his wife on their fiftieth wedding anniversary. Those were the good family times--before the accident, before all the deaths.

She packed her knapsack, checked out of the hotel and asked for a map of Toronto.

By one o'clock she was sipping a huge Tim Horton's coffee on the GO train to Burlington. The sky was dark and dreary, threatening freezing rain or snow. Typical southern Ontario fall weather. Or was it pre-winter? In any case the weather suited her mood. She could not have coped with a bright yellow sun and a cheery blue sky.

Her taxi let her off in front of the rambling bungalow, just as she had remembered it. A tall oak tree planted too close to the house towered over the picture window. She scraped away dead leaves and fallen cones with her boot as she walked up to the front door and paused before putting the key in the lock. How many memories would she encounter on the other side of the door?

She hung her coat beside her father's old ski jacket in the front hall closet and almost succumbed to tears again. Instead, she burrowed her face in its folds, savoring the musky, outdoorsy scent of him. How long would his odour remain on it?

The fridge was well stocked with health food, brands she had never heard of. Standing in front of the open door she sampled everything with a soup spoon, then drank a large glass of skim milk.

After rinsing the glass and spoon she called the lawyer's office to make an appointment, then set out to look around. The beautiful, pristine sunken living room-- the room that had always been off-limits to Carrie when she was a girl. Plush carpet at least three inches deep, white upholstered chairs and matching sofa positioned just-so around an ornate, mahogany coffee table. Overturned Stradivarius crystal wine glasses sparkled on a sterling silver tray. After pulling the heavy damask drapes open, she lounged on the verboten sofa and watched the dust motes track the light coming in through the tall windows. Her heavy eyelids slowly closed.

She jumped up at the sound of a harsh jangle, cursed when she banged her shin against the table, and hurried to the hall phone. She recognized the velvety tones of the lawyer's receptionist. The sleaze-ball lawyer Carrie had used when her father had helped her through the legal mazes years ago. Her mother had chosen him initially because he was some sort of distant cousin. Now he was expedient, but Carrie wished she had another option. She explained the situation to his secretary who was able to squeeze her in that afternoon.

Not trusting her memory of Burlington, she phoned a taxi. At the lawyer's she endured the many "sorry for your loss" greetings without shedding a tear. Good God, surely there were other expressions of condolences? When she was finally admitted into Stephen Sumpka's office, he stood, stiffly embraced her and told her what a great guy Vic was and how he would be missed. And how was her mother holding up? Without waiting for an answer, he related the important events he had gone to with her parents as he shuffled files on his desk.

"What do you need me to sign?" Carrie broke into his monologue.

He gave her a censorious look and opened a blue file. She carefully read each document before she signed next to the large red X. When he went through the will, she followed on her copy and gulped when he told her the monetary value of her inheritance. Her father had specified cremation, the church at which the funeral service should be held including the music to be played and sung. He had even written his own obituary.

When she got up to leave, Sumpka stopped her with a hand signal. She cringed at his phony smile and waited.

"There is one last document, but your mother should be here when we open it."

"That won't be possible. She's at a respite home."

He feigned surprise. "Oh, dear. No one told us. In any case, your mother will contest the will. That is a given."

"You mean you will contest it on her behalf while she's vegetating in a care home." She pursed her lips in a determined line, knowing she was only alienating this obnoxious man. Why was there no mention of her mother in the will? She did not trust this lawyer. Her mother's legacy must be in this mysterious document.

He looked uncomfortable and waved his hand in a meaningless gesture. "The document is sealed and still in our vault. I will make the legal arrangements to open it."

"Why all the mystery? Do you know what's in it?"

"Yes and no." Ignoring her first question, he checked his day timer, "Would three o'clock the day after tomorrow be convenient for you?" Not waiting for her answer, he stood up and extended his hand. "Again, I am sorry for your loss. That includes everyone in this office." He walked to the door and held it open for her.

She phoned a taxi to take her back to her parent's home which was as cold and sterile as it had been in the morning. She decided against a scotch. It seemed ages ago that she had switched from white wine to scotch. Jim's influence, definitely. She found a frozen dinner in the deep freeze and popped it into the microwave. Her mind seemed to be in a deep freeze too. After eating the tasteless dinner in front of an inane talk show on TV, she went to bed in the room that had always been assigned to her when she visited.

She woke the next morning surprisingly refreshed. After dressing in jeans and a sweater of her father's, she retrieved the "Globe and Mail" from the front porch to peruse over breakfast. Another to-do--cancel the paper. Her hunger finally satiated with scrambled eggs, toast and coffee, she noticed a missed call on the kitchen phone. Probably one of her mother's bridge buddies.

Wandering throughout the house she searched for items she could legitimately claim as her own. She lifted the lid of the antique bookcase in the hall and was engulfed in that musty, wonderful smell from the special mold that only grows on books. Could she claim it *and* the corner cabinet in the dining room? Over her mother's objections, her father had tried to persuade Carrie to take the bookcase west. It had belonged to her grandfather and Dad knew she coveted it. She browsed the books in her father's bedroom, marveling at his eclectic taste. Opening the drawer of his bedside table she pulled out the family Bible with its black soft, thick cover, its turned-in edges and gold-rimmed crisp onion skin pages, delicate as lace. The spidery signatures of three generations of Marchs on the fly leaf were barely legible and she noted her father's was missing. Retrieving a pen from her purse she added his name in bold letters. She didn't open his closet fearing she would be reduced to tears again at his familiar clothes carrying his special scent. Her mother's bedroom was as immaculate as the living room, and her closet immense--the skirts, blouses and dresses all arranged on separate wooden hangers by colour, all permeated with Chanel #5. How long had they been sleeping separately?

The sun had appeared from behind the clouds and was now shining brightly through the ornate bedroom windows. She decided to forego her list and get some fresh air. Donning her father's ski jacket and woolen mitts, she made her way down to the lake.

Her breath flowered and her chin tingled in the crisp air. The wind-formed frozen waves and mounds of jagged ice extended across the shore of Lake Ontario. The world seemed strangely beautiful in its frozen mobility. She was tempted to scramble up the ice to view the open water beyond. But remembering her father's dire warnings about the instability of these mini-icebergs, she kept to the path along the shore.

She walked and walked and when she decided to turn back, the sun was close to the western horizon. It was later than she thought. Head down, she hurried to beat the setting sun. The cold wind whipped against her face, and she tugged at her hat.

A familiar whistle startled her. Looking up, she saw Jim waving and walking towards her. She broke into a run and skidded into his open arms. He quickly backed them both into the lee of the bank.

"You came," She whispered into his ear.

"Carrie, I'm so sorry. I wish I could have met him." He cradled her head and bent to kiss her. They broke apart finally and he said "That was the best welcome I've ever had. Can we start over?"

His arms tightened again, and she laughed, "Let's go home. My feet are freezing. How did you ever find me?"

He took her arm and tugged it to his side as he steered her back to the path, "One of your nosey neighbors told me where to find you."

"The dogs?" She looked up into his homely, beautiful face and thought how much she had missed him.

He chuckled, "I knew that would be your first question. The Polish couple who usually take Tess have come to live in my house. Charlie warmed up to Mrs. Polaski immediately."

"He's such a ladies' man. How did you get here so soon?"

"I'm a frequent flyer with priority. And I did try to phone you--your parent's number and your cell."

"Oh. My cell is probably still in my other coat pocket."

He laughed, "Some things never change."

Back in the bungalow Carrie gave him a quick tour of the house, then showed him the liquor cabinet.

The flimsy glass and mahogany doors squeaked when he opened them and he said, "It's going to take a while to drink through all this." He held up her father's favorite scotch and shook his head. "This twenty-eight-year-old single malt Laphroaig is too expensive to drink. I'll just have a sniff." He carefully removed the stopper, bent his nose close to the bottle's spout, "Ah…. I can discern honey, apricots and a touch of anise. Do you know this elixir has been matured in bourbon and sherry casks?" He tipped the neck of the bottle under her nose. She obliged him by breathing in deeply, letting the familiar smell fill her senses and memories of her father flood her brain. He put the bottle down on the cabinet's edge with careful reverence and turned to her, "Do you have any beer?"

"You must be kidding. I can't imagine my mother ever allowing beer in her house." She tried to smile, "I'm sure Dad would want us to drink his special scotch."

"Okay, scotch it is. Are you joining me? "He examined the array of crystal and seemed confused.

"You know you've made me a convert." She reached for the Waterford special whiskey glasses. "However, if it's that expensive perhaps we should use shot glasses."

"Carrie, Carrie, I've missed you." He put the bottle down and wrapped his arms around her again. She tried very hard not to cry.

Drinks in hand, she led him towards the sunken living room. "I call this the Excelsior Room." They paused at the entrance. Jim took in its elegance--the dark raised panel walls with a decorative beveled edge at the chair rail, a stained-glass transom window, the silk Persian rug in burgundy and cream.

He shook his head, "I don't think either of us can relax there. Besides, I'd probably leave footprints in that rug. How about that comfortable looking room at the end of the hall?"

She smiled gratefully, "It was Dad's favorite room too—the rumpus room. He had it painted a sky blue, his favorite colour, then filled it with 1950's white furniture." She pointed to the white day bed in front of a concave, three paneled window. Snow glistened under the lantern-style pole lights set at the corners of the patio. She had always appreciated the room's simplicity and isolation from the rest of the house.

With their feet on the limed oak coffee table she filled him in on everything that had happened in the last two days--her mother's meltdown, the sleazy lawyer, all the papers she had signed, and lastly, the mystery document.

He placed his empty glass on the table, finished hers, and pulled her into his arms. "You never cease to amaze me. You've done all the tough stuff, but you must have your own lawyer." He sat back with his arm around her. "I phoned Dave before I left to fill him in, and I expect him to phone back tonight. It would be great if he would represent you, but he's very busy, especially having been out of the office for so long--he calls it his "Carrie week" instead of "ski week". He promised to take us to his favorite restaurant while we're both here in the east." He squeezed her bare knee through the rip in her jeans and grinned. "We've got reservations at the Carriage House in half an hour. Can you make it?"

"The most expensive restaurant in town? How did you…"

"Go, go!" He stood quickly and pulled her to her feet.

When she was presentable in her slightly crushed navy-blue pant suit and yellow frilly blouse, she emerged to find him talking on his cell phone.

"Here she is now, looking gorgeous." Jim extended the phone cutting off whatever Dave had been saying.

"Hi there, Carrie," Dave boomed. "So sorry about your dad." He harrumphed and said, "Look, kiddo, I've got to dash but my clandestine researchers have discovered something about Pete's life twenty odd years ago. Remember, you didn't hear it from me. Their digging has yielded fruit, a bountiful harvest. Gotta go. Ciao."

"Wait, Dave!" But the line was dead. She gave Jim his phone, "Really? How does he expect me to wait? Let's go to Toronto tonight." The thought of navigating that city in the middle of winter with its un-cleared, crowded streets was not appealing, but it was hard not to get excited about any new dirt on Cummings.

Jim shook his head as he pulled jackets out of the closet, "Let's have dinner and get a good night's sleep."

She started to put her arms into the coat Jim held for her, "This is Dad's. I'd better wear my own." She exchanged coats and her eyes searched the foyer, "Did you bring your bag in?"

"I'm not staying here, Carrie."

"Why not?" She couldn't keep her disappointment from showing. "There's oodles of room. You don't even have to sleep with me."

He chuckled as he shrugged into his ski jacket, "You've got enough on your plate without giving your neighbors something to gossip about."

"I only know one of the neighbors well enough to have coffee with, and she's in Florida for the winter." Carrie sighed, "You're probably right though--even if it's only out of respect for Dad." She blew her nose and asked, "Where are you staying?"

"A lovely stone house that faces the lake too. Cobblestone Lodge. The landlady seems to know you, your family and your history from day one."

Carrie groaned. "I get where you're coming from now, but she's a sweetheart. She's been here for years, and I always suspected she had her eye on Dad."

"The protective daughter." His gaze was affectionate as he took her hand, "Come on. You need some food in your stomach. When's the last time you ate?"

Chapter 26

The Burlington church was packed well before three o'clock. The town had turned out en masse for the funeral of one of their favorite sons. Carrie sat alone in the first pew directly across from a row of white lilies. The air was thick with their intense, aromatic odour and she had trouble breathing. Hearing a murmur behind her she turned and stood to greet her mother, who was supported by two sturdy women. Carrie dutifully kissed her cheeks then slid along the pew towards the windows, away from the lilies, and her mother.

There were songs to sing and prayers to be said, and the healing power of the rituals surprised her. Everything was laid out, the steps of grieving and loss circumscribed so that she could stumble ahead with her life in her own uncertain way.

She bowed her head, but her thoughts kept returning to the 'mystery' document. Lionel, the young lawyer assigned to her from Dave's firm, had wheedled it out of Sumpka. In it, her father stipulated that upon his death, his wife, Evelyn March, was to be admitted to Nightingale Manor, a long term care facility in Burlington. Dad had set up a trust fund to pay all her mother's expenses until her death. Carrie had enduring power of attorney over her mother and power of attorney of all his remaining assets. *But a nursing home? How could he have done this to the love of his life, his beloved wife who he loved beyond all others?*

....

The receiving line went on forever. She lost count of the number of people who asked why her mother had left right after the service. When she spotted Jim's grey head towering over the chattering women, she stood up straighter and smiled at the elderly man whose hand she was shaking. Before she knew it Dave was hugging her with Jim right behind. Her eyes misted when Jim bent to give her cheek a lingering kiss.

"Good job, Carrie," he whispered in her ear.

"It wasn't. You were right. I shouldn't have tried to give the eulogy." She pulled a damp white handkerchief out of her sleeve, "I couldn't believe I broke down…"

"Hey!" Jim pressed his hand on her shoulder. "It was a beautiful tribute to your Dad and it wouldn't have been so without a few of your tears." He turned to take the elbow of the tall, handsome woman standing a few feet behind him. "I'd like you to meet my mother, Alvena."

Carrie held out her hand as Dave said, "Hello again, Alvena" before he made a tactful disappearance. Alvena stepped forward. Wisps of silvery-blond hair curled around her angular face, and her violet-grey eyes were soft as she took both of Carrie's hands in hers and said, "I'm very glad to meet you, Carrie, but I wish it were under happier conditions. My sincere condolences." She started to say more, but Jim nudged her,

"Come on, Mother. We shouldn't hold up the line." He led her past Carrie who stood on tiptoes and scanned the room. He stopped, "Are you looking for someone?"

"Yes." Carrie hid her disappointment, "Will, Willard Kenyon, Dad's drinking buddy. He said he would be here." She sighed. "Oh well, guess not."

"I've looked after the tag ends here--minister, organist and a church fund of some sort." Jim glanced at the people behind him, "We'll see you at the punch bowl downstairs. Dave is waiting there for us."

She did not make it downstairs to the punch bowl, and it was dusk as they stood shivering at the graveside. Carrie felt everyone's eyes on her as she sprinkled the required handful of dirt on the coffin. When she stepped back, her heel caught the hem of her grandmother's long black seal-skin coat. *Why one earth did she wear it?* The minister held her elbow as she disentangled her boot. The coat weighed her down, making her sink into the soft snow, bringing her closer to Dad who lay in that cold wet ground. She shuddered at the thought of him there. Was he waiting for her? Just as he used to-- leaning on his poles at the bottom of the ski run, eyeing her stem christies and beaming proudly. A loud sob escaped from deep in her throat, and Jim was beside her, his arm encircling her shoulders. They watched the bouquets of flowers thumping on the coffin until they were distracted by the sound of pounding feet approaching the grave.

"It's Will!" Tears streamed down her face as Will yanked her away from Jim in a quick one-arm embrace and boomed, "Bet you thought I wouldn't make it." He lifted a 48-ounce bottle in the air and brought it crashing down onto the coffin. "Sniff that, Vic, old buddy! All the way up to the Great Reaper," Will's voice broke on 'reaper' but he flung his arms up and yelled, "Yeah, Vic!!"

The intoxicating aromas of Laphroaig scotch lifted in the breeze. Carrie could hear Jim and Dave's loud voices joining the mourners as they toasted her father on the fumes from the broken bottle. "Yeah, Vic! Yeah, Vic!"

Laughter and reminisces followed as Will stepped back to Carrie's side and asked in a low voice, "Where's Evie? Where's your mother?"

She hesitated, "She couldn't make it. She's…" How to explain?

"Tell me." Will demanded.

Jim was on her other side, "Coming Carrie?   Everyone's waiting. And freezing."

"Yes, yes of course." She tugged Will's hand. "Join us, please Will."

"No can do," Will shook his head. "I gotta get my rental out of the way--I've blocked the entrance." He jerked his chin in that direction and said, "Let's go, kiddo. We need to talk." He gave Jim a vile look.

She introduced Will to Alvena, Jim and Dave as they walked back to their cars. "Care to join us for dinner at the Carriage House, Will?" Dave asked.

Jim's face was stony.

"No thanks." Will called back. He hurried Carrie to the front seat of a red Ford parked at an odd angle in front of the open steel gates. The others had caught up and Will turned to them. "I'll get Carrie back to you in an hour or so." He ran to the other side, jumped in and the Ford took off, swirls of dust and loose snow in its wake. The eerie sirens from police cars split the air in the distance.

"Some bastard called the cops on me," Will muttered. "Hope I can hide this crate in your garage." He winked at her and grinned as they bumped onto the asphalt.

She looked back at her parent's friends who had come to the grave site and who were now scattering to their cars. She wondered how long they would remember her father. Was the funeral just another social obligation for them? At least this one would stand out in their memories. Would they gossip about her mother? Of course they would. Dad would have been shocked and saddened by his wife's condition. It would have broken his heart, and Carrie's breath caught.

Will glanced sharply at her and said, "Close your eyes, kiddo. I know the way."

She moved her car to make room for his rental and Charlie went berserk in the back yard. Will tried to cope with the exuberant dog while she unlocked the back door.

Inside, she handed him hangers. He stroked the black seal fur and said, "I remember this coat. Evie use to complain about how much it weighed but she loved how warm it was." He hung up both their coats in the closed, turned and said, "Let's sit in the kitchen. Can you make coffee, or shall I?"

"You do the honours. I need the washroom." She assumed he must know his way around this house and the coffee maker.

Seated at the kitchen table with mugs of steaming coffee she broke the silence between them.

"I don't understand Mom at all," she said before she ploughed into the description of her mother's strange behavior at her husband's death bed. Carrie expected a reaction from Will, but he just nodded and said,

"Evie's been worried about Vic for a long time. He tried to hide his medical problems from her, but she knew. She phoned to warn me."

"She told you but not me?" Carrie's tone was bitter.

He reached over to pat her arm. "Carrie, my girl, I have a confession." He took a large swig of coffee. "Your mother and I had been lovers for a good while when I introduced her to your father. Big mistake. The three of us did everything together, went everywhere together for a few months. Until it was just Evie and Vic."

"Oh, Will," She whispered. Her heart went out to him.

"She's still my gal. Always will be, fool that I am." His eyes were sad and his smile sardonic as he stared into space, "I will look after her as long as I'm able. If you agree."

"How?" She stammered.

"Well, I sure as hell won't put her in an old folks home." His censorious look sent a wave of guilt through her chest, but he did not wait for her response, "Yesterday I put my Toronto condo on the market and today I placed a deposit on a three-bedroom apartment in Burlington."

"Oh. Wow." Carrie, overwhelmed, felt grateful tears tighten her throat.

"It's a go then?" He placed his hands flat on the table as if ready to stand up and said, "You should see this place I'm gonna buy. Lots of room for you, too. All the major windows look out onto the bay, that little dip in Lake Ontario."

"Wait a minute." She sat up straighter. "There are legal…I thought you'd retired to a cottage on Lake Simcoe."

"Yeah." Will nodded. "Summers are beautiful there, but winters are shitty. Cold and windy and you never know what kind of weather is going to hit you from day to day. Not that the winters are much better in Toronto. Or here."

"You're sure Mom will go along with all this?"

"Very sure." He grinned happily.

"But Will, she's undergoing psychiatric treatment and the doctors--"

"Doctors!" He said contemptuously. "Believe me, kiddo, I will be much better for her than any shrink." He sat back, drained his mug of coffee, and gazed at her expectantly. His tone had changed, not so confident now and his eyes were pleading, "Let me try, at least. For however long--you decide."

Carrie put her face in her hands and rubbed her eyes. She looked up and smiled at him, "You're like manna from heaven. The last thing Mom wants around her now is me."

"As soon as Evie is able to travel, we'll come and visit you on that bald prairie. You two need to get back on an even keel." He picked up their empty mugs, rinsed them and placed them in the sink. Carrie remained engulfed in her thoughts and emotions.

Will noticed her bulging knapsack sitting in the hall when they retrieved their coats. Before he could comment she said,

"I don't want to stay in this house another night. I've made a reservation at Sutton Place in Toronto."

"How are you going to get there?" He asked.

"Your marvelous "Go" train. I'm so glad I only have a backpack."

He let out an exasperated sigh. "Jesus, Carrie. How old are you? That kind of luggage is for hippies." But he slung it over his shoulder and muttered, "My rental should be safe now. I'll drop you off, but you'll have to guide me."

In the car they exchanged emails and Will reminisced about Evie, not so much about Vic.

He drew up under the huge bright awning of the Carriage House. She waved to him and wondered how long he'd been waiting.

Jim opened her door but before getting out she touched Will's arm, "I'll deal with Mom's legal stuff. Be sure to keep me posted. On everything!"

He laughed, grabbed her in an awkward hug and kissed her soundly. When they pulled apart, she could not help laughing at Jim's scowl.

"Good luck, Will. You're certainly going to need it." She put her hand in Jim's as she stepped out of the car. Will reached into the back seat for her backpack and said,

"Same to you, kiddo. Whatever the hell you're up to."

Jim hugged her briefly and Will's red rental car disappeared, merging into the traffic. She took Jim's arm and smiled, shaking her head at Will's last remark. How did he know she was "up to something"? And did he know Peter Cummings?

Dave and Alvena, waiting in the foyer, hugged her and escorted her into the dining room while Jim took her backpack to Alvena's car.

The tuxedoed waiter showed them to a window table set with a blue tablecloth and blue candles. Carrie was sure she could smell those damn white lilies from the church. She sniffed her collar to check and leaned over to Jim, "J don't want to go back to that house tonight, so I made a reservation at Sutton Place."

He took her hand, "I understand." He paused, "You can come to Toronto with us. Lots of room in Mom's Mercedes."

"No need to whisper, you two," Dave said as he held Alvena's chair.

"Carrie's coming back to Toronto with us." Jim answered and grabbed the drinks menu.

"What will it be, Carrie? White wine or scotch?" Jim showed her the list of special drinks, "How about something exotic?"

"I'd better stick to white wine, but you don't have to buy the most expensive brand they have."

Alvena laughed, "You know my son!"

They chatted amiably until it was time to order dinner, Carrie contributing very little--she was intrigued by the casual, easy relationship Jim had with his mother. And Dave was, well, Dave was Dave. After being with Will for a few hours Dave's abrupt manner seemed almost mild by comparison. She wondered if Dave was as impatient to divulge his new information on Cummings as she was anxious to hear it. The conversation about the Blue Jays and the Ontario by-elections were of absolutely no interest to her, even in the best of times. Her cell phone vibrated in her purse and pulling it out she glanced up. Conversation was flowing freely. No one will notice. She switched it on and when she saw the caller was "anonymous" her curiosity got the better of her. Her whole body twitched at the message--

"When the cat's away the mice will play."

Jim noticed. Of course. She shook her head and attacked her dinner. "Anonymous" was Pete, she was sure. Just his style. The food was tasteless, and the conversation seemed to swirl above her. *What the hell has Peter Cummings done now?*

Alvena turned to Carrie as they sipped their coffees, "You are most welcome to stay with me when you're in Toronto. There's no need to waste money on one of those over-priced Toronto hotels."

Jim shook his head, "Peter Cummings would have no trouble barging into your lakeside condo, Mother."

"Peter Cummings?" Alvena set down her empty cup, and said pensively, "A man for whom evil is a daily activity."

"You knew him?" Carrie came alive.

"Just socially." Alvena repeated his name, "Peter Cummings. Who could forget that man? He was vulgar, he was ugly, he was tedious, but he was somehow charming."

192

Carrie choked. Jim rubbed her back and said, "And rich. That always helps in the social life of any city."

"Not always," Alvena contradicted her son. "He went bankrupt here years ago, but it seems he has bounced back. If you lose a fortune, you can always earn it back, but if you lose your good name, you can never get it back. James has told me, Carrie, a little of your encounters with the man. If I were you…" She paused.

"You would work on destroying his reputation," Jim finished the sentence for her.

"Or bring him to justice in a court of law," Alvena added.

Dave leaned across the table, "You are truly a wise woman, Alvena. No wonder Jim turned out alright."

The tension relieved, Dave pressed on, "The research is suggesting that Pete's actions became ethically corrupt after his bankruptcy. Not quite criminal behavior but…"

They waited for more and Jim said, "Come on, Dave. Spill the beans. You can trust my mother."

Dave shook his head, "Not here. Somewhere less public."

Carrie waved her Visa card at the waiter, "I'm paying for this dinner, and I will not broach any arguments from any of you."

"Ah, your father's will," Dave ducked as Jim's fist shot into his shoulder.

Jim saw his mother digging into her purse, "Forget it, Mom. When Carrie has that determined look there's no use arguing. I'll get our coats."

Dave took both the ladies' arms, "I came with Jim, so you've got me too. Thanks for the dinner, Carrie, and it's my treat tomorrow night. You will join us, ma'am?"

"Thank you, but only if you call me 'Alvena'." She flashed him a dazzling smile.

Chapter 27

A bitter wind off Lake Ontario whipped at their coats and faces as they waited for Jim to bring his mother's Aston Martin around. Carrie insisted on sitting in the back seat knowing Jim would find his way back to her Dad's house without any help from her. After picking up her backpack, they were on their way. With Dave's arm slung on the seat above her shoulders, Carrie stared out at the dark night as they drove east on Lakeshore Boulevard towards Toronto. No one made any attempt at conversation for an hour or so until Alvena swiveled and said, "You must be exhausted, Carrie. We'll get you a hot toddy."

"Mother, I doubt the hotel knows your recipe for hot toddies."

Carrie smiled, "Stop it, you two. Tell me about your life, Alvena. If we have to wait for Dave's revelations, I need a distraction."

"Well, that should put you all to sleep and James has to drive." She settled back, "I was born, bred and buttered in Toronto but I fell in love with a wild lumberjack from Quebec who changed my life. He made me deliriously happy for a short time and gave me a son who interrupted my career."

"Your career?" Carrie asked when Alvena paused. "I had been in the theatre with the Davis trio, Donald, Murray and Barbara, two brothers and a sister. They founded the Crest Theatre in the 50s, and I was one of the first actresses they hired." She clutched the arm rest, "James!"

Jim wheeled the big car onto a side street when he spotted two RCMP cruisers parked in front of the Sutton Place Hotel. He tore around corners and rushed yellow lights until they were headed south towards the lake again.

"That was my hotel! Where are you going?" Carrie looked out the back window.

"Carrie, have the RCMP contacted you?" Jim asked her.

"No. Why?"

"I just don't believe it's coincidental that a squad car was parked down the street from your Dad's house a few hours ago." Jim checked the rear-view mirror, "Hard to tell if they're behind us now."

Dave removed his arm from over Carrie's shoulders and straightened up, "I'll keep an eye out from back here." He shifted in his seat, "What have you done to warrant their interest, Carrie?"

"I don't know. Nothing." Carrie let out a shaky sigh.

"Are those explosives still in your garage?" Jim stopped for a red light.

Alvena sucked in an audible breath. Dave turned to Carrie and lifted her chin, forcing her to look at him, "Well now, the plot thickens. Explain please."

"They're not mine," Carrie protested. "They belong to the fishing club."

"They fish with semtex?" Dave asked.

"Only when the ice freezes over the pond. The trout will die anyway from lack of oxygen, so the fishing club guys harvest what they can after blowing up their, the trout's, favorite deep pool." Carrie pulled out her cell phone.

Jim shook his head in disgust as he pulled out his cell, "Let's see if we can get you into the King Eddie. It's old and innocuous, and closer to Mother's condo."

"If the RCMP actually saw the semtex, I'm going to have to face the music sometime, Jim." Carrie tapped in a number.

"Not tonight. We'll come into the hotel, let Dave hear about your fishing club, and help you with a statement so you're prepared when the Mounties do find you. They're bound to track you down eventually."

"The Mounties! You must have committed a federal offense!" Alvena shivered. "Come to my condo. No one will ever find you at Harbour Square."

Carrie had turned away and talked softly into her phone while Jim and his mother argued.

"Mother, your condo is one of the first places they will look. I'm sure they've connected the dots by now," Jim said as he stopped in front of an old stone building.

Carrie clapped her phone shut, "If they can, so can Pete. I am not getting your mother involved in the mess of my life, Jim. Let me out at the hotel and take your mother home. I will deal with the damn Mounties."

"Oh, but I *want* to be involved in the mess of your life." Alvena reached for the door handle. "We're coming in."

"Wow!" Dave whistled. "Alvena and Carrie--have you got your hands full, Jim boy."

The porter was at Jim's car door, and he assured them there were empty rooms in the hotel. He grabbed Carrie's pack as soon as Jim popped the trunk open and led them to the reception desk.

While they waited for Carrie to check in, Alvena wandered around the lobby admiring the décor. Coming back she said, "I haven't been in this hotel for years. They have maintained a semblance of its former elegance." She glanced behind her, "Here's Carrie."

"That didn't take long," Carrie joined them and waved a key card. "Are you coming up, or shall we sit here in the lobby?"

"We need privacy," Dave said taking their arms again and following Jim to the bank of elevators.

Jim let the bellboy take Carrie's pack and they all crowded into the elevator. Wisely, no one said a word. Instead, they listened to the bellhop's soliloquy on the glories of the Omni King Edward Hotel. Dave and Jim looked bored, but Carrie and Alvena displayed polite interest.

By the time the beaming bellhop, endowed with Jim's handsome tip, bowed himself out, Alvena was literally bursting with curiosity.

"Tell me all," she demanded but Carrie had turned her back and was speaking in a low voice into her cell phone. She hung up and heaved a sigh of relief.

"Carrie? I sense a new development," Jim said. "But wait, we all need a drink." He pulled a mickey out of his breast pocket, "Dave, can you find some mugs or something?"

"Ever heard of room service?" Dave grumbled but he found three glasses. Jim poured a few thimbles of scotch into each, reserving a swallow for himself, and raised his eyebrows towards Carrie.

"Well, here's what my phone calls have revealed," Carrie responded to his eyebrows. "Someone, Peter Cummings undoubtedly, told the RCMP the explosives were in my garage."

"How would Pete know about the semtex?" Dave asked before Jim could.

Carrie shook her head, "I could be wrong, but all is well now. Susan's buddies from the north are removing them. All is clear." She glanced at Jim. "Don't worry, the cops have to get a search warrant and probably won't get into my garage until tomorrow." She finished her scotch, "Let's hear from Dave."

Alvena, Jim and Dave were silent as they stared at her. Carrie couldn't decide whether they were in disbelief. She liked to think it was "awe".

Dave, sitting on the bed, twirled his drink and began. "Actually, it was Mrs. Mathews, Alvena, who suggested we look in the social pages of old Toronto newspapers." He pulled a folded photocopy from his breast pocket and read, "'What influential oil and gas executive hides his ex-wife in an exclusive private school?'"

"Jeanie," Carrie breathed.

"Right you are." Dave smiled at her. "Manning College in Bonneville, Ontario. It's old, not that posh, and Jeanie was there working in the kitchen for almost a year."

"And?" Jim and Carrie both asked.

"That's it, I'm afraid," Dave said shaking his head. "I haven't been able to find anything else. Somebody needs to visit the college and see if anyone there remembers Jeanie."

"I'll go tomorrow," Carrie said without thinking and turned to Alvena, an unvoiced request in her eyes.

Alvena nodded, "Of course you can use my car. It's in need of a good long run, anyway. But Carrie, my dear, it's too soon…"

"I will grieve my father the rest of my life. Will is looking after Mom. Getting evidence against Pete won't wait." Carrie was her determined self again.

"I'm coming too," Jim got up and pulled out his cell and his airline tickets.

"But your flight…" Carrie objected, secretly thrilled and grateful.

"I'll cancel." His phone rang before he had a chance to punch in any numbers. He turned his back to them, but the room was small, and everyone heard him swear into the receiver. In deference to him the others went quiet as he paced the small space and listened intently. "Okay, you've done well following the emergency procedures. I'll see you tomorrow."

"What's wrong?" Carrie stood up and touched Jim's arm.

"A fire at the plant. Nobody knows how it started and how much damage it caused. I have to go back. Sorry, Carrie." He kissed her hand, "Perhaps Dave or Mom could--"

"I'm fine on my own. After all…" Carrie's disappointment was immediately replaced by her suspicion of Pete. He could be, and probably was, responsible for the fire. *"While the cat's away, the mice will play."* It was Pete.

"You just got here, James." Alvena looked heartbroken but she turned to Carrie, "Here's an idea. I have the keys to my friend's apartment just off Avenue Road. She's in Arizona and I'm sure she wouldn't mind your using it. Her ex may be there on the weekends, but he can watch over you. Please. You'll be safer there than in this hotel."

"You may be right, Mother. But better still, Carrie, you should come back west with me. Forget about the college--how many years has it been? It's unlikely anyone will remember Jeanie. It may very well be a wild goose chase."

"You never know," Dave said and drained his glass. "It sounds like too good a lead to pass up. Count me in tomorrow, Carrie, but you'll have to drive. I let my driver's license lapse. Who needs one with all the subways in Toronto?" He heaved himself up, "We should be able to do it in one day, so let's get an early start. Meet at Alvena's at nine tomorrow. Okay, Carrie?"

"I'll have the coffee on." Alvena turned to Carrie, "Bring your bag tomorrow and I'll get it up to the Avenue Road apartment." She ignored Jim's scowl, "I'm dying to hear your story, Carrie."

"We've got time," Jim glanced at his wristwatch. "I know Carrie's rendition will be short and to the point, so I'll fill in the blanks." He winked at her and held up the empty mickey, "Sorry, gang. No seconds."

Well, now," Dave sat down again. "I have to hear this."

Chapter 28

The temperature had risen dramatically overnight, and Carrie reveled in the power of Alvena's Aston Martin as it growled softly along Highway 401 to Bonneville. The cold morning sun, an orange glow on the eastern horizon, rose before them. Dave, surrounded with files on the back seat, fired questions about her story of last night.

She put a bridle on his tongue by saying, "I have to somehow get this big car out of the city and onto the highway, and I can't do that with you needling me." She glanced out the rear-view mirror, "Dave, please. You're blocking my view. I thought you said you wanted the back seat so you could get some work done."

His face registered shock at her rebuke but sat back in the luxurious rear seat and opened his laptop. Poor Dave. She had never spoken to him so harshly, but it worked. He was obviously scrolling through his emails because he announced, "Here's one from Jim. He's just landed in Edmonton."

Two hours later large snowflakes began to fall. They melted into dribbles of water when they hit the windshield, but the visibility deteriorated, and steering through the heavy slush became a challenge.

Dave peered over her shoulder, "Sure you're alright? We can turn back and wait for a better day."

"Hey," Carrie eased up on the accelerator when the headlights of an oncoming vehicle appeared, "I'm an Albertan now, and I've driven in all kinds of winter conditions." She rolled her shoulders. "Get back to work. Does this classical music bother you?"

"No, not since I turned off the speakers back here." He swore softly and grabbed the shoulder of the front seat as they skidded on the edge of the tarmac. They saw two cars angled into the ditch and glimpsed the rear of a half-ton sticking out of a gully on the other side of the highway. The weather got steadily worse until she couldn't see two yards ahead or on either side. She slowed to twenty clicks, then fifteen. The driving snow whipped against the windows and the wind buffeted the car.

"I'm getting out to sit on the hood. I can direct you with hand signals." Dave had zipped up his parka and tied his hood.

"No, you're crazy! How will you hang on?" She lifted her foot off the gas pedal as she glanced in the rear-view mirror. The car following them dropped back to a glacial pace too.

He ignored her and said, "Close the door behind me." Pushing the car door against the wind he slid out and pulled himself forward with both hands clutching the bottom of the side-view mirror. The weight of his body closed the door, but it didn't click completely shut. Carrie unbuckled her seat belt to lean over and latch it, her eyes never leaving the road. She watched him maneuver his body to lay spread-eagled on the hood, his two feet braced against the side rims of the windshield and his arms reaching forward. Was he clinging to the radiator? He raised his left hand and jabbed it desperately to the left. Carrie overcorrected and they swerved and slewed on the slick, hard surface. One of his feet lost its purchase. He slid on the metal surface and his head sank into his shoulders in preparation for the worst, but she was able to get the heavy car back over the center line. Dave squirmed into position again.

They crawled at a walking speed for another twenty minutes. Through the snow squall Carrie could now see a line of weak headlights behind them. She prayed they would not meet another vehicle. Dave jabbed directions with his left arm and held on with his right hand and his feet. The wipers labored and clanked as snow and ice accumulated on them and on the windshield. She knew she should clean them off before they were completely inoperable, but she was terrified of stopping. Dave must be freezing. How long could he last out there? What if she couldn't see his signals? At least the Aston Martin seemed to be as one with the road now.

Without any warning they emerged from the white-out. Dave pointed to the passenger side, and she stretched to unlatch the door and push it open. He slid in shivering. With chattering teeth, he pulled off his mitts and blew into his cupped hands. A few minutes later he turned and grinned, "We're a team, you gorgeous gal!!"

Carrie had not been called "gorgeous" in over a decade. "If ever" was more like it. Embarrassed, she glanced at him, stared at the object he had pulled from his pocket and asked.

"What on earth is that?" The car drifted to the side, and she quickly refocused on her job of driving.

He unzipped his jacket, wiped the moisture off the object with his shirt and said, "The hood ornament—it came off when I was desperately grabbing for **any** hold during my last slide across the hood." He fondled it and looked at her neck, "I'm going to have it made into a pendant for you." He held up a silver feathered badge.

Carrie laughed and read the prominent brand name, "*Lagonda*. A quick glance will make people think it's a name tag and I'm an anaconda." She turned back to the road. "How did you manage to snag it?"

"On that great swerve of yours--what the hell were you doing? --my arm went around it and I held on. A desperation move, but a lifesaver. When you got the car on the road again and I was back on the hood I noticed that silver ornament was bent almost ninety degrees. I twisted and it came off easily." He put it back in his pocket.

They found a fast-food place off the clover leaf to Manning College, and over hamburgers and hot chocolates they planned their strategies. Dave drained his mug, dug in his pocket and showed her an eight- or ten-inch winged object, "What do you think? A gold or silver chain?"

"Silver, of course, to match," replied Carrie without too much thought. "You should give it to Alvena as a thank you gift for the use of her car."

"For wrecking her car, you mean. I prefer gold. The contrast would make this thing look like real silver. Look, you can even make out the feathers on the wing."

"Well, Alvena would probably prefer gold." Carrie put her mug on the tray and stood beside him, "Let's go. I phoned her and she's expecting us back for dinner."

Dave started to laugh and said, "I can just picture you handing this to her." He held out the ornament, "Thank you for the use of your Aston Martin and here's a little gift to show our appreciation." His chortles turned into horse laughs, and she stood up to shake his arm.

"It's not that funny." She leaned down and whispered, "You're attracting attention, you nut."

He reached up, pulled her down onto his lap and kissed her. A huge, mouth-open kiss. Before he let her go he whispered, "I love you, you wonderful old girl."

She reeled back, almost lost her balance, and Pete's words, *horny old maid*, rang in her ears. Grabbing her coat, she sought refuge in the washroom where she tried to collect her thoughts. Dave couldn't be taken seriously. He probably has a stable of women in Toronto. But still, the sensation had been pretty wonderful--she'd felt it right down to her toes. She licked her lips and tasted him! Dave probably knew Jim was somewhat sedate and that quality kissing wasn't one of his priorities. Was Dave taking advantage of her vulnerability? She really didn't care.

He was paying the bill when she emerged and she brushed past him to get outside. Looking up, as if seeking answers from above, she noticed the somber ceiling of the sky had lifted. White, fluffy clouds chased each other in a crowded sky.

As they walked to the car she mused, "How can the weather change so abruptly?" Not waiting for Dave's response, she stopped, "What if Mrs. Clark closes the door in our faces? What if her husband--"

He grabbed her arm, "We're committed. No more 'ifs and buts'." Leading her to the driver's side he said, "We both have to play it by ear. Anyway, as long as Pete doesn't find out where we are, what have we got to lose?"

"Quite a bit," she muttered but he did not hear her as he skittered around the car.

She steered the car south, turned west and followed Lake Ontario's shore to the Manning College. A long driveway, bounded on one side with a playing field, led to a Gothic style building. The tower that dominated the limestone façade that overlooked the lake's turbulent waters and its single spire gleamed in both sun and cloud.

"It looks formidable, more like a church than a school," Carrie said gazing up at the building as she locked the car.

"Not surprising," Dave rolled up his collar against the wind. "It was built as a seminary by one of those evangelical churches and re-chartered as Manning College in the mid-eighteen hundreds. It was named after some obscure politician."

"Yes, but not the Alberta 'Manning'. I did a little research as you obviously have."

He held open the big wooden door, "We stick to the plan--you talk to whoever is still in the kitchen, and I'll see if any of the administrative staff remember the former principal, Clark. We'll keep in touch by cell phone."

The kitchen was stifling with moist, heavy air from the churning dishwashers. Two young girls sat at a table rifling through magazines. They met Carrie's inquiries about Jeanie Archambault with baffled looks. The freckled one shook her head, "I've only been at the college two years, and Helen here just started a month ago," She licked her finger and flicked a page. Carrie nodded and turned to leave thinking Jim had been right--this was an exercise in futility--when Helen yelled above the noise of the machines,

"Hey, wait a minute. Molly might've known her. She's been here a long time, but she's left now, gone home for the day."

Twenty minutes of Carrie's wheedling extracted Molly's address from the girls, but they wouldn't divulge her phone number. "Ask at the desk" was their advice, and Carrie was sure *that* would be a no-go. "Freckles" gave her vague directions to Molly's house, which Carrie wrote down, omitting all the *'you knows', 'likes', and 'sort ofs'*.

Dave didn't answer his cell, so she left a message giving him Molly's address. Spreading out her map of Bonneville she traced the most direct route with her finger, memorizing the turns. She parked in front of a two-story clap-board house, badly in need of a paint job, in what Carrie believed must be the oldest section of town. Or was Bonneville a city?

A chubby, middle-aged woman came to the door. She wore a grey hand-knit sweater, unravelling at the bottom edges, over a flowered cotton dress. *My God, who wears house dresses anymore?* Her face was lined, tired and grey, and she smelled of cheap rye. She frowned, eyed Carrie up and down and said, "Yeah? Whaddaya want?"

Carrie took a deep breath, "Molly?"

"Yeah." Her upper lip curled, "Who wants to know?"

"My name is Carrie," she said in a faltering voice and mustered her courage against Molly's obvious hostility before she continued, "I would like to ask you a few questions about Jeanie Archambault."

Molly startled, her forehead furrowed and her face became a mask of suspicion. She recovered quickly but her eyes narrowed and her frown deepened, "How come you know my name?" She started to close the door, but Carrie held it open with her foot and tried a new tact,

"Can I buy you a drink, Molly? Is there a bar in that hotel at the corner?"

Molly hesitated, then grinned revealing a missing incisor, "Sure. Gotta get my coat." Her suspicions of Carrie had suddenly evaporated.

As they walked the short distance to the hotel Carrie looked back at the Aston Martin and asked, "Is my car safe here?" She saw two men in hats, gloves and heavy coats drinking beer on the porch across the street. A few kids dawdled on the way to school and a young woman with a shopping basket walked briskly around them. Carrie shook her head and thought, "What a stupid question. Of course this striking car is not safe here. It stands out like a sore thumb."

"You can keep an eye on it from the bar." Molly cackled, "But some of the kids around here might add a little artwork to it."

Except for a lone bald man sitting in a corner with his head bowed over his glass, the bar was empty. Carrie motioned to a window table, but Molly loitered to speak to the bartender.

"Hi, Fernie. This here is Fernandez, but we call him Fernie."

Carrie half-smiled at him, "Nice to meet you, Fernandez." She took Molly's arm and tried to lead her to the table.

Molly resisted, "You have to order here at the bar. I'll have a double rye and ginger. One ice."

The lingering stench of cigarette smoke combined with the smell of stale beer and vomit emanating from the carpet turned Carrie's stomach, but she wasn't about to give up now. Pointing to the bottle of Crown Royal she ordered Molly's double and a light beer for herself.

Carrie sat beside the window through which she could see the sleek black front end of Alvena's car. Fernie had the drinks on the table before their coats were off, "Here you are, girls." He threw down two packages of peanuts and added, "Enjoy."

Carrie's first question to Molly, "Do you know where Jeanie is now?" was followed by a long silence. Molly took a long swig of her drink and looked at her over the rim of her glass, as if she were weighing the pros and cons of answering. She opened one of the packages and munched on the peanuts.

Carrie sunk her head in her hands, but, a few minutes later heard Molly say, "No sleeping in the bar." Molly slouched over the table and her voice became low and conspiratorial, "Two big guys came in the back door, you know, of the college. They didn't say nothing, they just took her. She was scared shitless. I know because she went as white as a sheet and her broken cheek looked like it was going to disappear down her throat."

Carrie gulped her beer trying to hide her surprise, "Her broken cheek? Her cheek bone was broken?"

"Yeah." Molly pointed to her right cheek, "This side. Took away any prettiness she might have had, it did. She always wore a bandana over her nose and mouth and dark glasses, but her eye drooped something terrible. Sometimes under the bottom rim. I saw her once without that bandana, when she had a cold, and her face was lopsided. She never smiled, and sure didn't talk much. Some of the students caller her a freak. The mean ones called her worse." Molly slurped her drink and swirled it around her mouth. She swallowed noisily, "Nothing much to smile about around here anyways."

Carrie absently wiped the condensation off her beer glass with one finger and was musing on Jeanie's face when Molly demanded, "What do you want to know for? Do you know how long it's been?"

"Yes, nine years." Carrie took a sip of beer and signaled Fernie for another rye and ginger for Molly.

"Thanks, girly." Molly lifted up her drink, "Not used to this high class stuff." She took a few gulps, wiped her lips on her sleeve and got back to Jeanie. "She was a mess when she was dumped in our kitchen. Big bandage tied under her chin, shaking like a leaf, not talking, her arm in a sling. I took her to the college doc, and he fixed her arm – right there. Her shrieks were the strangest sounds I've ever heard when he pulled it right. Dislocated shoulder. Gave her pills, for pain or sleep, I don't know. He said she needed an operation to fix her cheek, but of course, that didn't happen. She was here about a year and wouldn't tell nobody nothing."

Carrie opened her mouth to ask a question, but Molly hadn't finished her story, "She liked to bake though, and she became the cookie maker. The kids, especially the girls, liked her for that, but she wouldn't cotton to them neither. She baked and cleaned, helped with the dishes and went to her room. End of story."

Carrie was intrigued, "She lived here at the college?"

"Yeah, a little room under the back stairs." Molly's words were slurred, and she repeated herself, "Her face was awful bashed, but she couldn't hide her droopy eye, even with dark glasses." Carrie grimaced when Molly pulled down the lid of her left eye to demonstrate. "Sometimes it fell down below the rim, like this. But from the other side you could see she'd been a beauty once."

"Do you think she's still...disfigured, still bashed in?"

"Oh, yeah." No doubt in Molly's mind, "For sure. The doc said he would have to report it, and she freaked out. She begged and begged him not to--shaking her head and moaning the whole time. Ended up bribing him. Told him her pop would pay, said he was a big TV star in Germany. She told him a whole lot of foreign stuff, stations that didn't mean nothing to me. I guess it must have worked because we never saw hide nor hair of any cops."

"Did..." Carrie was talking to empty air because Molly had drained her glass, jumped up, and grabbed her coat.

"Gotta go," Molly muttered as she braced herself on the table briefly and looked sideways. When Carrie followed her gaze, she saw a man in a heavy plaid woolen shirt at the reception desk. He turned from his conversation and started towards them. But Molly had left. She had slid behind a velvet curtain over a door that led to a small parking lot. Carrie watched her weave unsteadily through the cars, bumping into a few, her coat dragging in the dirty snow. She disappeared through a broken board in the fence.

The man in the plaid shirt rushed to the barely visible door, and in his attempts to open it became entangled in the heavy curtain. With a loud *carumph* the track separated from the wall and the whole apparatus fell on top of him. He cursed and thrashed around like a crazy man until he freed himself. Carrie made herself small. He pushed open the door and ran through the cars, bending down to peer underneath a few. She sucked in her breath when he walked the length of the fence. But he got into a green Mazda and drove slowly out of the parking lot.

Had Molly gotten away? Terrified and alone in the bar--even "Baldy" had left-- Carrie phoned Dave who still didn't pick up. She left change and her unfinished beer on the table and glanced out the window.

The Aston Martin was gone!

Chapter 29

Carrie couldn't believe her eyes. She panicked, stepped over the broken rod and curtain, pushed open the side door and ran to the spot in front of Molly's house where she had left Alvena's car. The street was now deserted. No old men, no kids, and no Aston Martin. Her heart was in her throat as she tried to imagine Jim's mother's reaction to her car being stolen – that serene, Bach aficionado who lived for symphony concerts. Well, and for her son, of course. How could Carrie break the news to her, not to mention to Jim? Damn, damn, damn. She knew she shouldn't have left it in that questionable neighbourhood, but she had, and now she was forced to face the music. She went back the bar to retrieve her coat and talk to the hotel's receptionist. "Do you know the man in the plaid shirt who was just here?" Carrie asked her.

The girl, who looked to be beneath the legal age in any province, shook her head and pretended to be busy at the switchboard.

"But he talked to you. What did he say?" Carrie persisted.

"He, he..," the flustered girl stammered. "He wanted a room." A self-satisfied smirk at her blatant falsehood replaced her confusion.

"You're lying," Carrie hissed. "What…"

The familiar strains of Bach's "Toccata" blasted from a car's horn at the front of the hotel and both women jumped. The girl stared through the window. Carrie whirled, dashed out the front door, ran to the car and dove in. Slouched against Dave's shoulder she said,

"Cloak and dagger, what the hell?" She could have wept with relief.

He glanced at her, not amused, and said, "God damnit, Carrie, I was so worried about you." He swung the car right at the corner ignoring the stop sign and the honking from the truck driver who swerved to miss them.

She straightened up and looked back. No sign of Molly, the bald man or *plaid shirt*. Dave seemed to know where he was going but his body was as rigid as a wound-up spring. She reached over to touch his white knuckles, "Loosen up, Dave. Do you know where you're going?"

"Sort of. I memorized the route here in the cab so I think I can get us out."

Her eyebrows rose, "Your driving seems adequate. I thought you said--"

"Look, Carrie, I'm a lawyer. I say a lot of things."

She had to smile and he grinned when she asked, "How did you get it started? And don't tell me Alvena gave you a second set of keys because I won't believe you."

"I couldn't see you anywhere, so I talked the cab driver into using his engine to jump start the Aston Martin. For big bucks, I might add."

"Keep a tab," she advised. "How did you get in?"

"The back window was still open a bit and his hands were a lot smaller than mine so he was able to get the door open. Thank God you left me that message on my phone." He glanced at her, "You're obsessed with this girl, Jeanie. For no valid reason that I can see."

"She was married to Pete and he ditched her," Carrie replied. "Remember he's vowed to get back at me? Well, I'm just going on the offensive rather than sitting back waiting to see what he'll do. My immediate plan is to find out everything I can about the bastard's past life."

"You're playing with fire," He shook his head. "And I'm not sure I can protect you."

"Thank you for your concerns, but I'm a big girl--"

"Okay, okay. I'll hang around for a bit longer. All right?" His lips curled in a seductive smile. He winked at her but she turned away refusing to submit to his charm.

They passed a Starbucks, a Winners and a few other shops whose names she didn't recognize. At least they were out of the crummy section of Bonneville. When the car started up a steep hill she asked,

"Where are we going? Doesn't this car have a GPS?"

"To the Clarks. I phoned ahead and Mrs. Clark agreed to meet us on the condition we keep our visit short. Yeah, here's the address." He dropped his notepad into her lap. "Can you punch it in? I hate the damn GPS so I still may need your Bonneville map."

The car shifted gears automatically halfway up the hill and he explained, "After a little persuasion, the cute gal in the principal's office let me go through the school's back files. And guess what? I found a receipt for twenty grand from Pete in the donor's file, circa 2007."

"Pete? Donating to an educational institution?" Her voice rose in disbelief.

"Yes, strange as it--"

"Turn left at the next intersection. Proceed east for ten blocks." The domineering woman's voice on the GPS interrupted Dave. He turned the volume down and continued,

"And even more surprisingly, Mrs. Clark has agreed to talk to us."

Carrie could envision *the persuasive methods* he had used on the two women. His mischievous eyes and broad grin were enough to get their knees melting. She gazed out at the lovely stone houses and mused, "So vintage old Ontario--the upper class on the top of the hill." The GPS voice came on again and Carrie shouted, "There it is!"

"Easy, old girl. I'm right beside you."

"Old girl?"

"Sorry." He parked in front of a two-car garage and the door of the left one rose, almost automatically. "She said she'd open it for us when I explained it was a borrowed car, very expensive, and could we park in her garage?" He wiped his forehead with a white handkerchief, "Good to get this damn car tucked away. It's way too conspicuous. Let's go." He found the garage door switch; they ducked out quickly before it came down on them and started up the walk leading to the front porch.

He took her arm to help her up he stone steps, "Let me do the talking."

She smiled, "I wouldn't dream of intruding on your lawyerly skills."

"Lawyerly?" He rang the bell and bent his head to kiss her, but before their lips made contact the door was opened by a stern, older woman. She was tall with carefully coiffed grey hair and a gloomy demeanor. With a glassy smile she stepped back and said,

"Please come in." Closing the door, she pointed to the closet and bench.

"Would you like to leave your coats in the closet? I am Paula Clark. And you are David and Carrie." She chatted nervously about the weather as they hung up their coats and took off their boots, then led them into a small sitting room. A white-haired man, whose hands and feet shook uncontrollably, sat in a straight-backed chair. Putting her hand lightly on his shoulder she said by way of introduction,

"My husband, Douglas Clark. You promised you would not upset him." She did not offer tea or coffee for which Carrie was grateful.

Dave perched on a foot stool in front of the old man. Mrs. Clark and Carrie sat on the loveseat on his left side, their knees almost touching. The two men eyed each other for a moment before Dave pulled out two cards which he flashed before the couple and said,

"As you can see, I am an attorney authorized by the RCMP to question you." Carrie did a double take--an outright lie? He ignored her and continued, "I am specifically interested in your dealings with Peter Cummings nine years ago."

Mrs. Clark sucked in her breath. Mr. Clark raised his watery eyes to his wife's, as if beseeching her. She shook her head and her shrill voice resonated in the small room, "I knew this would come back to haunt us someday." Her husband bent his head and gripped the arms of his chair. His whole body shook now and Carrie thought,

"Parkinson's disease."

Dave's lawyerly voice became gentle and kind as he questioned the Clarks about mundane topics, how long they'd lived here, when they were married. Mrs. Clark answered in monosyllables when she could, but Carrie sensed that Mr. Clark was following closely and anxious to speak. Dave turned to him,

"How long had you known Peter Cummings when he made his generous donation to Manning College?"

Before her husband could answer Mrs. Clark stood up, "Why waste time? My husband paid that man to cover up his love affair." To clarify she added, "My husband's sordid affair."

An embarrassed silence followed that was broken by Dave, "But why is there a receipt from Cummings in the college files for twenty thousand dollars?" Dave looked from Mr. to Mrs. Clark and waited.

"It was complicated," Mrs. Clark said sitting down again. Dave nodded knowingly. She flashed him a vile look and said, "His mistress was the wife of…" Her husband groaned and grasped her arm. She peeled off his hand and Carrie was surprised to see her hold it lovingly for a few seconds before she continued, "The accountants took care of all the details, but I can assure you that the college didn't see any twenty thousand dollars from Peter Cummings. It may be in the files, but it did not happen."

Dave's bushy eyebrows rose and he asked, "So it did not appear as a donation in that year's annual report?"

"No, it did not." Mrs. Clark was adamant. "Now, if that is all…" She stood up and as if on cue, Dave got to his feet.

But Carrie couldn't restrain herself, "Do you know anything about Jeanie, the young girl who worked in the college's kitchen at the time?" She remained seated as a long silence halted all movement in the room. Dave and Mrs. Clark stared at her.

"Jeanie," Mrs. Clark breathed the name. "The girl with the unfortunate face." She seemed relieved at the change of subject and said, "I didn't know her of course, but there were all sorts of speculations about her face. She wore tinted glasses, but one eye was pulled down below the rim of her spectacles. It was bloodshot and, and…ghastly. When she blinked," Mrs. Clark made a disgusted face, "that one eye…well, it was quite awful. I looked anywhere but at her face the few times I had to speak to her. We were all glad when she was taken away."

"Taken away where?" Carrie sat forward. "By Cummings?"

"Not him personally, no. By two respectable-looking gentlemen."

Mr. Clark raised his tremulous hand as if warning his wife, but she looked down at him disdainfully, "The rumour at the time was that she went north, far north. There was also speculation that she was murdered." She sat down heavily.

"Murdered?" Carrie was stunned into reiterating the word.

"Well, she just disappeared, and college gossip is like a small town's." Mrs. Clark shrugged her thin shoulders, "Who knows? Why are you interested in her?" Without waiting for an answer from either Carrie or Dave she said, "I often wondered if Cummings was involved in her disappearance because all of this happened at about the same time. I mean, Peter Cummings appeared as my husband's savior demanding a bribe of twenty thousand dollars, and Jeanie suddenly left or was forced to leave. But it didn't make any sense. Why would a rich and powerful man care what happened to a kitchen maid?"

"Indeed." Dave got up and held out his hand to the older man, "I hope we haven't tired you too much. Thank you for your time."

Paula Clark was only too happy to see them out the door. "I've opened the garage for you and will close it behind you." She held up a remote.

The wind had picked up and snow swirled around their ankles as they walked to the open garage. Carrie apologized, "I know, I know. I was to keep quiet, but I couldn't resist..."

"No worries, Carrie. Your questions revealed another mystery--the Clarks, Pete, and how it all relates to Jeanie. You were on the right track the whole time. We have to find Jeanie--if she's still alive." He stood at the passenger door, "I made a reservation for dinner at the Holiday Inn. You drive, I'll guide."

Dave, in the passenger seat, directed her back down the hill and then to a playground.

"You wanna turn on the swings?" Carrie quipped as she put the car in park.

"Funny girl." He pulled out his phone. "So, our friend Peter Cummings covered up a love affair between the former principal of the college, Douglas Clark and the wife of the Chairman of Manning College's Board of Governors. In exchange Clark hid Jeanie in the college's kitchen and gave Peter Cummings a generous bribe to keep his extra-marital affair hushed up."

"You think?" Carrie's tone was laced with doubt. How could it have been that simple? To cover up an illicit romance in a closed society like a private school? Kids and teachers would gossip, and the scandal would undoubtedly get back to the parents. But miracle worker Peter Cummings had managed to sweep it all under the rug.

"I know. I copied some of the college's back files onto my smart phone." He pointed to it, "And I've been reading the photographs I took on this little gadget. The reproduction is lousy, and reading was an ordeal--I had to squint, even use my flashlight to make out some of the words and figures. It was the weird accounting that had me flummoxed and aroused my interest."

"Did Jeanie sleep in a closet or a cedar chest at night?" Carrie was unconvinced.

"She was only at the college a year. I agree it would have been difficult to hide her there indefinitely."

Carrie put the car in gear, "The newspaper article Alvena found?"

"Indeed."

She misquoted the excerpt from the gossip column, "What influential CEO hides his former wife at a private college in rural Ontario?"

He put his hands together, clapped twice and said, "Close enough."

Chapter 30

The hotel, situated on Lakeshore Drive, was not difficult to locate. During the short trip from the Clarks, Dave convinced her they should stay overnight to avoid a drive back to Toronto in the dark.

"Let's wait and see if we can get a couple of rooms." He had said. "You must be tired, and you did tell me during that famous golf game that you avoided driving after the sun went down. Besides, the weather forecast isn't great. Just look at those dark clouds." He pointed out the rear window to a black mass that had appeared on the horizon.

"All right," she acquiesced, yawned and said, "What we don't need is another damn storm". In ten minutes, they were parked in the Holiday Inn alcove. She popped the trunk.

Dave opened his door and glanced back at the vehicles inching up the ramp. "Looks as if Lakeshore Drive and the 401 are disgorging here." He stopped by her window, his overnight bag and her backpack slung over his shoulders, "I'll wait for you at reception. Wish me luck."

Yearning for her compact car, she finally squeezed the Aston Martin into a tight spot in the underground parking. A young delivery boy showed her how to get to the foyer, which was a madhouse: screaming babies, kids chasing each other between legs and bags of all shapes and sizes, and adults venting their frustration and annoyance.

Dave emerged from the pandemonium and, picking up his bag and her backpack, he gestured to her with his chin. She followed him down a long hall into a corner room. A double bed with a brown quilted bedspread, two fake-mahogany end tables that held impossible-to-read-by lamps, a single chair at a student desk, and the ubiquitous TV was the sum total of the room's furniture.

"The last room--the only one I could get." He dumped the bags on the bed.

She stared at the double bed and imagined banking a wall of pillows down the middle, leaving, at the most, two feet on either side. Her jaw tightened and she wore the calm stupor of disbelief, "I'll sleep in the car." She reached for the door handle.

He grabbed her hand, "I promise to behave." He grinned sheepishly and she cursed herself for the effect his boyishly-manly good looks had on her, as they had, she was certain, on women of all ages. She jerked her hand from his and glared at him,

"If you think for one minute that I will come tumbling into your bed, you have another think coming." Sounding like the perennial mother.

He laughed but seeing the look on her face, he turned and opened his bag, taking out his shaving kit and pajamas. He headed for the bathroom, "Gotta get these warmed up. I suggest you do the same."

The contents of her backpack were as cold as ice. She was pressing her nightgown against her chest when he came in with two glasses.

"Our reservations in the hotel dining room aren't until six." He pulled a mickey of scotch out of his case and unscrewed the top, "Can I interest you in a pre-dinner drink?"

She relented, threw her nightie on the bed, and forced herself to accept the situation she was in. After all, it wasn't the end of the world and she said, "You must fill up that bottle every night." She sat rigidly on the bed beside their bags and asked, "With ice? I saw an ice machine down the hall."

He placed the bottle and glasses on the desk, "Try and get comfortable in this god-awful room while I see about the ice."

She moved to the hard desk chair and reviewed what she knew of Dave. He was fun during the golf game, polite, and had tried valiantly to relieve the tension between she and Cummings.

He returned with a bucket of ice and set them on the desk, then plumped up the pillows against the flimsy headboard and said, "Come and sit here. I'll take the chair."

She smiled up at him and didn't budge, "I got it first."

Accepting her stubborn refusal with a shake of his head, he mixed the drinks, handed her one and settled back against the pillows with the remote, "Want to watch TV?"

"God, no!" She sipped at her scotch, "Tell me about your life."

The wind rattled the windows and hail started to pound the tin roof. Or was it aluminum? In any case, by the sound of the storm's fury the Aston Martin would have been pock-marked at the very least if she had left it outdoors.

He swirled the ice in his glass, "Well, it wasn't your typical Canadian upbringing. My father was in the diplomatic service, so we moved around a lot. My brother and I ended up with a smattering of Italian, German, Hungarian and a few others. Dan stayed with the German, but I didn't get expert in any of them. The smatterings have served me well in my career though."

"Your career as a lawyer? Or working for Peter Cummings?" Carrie's voice carried an edge of sarcasm.

213

He shook his head, "Pete is only one of my clients. I got stuck with coming out west because of staff shortages. Too many lawyers having babies." He backtracked when he realized his unintended slur on her province had provoked her. "Nothing wrong with Alberta but I love Toronto--lived there all my life." He expounded on maternity and paternity leaves and the effects they had on his law firm. Dave had a pleasing baritone voice, he loved to talk and Carrie was a good listener. Six o'clock came all too soon.

The chaos in the foyer was in partial retreat as they passed through it to the dining room. Seated with a bottle of white wine wrapped in a cold towel beside the table, they clinked glasses and he apologized for his motor mouth.

"Not at all," Carrie objected. "Your life sounds interesting. Do you get to see your brother at all?"

"Yes, we meet for a skiing holiday pretty regularly. A different country each year and we try to avoid civil wars and revolutions. We skied Japan in 2014. But enough about me...."

"Excuse me, sir." The waiter interrupted with menus and topped up their wines.

After a quick glance, Dave closed his, "I'll stick with a hot turkey sandwich. Surely they can't bugger that."

"Make it two. With French fries." She held up her wine glass, "Even though it's not up to your standard we can still toast to good luck and success."

He touched his glass to hers, "In getting back to Toronto or in finding Jeanie?"

"I know you think I'm obsessed with Jeanie and perhaps I am." Carrie sat back with her wine glass and took small snips. She was about to change the subject when he said,

"Tell me everything you know about her, and no editing, please."

She thought back to her first encounter with Jeanie and tried to come up with a comprehensive picture of her and why she, Carrie, was anxious about her. Dave listened without interrupting and admitted he had met her a few times when she was married to Pete.

"Well," Carrie said. "You know how beautiful she was."

"Yes, but..."

"But?" Carrie asked.

He shrugged, "Just not my type. And Pete is not a guy you want to cross."

The waiter placed a warm plate in front of her that held a heaping mound of French fries wedged against a pile of sliced turkey brimming with rich brown gravy.

"Mmm…" She leaned forward as her overloaded fork dripped gravy, narrowly missing the front of her sweater. "My apologies for eating like a slob. Don't know why I'm so hungry and this smells so yummy."

He chuckled as he filled her wine glass, "It's a treat for me to see a woman actually enjoying her food. Can we talk about your life, your interesting career, and how you acquired those fascinating eyes?"

She held her hand over her mouth as she laughed, "From the eye bank, of course. And no, my life is boring. Let's figure out how to find Jeanie."

He looked at her askance, "About thirty-five million people are scattered across the area of Canada. That is a very large haystack and Jeanie is a very small needle."

She smiled, "Yes, but if we approach the problem logically, we can at least formulate a tentative plan."

He nodded his approval, "And you are assuming she was whisked away by Pete?"

"Yes, of course. What else? Who else?"

"I thought you, or Jim, told me that Don had had a thing for Jeanie. But assuming you're right, why would Pete want her out of the picture in the first place?" He poured more wine into her glass.

"Well," Carrie's mind was getting foggy and her words did not come out clearly, "F..f..financial or p..p..personal." She finished her glass of water and reached for his. She was getting drunk. Her limit was eight ounces of wine. God knows how much she'd had with Dave adding more every time she set her glass down. And the damn scotch before dinner! What was she thinking? Obviously, she wasn't thinking at all.

He shook his head, "I cannot imagine how he could have benefitted financially, and I am pretty familiar with that aspect of Cummings Consortium."

"What about girl friends, lovers? Could they figure in somehow?" She drew out her question slowly, trying not to slur again as she sipped his water.

"Hard to keep track of those," Dave chuckled. "He's a pretty promiscuous guy and still in his prime. Or so he says." He put his hand on hers, "Come on, Carrie. Talk about you."

She picked up the dessert menu, "Want something gooey or wholesome?"

"Yes, another scotch." He tipped his glass at her, "I'm waiting to hear your story."

She finally obliged him and made an environmental regulator sound like the most fascinating job in the Alberta government.

The waiter hovered, Dave signed the bill, but when they got up to leave Carrie tottered and held on to the top of her chair.

Taking her elbow, he led her to the elevator and the second floor. "Let's walk a bit. The shops don't seem to be open so we won't be tempted. You really didn't have that much wine, but we'll walk it off." He kept his grip firm as they paced up and down the corridors at least six times. Her head cleared considerably but she wanted to sit, anywhere. On the seventh he swung her around a corner and opened the door to Saks Fifth Avenue and said,

"What do you know? It's open." He gently pulled her forward, but she resisted.

"I'm not interested in jewelry," She held out her ring-less hands. "You go in, but I'll window shop." She could foresee all the bored salespeople descending on him.

He let go of her arm and said, "A girl without rings is like a night without stars." He smiled down at her, "I'll just take a quick gander. Be right back."

She looked briefly at the window displays--glittering diamonds and rubies. She prayed to her non-existent God that he wouldn't buy her a ring and noticed he was at the till with his wallet open. She leaned her back against the plate glass window and closed her eyes. The next thing she knew her feet gave out and she was sliding. Two hands appeared under her armpits before she hit the floor.

"Jesus, Carrie. Don't fall asleep here." Dave lifted her to her feet.

She grabbed his shoulders, "You sound just like Jim."

He supported her body against his and said, "Why didn't you tell me you were so tired?" He practically carried her back to the room, opened the bathroom door and pointed, "You first. I'll phone Jim so he can let his mother know where we are."

"I have Alvena's number somewhere," she mumbled as she put her cell phone on the bedside table. He pushed her into the bathroom and closed the door. Her nightgown was on the edge of the bathtub (did Dave put it there?) and she managed to struggle out of her clothes and force it over her head. She brushed her teeth with his toothbrush, wiped a wet cloth over her face, stumbled back into the room and climbed into the double bed. She was vaguely aware that Dave was watching TV with the sound very low.

She woke up when the mattress sagged, and Dave tucked the covers around her. Rolling over, she murmured, "Alone again with a man I hardly know…"

"Go back to sleep." He stroked her hair, "Sweet dreams, sweetheart."

She turned towards him, and he kissed her. A lovely soft kiss that she couldn't help returning and they rolled into each other's arms. His hands were everywhere and when he took her nipple in his mouth she moaned and lost it. Her legs clamped around his body, his mouth moved back and forth between her breasts--and her cell phone jangled.

Dave's head shot up and with a curse he reached over her to turn on the light and hand her the phone.

"Carrie?" Troy responded to her fuzzy 'hello'.

She sat up, inadvertently kicking Dave in the stomach, "What the hell, Troy?" She glanced at the clock. After midnight. A shiver of apprehension slid up her spine, "What's wrong?"

"My mother. You need to phone her." Troy sounded worried. About Susan, his mother? Not bloody likely. Without any explanation he rattled off a phone number.

"Just a sec. I need a pen." She took the pen and pad that Dave handed her with a nod of thanks, "That's not her cell number. Where is she?"

"She's in a RCMP office in Tuk--Tuktoyaktuk. Did I say it right?"

"Oh God! Has she been arrested?" Carrie tucked the bulky receiver against her bare shoulder and neck and pulled the sheet over her exposed breasts.

"They picked her up with a bunch of natives for blocking an access road to a pipeline that's under construction."

"Pete's pipeline?" Carrie glanced at Dave who was close, touching her shoulder with his and listening to both ends of the conversation.

"It's not really his, but I think he does have a few bucks in it. Here's the phone number to call." He told her again, more slowly. "Gotta go now."

"Wait!" She held up the pad, "Let me read it back to you." She could hear his impatient breathing as she slowly repeated the numbers and she said, "The Indigenous people do not like being called 'natives'. You should…"

"Whatever," Troy cut her off. "You got the number right."

"Okay, why does….?" But Troy had hung up and she was talking into static. She wrapped herself in the sheet and stood up, "We have to leave. Right now."

"In the middle of the night? You hate driving in the dark."

She turned, her hand on the bathroom doorknob, "If we leave now, we can be in Toronto by breakfast."

He moved quickly to put his weight on the door, and they wrestled briefly, she pulled, he pushed. She gave up when he said,

"Let me talk to the police up there. Maybe I can get her released." He picked up the hotel phone.

She sat on the hard chair listening to his persuasive voice convince the RCMP officer that Susan Wright was innocent, only swayed by her environmental concerns and convictions. She was sober, right? She had no record, right? (Carrie crossed her fingers and prayed). And finally, "Yes, I will get back to you as soon as she's booked on a flight to Edmonton."

"Good work!" She gave him a thumbs up. "Now let's see if Jim can get her home." She rattled off Jim's number from memory and he looked at her quizzically.

With no preamble, he told Jim about her dislike of driving in the dark and gave him the details about Susan's predicament. Dave held the phone out as Jim said, "I'll get her to Edmonton." Before Dave signed off, she heard Jim ask, "You said you could only get one room. Are you and Carrie sharing a hotel room?"

She snatched the phone out of Dave's hand, "Yes, Jim. Do you have a problem with that?" She slammed the receiver into its cradle, dug into her purse and threw two hundred--dollar bills on the bed, "That should cover my portion of the meal. I'm leaving."

He stood by the bed, "It's late, you're tired, I'm tired. Let's try and get a few hours of sleep."

She knew he was right. But his pajama bottoms hung low on his hips below his belly button, and she had to tear her eyes away from curly grey hairs peeping over the waist band. Disgusted with her thoughts, she climbed into bed, pulled up the covers and rolled over, her back towards him. By the time she had counted to thirty-nine she was asleep.

They breakfasted in the coffee shop, saying little to each other except to share the Globe and Mail. They were on the road by nine o'clock. It was a cold crisp day, and the first pale streaks of morning were brightening the sky. They turned onto Lakeshore Drive with the yellow globe of the sun glowing brightly behind them. The highway was blissfully clear of snow and ice. Dave sat in the passenger seat reading and making phone calls. Their only stop was to have the car washed and filled up.

Alvena buzzed them in and Carrie pulled into the basement parking stall. Turning the engine off she pushed the seat back, "I am so-o-o relieved to get this gigantic car back where it belongs."

"You've done a great job, Carrie." He gently squeezed her shoulder. "I'll just pop up to say a quick 'hi' to Jim's mother." He slung his bag and her pack over his shoulders and grunted a cynical laugh, "A three--day backlog to tackle at work. Oh, joy!"

Alvena welcomed them both with hugs but could not prevail upon Dave to stay for lunch. He waved to Carrie from the door, "It's been grand, old girl, even though your problems may get me disbarred." His laugh gradually faded as he hurried down the hall.

Carrie brought her hostess up-to-date and as they lingered over coffee she lamented, "So many unanswered questions and still no idea where Jeanie might be."

Alvena looked pensive and asked, "Do you think your friend Susan might be able to make inquiries in the north? Cummings Consortium is one of the stocks I hold so I'm aware of the company's northern pipeline. I know all those communities are widely spaced geographically, but close socially—Inuvik, Yellowknife, Norman Wells…"

Carrie jumped up, "Why didn't I think of that?" She pulled her cell phone out of her purse and flashed Alvena a grateful smile.

Chapter 31

"Hey Carrie, how goes it?" Susan's voice boomed over a background of laughter, loud voices and a three-piece band.

"It's taken me hours to track you down in Yellowknife," Carrie complained.

"Yeah, we're weathered in here--the fog is so bad nothing is flying in or out for God knows how long. So I'm sampling the bars." Carrie groaned and Susan laughed, "I'm at the Wild Cat Café--came over here with a bunch of dudes from the Strange Bar. I love this town--maybe I'll move up here to The Knife."

Cheers, a few "yea Sue's" and stomping feet did not prevent Carrie from hearing Susan gulp a mouthful of beer and ask, "What's so important that you need me?"

"Do you remember Jeanie?"

"Yeah, the yellow warbler and my encounter with that creep, Cummings. How could I forget?" Sue paused and sighed, "Jeanie, this current mania of yours." Carrie heard the scrapping of a chair, calls to Susan as she moved through the bar and finally her voice again, "I'm going to the loo so I can hear you better. Hold on."

Carrie kept the receiver to her ear and could almost smell the bar. A few minutes later she heard a toilet flush, a gush of water and Susan was back,

"Okay, here I am. What's up?"

"Cummings may have tried to hide Jeanie in the north." Carrie yelled over the background noise--loud female voices entering the bathroom and the band had started up again, "I know it's a long shot, but could you inquire up there if anyone remembers a girl, or a young woman with an eye patch or a face scar, or both?"

A long pause and Susan finally replied, "How long ago? How old is she now?"

Carrie did a little mental math, "Early thirties is my guess."

"Cripes, do you know how many thirty and forty year old women are up here looking for a man?"

Under normal circumstances Carrie would have laughed, but she asked, "With scars and eye patches?"

"Well, most of the scars here are invisible, and you know I'm not very observant. I really don't remember her very well. Height? Weight? Eye colour?"

After describing Jeanie as well as she could Carrie added, "Under the high-brow British diction she sounds a little mid-European. That accent may not be discernible-- hard to detect."

Susan snorted, "I know what discernible means, you klutz. I'll ask around. The Knife is some kind of truck hub, so you may luck out. Anyway, I'll give it a shot."

"Thank you. Thank you." Carrie's ebullient response was partly relief that her friend sounded sober. "Phone me on my cell 'cause I too am trying to get back home."

"Where are you?" Susan sounded surprised.

"At Jim's mother's. Her condo in Toronto."

"Christ, not him again."

Carrie bristled and retorted, "He's getting you out of the north. He can work miracles when it comes to booking airline tickets."

"Like his miracles in bed?" Susan's horse laugh bellowed over the line and Carrie clapped her cell phone shut to cut it off.

"What's wrong? Won't she do it?" Alvena asked from the doorway.

"Yes, she'll 'give it a shot' she says." Jim's mother now looked old and tired with creases between her eyebrows, a corrugated forehead and deep lines above her mouth.

"I thought you were going for a nap," said Carrie.

"Just a lay-down. But I wanted to hear the next episode in your quest for Jeanie." She gave a little chuckle, "I hope I get to meet your friend Susan someday. Her language is as bad as my son's."

"Alvena, you shouldn't be worrying about my problems. Go for your lay-down. Please." Carrie gently took her elbow, turned her around and watched her weave down the hall with one arm extended for support on the wall.

Carrie washed the lunch dishes and wondered if Jim knew how frail his mother had become. The hall phone rang as she was hanging up the dish cloth and she ran to answer it before it disturbed Alvena. "Hello?" she whispered.

"Hi Carrie." Jim's voice sent a pleasant shiver up her spine. Without any preamble he read off the flight number and time of Susan's rescheduled flight from Yellowknife. "That's assuming the fog lifts by then."

"Thanks for doing this, Jim. I just talked to her. She seems to be enjoying herself up there." Carrie opened the little drawer of the phone table and pulled out a pen and pad, "Okay. Again please."

He repeated the information and waited while she wrote it down. "I, uh, I hope you don't mind but I changed Mom's tickets so she could fly with you. She was planning on visiting me next week, but I know she hates all the rigmarole at the airport…"

"That's great." Carrie had never heard a hesitant Jim. "She's resting now, but I can wake her up--"

"No, no, don't. I forgot this is her lay-down time. I'll phone later." The phone went dead.

Does he hate me now so much that he can't bear talking to me? She wandered into the living room and sank into the first armchair. The sun streamed in on her face and to prevent herself from falling asleep she opened her smart phone and searched 'Yellowknife.' To her surprise she discovered the 'yellow' did not refer to the hundreds of tons of gold Yellowknife's Giant Mine had produced, but to copper. A local Dene tribe had traded tools made from copper deposits found near the Arctic Circle and they were known as the Copper Indians or the Yellowknife Indians. The tribe is now incorporated as the Yellowknife Dene First Nation. The former settlement, located on the northwest shore of Great Slave Lake is now a business center, the capital and only city in the Northwest Territories.

She closed her eyes and thought about Sue. With her experience and outgoing personality, she would have no trouble getting a job up there. Carrie fell asleep smiling, imagining the environmental protests her friend would bring to the north--the havoc she would wreck.

"Wake up, dear. It's drink time." Alvena gently squeezed Carrie's shoulder.

Sitting up quickly she blinked a few times and said, "And then I'll take you out for dinner. Do I need to change?" Carrie scratched a piece of hardened food off the thigh of her dark blue jeans.

"No, I just talked to James and he recommended that we not go out. He wants to keep you hidden and he has ordered Chinese for us." She went to the sideboard and pulled a bottle of Oyster Bay sauvignon blanc from the little fridge. "I have it on good authority that this is your favorite wine, and that you love ginger beef." She poured a generous portion into an intricately patterned crystal wine glass.

"You talked to Jim?" Carrie nodded her thanks as she accepted the wine, noting that Alvena looked one hundred percent better than she had a few hours ago.

"Yes, on my bedroom phone. He told me about changing my airline tickets. You did know that I was planning on visiting him next week, didn't you? I hope you don't mind being saddled with an old woman on your flight."

"You better not let Jim catch you calling yourself that." She gave Alvena a little hug and headed for the washroom. "Be right back. Nature calls."

In twenty minutes, Carrie was pleasantly happy even though she tried to take small sips of the delicious wine. She noticed Alvena put her glass to her lips but did not swallow.

"Let's make a to-do list," Alvena pulled an old school scribbler from the magazine rack beside her chair. "I have to make notes on everything now, but I'll start a fresh page. Item number one: find Jeanie."

"Just like that!" Carrie laughed as she popped open her laptop. "Okay, assuming we find her, how do we hide her from Pete?"

They discussed various possibilities, none of them feasible until Alvena mentioned that she had the key to her friend's condo on the twelfth floor. Her friend who was in Florida for the winter.

"Perfect!" Carrie was enthusiastic. "We should be able to keep her away from Pete's spies for one night anyway."

Their Chinese dinner was delivered and over ginger beef and spring rolls they bandied ideas back and forth; Don needed to be involved, but did he want to be? Was he still in love with Jeanie or had he moved on in his life? And Troy, could they trust him now and, if so, how could they use him? How long could they keep Pete in the dark? What will he do? Jeanie will obviously be in danger from him, especially if she goes to the police. Cummings would, without a doubt, have a well-rehearsed rebuttal to any charge of kidnapping Jeanie.

As they dumped leftovers and used boxes into the trash, Carrie's cell phone rang and Dave's irate voice took her by surprise,

"What the hell have you been up to now?"

She reacted without thinking, "God damn you. Who do you think you are? My mother and father combined?" She forced herself to be a touch more civil, "Hi Dave."

"Haven't you been watching the news?" He did not wait for her response, "Somebody blew up a section of Pete's pipeline in northern Alberta and diluted bitumen is spreading over hundreds of acres of permafrost. The RCMP are trying to trace the explosives as I speak."

"Oh, boy."

"Check your garage. Jim told me…"

"I can't. I'm in Toronto. The fishing club…"

There was a long pause before he sighed, "What a mess. Where's your friend, Susan Wright?"

223

"I talked to her yesterday. She was at the airport in Yellowknife where she was weathered in, fogged in, but she is on her way to Edmonton."

"If she made it to Edmonton, is it possible she could get in your garage?" Dave did not sound anything like the loving guy of a few nights ago.

"Probably."

Dave sighed, "And is it also possible that the explosives the natives used came from your garage?"

"Probably."

"You are in big shit." He sounded almost sympathetic.

"Probably" she conceded. "You are assuming the Indigenous people blew up the pipeline. But the timing is all wrong. How could Sue get the explosives to them so quickly?"

After a long pause Dave said, "She could have told her buddies how to get into your garage. We need Jim, or someone, to check."

"Jim knows where I hide my emergency house key." She hated to admit that fact to Dave, but there it was. His response was as she expected,

"Why in hell does he have access? Don't answer that." She heard his fingers tapping on wood, and when he came back on the line, he sounded more like the good-natured Dave she had come to know, "I'll get him to have a look. Don't worry, Carrie, we'll get this sorted out somehow."

She listened to the dial tone, gave Alvena a despairing look and moaned, "I need another drink."

"Tell me." Alvena handed her the wine bottle and sat quietly as Carrie related her conversation with Dave. "Should we talk to Jim now or wait until he's looked in your garage?"

Carrie glanced at her watch, "Let's go to bed."

"Don't be silly. Neither one of us will sleep until we know--"

"It's after midnight in Alberta. Surely Jim will wait until morning. If he even picks up his phone for Dave."

"He will pick up for me." Alvena dialed and she held the receiver out as Jim's worried voice filled the space between them,

"Mom? Why aren't you asleep? The doctor said--"

"I'm as fit as a fiddle, dear. Have you looked in Carrie's garage?"

"I'm on my way." Dave was pretty insistent. "Now go back to bed and put Carrie on, please."

Carrie swallowed a mouthful of wine before she accepted the phone from Alvena. She immediately apologized, "Jim I'm so sorry I yelled at you and have gotten your mother involved. She won't listen to me and refuses to go to bed."

"I understand completely. I've lived with her off and on for many years." He paused. "I'll phone you when I get into your garage." And the line went dead.

Carrie stood and banged the phone down, "I am so completely fed up with men hanging up on me. I know fifty is a watershed and I'm now a useless old maid, but I need to be in control of my situation, not be a bystander to it." She flopped in the easy chair and said dully, "Jim is on his way to look in my garage."

"Well," Alvena was the picture of patience, "It seems to me that we just have to sit tight. I told James your whole story, including the woman Molly and the bribe Cummings negotiated. He will phone back as soon as he gets to your garage."

"For your sake, not mine. But whatever? Shall I make coffee?"

"Come and sit beside me and tell me about you, your early life and your family." Alvena patted the cushion beside her.

Carrie took Alvena's hand and let her mind drift back to her father, Bobby and Cliff--before disaster hit, before the accident, before her life dissolved. By the time she finished talking tears were streaming down her face, and Jim was on the phone again.

"No explosives here. Could your fishing buddies have collected them?"

Carrie wiped her eyes and blew her nose.

He gave up waiting for her to answer, "What's the date of the big fireworks at the fishing pond?"

"The long weekend." She swallowed, "But Jim, haven't you listened to the news either? The natives have blown up a pipeline in the north, one of Pete's pipelines."

"Yes, I know. And the means to do that may have come from your garage."

"Yeah. Dave phoned and said the RCMP are trying to trace them, the explosives."

"That sounds like a nearly impossible job." Jim swore. "Look, Carrie..."

"Well, it may not be." Carrie took a deep breath. "They may be the same people that Susan was helping blockade the road to the pipeline two days ago."

"Why the hell didn't he tell me about Susan being arrested?" Jim mused.

Carrie snorted, "Maybe because he knew you wouldn't help her get out of the north?"

"Perhaps. I want to help you not Susan, not the Indigenous people, only you. How can I do that?"

"I don't know. Dave thinks I'm in big sh..." She glanced at Alvena. "Well, your mother and I have brought it down to two major problems. If Susan's friends are able to find Jeanie, how do we identify her and get her to safety? Don and Helen are the only ones who would recognize her now, but Pete is watching Helen. Do you think Don still cares enough for Jeanie to go north without Pete finding out? And where on earth can we hide her if he brings her south?"

"You and Mom—what a duo! You must realize finding Jeanie is a long shot. Susan has no positive proof that Jeanie is in northern Alberta. God damnit, Carrie, she could be anywhere." What could Carrie say to that? So she said nothing, and he blew out a sigh, "Okay, I'm on my way home. Let me think. I can definitely sound out Don. We have to presume he's still in cahoots with Pete, but who knows? Any idea when Susan will get back to you?"

"That depends on her trucker friends. Perhaps Jeanie has had surgery by now..."

"Surely she'd have to come south for that. But, good point. Look, I just had a brainwave, but it will have to wait until I see you. You are so heavily involved now your phone may be compromised."

"Oh, God! That thought never occurred to me."

"Guess you won't make the detective grade after all." He chuckled, "I'll be at the airport the day after tomorrow. Anything else I can do between now and then?"

"Yes." Carrie hesitated, "Charlie is at that animal boarding kennel on Highway 21..."

"Done that. I can keep him here until we know if you end up in the slammer."

"That's not funny, Jim."

"Well, it's not as if you set the charges. You used to like my sense of humour." There was an awkward silence. "See you at the airport. Good night." And he hung up.

"Your son has the weirdest sense of humour of anyone I know. But..." Carrie got up to replace the receiver.

"But you love him?" Alvena asked hopefully.

"Probably," Carrie sighed. "Time for bed."

"Let's take the phone off the hook," Alvena suggested with a broad smile.

Chapter 32

Carrie couldn't sleep. Way too early a bedtime for her. She put on her travel dressing gown, slipped her cell phone into her pocket (in case Jim phoned), and padded into the kitchen to pour herself another glass of wine. After filling it well past the acceptable level she stepped carefully into the living room. Her toes curled deliciously in the thick carpet, and the moonbeams spilling through the wide picture window beckoned her. She watched a few lights dart across the dark waters of the lake below. Isn't it dangerous to boat at night? A terrible thought crossed her mind. What if Cummings had drowned Jeanie? No one would ever find her, but surely even he wasn't that malevolent. She realized how little she knew about the man.

As she tipped the last of her wine to her lips her phone vibrated. It was Dave.

"Hi, Dave. Are you a night owl too?"

He chuckled. "I'm outside in a cab. May I come up? I need to talk to you. Is Jim's mom asleep?"

"Yes, but she's a light sleeper." She lowered her voice to a whisper, "I'll buzz you in. Number 1909." She found the panel beside the front door, rang him in, then hurried to turn a few lights on. She tightened the belt around her waist rejecting any idea of touching up her face or brushing her hair. It was only Dave. After letting him into the building she stood at the open condo door watching the numbers above the elevator rise.

He burst out and setting down his briefcase he crushed her to him. Putting her arms around his broad back she walked backwards pulling them both into the condo. He bent to kiss her, but she broke away, brought his briefcase in, closed the door and said,

"You're incorrigible." She hung up his coat as he wandered into the living room.

"What a view! Much better than mine." He smiled down at her when she joined him at the window. "But if you come to live with me, I promise to upgrade."

She laughed and let him lead her to the sofa. Sitting very close, he drew a blue box from his breast pocket and placed it in her lap.

"A little something for you to remember me by." He grinned.

She opened the lid and gasped, "You didn't!" She lifted a silver chain and gazed at the "Anagonda" emblem. "It does look, uh, unique. Alvena may even wear it."

"What do you mean, "Alvena"? It's for you." He leaned back, "If you want it…"

"Oh, Dave!" She reached for him and kissed him lightly on the lips. "Here, put it on for me." Holding the two ends of the chain out to him, she bent her head down.

He fumbled with the clasp and said, "Why do they make these things so damn small?" His large hands were not meant for such a task, but he persisted. He stood, dug in his pocket and handed her a long gold chain, "I got you a gold one too—just in case."

"You crazy guy! Thank you, thank you. Two gifts in one--"

He grabbed her, the two chains fell to the rug, and he kissed her as only Dave could. They settled back in the sofa for some serious love-making. Thirty minutes later Carrie surfaced, flushed and breathless. She picked up the two chains. Tinges of guilt clutched at her like a lion's claws. She escaped to the bathroom and tried not to think about Jim. Leaning on the sink she looked into the mirror and asked herself, '*Do I look like a duplicitous woman? What the hell am I getting myself into? How can I enjoy two men at the same time? But I do, I do!*' When she emerged, Dave was holding an open folder on his lap. He winked at her and said,

"Now we have to get down to business."

"Business?" Aping him, she cringed.

"Yeah, the business of finding Jeanie." He tapped his finger on the folder.

"You're going to help me?"

He pointed at the first document in the folder, "Read it. Please." And he waited.

"Pete's birth certificate?" She handed back the photocopied document. "How is this significant? Does he know you're here, showing me this?"

"I'm Pete's lawyer, not his best buddy. You seem so certain that he has Jeanie hidden away you've almost convinced me." He carefully replaced the birth certificate and said, "Pete never talks about his childhood, so I did a little research. He was born in Outremont, Montreal, in case you didn't notice that."

"He's Jewish?" She pictured Cummings, with not a little repugnance. "He has the nose and dark hair, what's left of it."

"His mother was beautiful. Look." He slipped a 7x10 black and white photograph from the folder.

"Wow." She held it up for a closer examination. The image was a little blurred, probably because it had been magnified from the original. She gazed at a lovely young woman in a form-fitting strapless evening gown. She was smiling and holding out a corsage as if she was asking her date to pin it on her dress. Her hair curled in a soft page-boy against her bare shapely shoulders. And her eyes, they must have been luminous!

Dave took the photo back, "Apparently, she was the toast of Outremont, even the belle of Montreal for a few years. She reminds me of you."

"What? Her nose?" She pulled the open folder onto her lap and looking at him with a question mark in her eyes, put her index finger on the letterhead of the next document. It featured a pipeline winding through round hills and the address was St. Catherine Street, Montreal.

Dave nodded, "Our friend, Cummings, is one of its shareholders."

"A pipeline company. No surprises there." Carrie was disappointed.

"Yeah. It's small potatoes now, but that's where Pete got his start. At one time there were six oil refineries in Montreal, and the interprovincial pipeline was extended there in 1976. Cummings Consortium got its start shortly after that."

"So? You think he hid our Jeanie there?"

He nodded. "Makes more sense than Toronto, Vancouver or Calgary, and she'd be too conspicuous in a small town. Besides, he has a cousin on his mother's side who still lives in the old Outremont neighbourhood."

"And you found a woman with a scarred face there?"

He winced at her sarcastic tone. "No such luck. But one of our paralegals, Marie, is French-Canadian and I have persuaded her--"

She interrupted him with a snort, "'Persuaded' her? And how did you do that?"

"Come on, Carrie. Get your mind back on track." His smile did not carry any amusement, and she realized she was pushing the envelope. She might lose his help and support with her smart-ass remarks. She mumbled an apology and he continued,

"Anyway, Marie is paying one of her former schoolmates to go ask around and they have come up with a possibility. The woman they found fits Jeanie's description except she doesn't have a scar, just a lop-sided smile, and she apparently doesn't smile very much." He clipped the photo to the other documents and handed her the file folder. "Good luck, old girl. The ball's in your court, so to speak. I think I'd better back away for a while--possible conflict of interest or something close to it. I can't afford to lose Pete's business, either for my sake or my law firm's."

She watched him re-organize the contents of his briefcase and when he stood up she stopped him, "Wait. Thanks so much for all this, Dave. May I contact her, Marie?"

"Of course. Her home phone number is in the file and she's expecting your call." He bent to touch her shoulder just as she turned to put the file on the side table. He sighed and straightened but she jumped up, threw her arms around his big chest and hugged him. His quick response forced the air out of her lungs, and she gasped. He held up his hands in remorse, then cradled her head gently, "Sorry, sorry, sweetheart. You surprised me, and I kind of lost it. Did I hurt you?"

He looked so chastised that she kissed him quickly and eased herself out of his grasp. The sash of her dressing gown had come untied, and her nightgown had twisted baring some pale skin. He gazed greedily at her exposed breast, and for some reason she thought of Charlie with his mouth open and his tongue lolling out. She swallowed her snicker, wrapped the front of her gown closed and said, "You'd better go before we wake up Alvena."

"Yes, okay." With his hand on the door handle he asked, "What are your plans?"

"I've only got one day to get to Montreal, talk to Marie and get back here for my flight home. That's assuming she will see me tomorrow." Carrie shook her head.

He glanced at his watch, "It's not eleven yet. Phone her now."

"No way. I would never phone anyone at this hour of the night." She thought for a moment, "But perhaps Marie would be delighted to hear a male voice on the line."

He pulled his cell phone out of his briefcase, scrolled and within seconds he was speaking into it, "Bonsoir, Marie. Did I wake you?"

A high-pitched squeal of laughter emanated from the phone. Carrie listened to Dave partially explain the situation and waited. A few minutes later he handed his cell to her with a nod. She swallowed and introduced herself,

"Hi, Marie. I'm Carrie. Thank you for agreeing to help me and I apologize for the time, but Dave, well, he said it would be okay." She glanced down the hall fully expecting to see Alvena emerge from her room.

"Enchanted to meet you, Carrie. Un moment." They heard her put her phone down and shuffle papers before she picked up again. "We may be lucky. This is what we have found." Her accent was heavy, but her English was precise. "In Outremont we found a woman who speaks both English and French with a funny accent. This is not unusual because we are close to the University of Montreal which has many foreign students. But she fits how David described her--height, eyes, hair. She looks like the red picture except she is no longer elegant. Her name is Betty Smith. Suspicious, no? Many Bettys, many Smiths, here in Quebec." She paused.

"But?" The ever-hopeful Carrie was now apprehensive.

"She has no scar on her face, but her smile--I only saw it once but it is, how you say it, it is not right." In her uncertainty, Marie's English had deteriorated.

"Twisted? Her smile is twisted?"

"Oui. Twisted. She is a typist for a big company, Alcan, the aluminum company here in downtown Montreal. She is living, pardon, she lives in a small apartment in Outremont. She never goes out, except to her job. She looks scared when we talk to her, and we know she wants us to leave, to go away." Marie took a big breath and asked, "Are you coming here?"

Carrie hesitated. She had to check this out even though it sounded too good to be true. Was someone setting her up? Dave on Pete's orders? But no, she had to trust Dave. So what if she got lost in Outremont, or in Montreal? Her French was passable. She would stay on the main streets and warn Jim. Ask him to be sitting on his phone while she was there. She was conscious of both Dave and Marie waiting for her answer, so she said, "Yes, I think so, but do you think Betty will talk to me?"

"Peut-etre. Maybe. When are you coming?"

"I, uhm, I will phone you back. How late may I call?"

Marie chortled, "I will wait to hear from you tonight." And she hung up.

Dave was back in the living room, shoes off, feet up on the coffee table, "So you're going to Montreal?"

"It could very well be another goose chase." She sat down beside him, not too close. "Do you think I can get to Montreal, find Marie without getting lost, talk to her and get back here in time for our flight to Edmonton?"

"Sure, no problem. There's a train at six, Via Rail express. I know because I've taken it."

"A train?" That mode of transportation had not occurred to her.

"You know how long it takes to get to and from airports and then wait for the take-offs. The train between Toronto and Montreal is probably more expedient than air travel, and CNR is fairly reliable." He consulted his cell, "You and Marie could take your mystery woman out for lunch and catch the late afternoon train back to Toronto. How much time do you need to quiz her? To ID her?"

"You don't believe it's Jeanie, do you?"

He shrugged, "Why should you care what I think? I know you are putting yourself in danger. From Pete. And for what? Maybe this girl/woman likes her life just fine the way it is. Have you thought of that?"

"Doesn't sound as if her life is a bed of roses—scared and living alone, no social contacts. You haven't told Cummings, have you?"

"Carrie, Carrie, have faith. You know how I feel about you and betrayal is not my bag. I want to protect you, but I'm completely baffled as to how in hell to do that. Do you want me to come to Montreal with you?"

"No, but thanks. It should only take a few minutes to identify her."

"Yeah? From the photo of the portrait that Jim sent? It must be ten years old." Doubtful Dave.

"Yes, mainly that." She hesitated, suspecting he'd laugh at her but she explained, "Helen, Jeanie's sister, spoke of a poem she and Jeanie used as a signal when they were young. I've memorized it."

"Poetry? This is why I love women." He grinned and took out his phone, "Shall I make a train reservation for you?"

"And for two on the return trip, please."

He laughed. "You are really something, and your optimism is laudable." He punched his phone and took out his pen, "Here, write down the details. Union Station. Car and track number. You'd better be there by 5:30."

"I can walk from Alvena's--"

"No! And have Pete or his goons run you down? Take a cab. Or I can pick you up in a cab. Or I can stay here for what's left of the night and…"

"Dave." Carrie waved her hand in a 'no' gesture. "I think I'm old enough to get on a train by myself, Pete or no Pete. Go home. I need to get a few hours of sleep." She went to the closet and handed him his coat, "Merci beaucoup. I'll let you know how I make out."

Again, she stood in the hall as he waited for the elevator. It dinged, he got in, turned and gave her a thumbs up as the aluminum doors swished shut.

She went back to the window, and recited the poem to the moon, "You do not sing as I do, it is a different tune. You to me like music, as bumble bees of June."

Closing her eyes, she imagined Jeanie and Helen as young girls, hugging each other and giggling as they plagiarized Emily Dickinson's poem.

Chapter 33

At 5:15 the next morning Carrie wrote a note for Alvena and let herself out of the condo, her backpack tight on her shoulders. She had barely slept--worried about missing the train, anxious about the arrangements to meet Marie, the possibility that Betty Smith was not Jeanie, and finally the big one--if Betty turned out to be Jeanie would they be able to talk her into coming back west where the menace of Peter Cummings would loom large?

She emerged from the building to see Dave waving at her from the side of a yellow cab. Her heart was in her mouth as she ran to him, "What's wrong?"

"Change of plans, but we need your consent." He hugged her briefly, helped her into the back seat of the cab and climbed in beside her. He gave their destination to the driver then made sure the partition between them and the front seat was firmly closed.

"Consent?" Carrie aped. Again. You have to stop doing this.

"Yes, consent." He settled back, pulled a thick brown envelope from his breast pocket. "I talked with both Susan and Jim. Way into the wee hours this morning. Jim had brought Susan out to his plant to make sure the phones were secure."

She smiled briefly at the incongruous thought of Jim and Susan together.

Dave opened the envelope. His expression was grim as he explained, "To complicate matters Peter Cummings was in the office yesterday asking for Marie." He gave her the envelope, "Your instructions, Madame."

"Oh, no! Pete will find out Marie is in Montreal..."

"Not necessarily. Marie booked off sick--her monthlies." He pulled a coloured photograph from the envelope and showed it to her, "Cute gal, eh, our Marie? Everyone wants Marie working on their files. She's the best paralegal we have. So we have to get her back here in Toronto ASAP. Anyway, Pete is headed back to Calgary tonight."

Carrie shook her head, "I don't like it--"

"I know. That's one of the reasons we decided it wasn't safe for you and Jeanie to go back west with Jim's mother. If this gal is indeed Jeanie, that is. That and the fact that this Betty has no ID, and we haven't got time to get her a fake one." He drew her under his arm and lowered his voice to a hoarse whisper. She pressed her head into his chest with growing apprehension as he continued,

"Marie and Betty/Jeanie have spent the night with one of Marie's cousins who will also lend them a car. Marie will drive to what was once Windsor Station. That's where you'll meet them. It's been called Gare Lucien-L'Allier since the quiet revolution. How's my French? Anyway, the old train station is now a heritage site. We tried to make your route as meandering as possible under short notice. Do you know Montreal?"

"Sort of. I know there's an underground city, la ville souterraine, under downtown Montreal now. But…" She pulled out the contents of the brown envelope.

"Marie drew a map for you. We figured Pete & company would never look for you in a place dripping with history. The problem is, can you find your way to it? Best to use the metro--it's all in your instructions and I know you're a smart old girl."

"Yeah, right." Carrie quickly read down the list of instructions. "Okay, then what?"

"From there the three of you will take a taxi to Bully's Truck Stop in the Kahnawake Reserve. It's only a fifteen-minute drive from the Gare Lucien--whatever."

"How the hell do we get there without Pete finding out?"

He bent down to her ear again and repeated, "Take a taxi from Montreal's Central Station to this Gare Lucien. Always get the second taxi in the line if you can. Remember, you're the boss--be assertive--I can't imagine that being a problem for you." He smiled and continued, "Take another taxi to the restaurant at the truck stop on the reserve. We've arranged for your truck driver to wait for you there. Marie has the fare because the trucking company insisted on collecting up front. She'll make sure you and Jeanie are comfortable in the truck." He hesitated, "in the bed of the truck."

"In the bed of the truck," Carrie repeated, her voice dull and lifeless.

"Yes, well, the driver assured Marie you would be okay. He's supplying the food and water, or drinks."

"A truck? How is that safe? Don't they have to stop and be inspected along the way?"

"You will be well hidden among the boxes which are tied down and secured on pallets. Immovable pallets." Dave sounded so confident.

"Jesus Christ." Carrie's head fell back in disbelief.

"If you can think of any other way…" His voice trailed off.

She bit her tongue before she voiced any number of sarcastic responses, "How long is this pleasure trip going to take?"

"Thirty-seven hours nonstop on the TransCanada Highway. Better than Via Rail."

"A day and a half. Plus." She mentally counted her remaining codeine pills. As if he could read her mind Dave asked,

"How's the leg?"

"Okay. Doesn't he stop for pee breaks?"

"I'm sure he must. And probably a change of drivers because they insisted the thirty-seven hours is non-negotiable." He tipped her face up. "We can call it all off right now. It's not too late."

"And leave Jeanie in the lurch?" She sighed, "No, I'm committed."

"Look, if it's any consolation your truck driver has had experience doing this sort of escapade. He's brought refugees from Honduras into the states through Mexico." The cab had stopped. "Here we are. I'll go in with you."

"Me and the Mexicans," Carrie grumbled as she tucked the brown envelope into her bag then leaned on his outstretched hand to get out of the taxi.

He steered her into the station and, finding her gate, Dave muttered, "Be a bloody miracle if Via Rail leaves on time." They loitered at the end of the line-up. "This is as far as I can go." He turned her shoulders towards him and kissed her. Hard and sweet. "Phone me as often as you can. Please."

He waited in line with her and suddenly said, "Look, old girl. It's not too late to bow out."

She had just started thinking of all the things that could go wrong but she replied, "What kind of a wimp do you think I am?"

His laugh was wimpy, and he looked exhausted. "You are the bravest old girl I know, but I will be worrying constantly about you. Promise you'll phone."

"Okay, if you promise you'll go home and get some sleep." She smiled hoping to cover up her fears with false cheerfulness as she watched him leave. He waved in a back-handed gesture when he got to the exit.

She was in her assigned first-class seat in the club car when the train pulled out at 6:05. So much for Dave's pessimism. Suits prevailed amongst both male and female travelers. It would seem that travel had not been curtailed even though the oil and gas industry was tanking in the west. The chubby, middle-aged man in the next seat wished her "'good morning" before he dove into the financial pages of The Globe and Mail. As the train whished out of downtown Toronto, she picked out a few landmarks through the filthy window. She examined the package Dave had given her, closed her eyes and slept.

She woke at Kingston with a stiff neck and a sore arm. Her seat mate smiled,

"I tried not to rustle the paper. Did you have a good rest?"

"Yes, thank you." She found her purse and joined the lineup for the washroom. By the time she had splashed cold water on her face and rubbed it dry with the complimentary towel, she felt somewhat refreshed and ready to face the day.

She and her chubby seatmate chatted, and they had barely finished their coffee and muffins when the conductor passed through the aisle announcing, "Montreal Gare Centrale, Montreal Central Station."

The passengers stood to look for their bags and briefcases well before the train pulled to a huffy stop. She joined the crush in the aisle. After sitting for so many hours she had almost forgotten her sore leg until she gingerly stepped down the metal steps to the platform, grateful for the porter's helping hand.

Her name blared over the loudspeaker system, echoing in the hall. So much for subterfuge. If Cummings didn't know she was in Montreal, he certainly does now.

Marie, it could only be her, running against the tide of arriving passengers, called in a shrill voice, "Carolyn! Carolyn!" Wild black hair spread out like a windblown string mop from a pert, pretty face that Carrie recognized from her photo. With a bright red smile Marie grabbed Carrie's hand and pulled her towards the exit, as she said breathlessly,

"Come, viens-citte, depeche-toi."

They ran to a waiting taxi. Marie pushed her into the back seat beside a pale, frightened-looking young woman. Jeanie.

Carrie got her act together quickly. She extended her hand and recited softly, "You do not sing as I do, it is a different tune."

Jeanie's eyes widened and filled with tears. Carrie had her positive identification.

Marie sat in the front seat and talked a mile a minute in French to the taxi driver. The car took off with a jolt, sending Carrie sprawling beside Jeanie.

"Where are we going?" Carrie asked as she straightened up and looked at the surroundings they speeded past. They were going east, not south. She turned to Marie, "Is there a change in plans? Dave said--"

Marie turned, "Sh. Dave, he says to be very careful. Des yeux, des oreilles, they are everywhere." She glanced sideways at the driver.

What the hell? Dave wouldn't like this. Carrie tried to phone him, but the traffic noise, the car radio and Marie's chattering made it impossible to hear. Besides, Dave didn't pick up--only his answering service. When she'd phoned an hour earlier, he had said he was going into a meeting. Looking through the windscreen, she realized she had no idea where the hell they were.

Thirty minutes later the taxi pulled into Bully's Truck Stop in the Kahnawake Indian Reserve. Carrie breathed a sigh of relief. So far so good. Marie pulled both of them out of the taxi and hustled them into the truck stop's small restaurant. A burly heavy-set man stood up to meet them as Carrie tried dialing Dave again.

"Let's go." Without another word he led the way to the back door. Carrie pocketed her phone, and she, Jeanie and Marie followed him past a line of trucks of all sizes and descriptions. Marie's high heels clicked against the wooden deck as he three women ran to keep up with him. He stopped at the last one, a very long transport truck with blue fleur-de-lis and red maple leaves painted on the sides. He jumped down to the dirt surface of the lot and motioned them to follow him to the rear of the truck. He pulled up the back door and it slid into the top of the truck with a loud bang. He held out his hand,

"Give me your cell phones." His voice was gruff, like Red Riding Hood's wolf.

Carrie reluctantly parted with hers and, gesturing towards Jeanie, said, "She doesn't have one."

"Yeah?" He grabbed Jeanie, covered her mouth with one hand and ran the other over her squirming body. He released her, "Too skinny for me." Pointing to the truck bed, he ordered them, "Get in. Keep down. Keep quiet. There's a place for you about halfway down. Find it. If the truck stops, cover yourself with that rug there."

Carrie practically lifted Jeanie in, whispering assurances in her ear. She put her knee on the back of the bed but couldn't get any purchase. Why didn't it have a tailgate or a ramp? Glancing at the driver she saw him smirk at her attempts to get in, and he said,

"I only agreed to one. Where the hell do you think you're going?" She dropped back down and waited. Marie handed him a roll of bills and said,

"Here's extra. Lots extra, more than enough for two passengers." She too, looked terrified. She backed away. Carrie knew she couldn't wait to be gone.

Taking the money he started to count it. Seemingly satisfied, he stuffed it into his pants' pocket and jabbed his finger at Marie and ordered, "Get going, sister. And keep your trap shut. Ferme ta yeule. Know what I mean?" He watched Marie disappear among the trucks as Carrie tried again to get her knee up.

Suddenly she felt his hand between her legs. His other hand clamped on her chest. He held her against his body in an iron clasp, finding and stroking her clitoris with his right hand and finding and squeezing her nipple with his left. Before she knew what was happening, she was sailing into the bed of the truck. Her head struck something metal and she sprawled against Jeanie. His jubilant laugh soared over the reverberations of the rear door slamming down.

238

Carrie lay stunned. The engine of the truck coughed into life, and she struggled to sit cross-legged on the hard floor. She held out her hand and her shattered watch dangled from her wrist. She groaned in despair.

They bumped onto the highway. Jeanie's eyes were as wide as blue cereal bowls, but Carrie couldn't meet them. Her clit had responded! God damnit, her dormant clitoris had sprung to life under that animal's manhandling. Shaking her head in disgust at herself she found her voice, "You okay?"

"Yes, but there's blood on the back of your head." Jeanie said pulling a tissue out of her pocket. She reached out to dab at Carrie's disheveled hair.

"Don't touch it." Carrie brushed her hand away. "That asshole is going to come after us again." She regretted her words as soon as they were out of her mouth. Jeanie looked stricken and terrified, but instead of comforting her, Carrie crawled forward to look for the spot the driver had indicated. Boxes and equipment were strapped onto pallets of varying sizes. She had to admire the care and economy with which the truck had been packed. With no difficulty, she found an enclosure between two pallets of five-foot-high boxes. Standing on the six foot by six foot square of thin foam covering the space, she reached up to push at the three metal bars crossing the top of the boxes. They didn't move. They were stationary. How she had no idea, but they seemed unlikely to fall or come apart. Two blankets and a pillow had been tossed on top of the foam. She turned to find Jeanie had followed her into their sanctuary.

They arranged the pillow and blankets against one of the pallets and sat beside each other on the foam which provided little protection against the hard surface of the truck's bed. The driver's loud voice reached them through his open window as he sang along to his truck radio.

"Do you know the words?" Carrie asked Jeanie.

"Yes. I like country and western," Jeanie said. "But not the way he tries to sing it."

"Then sing it your way, please." Carrie swallowed the tears in her throat and tried to stay calm. They were stuck here for thirty-seven hours. She looked for a stick, anything she could use to defend herself and Jeanie. Maybe their shoes?

He stopped singing to yell curses at the car that had passed them. Jeanie's voice was soft and soothing as she continued to sing the plaintive love song that pleaded for the return of a lost partner. She kept on singing through the radio's commercial and Carrie squeezed her hand in thanks.

"Can he hear me?" Jeanie asked.

"I doubt it. He's too full of himself. Let's try and sleep for a bit." Carrie slid down into a prone position, but Jeanie shook her head,

"I'll keep watch over you."

The steady drone of the tires and the rocking of the truck lulled Carrie into a drowsy state not quite resembling sleep. How could anyone sleep when the damn driver leaned on his horn at every opportunity?

She woke when she felt Jeanie's hand on her shoulder. The truck had slowed. It pulled over and stopped. The rear door came up with a clatter and the driver handed them a roll of toilet paper. He pointed to the side of the truck,

"Right here. Hurry up."

Before they jumped down, Carrie whispered to Jeanie, "Better do it. Might be our only chance for a pee." She grabbed the roll with one hand and Jeanie with the other. They heard him shuffling the pallets and boxes. Checking their stability, Carrie hoped. They pulled down their jeans and underpants and squatted.

Carrie said in a low voice, "God, what a relief. My back teeth were floating." She tore off a strip of toilet paper and looked back to see the driver ogling her.

He nodded his approval, "I like a little meat on my women."

Jeanie looked at him in horror, "I can't. Nothing comes." She sounded like a two-year old and she started to pull up her jeans.

Carrie quickly finished and turned her back to him. Trying to shield Jeanie from the trucker's eyes, she coaxed Jeanie, "Try relaxing and squeezing like crazy." And thought, '*A true oxymoron.*'

"Nothing comes," Jeanie repeated in a strangled voice.

He slapped the side of the truck, "One more minute 'til I come to help you."

"Do it, Jeanie. He can't see you." Carrie crossed her fingers and heard a few spatters on the dry dirt underneath Jeanie.

He had put a step stool in front of the rear door (where the hell was it the first time?) so they made it back to their cubby hole without his touching either of them. They rearranged the pillow and blanket and sat beside each other holding hands. The driver merged the truck into the traffic, and they were off again.

"How many hours do you think I slept?" Carrie asked.

Jeanie hesitated, "Maybe a couple?"

Carrie sighed, "Thirty-five hours to go. Your turn to sleep."

"Are you kidding? There's no way on God's earth I could sleep here."

A few minutes passed. Carrie asked Jeanie to relate the story of her life. "Just what you're comfortable with. Before and after Peter Cummings."

Jeanie was silent for so long Carrie regretted asking. It was too painful for her, Carrie thought and had almost given up waiting when Jeanie took a deep breath, and in a strong voice started relating the history of her life.

Chapter 34

"I was born in Belgrade, before the Yugoslav wars. Helen is six years older than me, and she has always been my protector, my big sister. We grew up in a happy family with grandparents, cousins, and friends. My father taught economics at the university before he was drawn into politics. My mother was the home maker, but she was active politically too. It was a pleasant life until Papa was asked to work for the Prime Minister, Dindic. This made my mother very proud. I don't know whether Papa had a choice whether he could have refused Dindic. Soon he and Mama both became worried about the future of the country and for us, their daughters. On our last trip to England, they left us with a cousin in Dartmouth. *Just for an extra week*', they said. The weeks went on and on, but they wrote often. Until Dindic was assassinated. The letters stopped, and we never saw our parents again."

"Our cousin and her husband were kind to us. They had no children of their own and my father had left a trust fund in England for our education and upkeep, our maintenance. We eventually received a formal letter from the embassy to tell us that both our parents had been killed in the uprising that followed Dindic's assassination."

Jeanie paused to take a few sips of water. The truck driver had been generous to a fault with water bottles. As if he wanted them needing to urinate more often.

"I cried for days and nights and only stopped because everyone shouted at me to stop my mewling." Jeanie hung her head but continued. "Helen had always wanted to be a model. She poured over American fashion magazines, and she went to London for training. She was beautiful and had always been careful to maintain her figure. She came back to visit me even though her modelling jobs took her all over the country.

I finished high school in Dartmouth, and I was offered a scholarship to one of the British colleges. But my sister was against it and she and my cousin insisted I take a secretarial course instead. "Look at all the university graduates who don't have jobs. But any woman who can type will always find employment."

So I learned how to type and a few word processing programs while Helen became more in demand as a model. By the time I graduated my father's trust fund was getting low, and I think my cousin was anxious to get rid of me. Her husband was able to get both Helen and I sponsored to Canada on some humanitarian cause."

The truck and a passing car had a brief horn blasting contest and Jeanie was unable to compete. She shifted uncomfortably and Carrie suggested they do squats.

"It's cramped, I know, but we need some exercise." She got up to demonstrate and Jeanie joined in, somewhat tentatively. They collapsed after the count of twenty, and after deep breathing for several minutes Carrie asked,

"How many languages do you speak?"

"Serbian of course, a few Yugoslav dialects, German and some French."

"And perfect English." Carrie added. "Carry on."

"It wasn't hard for me to leave England. I was always treated as an inferior because I wasn't British, but Helen was so outgoing she fit in everywhere. She had always wanted to go to the States, but she agreed to Canada under the circumstances. I read a lot, mainly library books, so I knew there had been large migrations of Ukrainians in the late nineteen hundreds to Canada. It was very exciting--starting a new life in a young, big country. And with Helen, my favorite person in the world."

"And you met Peter Cummings?"

"Well, not right away. We went to Montreal because Helen was able to get a job modelling there. Oh, I should tell you about the boat trip. We sailed in the winter and the sea, the North Atlantic, was rough. Helen was sick the whole voyage, very, very sick, but for some reason I was not. I wandered the decks, freezing I might add, trying to find someone I could practice American or Canadian English with. I wanted to get rid of my accent, so I struck up a friendship with a Canadian sailor. And he taught me."

Jeanie smiled at the memory and Carrie wondered what else he had taught her.

"Our sponsors lived in St. Lambert, just off the island of Montreal. We both got jobs right away, mainly because we could speak French. Helen adored Montreal. She had men, both French and English, buying her gifts, taking her to dinners and dances. You know, the usual. I met Peter Cummings at a private club that one of Helen's admirers had taken us both to. Pete was charming. He devoted all his attention on me, not Helen. We dated, and it soon became a daily, or nightly event. After four or five months he wanted to get married. He was very persuasive, so we were married in a court, not a church. He and Helen had a big argument about that, but I didn't care. I wouldn't have to type any longer. Besides, Pete treated me like a queen, or tried to make me over into a queen. I went to elocution classes, and I took tennis, skiing and dancing lessons. Pete assigned Don to practice all these activities with me, even the elocution."

"You got to know Don pretty well," Carrie interjected to give Jeanie a break.

"We fell in love. He kept saying he was too old for me, but I thought I would always love him. It was Don who arranged for that portrait--the one you found in the attic." She made a face, "Pete paid for the commission, of course. I was a show-piece on Pete's arm and Don came with us everywhere we went—France, Italy, the Alps, even China."

"Has Helen seen the portrait?" Carrie asked.

"Yes, of course. Why do you ask?

"Just curious. Carry on, Jeanie."

"Well, Pete made a lot of business trips, and he usually took Don with him. But when he didn't…"

Carrie snorted, "'When the cat's away, the mice will play.'"

"Exactly. We tried to be very careful to keep our love secret, especially from Pete of course. Both Don and I had experienced Pete's terrible temper. But we were so much in love, and we became careless. And I became pregnant. Pete was ecstatic when I told him. He was going to have a son! He was bursting with pride and treated me with kid gloves. I convinced Don it was a little Cummings growing in my belly. I hated to do it, but I had no choice. For the baby's sake--you understand?"

Carrie nodded and said, "And Don?"

Jeanie snuffled, "It was awful to see Don so sad."

"Did you know whose child it was?"

Jeanie nodded her head vehemently. "Yes, I know he was Don's. Pete always had trouble getting it up, as you North Americans say."

"He was impotent?" Carrie was surprised. Cummings seemed like such a jock.

"Not quite. He wanted a son in the worst way. He had gone through a succession of mistresses trying. I think he married me because I was young and inexperienced. I lied to him about my periods when he tried to map out my fertility times on the calendar. You have no idea the lengths I went to trying to fool him. When we did have sex, he could sometimes produce a few squirts, usually on my stomach, which he rubbed into my vagina. Romantic, n'est-ce-pas?"

Carrie winced. Jeanie continued in a bitter voice,

"Pete paid no attention to the baby, and that worried me. He said he would spend time when 'the kid' could talk back to him. He always called him 'the kid', even though he was the one who named him "Joseph" after his own father. But he bragged about his son to everyone, and everywhere--even at business dinners."

"And Don?" Carrie asked. "Didn't he question the baby's parentage?"

"Don was terrific with Joey. For my sake I suppose. He even changed Joey's diapers, and he loved to rock him to sleep. He didn't suspect it was his because he had practically always used a condom. Besides, it's probably difficult to pick out your own features in a baby."

"You think?" Carrie was circumspect.

Jeanie nodded knowingly. "I don't know much about Pete's business except it involves pipelines and oil and gas. Right after Joey's birth he moved us all, including

Don, to Edmonton. We lived in a magnificent house in a beautiful neighborhood. Everything was fine until Joey started growing hair, red hair. It was just a light auburn fuzz, but even his little eyebrows were auburn. They seemed even redder against his pale skin and blue eyes. I kept hoping for summer when I could get him tanned. By six months he was the spitting image of Don especially when he smiled. And Pete noticed. Of course. He started spending more time with Joey, tickling his toes to make him laugh, and staring at him."

"Oh, boy," Carrie breathed. Her heart went out to Jeanie.

"Pete sent Don on a six-month round-the-world business trip and arranged for a Vancouver couple to adopt Joey. For a big price, I'm certain. I pleaded and pleaded with him, but he repeatedly told me that the baby was better off without me. I was too young, too immature, and a foreigner. He promised that I would be able to visit Joey when he was a little older. I became hysterical and he slapped me so hard my teeth rattled." Tears rolled down Jeanie's cheeks, but she swallowed and carried on,

"Pete and I slept in the bedroom across the hall from Joey's room. At about six months he was sleeping through the night until five or six in the morning. But the night before the Vancouver couple were coming to get him, Joey started to fuss about midnight. I got up to go to him and I noticed Pete was not on his side of the bed. And Joey wasn't in his crib. I heard footsteps going down the stairs and I ran. I caught up to them as Pete was opening the back door. I yelled at Pete, he slammed it shut, and opened the basement door. By the time I reached them Joey was screaming. Pete literally kicked me down the basement stairs."

"Jesus." Carrie whispered.

Jeanie started to sob and through her tears she finished her sad tale, "Over the years I have imagined Joey in all the stages of his life--taking his first steps, learning to talk, his first day at school. I read everything I could about Vancouver to help me envision Joey alive in my dreams."

Carrie was at a loss for words. Should she try to comfort Jeanie, but how? She was relieved when Jeanie blew her nose in the remnants of the tissue and started talking again,

"The rails to the basement stairs had always been a little shaky. I went sailing down the stairs headfirst. I must have grabbed at one of the metal spindles and pulled it loose because all I remember is lying on my stomach at the bottom of the stairs with a spindle jammed into my face. I know I passed out. The cleaning woman found me in the morning."

Carrie gulped and said, "You know that's assault, maybe even attempted murder. Cummings could go to jail for life."

Jeanie snorted, "Fat chance that will happen. He's filthy rich with connections."

Carrie, appalled, stared at her, "Surely in Canada money and power can't flout law and morality."

Jeanie shook her head, "Oh, Carrie. You think Canada is so special?" She took Carrie's hand. "But you are special. I've never told anyone this and you mustn't breathe a word about it. If Pete finds out, you know…"

"Don't worry." Carrie gave her hand a light squeeze. "I've got my own cross to bear with that monster. Tell me the rest."

"I told the people at the hospital that I had tripped and fallen down the basement stairs. Nobody doubted my word. Except the cleaning lady who found me. She kept asking about Joey, but somehow Pete shut her up." Jeanie got up to do a few squats and Carrie joined her in the dark. They sat on the foam and Jeanie resumed her sad tale,

"A month later he sent me on the plane to work in the kitchen of a private school in Ontario. What's that expression? Out of sight, out of mind."

"I know about that year," Carrie said. "I talked to Molly."

"You did?" Jeanie perked up. "Molly was always kind to me. Did she tell you about the two goons who took me away from there?"

Carrie nodded, "Where did they take you?"

"To a Toronto hospital for plastic surgery on my face. Where Pete put the fear of God into me if I ever spoke a word about my past. Anything in my past. If I did, I would never see my son again. He said the Vancouver couple were happy with Joey and agreed I could visit in a few years if I pretended to be a relative of theirs. But I could never tell Joey I was his mother. I would never be with him alone, just in case. And I would never see him again if I didn't go along with Pete's charade."

They were both silent as the truck powered into the black night, its engine emitting the occasional explosive charge. Until Carrie asked,

"Who paid for the surgery? Surely not Pete."

"He said I was covered by Ontario's health plan because I had worked for over a year at the college."

Carrie had her doubts. No health plan would cover the complete costs of something as complicated as reconstructing a damaged face. But if anyone could swing it, Peter Cummings could. "And you went back to typing?" She asked.

"Yes, Pete got me a job at Alcan, and I lived like a hermit until Marie found me."

Carrie leaned over and hugged her, "I am going to make sure you are safe from now on. My friends and I will see to it."

Jeanie said sadly, "I will never be free of that man."

Carrie dozed while Jeanie slept fitfully. The sun's rays peeped through the narrow slits and the truck slowed to a stop. They heard voices and the gurgling of gas as the truck was refueled. Carrie stood up in a crouch, but she could see nothing.

"You should do this too. Get the circulation going." She did a few squats and apologized when she passed gas. "Sorry. I didn't mean to foul the air even more."

Jeanie smiled and followed Carrie's example, except for the farting. She asked Carrie to relate her life story. Carrie said she was too tired, so they sat in silence, each with her own thoughts, dozing, until the truck rolled to a stop again.

After a little while the rear door slid up and the trucker said, "Here's some grub. I'm not stopping again, so if you drink too much, you'll just have to wet your pants." He honked his mirthless laugh and slammed the door down.

Carrie crawled to the smell of the pizza and brought back two tall coffees in a cardboard tray and a pizza box. "I'm famished. Do you like cream in your coffee, ma'am?"

"Very funny, but yes please." Jeanie opened the box. "Ham and pineapple, the cheapest pizza you can get."

"It's a wonder it isn't the kids' size," Carrie commented. "Wish I could see the sun." She chewed on a large slice and thought fondly of her pizza and beer dinner with Jim. "The damn pizza is making me thirstier, but I'm afraid to drink."

They talked about books they had read and movies they had seen as they chewed slowly, trying to prolong their meal break.

"Look," Jeanie exclaimed. "We've demolished the whole pizza."

"And the sun isn't beyond the yard arm yet,"

"What does that mean?"

Carrie tried to laugh, "It means it's not time for our afternoon cocktail."

"Oh, Carrie. I'm so grateful you're here. I'm sorry you are caught up in this, but it would be unbearable to be alone. Here."

Carrie smiled, thinking that Jeanie's language revealed her extensive reading and said, "Hey, I asked for it. My mission was to find you." Carrie wondered for the umpteenth time what was in store for them. If they didn't get out of this truck safely

Jeanie would be much worse off than if Marie had left her pounding on a keyboard in Outremont. Or was it Montreal? It must be at least twelve hours now they've been in this moving box. Maybe fifteen? A long way from thirty-seven.

Jeanie sniffed at the drinks, "I don't think we should drink the coffee. What if he put something in it?"

"You may be right, and I hate cold coffee." Carrie giggled. How ridiculous is that? Cold coffee. Hot coffee. I'm getting dippy...

She tossed the empty pizza box towards the back, and they carefully stored the coffee between two tight boxes, squashing the thin cardboard mugs so that they overflowed filling, the small space with its delicious aroma.

They talked and dozed, did some squats and arm exercises, then repeated the routine until they were bored and tired. It had been dark for a while and they both needed a pee break, despite having eschewed the coffee. They finally dozed off sitting up, their arms linked, and their hands entwined.

Sirens, harsh and piercing, split the air. The air brakes squeaked as the truck slowly stopped. They heard the driver arguing, then yelling, and suddenly the rear door slid back. Jim, flanked by two RCMP, held out his arms.

Carrie jumped down into them and hugged him as if she would never let him go. He held her and whispered, "Carrie, Carrie". He stroked her dirty, greasy hair until his hand found the dried blood. He looked at his hand over her shoulder. "You have a mammoth lump there. Is that blood?"

"I bumped my head. No big deal." She was conscious of Jeanie's voice behind them, saying over and over "I'm fine. I'm fine" to male and female questioners. Carrie released her strangle hold on Jim and looked sheepishly at the two RCMP standing on either side of Jeanie.

"Get your f...... hands off me!" Two other RCMP dragged the yelling truck driver to a squad car.

The two women looked at each other and smiled but neither one could laugh at the trucker's predicament.

Within minutes Carrie and Jeanie were on their way to the Royal Alexandra Hospital in Edmonton under a police escort. Jim followed in his truck. Three hours later, with five stitches in her head, Carrie lay in a dazed state. A tired, wan Jeanie, slouched in the stuffed chair opposite her bed, waved a hand,

"We made it, Carrie."

Carrie nodded and tried to smile. Jim, his deep-set eyes still worried, came to sit on the side of her bed. She reached out a shaky hand to smooth his unruly eyebrows and said,

"Here we are again, Jim."

Chapter 35

By Tuesday Carrie was fit to be tied with the damn hospital, the incessant beeping, the constant medical call-and-response, the nurses hollering to one and another, and irritable patients complaining constantly. Not to mention the terrible food. When Jim arrived for his daily visit, she pleaded with him,

"Get me out of here. Please Jim, before I lose my mind."

"Me? I don't exactly have any pull in this hospital." Noticing her disappointment he sighed, "Okay, I'll give it a whirl." He brushed the back of his hand against her cheek and headed for the door, but she stopped him,

"How's Jeanie? Is she okay?"

"We've got her hidden. She's fine. I can't say anymore here, you know that." And he was out the door.

Carrie read her book, worked another crossword, drummed her fingers against the tray and stared at the white walls.

Jim rushed in five minutes before the end of visiting hours. "You're out of here tomorrow. That's the best I could do. Can you survive another night?"

"Oh, Jim, thank you." She could have hugged him but stopped herself from holding out her arms.

"But" he warned, "You can't go home. You can come to mine in Fort Saskatchewan with the proviso that I hire a full-time nurse. They convinced me that you need to be under observation because of your concussion."

Carrie groaned and complained about the cost but he assured her his company medical plan would cover everything. Her quizzical eyebrows shot up. He read her dubious thoughts, laughed and said,

"I'm the boss, remember?"

"Your house is going to be very crowded. Is your mother still there?"

"Yes and no." Jim pulled a chair closer to Carrie's bed. "She's staying with Aunt Lottie at the moment. And so is Charlie. He wants to play with Tess constantly even though he's still recuperating from that vaccine. We thought both Mom and Charlie would be better off at Aunt Lottie's. So there's lots of room for you, and Tess knows you now, so she will be your guardian angel."

"Oh, okay." She tried to hide her disappointment at not seeing Charlie. "Aunt Lottie and Alvena? Can they handle my dog? Charlie is so--"

"Charlie is having a ball," he interrupted. "And those two elderly ladies are delving into Pete's past. They've found the old assault case against him that was dismissed. Aunt Lottie has even assembled most of her old investigative team." He bent to kiss Carrie before she could start firing questions, and said, "Mom and Alvena love having Charlie-- they argue about who will feed him, whose turn it is to walk him. His water bowl is always filled with fresh water. I lecture them every time I see them about restricting his treats, but neither listen to me."

Oh, boy," Carrie breathed, and let the side of her head fall back against the pillow. "I wish I could tell you he'll protect them, but he barks at strangers with his tail wagging."

The piped voice announcing the end of visiting hours cut off her words and Jim stood and pressed the big toe of her good leg. "Try not to worry. Have the nurse let me know when you're ready for pick up tomorrow. Ciao." At the door he turned to wave.

....

Twenty-four hours later, they were sitting in front of his picture window, eating take-out meatballs and drinking beer.

She took a big gulp and grinned at him, "This sure goes down a lot better than the last time we were here. When does my nursemaid arrive?'

He glanced at his watch, "In two hours."

"She's staying overnight?"

"Well, yes, Carrie. Round the clock nursing care, remember? I've moved down to the basement and cleaned up my bedroom for her. Another helping?"

"It was great but I'm full," she patted her stomach and yawned. "A full-time nurse seems excessive. I'll be sound asleep when she arrives. At least you'll have someone new and different to entertain you tonight."

"Yeah?" He shook his head. "I'll be getting caught up at the plant."

In the next week Jim made time to visit Jeanie at Slim's. To indulge Carrie's worries, he used circuitous routes each time in case Pete was having him watched. He became the courier of their letters to each other because email was too traceable. Carrie was often asleep when he got home, and he refused to wake her. He arrived at four thirty on Friday and she jumped at his offer of dinner at the Alberta Hotel. The nurse objected volubly and went on and on about the dire results to Carrie's head wound if she went.

Jim, his mouth set in a firm straight line, broke into the nurse's diatribe, "Enough of your verbal diarrhea." He pulled out a leather folder, scribbled a cheque and handed it to her saying, "We won't need your services any longer." He put the folder back in his breast pocket, "This should cover everything. Get your things and I'll show you to the door."

Carrie was still chuckling as they sat across from each other in the Alberta Hotel's bar. To be sipping Oyster Bay sauvignon blanc away from the prying eyes and ears of her nursemaid--what heaven! She asked about Jeanie.

"Let's order first." He added, "I'm told the safest item on the menu is steak."

"Sounds great. Medium rare, please." Carrie said settling back with her wine.

He took their orders to the bar, and answered her when he sat down again, "Jeanie is okay. She seems content with our arrangements. I know you wanted a doctor to check her over, but the best I could do was get her blood and urine tested. And I swear old Slim has fallen in love with her. But--"

"Oh, no!" Carrie frowned, "Not another but."

"Even though Pete is fully occupied fighting the court order..." He waited while the table of five rowdy men next to them got up and left before he continued, "Dave and I think we should move her."

"Dave?"

"Yes, Dave and I have been on the blower every day for the last week. He flew in yesterday on Pete's orders. Although Dave can only practice law in Ontario, Pete wants him here to help the two lawyers he's hired get up to speed." He nodded to the bar and got up, "Our steaks are ready. Must be the speediest service in Alberta."

Carrie gazed at the mixed crowd in the bar while she waited for Jim's return. Although a few old grizzles winked at her, she could not identify any suspicious looking characters. But what the hell did she know? Any one of these men could be Pete's informant.

Jim set down the two plates of simmering steaks and mounds of French fries, "Dig in. Do you want more wine?"

"No, thanks. This looks absolutely marvelous." She smiled at him as she sliced into the steak.

"Beats hospital food, does it?" He watched her for a moment before attacking his meal and said, "Dave and I think..."

"And speak of the devil." Jim stood up to shake hands with Dave who then bent to kiss Carrie. She was so surprised she didn't have time to present her cheek and he took advantage of her slightly open mouth. She broke away laughing,

"Dave, you are unreformable." But what a marvelous smoocher!

"And you are looking gorgeous, as usual, in spite of that ugly plaster in your hair." He had turned her head gently and let his fingers linger on her cheeks and neck. She sank back, embarrassed, and asked him,

"How did you get to the Fort, Dave?"

"Taxis. Terrible drivers. I thought I was in Quebec." He turned to pull a chair over to their table. "I ordered what you two are having on my way past the bar. It better be edible," he warned, looking skeptical. "Because I'm famished."

Jim pulled his chair closer, "Can you two eat and talk? We have a lot to discuss."

"Couldn't you have found a quieter venue?" Dave glanced with distaste at the bar's clientele, "How can we discuss anything in this place?"

"Well, at least we won't be overheard." Carrie's facetious remark evoked an amused smile from Dave, but Jim remained serious and his voice grim.

"Jeanie has told me a little of what happened between she and Pete, but it was pretty disjointed. Slim keeps her hidden--she works in his little kitchen making sandwiches and stuff, but she's not invisible. She's kind of cute and the bar regulars are kind of horny. We're hoping she'll be okay while Dave and I are away for a few days searching for her child, her boy."

"You--" Carrie gasped.

"I know," Jim interrupted. "Probably another wild goose chase. My cleaning lady and her husband are going to stay here with you, okay?"

She nodded dumbly as Jim continued, "We're starting with the night watchman at the property next to Pete's. Dave's staff came up with a telephone number, and he's agreed to talk to us tomorrow."

The barman came over with Dave's steak, and the three of them concentrated on eating until Carrie put down her fork and knife and demanded,

"Why this night watchman?"

Dave leaned forward, "Because we found out he had phoned in something unusual the night Jeanie disappeared. We talked to the security company he worked for, and they confirmed that it's part of their protocol--their security guards must report everything that occurs on their shifts, especially anything out of the ordinary. This particular guy, this night watchman, was guarding the property adjacent to Cummings Consortium and he reported a strange occurrence at Pete's tailings pond. The security company disregarded it because it was not in their jurisdiction. But considering the place, Pete's property, and the time--the night Jeanie disappeared, Jim and I think it's worth investigating. You've listened to Jeanie's sad tale. Can you think of anything that could help us when we interview this night watchman?"

"I'll think about it. When do you leave?"

"We're aiming for eight a.m.," Jim answered. "I wish you could check on Jeanie, but that's too dicey." He paused and looked into her eyes, "You can help by delving into Troy's past and current activities."

Jim's abruptness should not have surprised her, but she was speechless as Dave, grinning at her open mouth, followed up on Jim's request, "Find out everything you can about Troy's movements in the last few months. Check his gas mileage, his expense accounts. And Susan, is she funded by American anti-pipeline or environmental groups? Check all her activities, the names of people she's talked to, seen and met with--"

Carrie's head jerked up in anger as she interrupted him in a loud voice, "Susan and Troy are my friends and business associates. Do you really think I would go so far as to snoop into their personal lives?" Her sudden anger was fortified by the frustration of being controlled by these two men. How had she let that happen?

"Carrie," Dave's voice was urgent. "This is critical. Pete's on the warpath. He's hired extra staff to fight that court order to drain his tailings pond, which, by the way, he blames on you. We hope he doesn't know about Jeanie yet, but--"

"Oh God! Jeanie, Alvena and Aunt Lottie! They're all in jeopardy!!" Carrie felt as if the world was collapsing around them. "And Charlie. Do you expect him to protect two elderly white-haired ladies?"

Jim leaned forward, "Perhaps. Dogs are strange that way." He sprinkled more salt on his fries. "We're more concerned about your safety now than Jeanie's, or my mother's. That receptionist at the entrance to your building won't be able to stop Pete, and it takes time and a good reason to get any police surveillance. Dave doesn't think the couple I hired are much in the way of protection. We need to get you out of town. Right now."

"Out of town?" Carrie hated her shrill voice and she lowered it a few decibels, "I've got Tess here, and you--"

"Don't say it," Jim shook his head. "I'd be pretty useless against Pete or his so-called assistants." He nodded at Dave, "We thought of my mother's but--"

"Are you crazy?" Carrie did shout this time. "You would put her in Pete's path?"

"No, Carrie." Jim's weary tone made her wince. "Of course not. I just told you I'm worried about her, and now Aunt Lottie. We'd like to move you, and perhaps the two of them, to an apartment here in the Fort."

Dave placed his hand over hers, "How about it, kiddo? It's the best we could come up with at the last moment."

She snatched her hand back, "I am not a "kiddo", and I have to be at work tomorrow to organize--"

"No!" Both men objected in unison. After a long silence, Dave went to the washroom, and Carrie and Jim finished their dinners. They were quietly discussing Alvena and how to persuade her to return east when Dave rejoined them. He listened but did not offer an opinion.

On the drive back to Jim's, Carrie did her best to convince the two men that she was back to normal. She told them about the stretches and exercises she'd done after the nurse went to bed and said, "I feel so much better after that steak dinner."

Jim nodded, "Let's wait and see how you feel tomorrow morning. Dave, how about staying at my place tonight?"

"Thanks, but I need to rent a decent car for tomorrow."

Jim chuckled, "I'll get you a good car for tomorrow."

"Okay. At least I have my bag here, but I don't want to crowd you--"

"Look, if it's beneath your dignity to sleep in my basement you can have my bedroom. I cleaned it up for Carrie's nursemaid."

"Who you fired." Dave laughed softly and added, "Wish I'd seen that!' He grinned at Jim and said, "I always carry a mickey to help me through nights in questionable locations." He winked at Carrie, "How about it, Carrie? I'm happy to share it with you down there in the dungeon."

"No, thanks. I'm a white wine girl. Even though that dungeon has real character," Carrie said in all seriousness.

"Yeah?" Dave's eyes narrowed in suspicion.

"Yes," Carrie explained, "It's where Jim's dog sleeps at night."

Dave grimaced, "Whatever."

Chapter 36

Carrie jerked awake to Tess's long, raspy tongue stroking her face. The bedside clock read 4:45 am and she whispered, "Tess, what are you doing up here?"

The dog's jaws encircled Carrie's upper arm and gently pulled, using the 'soft mouth' technique for retrieving a downed grouse. Jim's hours of training Tess had paid off.

"Okay, okay. I'm coming." She dressed quickly as Tess paced. Shushing the dog's whining she threw on her ski jacket and shoved her bare feet into her boots. Grabbing the leash, she let them both out the side door into the back yard. Her teeth chattered in the cold morning air, and she muttered to the dog, "All right, girl. Do your business and let's get back where it's warm."

But Tess did not pee on her favorite poplar tree. She sniffed the fenced-in area quickly then trotted to the gate where she waited for Carrie. The dog's eyes were expectant and bright in the yellow beam from the streetlight as she looked back at this friend of her master's. The breaths from her open mouth formed a misty halo in front of her muzzle.

"What's the matter with you?" Carrie hissed as she opened the gate. Tess made a bee-line for the school playground. Carrie ran after her, stuffing the leash in her pocket. Surely no dog of Jim's would pee in the playground's sand. Keeping her eye on Tess, Carrie pinched her buttocks into one of the heavy rubberized swings, dug her toes into the sand and pushed off. She watched Jim's dog as she pumped higher and higher. The cold breeze on her face and in her hair brought her to a complete state of wakefulness.

Tess seemed lost in a geography of smells as she covered the school's yard. But she kept returning to one particular caragana bush. She poked her head underneath it, backed away, repeating the sequence over and over.

"I should check out that bush," Carrie murmured and stretched her legs out straight to slow down. She gasped when, at the apex of her next backward arc, she was grabbed around the waist and pulled roughly backwards out of the swing.

"Gotcha!" A muffled male voice spoke against her hair as a big hand covered her mouth and a powerful arm encircled her. Her back was crushed into a fat belly and a hard chest. His lips tickled her ear when he said, "We need to talk and--"

His words became a curse when Tess threw herself at him knocking both he and Carrie to the ground. The big dog latched her jaws around the back of his neck securing his neck in the sand. She stood, growling deeply, over the man's squirming body, and waited for the "kill" command.

Carrie scrambled to her feet, grabbed Tess's collar, and hesitated. She was enjoying the sight of her attacker's desperate struggles under the big Shepherd's body. She reluctantly pulled the leash out of her pocket, clipped it on Tess's collar, and stepped back pulling the snarling dog with her. It was Pete. She caught a glimpse of his profile before he adjusted his skewed mask and toque. He got to his knees and frantically pawed his bulging hip pocket. Tess lunged forward and clamped her jaws around his throat this time. The leash went taut and Carrie almost lost her balance. Pete seemed to be frozen momentarily in fear. His eyes were wild as he stared at her over Tess's head, and his body was rigid, as if he was afraid to move an inch under the dog's teeth.

Carrie's common sense trumped her hatred of this man. She yanked the leash, giving Tess the proper order, "Tess! Off!"

Tess raised her head, released her hold on Pete's throat and let Carrie pull her back. Pete rose quickly to a kneeling position and fumbled in his back pocket. Carrie caught a glimpse of the barrel of a pistol. She let go of the leash, leapt forward and brought the heel of her boot down on his wrist. He yelped. The gun fell out of his hand and Tess's jaws encircled Pete's throat again. Carrie snatched up the gun. She stared at it for a second before slipping it into her jacket pocket. She picked up the leash and with two hands on its handle she backed up repeating the "off" command until she was six feet from Pete. Tess was much closer to him. She snarled, her white teeth glistening in the dark, her jaws dripping saliva as she strained at the leash.

He slowly stood up. His eyes never left Tess as he brushed the sand off his jeans and jacket. "You were ready to let that damn dog chew me up." His voice was gravelly, guttural.

"It was tempting," she admitted.

"We need to talk," he said again, his eyes on Tess.

"Yeah, with a gun. Stay right there." She tightened her hold on Tess. "You can remove the camouflage. I know who you are, and I have absolutely nothing to discuss with you." She wanted, in the worst way, to run back to the safety of Jim's house. But if she kept Pete talking long enough there might be a chance to corral him if help came by. Too many "ifs". Why the hell weren't Jim and Dave up and looking for her? But it was very early. Still dark. She grasped the handle of the pistol in her pocket and pointed it at Pete.

Keeping Tess on a short lead and the gun on Pete she shuffled sideways to the bank of seesaws and, letting go of the leash, flipped each one down. She pointed the gun to the last seesaw in the row she said in a stern voice, "Sit there."

She hoped she sounded more confident than she felt. Tess, thinking the command was for her, followed Pete to the seesaws. Carrie thought briefly of Aunt Lottie and her so-called "resources". Could Jim's aunt help her bring down this man? Pete hesitated, glanced at Tess, and, with loud grunts, lowered himself down to ground level.

Peter Cummings was a big man and he looked very uncomfortable, his knees higher than his nose, as he balanced on the small seat with one hand in the sand. He reached backwards to grab the handle of the seesaw for balance. Four downed seesaws and a drooling German Shepherd separated him from Carrie.

She waved the pistol and said, "So. Talk."

The black night was quiet except for the regular churning of a motor in the distance. *From Jim's cobalt plant?'* Carrie wondered. The sun would not be up for another couple of hours, but kids went to school in the dark at this time of the year. They'd be here soon. Maybe.

"For Christ's sake stop waving that gun around," Pete wheezed. He shifted his buttocks and said, "I have a deal for you. You get that court order to drain my tailings pond rescinded and I promise I won't press assault charges against you for dumping me into that filthy pond on the golf course."

"Promise?" She scoffed. "Do you even know what the word means?"

"I will put it in writing, if that's what you want." Hatred suffused his frowning face as he added, "I'll even get it notarized."

She detected no trace of pleading in his words. It was as if he was certain she would meet his demands. Holding the gun at her side she asked, "Why are you so concerned about your tailings pond? What lethal chemical are you dumping?"

"Just do it, b…" He caught himself from saying "bitch".

She played for time and said, "The many sloughs in the province are attracting heightened regulatory scrutiny. The Environment Department has ordered the draining of all sloughs that have the potential of seeping effluent into the North Saskatchewan River. Your company is near the top of the list. Perhaps because yours is the most toxic?"

"I know you instigated that order." He scowled up at her, "It was issued under your watch, and don't try to deny it."

She shrugged and asked, "Where is Jeanie's child, Joey? The baby you stole from her after you pushed her down the cellar stairs."

He jumped up and stepped back. Tess snarled and bared her teeth. Carrie knew that if Pete had the gun, Tess would now be dead.

"Jeanie." His voice was bitter. "I should have sent her back to that shit country she came from." He paused, glanced at Tess and with a menacing scowl said, "Get that court order rescinded or Jeanie's messed up face will be the least of her worries."

Carrie shivered and tried to loosen her grip on the gun. She had been holding it so tightly her fingers were numb, but she said, "The crews and equipment should be on site in a matter of days. Depending on what they find is there a possibility that you could end up in jail with a big fine?"

"You bitch! Rescind it or else!" Pete pulled a knife from his pocket. Carrie screamed, and Tess scooted under the metal seesaw support to come up behind him. Pete whirled on the dog. Carrie raised the pistol, released the safety and stretching both arms straight out she pulled the trigger. When she opened her eyes, Pete was grinning and Tess was crouched stock still behind him.

"You missed!" Pete's grin evaporated when Tess barked and lunged at him. He ducked sideways and Tess sailed past him. Pete almost tripped but recovered quickly and ran in the opposite direction. Tess slid to a halt, turned, but was indecisive when she heard Jim and Dave's shouts,

"Carrie!"

"Tess!"

"Over here!" She cried and realized her shot had gone wild. Tess started to run after Pete, but Carrie called her, "Tess! Come! Come!"

She dropped the gun, sank to her knees and hugged the excited dog. She was so sure she had shot Tess that she sobbed in relief into Tess's thick, furry neck.

Dave reached her first. "Carrie, why are you out here in the dark?" He lifted her and wrapped her in his arms. "Don't cry, sweetheart. What happened?"

Jim, fending off his exuberant dog, picked up the pistol. "That was a shot we heard!"

Carrie pushed herself away from Dave, snuffled, wiped her nose on her sleeve and said. "It was Pete. He's going to hurt Jeanie and…"

"Let's get him," Dave yelled. He started to run towards the edge of the playground but they all heard a car's engine start up on the next street over.

"Too late," Carrie said. "He's long gone." She stared at their bare feet and chests, "Oh my God! You must be freezing!" She grabbed an arm of each of them, and with Tess galloping ahead, they ran to Jim's house.

"I could do with that Glenfiddich now," she said to Jim as she ducked under his arm holding the side door wide open.

Dave showered while Jim phoned the police. He poured her a scotch and disappeared upstairs to dress. She sat in front of the picture window sipping her neat scotch and listening to Tess gobble down her reward of kibble.

Two squad cars screamed up to the playground. She finished the scotch, stood up and grabbed the arm of the chair for support. Scotch on an empty stomach was not a good idea, but she had to talk to these RCMP. She stepped outside and quickly realized balance was no longer a given as she teetered across the street.

Barry saw her coming and hurried to steady her. She grabbed his meaty arm for support and pointed to the caragana bush, demanding they search underneath it. He hesitated, and she knew he was skeptical. He could probably smell the scotch on her breath. But he signaled his cohorts and they flitted their flashlights around and under the bush.

Moments later Barry held up a handful of dog treats. "Greenies," he announced, dropping them into an evidence bag. "We'll have them tested in the lab."

"How much do you want to bet they're filled with poison?" She knew greenies were used by dog owners to get meds down their throats, like pills ensconced in peanut butter for kids. "With potassium cyanide, maybe?" she added.

Barry nodded and smiled at her indulgently. He took her arm and escorted her back to Jim's house just as Jim and Dave appeared on the porch looking for her.

"The lady will explain," Barry said in answer to their questions. He joined the other RCMP officers who were scouring the whole of the school yard now.

"Come and eat," Dave said. "And tell us over coffee. You look like you need it." He disappeared into the kitchen and called, "Somebody set the table."

Ignoring Dave, Jim put his arms around her and said, "Let me hold you 'til you stop shaking." She leaned gratefully into his body.

Carrie felt quite sober sitting with Jim and Dave over a breakfast of eggs, toast and bacon. She took small bites with lots of coffee and told them every detail of her encounter with Pete. When she sat back, coffee mug in her hand, Dave warned her,

"Finish your breakfast, old girl. Those men in blue are going to quiz you like there's no tomorrow."

"Their dress uniform is red," Jim commented.

Dave was right about the questioning. By the time the RCMP left, Carrie's throat was parched from talking. She had to explain who Jeanie was, but she kept it brief. She knew they could not understand Pete's threats, but they certainly knew who Peter Cummings was. Before leaving they advised her to hire a lawyer.

"Jesus, Carrie," Jim said. "We can't leave you alone for a minute." He put his arm around her, but she pulled away and asked him, "Jim, I have a favour to ask of Aunt Lottie, but it may be an unreasonable one."

"Let's hear it," He sat down at the table and Dave poured more coffee.

"Do you think Aunt Lottie could use her influence to speed up the execution of that court order to drain Pete's tailings pond? Or prevent Pete from getting it rescinded?"

Jim thought for a few moments. He pulled out his cell phone and said, "We can only try." He greeted his aunt and said, "Here's Carrie. She'll explain."

Carrie gave Aunt Lottie a brief precis of her encounter with Cummings and the court order to drain his tailings pond before she said, "I know he may be able to use all his connections to get the court order delayed, or even rescinded, but can you use your resources to counter him and get it speeded up?"

Aunt Lottie said immediately, "Let me think." Several seconds later she said, "Carrie, my dear, you absolutely must be free of this human gorilla. If you think there is something incriminating in that pond, I will see what I can do." She paused. "Perhaps Alvena can help too. She has a different set of resources. Do you have a lawyer, dear?"

Carrie hesitated and Aunt Lottie jumped in, "I'll phone mine. We'll get you set up. Ready to do battle."

Jim, Dave and Carrie high-fived and Jim repeated himself, "You can't be alone, Carrie. You could come to the plant with me for the day."

"Or I could stay here with Tess and sleep," she countered.

"No!" Dave and Jim said in unison, and Dave added, "Come with me, old girl. You can sleep in the car. I'm meeting the night watchman and his wife in a few hours. The Padoroskis. You may think of questions that I don't have in my arsenal."

"Good plan," Jim said as he cleared the dishes. Tess stood up, expecting leftovers.

"You just need me to drive," Carrie grumbled.

"No, you're off the hook. I found a driver's license," said Dave with a wink.

She smiled, laughing was beyond her capabilities at the moment, and asked, "Can Tess come with us?" She was bonded to the dog now.

"I suppose," Dave grumbled.

Chapter 37

Tess was delighted to be included. Her tail thumped against the back seat of the Chev Jim had provided from his company's rented fleet of two. They headed west to the bridge crossing the North Saskatchewan River. Behind them the warm orange glow on the horizon was burning off the late autumn fog, promising a sunny day. Carrie snuggled down into the front seat and closed her eyes, but Dave placed a folded map in her lap and said,

"I know the way to the bridge, but you'll have to direct me from there."

She sighed. So much for a snooze. She sat up, unfolded the map on her knees and asked. "No GPS with this car?"

Dave searched the dash and replied, "Doesn't look like it."

When they turned onto the approach to the bridge, Dave glanced back and swore at Tess, sliding happily on the maroon leather seat,

"She'll probably leave scratches on that leather, if not tears," he complained.

"It's only a rental," Carrie said dismissively as the car glided smoothly down the ramp. She squinted at the squiggles on the map and said, "God, you're a terrible writer." After finding the red tick that marked the Padoroski, farm just beyond Redwater, she struggled to read Dave's handwritten instructions. Several minutes passed before she looked up and cried, "Turn here!"

"I'm right beside you, old girl." Dave backed up and muttered under his breath when he saw the narrow dirt road. It bisected a small field of harvested corn and a sparse pasture where a few Jersey cows stared at them with their dull, listless eyes. Dave fought the wheel around the potholes and bumps, and finally the car crested a small hill. They gazed down on a chorus of red roofs. The Padoroski farm and its outhouses stood out on the flat prairie like a huddle of painted ships floating on still water. Dave parked in a cloud of dust in front of a small stone house with a bright red tiled roof.

"You'd better park around the corner," Carrie pointed. She tried to calm Tess who was almost giddy at the sight of the hens and chickens pecking casually around and underneath the porch.

"The car is going to be covered in shit," Dave muttered as he carefully maneuvered the car away from the house and parked out of sight of any living creature. Carrie spoke sternly to Jim's dog as she opened the back windows ten inches. They picked their way from the car towards the front porch trying to avoid mud puddles and strings of feces.

"Let's get the hell out of here," Dave said but Carrie pulled his arm. The mix of poultry moved casually out of their way.

The elderly couple greeted them warmly and led them into a small parlour where bookshelves and family photos covered the walls. Sheer white curtains blew in the light breeze from the two partially opened windows. The furniture was covered with brightly coloured doilies and afghans, which gave the room a decidedly cheerful atmosphere. Mrs. Padoroski insisted on serving them coffee and poppy seed cake. They sat balancing plates on their knees and steaming mugs in their free hands. Carrie stifled a giggle at Dave's obvious discomfort. After exchanging a few pleasantries Dave started firing questions.

They learned that Albert, from the Ukraine, and Constancia from Portugal, had fallen in love on the steamship to Canada fifty years ago. Free from parental objections, they had married when the boat docked in Quebec City. The Padoroskis now had two successful sons and four adorable grandchildren.

Albert put his fork and empty plate on the coffee table and asked in his near perfect English, "You want to know about that night back in two thousand and six? I am old and my memory is fading but I will try to answer your questions." He motioned for his wife to sit beside him on the love seat. Carrie and Dave sat on either side of them in two matching armchairs.

Carrie leaned forward, and before Dave had a chance to renew his assault on the old couple she said to them, "We do appreciate your seeing us here in your home on such short notice. It's on behalf of my friend who can't be here--"

"Why not?" Albert interrupted her.

She hesitated, "Because she's in hiding. From Peter Cummings."

Constancia sucked in her breath and her husband sighed, "So. The chickens have come home to roost." He smiled sadly at Carrie, "Is that correct? My English?" He waved his hand at the bookshelves, "I read English books all the time but--"

"It's perfect, Mr. Padoroski." Carrie reached over to pat his arm, "Can you tell us what you remember of that night?"

He looked at her kindly, "If I call you 'Carrie' you must call me 'Albert'."

"A deal." Carrie settled back and waited.

"It was a cold and windy night," Albert began, and Carrie tried to remember what English classic started with those very words. "The rain cut into my face like it was hail. I wanted only to get home to my warm bed and my Constancia, but I made my last round in that foul weather. My employer's property ran down to the river right next to the Cummings' tailings pond. I thought about skipping it just this one time. But I am not a shirker, and I knew my boss would ask about the level of the Cummings' tailings. He always worried about it spilling over onto his property. With all the rain, it needed to be checked, and Cummings never bothered to do it. I knew the way on the gravel path, so I did not need my torch, my flashlight. The wind was howling, and the trees were moaning." He glanced at Carrie who nodded encouragingly,

"Your English is excellent, Albert." She smiled and he went on,

"I approached it from the north and when I got near, I heard somebody on the other side of the pond. He was cursing--at the slippery mud or the rain, or both maybe. I switched on my torch just as a bulky figure threw a bunch of chains into the tailings. I knew it was chains by the sound. Why would anyone throw chains into that muck? I yelled at him, and my torch found him on all his fours." He looked inquiringly at Carrie.

"On all fours," she corrected him. "Go on." She glanced at Dave and suspected he was using his smart phone to record Albert's words. Wasn't that illegal without Albert's consent?

"On all fours," Albert repeated. "You know Alberta mud, it's like slime when it's wet. He had trouble getting up because he kept tripping on his long poncho. And the rain and the wind beat down on him. On both of us. I yelled again and he pulled up the hem of the poncho and ran. Fast. He went east. I was on the other side of the pond and there was no way I could catch up to him. I didn't hear a car start up, but I had my cap over my ears and the wind howled and the trees snapped--"

"Could you see the chains in the tailings pond?" Dave asked, obviously impatient with Albert's repeated allusions to the weather.

"No." Albert was certain. "I shone my torch around the surface, but chains would sink to the bottom, even in that thick sludge. A piece of cloth floated for a little while near the edge and then it disappeared too." Albert spoke sharply at his wife when she got up to open a drawer in an old armoire, "Constancia?" He stood up to restrain her, but he was too late.

Constancia held out a gold ring to Carrie who took it and exclaimed, "It's a blood stone. A man's." She bent down to read the letters in the dark green stone, "P.C. Peter Cummings!"

"Let's see. Don't jump to conclusions." Dave held out his hand and squinted at the ring, "You are right, Carrie my dear. As usual." He put the ring on the coffee table and said to Albert, "So you knew it was Peter Cummings who had thrown the chains into the pond. Do you think it was just a bunch of chains? Or were they holding something? Wrapped around another object so both would sink and disappear?"

Carrie glared at him. Now who's jumping to conclusions? Out of the corner of her eye she saw Constancia sweep the ring off the table into the apron that covered her knees. With her shaking, arthritic hands, the old lady bunched the cloth around the ring.

Albert shrugged, "Perhaps. I was lucky to find the ring. I went back the next day to check on the other side of the pond and this ring was face down in the wet mud. The gold on the side under, the underside?" He waited for Carrie's nod. "That gold had been washed clean by the rain and it shone, it glinted when the sun broke through the clouds."

Carrie could see Constancia was getting weary, but Dave persisted his barrage on Albert, "Did you ever talk to Cummings about that night, or the ring?"

"Are you crazy?" The old man was angry now and he sat up straight. "We are poor people, as you can see. It was the only job I could get at the time. Cummings was rich. He could buy another ring." He looked sadly at his wife, "Constancia. Why did you not sell the cursed ring? You told me it would pay for Christmas presents for the grandchildren." His head drooped and he muttered, "What would he do if he knew I had his ring? Everybody said he was mean and powerful. I was afraid he could stop my job, even my pension."

Constancia took his hand and her chin wobbled. He stroked her wrinkled cheek and said gently, "Do not worry, my Constancia. Give me back that damn ring so I can throw it away. Far away." He tried to pick it out of her apron, but the ring fell to the floor with a loud clunk. "This time it will be lost forever." He reached down, but Dave was faster. He plucked it off the floor and held it up saying,

"Too late for that, I'm afraid. All ponds seeping into the North Saskatchewan River are scheduled to be emptied, one way or another." Winking at Carrie he put the ring in his pocket and his voice became lawyerly, "Although I need to keep the ring for now, it is not conclusive evidence, and you will have it back eventually. Don't worry. You'll be safe." He reached for his briefcase.

"Yeah?" Albert stood and took a menacing step towards Dave, "Easy for you to say. I want that ring."

Carrie quickly put herself between the two men and said to Albert, "My friend is a lawyer, an attorney. He can help you."

Both men backed up, afraid now of hurting a woman. Carrie took advantage of their reticence to cajole Albert. Dave joined her and they used all their powers of persuasion on the couple to give up the ring willingly. When they finally received Albert's consent, Dave wrote up a semi-legal document ensuring that they would not be implicated in any way for having kept the ring almost ten years.

The ring is legally yours. You found it." Dave told them. "I will make sure you get it back."

Carrie and Dave took their leave, the ring secure in a zippered pouch of Carrie's purse. Tess had been sleeping in the front seat. Her tail wagged against the steering wheel when she saw Carrie. Dave approached the car on the driver's side, clicked on the engine with his key fob and Tess's tail started the horn blasting.

Dave was livid. It wasn't until they were well on their way that Carrie dared to suggest they stop to let Tess pee at the side of the road. He pulled over immediately. When Carrie and Tess got back in the car he apologized for his anger and added,

"You are some gal. You had those two old guys eating out of your hand."

She shook her head, "The important questions have not been answered: Why did Cummings throw chains into the tailings pond?"

"Neither the ring nor the fact the guy was bulky is conclusive evidence it was Pete. A lot of men, or even women, could fit that description" said Dave, the lawyer.

"You're kidding," She stared at him, "How much evidence do you need?"

He gave up trying to explain the legal process to her because she closed her eyes. Exasperated, he expounded on her need for safety measures. They argued the rest of the way to Fort Saskatchewan; Dave finally conceding she was probably secure at the Federal Building in Edmonton. He pulled up in front of Jim's house, glanced at the back seat and exploded,

"Jesus Christ, I thought you'd cleaned her feet."

"Well, I tried. It's just Alberta black dirt from which has sprung riches galore."

He did not laugh. When she came back to the car after putting Tess in Jim's back yard and throwing her things in a bag, Dave was talking to Jim on his phone. He hung up and asked her,

"Do you have a safety deposit box?"

"Yes, but my bank is in North Edmonton. You have a plane to catch. I can do it--"

"Jim and I think it's the best place for that damn ring right now."

Carrie agreed, "Good idea. But we'll have to hurry. And how do we get Jim's car back to him?"

"He's made arrangements for it," Dave said shortly. "I need to concentrate on getting to that bank and staying within the speed limit."

They just made it before the bank closed. With the ring folded into a bank envelope in her safety deposit box, Carrie sighed in relief, but Dave was still worried about her and he announced,

"Jim and I think you should alternate public transit and your car to and from work."

"Why is the LRT, a subway, like safe?" She winced at her use of like.

Dave shrugged, "I agree it's a toss-up. We just feel you'll be safer if you don't keep to a regular schedule. Being in a crowd could be dangerous, but so is being alone. Make sure you go to and from work in rush hour. Keep your eyes open for Pete or his henchmen. We're assuming you know a few of them now. Look for anybody who is eyeing you unnecessarily."

"Oh, boy." Carrie banged her head against the backrest.

"Yeah, I know." Dave let his hand rest on her knee for a moment. "We're meeting Jim at the Mac again. He's got me on a later flight."

An hour later they were in the Harvest Room bringing Jim up to speed on the Padoroskis. After two glasses of wine Carrie could not keep her eyes open, so Dave said his farewells and Jim drove her home.

He walked to the door and said, "I'd love to tuck you in."

She barely had the energy to unlock her front door, but she gave him a tired smile and said, "Some other time."

Chapter 38

"Another Alberta government boondoggle," Susan commented when, four weeks later, Carrie met her in the atrium of the newly restored Federal Building.

"You don't like our living wall?" asked Carrie in surprise. "I think that waterfall and expanse of greenery look magnificent. It enhances the government's image and gives me a sense of peace every time I walk by."

Pointing to the signage above the door, Susan read, "The Alberta Federal Building. A true oxymoron." She headed to the revolving doors, waved to the receptionist, and called, "Thanks, Irma."

"You know Irma?" Carrie asked.

"Yeah. She recommended a bar at the corner of Jasper and 107 St."

"Let's get the LRT. It's faster." Carrie zipped up her ski jacket.

"Oh for God's sake. You travel that subway every day. The fresh air will be good for you."

Susan linked Carrie's arm in hers. The cold wind from the valley blew them up 108th Street to Jasper Avenue where they turned east. Dodging the few pedestrians and icy patches on the sidewalk, they hurried along Edmonton's main downtown street to the bar. It was filling up with the TGIF (Thank God it's Friday) crowd, but they found a small corner table. Susan sat facing the entrance (she never had her back to the door in any bar) and pulled out a twenty from her pocket (she never carried a purse). Waving it at the bartender, she motioned for two draft beers.

Carrie shrugged off her jacket and asked, "How was your trip to Prince George?"

"Okay. Your emails read like a suspense novel. I got so curious I've been doing my own research into Cummings Consortium." Susan blew on her cold fingers. "Prince George was fun. Those northern guys sure know how to drink." She paused, "But. I was only gone two weeks and all hell has broken loose here. And I'm not referring to your activities."

"Really? How so?" When Susan did not respond Carrie fidgeted, glanced at her friend's worried face, and cleared her throat. Before she could speak Susan declared in a tortured voice,

"My son is in love." Susan's shoulders sagged and she wrung her hands. Literally.

Carrie took in Susan's tragic face and managed to halt the maniacal laughter that threatened to erupt from her throat, "Sue, for God's sake, get real. Troy is a handsome young man. It was bound to happen sooner or later."

"Not this way." Her grumpy reply left Carrie at a loss for words. She wondered how many ways one could fall in love.

Susan's tone was flat and dejected as she carried on, "He's in love with your refugee, Jeanie."

Carrie's mouth fell open, "Oh my God! We had her hidden. How? What--"

The waitress set two foaming beers on the table. Susan thanked her, quaffed a swig of beer and said,

"Peter Cummings gave Troy big bucks to find Jeanie." Susan sighed, "And you gave him an extra two days off on the long weekend. Money inspires Troy like nothing else does." She swigged her beer. "Cummings' doctor has put him on a diet--he said Pete was a coronary waiting to happen--and Troy was anxious to escape his foul moods. You know how diets can make you crabby. Even Pete's chauffeur has quit, so Peter the Great is reduced to taxis or the subway. Troy had to show him how to use the LRT."

Carrie crowed in delight, "I just cannot imagine Peter Cummings on the LRT. But how the hell did Troy find Jeanie? We had her well hidden."

"So you thought," Susan gulped her beer, wiped her upper lip and replied, "Troy followed Jim to Slim's bar. He spent several evenings there drinking and watching and, lo and behold, Jeanie appeared. It was a busy night and Slim was short-handed. Jeanie was only too happy to help out at the bar rather than toiling as a kitchen maid. Better not tell Jim or Dave 'cause they're probably paying Slim a king's ransom to seclude her."

"But I bet Pete knows," Carrie said.

Susan was interested only in her son. She ignored Carrie's comment and continued, "Anyway, Troy said it was love at first sight. As if there is such a thing. Apparently, the two lovers kept your pal, Slim, in the dark. Even though they had several tete-a-tetes in the back room of his establishment."

"God," Carrie breathed.

"Yeah, well, He, the Big Guy in heaven, hasn't put in an appearance even though Slim was on his knees in the Catholic Church asking for guidance. He, Slim, not God, phoned Dave when he couldn't get hold of you." Susan gave her an accusatory glance.

Carrie pulled out her cell and noted the calls waiting for her response. "I never answer my cell at work." She flipped it shut and asked, "What about Cummings? Does he know Troy found Jeanie?" She was still having trouble getting her head around Troy and Jeanie as an item. And Don? Jeanie was supposed to be in love with him. What the hell is this girl up to? Where can we move her now?

"Apparently Cummings doesn't know. Yet." Susan answered. "No action from the enemy's camp. I'm afraid your big problem now will be hiding her again."

"I wondered why Troy has seemed preoccupied lately," Carrie mused. "When I think of it, he's had this stupid grin on his face ..." She shook her head, "But I've been too busy--"

"You're always too busy--for a civil servant anyway." Carrie bristled and Susan lowered her voice to a conspiratorial level, "Those two, Troy and Jeanie, are up to something. I'm sure of it. And I shudder when I think of some of the possibilities."

"The shit will hit the fan when Pete finds out his dollars went to initiate this love affair," Carrie said with an air of triumph.

"Exactly. Your guys should have moved her sooner," Susan accused her.

"Jim and Dave must know of this budding romance."

"Perhaps." Susan's finger played with the condensation on her beer bottle. "According to Troy, those two executive-types were never around--Jim busy, busy at his cobalt plant, and Dave back in Toronto. Which suited the two lovers just fine."

The outside door to the bar opened. A cold wind swept into the bar which resulted in yells and mutterings, "Shut the damn door!"

The freezing draft ruffled Susan's bangs when she turned to see who it was. Not bothering to mask her disapproval, she said, "Speak of the devil. Once again."

A folded newspaper smacked down beside Carrie's beer making her jump and explain, "Jim! What are you doing here?"

He bent to kiss Carrie's cheek as Susan asked in a tone that could have emasculated the toughest cowboy,

"How did you find us, wonder boy?"

Jim smiled, pulled out a chair, sat down and helped himself to Carrie's beer, "Good to see you, too." He tapped his index finger on the paper, "You must read this article." He shrugged out of his coat and added, "Irma told me where you were headed."

"Irma." Carrie picked up the newspaper, "How come everyone knows Irma?" She started reading the article circled in red, "Oh, no!" She brought the page closer.

"Yes," Jim signaled for three beers. "Some enterprising journalist picked up that Pete's tailings pond contained more than sludge and toxic chemicals. They found bones--the bones of a six or eight month old child."

Carrie gasped and Susan asked,

"How do they know they're human bones?"

Jim shushed her as the waitress placed three beers on the table and scooped up the empties.

"And?" Carrie managed to whisper as soon as they were alone again.

"And I phoned Barry. He was already on it." Jim swallowed a few mouthfuls of beer, "Ah! Tastes good. To continue, as you can imagine all hell is breaking loose in Pete's office. Dave is on his way back to Edmonton, and did you know, that the long lost Jeanie has been found, but is now missing? What else could possibly go wrong?"

"Oh, boy," Carrie handed the newspaper to Susan.

"Right." He placed his hand on her arm, "Where is she, Carrie?"

"I...I don't know." She glanced at Susan and added, "Probably with Troy."

"Troy?" Jim's eyebrows arched and Carrie's heart skipped a beat. He continued, "So, why hasn't Troy handed her over to Cummings? Or has he?"

"My son would never betray her!" Susan yelled, bar patrons stared, and Carrie gripped Susan's shoulder and shushed her.

The bartender frowned a warning at them. Susan shook off Carrie who tentatively reached for Jim's hand. He gave it up willingly. Stroking the hair on the back of his hand seemed to calm Carrie and she said,

"Here's the scoop, Jim. Jeanie and Troy are in love. If Jeanie is missing, your best bet is to find Troy."

Jim stared at her, burst out laughing and said to Susan, "Wedding bells next? Funny, but I just can't imagine you as a grandma."

Your friend Cummings may not find this so amusing. His ex-wife--"

Jim leaned towards Susan. Gone was any trace of humour as he scowled at her,

"I am not a friend of Peter Cummings. I am a business associate. Period."

"Okay," Susan waved him back, "Don't get your britches in a bundle."

"Sue! For God's sake!" Carrie noted Susan's flushed face and suggested they get something to eat. Freeing her hands, Carrie plucked a menu from an adjacent table and read out the entrées, "Standard Alberta fare--hamburgers, pizza, fries--"

"I'll have a hotdog and fries, "Susan's voice overrode Carrie's.

"Carrie?" He turned to her.

"Hamburger, loaded and fries, please."

"Good." Jim grinned, "Nobody on a diet here." He signaled to the waitress. Carrie and Susan found the loo, whose state did not encourage lingering or small talk.

The bar had filled to overflowing which raised the noise level by several magnitudes. The three of them made no attempt at small talk as they devoured their food and drank their beer.

Jim pushed his empty plate away and spoke loudly to be heard over the din, "If we ever get through these increasingly complex scenarios involving Pete, I promise you Carrie, the best dinner in Edmonton." He used his paper napkin to wipe the ketchup from his upper lip before he carried on, "You'd never guess who paid me a visit at the plant today." Not waiting for either of the ladies to guess he added, "Don, the boy scout who took care of you after your coyote attack. "

Carrie chewed voraciously and swallowed noisily, "And who works for Pete. I wish you wouldn't call him a 'boy scout' so derisively. He's--"

"He knows Jeanie has resurfaced," Jim interrupted. "After your experience at the playground, Carrie, and assuming your assailant was Pete, it's not surprising Don knows. He is following your movements, as is Pete, the difference being Don wants to help Jeanie in any way he can. He swears he's not acting under Pete's orders."

"And you believe him?" Suspicious Susan asked.

"Yes, I do. I tried to warn him that Jeanie is not the young innocent girl he once knew, and that she's experienced a whole world of heartache. I didn't need to mention her terror of Pete. This is what I've come to tell you and--"

"And?" Carrie echoed when he hesitated.

"I hate telling you this, Carrie, but…come closer." He put his arms around both their shoulders and drew them into a huddle. "Remember my RCMP friend, Barry? He finally got the lab results back on the greenies they found at the playground."

"What the hell are 'greenies'?" demanded Susan.

Carrie answered for Jim, "They're dog treats that vets and pet owners use to hide the pills the dogs need to take. It beats forcing the medication down their throats." She turned back to Jim, fearing the worst.

"They were filled with poison." Jim paused, "Barry told me the chemical name…"

Carrie's emitted a strangled sob, "A poison pill for Tess! So he could attack me! Is Tess, Oh God! Is Tess okay?"

"Glad you filled me in on the playground incident, too," Susan muttered.

"Tess is fine. You know she's trained to take food only from me, the vet and now you, Carrie. The RCMP roped off the whole area for two days. Parents and teachers were in an uproar, but the police are confident they've found all the greenies. Now they're searching all the parks in the city."

Jim dropped his hands, releasing the two women, and sat back. "Think of all the kids you saved by telling Barry about those greenies. How do we prove that Cummings filled them with poison? An impossible task." He gazed at Carrie, "But good on you for insisting Barry look at that caragana bush."

"If kids would actually eat the greenies, that is. Poor Tess. How many lives has she got left?" Carrie's throat thickened and she blinked away her tears. She loved that big dog almost as much as Charlie.

"If cats have nine lives, dogs should have more, right?" His smile was bleak as he continued, "One more thing. We're going to outfit you with a GPS monitor. It won't be cumbersome. Please don't argue."

"Me? Argue?" She attempted a grin. Jim had her back. Again.

"You." He stood up, "I should get going." He put his hand out as if to touch Carrie but thought better of it, "See you at dinner."

Carrie reached up and hugged him around his waist, "Watch out for Cummings. He may come after you, too."

She broke away but he grabbed her and kissed her long enough for her to kiss him back.

Susan snorted.

Chapter 39

Instead of waiting for Carrie at the bar for their Friday drinks, Jim met her at the Churchill LRT station. She hardly recognized him--his black fur hat was pulled down over his ears and halfway down his forehead.

"What kind of fur is that, rabbit?" She greeted him.

"My dear," He said haughtily, mimicking an unknown accent. "This is a genuine Cossack Ushanka hat. It belonged to my father. That's why it's a little ratty now."

"I think it looks very warm, and quite smashing. If only I could see your face."

"You don't know when you're well off." Looking down at her with his dodgy Jack Nicholson grin he took her arm, "Plans have changed. Sorry I didn't have a chance to phone you, but Aunt Lottie has invited the three of us to dinner."

"Really? That's wonderful!" She was so pleased she hugged his arm against her side. The bitterly cold wind blew against them as they hurried down 100 Street.

"I'm parked at the Mac and Dave is waiting in the bar." His voice was husky as he continued, "I want to thank you for looking after Mom yesterday."

"Jim. I didn't look after her. We had lunch together and toured the art gallery." Carrie pulled down her toque with one hand. "I switched my E.D.O. for a Thursday. Did she get off alright this morning?"

"Yep. She praised the bright blue western sky but said she didn't regret leaving the sub-zero weather for southern Ontario's rain and sleet." He steered her around an icy patch. "What's an EDO'?"

"Earned Day Off. You work an extra few hours during the week and get every fourth Friday off." She glanced up at him, "As an employer, Jim, you should get up-to-date, get with the game." She laughed at his surprise and wondered when and if Alvena would be able to work on her request for information.

They stomped their feet as they waited for the lights to change, their breaths puffing into the dark sky like white smoke. She moved automatically on the green, but he pulled her back as a black Buick ran the yellow. He gripped her firmly and they slid across the wide street to the entrance of the MacDonald Hotel.

Dave waved from a corner table and Carrie prepared herself for his enormous hug.

"You look marvelous." He embraced her as if he did not want to let her go. Holding her shoulders he gazed down at her face, "Pink cheeks, red nose running--"

"Enough!" Carrie pulled out a tissue. Her superabundant blow disintegrated the flimsy paper handkerchief. Jim looked away in embarrassment for her, but Dave bent over in laughter, his loud guffaws raising a few eyebrows.

Without sitting down Jim handed Carrie a napkin for her runny nose. He finished Dave's scotch in two gulps, threw Dave his coat, grabbed her hand and said, "Let's go. The five o'clock traffic will be terrible in this weather."

"Hey, man. Buy your own drink," Dave left a twenty on the table, put on his ski jacket and hurried after them. He caught up to them at the door to the parking garage and suggested to their backs, "Then why don't we grab a cab?"

Jim held the door for him, "We'd never get a cab at this hour of the day in the middle of a snowstorm. Lots of room in my truck."

"Yeah, right." Dave growled, but Carrie was thinking how great it was to be with these two again. Had it only been a few weeks since she had seen them? She had settled into a routine of working standard business hours and meeting her escorts to and from the Clareview LRT station, the northernmost Light Rail Transit station. It was only a two-block walk, but Dave and Jim had insisted she have protection both ways. Two hunky high school boys, anxious for the extra cash, escorted her in the mornings. A married couple who worked downtown and who lived across the street from Carrie accompanied her in the evenings. She was strictly forbidden to go out alone at night, not that she ever wanted to. Although she was fed up with the baby sitting, she knew regaining her freedom meant she would be constantly looking over her shoulder for Cummings or his goons.

They crowded into the truck's front seat and Dave commented, "You are my squeeze now, Carrie, in every sense of the word."

Jim reached over to pat her knee, "No way. Carrie is my squeeze." He chortled at her sour expression as he swung the truck around a curve. The back end slipped on the snow-covered icy road, but Jim skillfully manhandled his truck back into the right lane. Not before, however, evoking a few irritated honks from behind and beside them.

"Jesus!" Dave exclaimed. "You western drivers!"

Carrie eased the tension between the two men by asking Dave about his ski trip. They listened to his tale of woe about having to ski on barely covered Ontario hills instead of the abundant velvety snow of the Rockies.

Jim pulled into Aunt Lottie's street, "Almost there. Safe and sound."

"Tell me what I should know about Aunt Lottie," Dave said.

Carrie put her head back and sighed, "She's beautiful, old and perfect."

"You sound as if you're in love," Dave said as Jim parked and cut the engine.

Dave got out and turned to help her, "How's your leg?"

Without answering Carrie shimmied over the seat and jumped down from the high seat, making sure she landed on her good leg. "See? Right as rain."

Dave smiled tightly as he took her arm. With Jim leading the way, they walked up the narrow flagstone path to the front door.

Aunt Lottie opened the inside door before Jim had a chance to ring the doorbell. He gave her a gentle, loving hug as she kissed his cheek and murmured, "My boy."

Jim, embarrassed, started to introduce Dave but the dogs, from somewhere in the house, recognized his voice. Hearing their barks Carrie cried,

"Charlie!"

She whipped off her boots and rushed into the kitchen to smooch with the dogs, then brought the wiggling, happy pooches into the small living room. They all had to re-arrange themselves to make room as Carrie ordered Tess and Charlie to sit at her feet. Jim handed her a glass of wine, and Aunt Lottie demanded to know all new developments.

"All is quiet," Jim responded. "Except that Cummings has fired Dave."

Carrie gasped and turned to Dave who said, "That's why I'm back in Edmonton." He sipped his scotch and water. "Pete found out about our visit to the Padoroskis and made some inquiries. His knowing where I stand with regard to you, Carrie, makes helping you much easier." He hugged her shoulders and added, "Although I do expect a bit of a battle to protect my legal reputation here in Alberta."

"Oh, Peter Cummings is such an evil man," Aunt Lottie chimed in. Her winter-white hair was cut short in an easy-to-care-for bob, making her look chipper and younger. But her parchment facial skin, creased as a scrunched-up vellum ball, confirmed her age.

"Do you know that Troy and Jeanie are now a, um, a twosome?" Carrie asked.

"Yes, I did hear something to that effect." Aunt Lottie sounded mysterious. She paused and turned to Jim, "I know you asked me not to get involved, James, but Carrie was up against impossible odds, so..."

Jim groaned, "Aunt Lottie, what have you done now?"

Carrie noted the deep worry lines at the corners of his eyes before Aunt Lottie began talking again in an apologetic tone,

"Alvena and I put our heads together and came up with a plan. You are aware that because of all the volunteer work I've done over the years, plus the charities I have supported, I have garnered a few friends in high places. I referred to you, Carrie, when I contacted Bramwell, the former deputy minister of the Alberta Department of Environment. And although he is retired now, he was able to speed up the court order for the draining of the Cummings tailings pond." She paused to catch her breath.

Carrie cheered and shook her fist, thumb up triumphantly.

But Jim was worried, "Don't overtire yourself, Aunt Lottie. We've got all night."

Aunt Lottie smiled, "I may be old but I think I have a few useful years left. Bram was present when the Cummings tailings pond was drained. He was the first one to notice the bones and he helped dig in that muck for more. He knew the department would have to hand over the bones to the RCMP, and he also knew from experience that their lab would take months, if not years, to perform a forensic analysis on them."

Carrie sighed, "So Cummings will get away with it."

Dave gave her a sharp look, but Aunt Lottie shook her head and said, "Not necessarily. Alvena has contracted with a private lab in the US who specialize in DNA testing."

"I can't believe the RCMP released the bones to you and Jim's mom." Dave said.

"You are right, young man." Aunt Lottie smiled at Dave again. "But Bram had found a large piece of the skull and he also knows something about anatomy. He was able to pocket the petrous bone from the skull's inner ear. That's where DNA concentrates. Apparently."

Carrie gasped, Jim grinned, and Dave muttered, "Inconceivable."

Aunt Lottie threw and indignant look at Dave, and Jim moved quickly to mollify her, "We're all amazed at you, Aunt Lottie. Is there more?"

The elderly woman nodded, "Yes. Your mother took that little bone down to an American lab, somewhere in the state of New York."

"I wondered where she'd gone. She bought her airline ticket east without my help. How long will the DNA analysis take?"

Aunt Lottie picked up a legal envelope from the side table. "Here it is. Your mother is still down there but she emailed the results--conclusive evidence that Jeanie's DNA matches the DNA of the body in the tailings pond."

Carrie stood up, "And Pete? Can he be indicted now?"

"No," Dave said with emphasis. "Definitely not. The RCMP questioned him earlier, but he pleaded innocence, of course. I'd hoped they would put an investigator on the case, but that's a no go. When they asked Pete about the baby's whereabouts, he gave them the name and address of the couple who'd supposedly adopted the child. That turned out to be a dead end although the address was a valid one. The Vancouver RCMP are checking the past owners and adoption records, but I doubt they're giving it much priority."

"So he's free," Jim said bitterly. "To hurt Jeanie or Carrie, or both."

"Some justice system we have," Carrie grumbled. "Peter Cummings killed Jeanie's baby, almost killed Jeanie, and he gets off scot free."

"Look, old girl," Dave took her hand. "We're as frustrated as you are, but the evidence is just not conclusive. No witness has identified Pete as the one throwing what might have been a baby into the tailings pond."

Swearing under her breath, Carrie snatched her hand back and knelt beside Aunt Lottie. She bowed her head on the older woman's knee and murmured, "Thank you, Aunt Lottie, thank you. You are truly a wonder. Will you be my aunt too?"

Jim pulled out his cell and took a photo of the two of them. "For posterity. I don't know whether Barry will bless you or curse you, Aunt Lottie." He pocketed his cell and became serious, "Carrie. How are you going to tell Jeanie?"

"Oh God!" She went back to her chair and hung her head in her hands.

Dave held up a warning hand, "Come on, you two. How old is this Jeanie? She must be close to thirty. After years under Pete's thumb, she must be a seasoned woman by now."

"A seasoned woman? What the hell is that?" Carrie stood up again to pace the small room. She stopped in front of Dave, "Jeanie thinks her child is being happily brought up by loving adoptive parents." Her voice broke, tears swelled in her eyes and Aunt Lottie took over,

"James and Carrie, help me get the dinner on the table. "She struggled out of her chair and waved a hand at Dave, "You, sir, can keep these two dogs amused and out of the kitchen."

Carrie had to smile at the changes in Dave's expressions-- annoyance, confusion and finally, resignation. Jim rose to follow his aunt. He gripped Dave's shoulder on his way past and said,

"You can do this, man."

Dave sat up straight making ready for his charges. He called to Aunt Lottie, "I smell lamb cooking, ma'am. I will do anything for a dinner of roast lamb." And he muttered under his breath, "Even look after the damn dogs."

They made a pact to exclude Peter Cummings from their dinner conversation. When Carrie expressed her surprise that Aunt Lottie was able to get lamb and mint sauce as a take-out, Aunt Lottie responded,

"All it takes is money, my dear."

Their little dinner party was a convivial affair. Carrie relaxed under the influence of good white wine, Dave and Jim's repartees, and Aunt Lottie's down to earth comments. Jim and Carrie washed up while Dave put together the GPS, explaining how it worked to his fascinated hostess.

"We should get one for you, Aunt Lottie," Jim commented from the doorway, wiping a plate with a tea towel.

"Not on your life. I value my privacy," she retorted and added, "Poor Carrie."

Carrie smiled at her compassion and noticed one of Aunt Lottie's eyes looked a little milky. She bent down to kiss her cheek, "We must go and let you get to bed. It's been a wonderful evening. Thank you so much."

When they said their goodbyes Aunt Lottie murmured, "Come back soon."

As they settled into the front seat of Jim's truck Carrie fingered the small GPS on her inside collar, "If Jim is in Fort Saskatchewan and you're in Toronto, Dave, how can you possibly help me if Pete attacks me in Edmonton?"

"Jim and I both have tracking devices," Dave responded hugging her shoulders. "And I will be here until I get things sorted out with Pete. But…" He paused.

"But?" Carrie asked. Not another but.

"Pete's health must be failing. He's lost a ton of weight and he does not look well."

"That's what happens when an older person goes on a diet. The weight goes off the face first, but he's not that old." Carrie snickered, "About the same age as me, I suspect."

Chapter 40

Four days of thawing, followed by freezing rain, made for treacherous walking and driving, in addition to dashing every kid's hope for a white Christmas. Jim phoned to say they were pulling off her guardians because Pete and his two main henchmen had gone to the Cummings' retreat in Arizona.

"Hurray! I'm free!" When one of the lawyers passing in the hall gave her a startled look, she stretched the phone cord and pushed her office door closed with her toes. Back behind her desk she asked Jim, "Jeanie? Has she been liberated too?"

"Slim is driving them to Susan's as I speak. I've invited she, Troy and Susan to our celebratory dinner tonight. Hope that's okay. Our reservations are for six." His voice became muffled, but she made out his saying, "Be right there." He came back to her and asked, "Carrie?"

"I'm in a bit of a shock. Everything's happening so quickly. But I'll be fine. Go to your meeting. Attend to your pipes."

"That's my gal. See you at six at the Mac."

The phone went dead, and Carrie leaned back in her reclining chair hardly able to believe she would no longer have babysitters, no longer have to constantly look over her shoulder and in her rear view mirror for Cummings. It would take getting used to.

She attacked her pile of memos and documents with renewed gusto. Half an hour later Susan popped her head in to say,

"Just because the creep is in Arizona doesn't mean you can relax. I told Troy and Jeanie the same thing a few hours ago, but who listens to a mother? You never know what Cummings has up his sleeve."

"Thank you for that vote of confidence." Carrie slammed down the report she was reading but Susan was impervious to her sarcasm and continued,

"Those kids are acting as if they've just been released from prison. You better expect them at your office anytime soon." She waved, "See you around."

Carrie did her best to concentrate on the report, but she finally put down her pen and stared out into space. Why wasn't she more elated at the news that Cummings was in far off Arizona? Because it was unfinished business. Could she go back to her former life as she had described it to Dave? Work, golf and skiing, fun and games until she retired and then more of the same? She realized with a jolt that her war with Peter Cummings had vitalized her existence. Her grieving had been put on the back burner as all her energies had been focused on defeating her enemy. She needed some sort of closure with the bastard. Almost like ending an affair. She shook her head to dispel the thought.

Ten o'clock. Coffee break. She grabbed her mug and rounded her desk just as Dave stepped through her office door.

"You're still here!" She cried in delight, but he did not smile. He gripped her arms and asked,

"Can we talk here?"

Carrie looked at his grim face and nodded, pointing to her conference table. He closed the door, sat down heavily across from her and said in a dull, lifeless voice,

"It's the Padoroskis. They're dead. Both of them."

Carrie stared at him, unable to process the meaning of his words. She finally stammered, "How?"

Dave hunched forward, his arms on the table, "They were coming back from an early morning medical appointment when they hit a moose on that dirt road. Just over the rise. Do you remember the little hill before the farm?"

She nodded vaguely. He pushed back from the table and leaned his elbows on his thighs. She had never seen Dave so twitchy. He directed his words to the rug,

"This is what the RCMP have pieced together. The Padoroskis hit the moose as they were accelerating down the hill. The moose slid across the hood into the windshield. The impact caused the truck to swerve off the road and they probably lost the moose at this point. The truck hit a telephone pole, blew up and burst into flames. The fire eventually took down the pole and all its wires. By the time the firefighters and police got to the scene, it was just a smoldering mess."

Carrie broke the long silence that followed, "That lovely old couple. They must have been terrified." Tears welled in her throat as she envisioned Constancia's eyes wide in fright and Albert's frantic attempts to do something.

Dave shuffled, "I don't think they would have had much time to be terrified. It would have been quick."

"Quick?" Carrie shouted at him. "Burning to death is quick?" She bent her head and swallowed a few sobs in tight gulps. A concerned typist looked through her window and knocked at the door, but Carrie waved her off. Dave rose to put his arms around her, trying to soothe her.

She shook him off impatiently, "So nobody actually witnessed the accident?"

"It appears not," Dave answered. "The lady on the neighboring farm saw the flames and smoke and phoned it in. I'm just regurgitating the RCMP's initial report." He reached for her hand, "They found the moose in the bush by following the blood drops in the snow." Stoking her fingers he added, "They had to shoot it."

Carrie shook her head and stated emphatically, "Cummings did it."

Dave's head shot up, "Carrie, my love, Pete is in Arizona."

"I don't know how he did it, but I know, I just know with the certainty of death that Peter Cummings is responsible for the Padoroskis' murder." She stood and paced the small area between the conference table and her desk, back and forth until Dave, blocking her path, said in a pleading voice,

"Come here and listen to me."

She ignored him and went to the window as he tried to reason with her, "Do you really think Pete somehow penned the moose and set it free when he saw the Padoroski truck come over the rise?"

"Yes, it's possible." She turned, "You worked for the man. Surely you know that he is capable of any felony." She looked up when Jim entered without knocking. She did not acknowledge him but placed herself, arms akimbo, directly in front of Dave and said,

"How convenient for Cummings. How expedient. The only witnesses to his throwing Jeanie's baby into the tailings pond are now dead. Silenced. Pete is an extreme opportunist, and he always believes the ends justifies the means. He adopts practices regardless of the sacrifice to moral principles. Because he hasn't got any. His only system of values is money." She turned to lean against her desk, "Hello, Jim."

Both men were silent as they watched her walk around her desk, sit down and pick up the abandoned report. She did look up when Jim started to speak,

"I only heard the last of your...of your spiel, Carrie, but I tend to agree with--"

"Pete did it, Jim." She slammed down the report. "Now it's up to us to prove it."

Dave and Jim nodded to each other and pulled the two chairs from the conference table to sit across from her. The three of them threw out suggestions for a course of action.

"Like The Three Musketeers", Carrie thought, "Prepared to face the foe."

"Damn," Dave commented. "We need a critical path here."

Carrie passed him a sheaf of paper and for the next few hours they came up with several possible courses of action to bring Peter Cummings to justice. Jim's cell phone rang, and they listened to him arrange to meet Barry at one o'clock.

Dave glanced at his watch, "I've got a lunch date. I'll meet you at the Mac at six."

Carrie nodded and gave him a bleak smile, "We'll have to work at making it a celebratory dinner now. But with Jeanie and Troy, you and Jim…" She stopped and turned to Jim, "Why don't we invite Aunt Lottie?"

"Don't think she'll come but I'll give it a try." Jim waved as he went out, "Ciao."

Her egg salad sandwich tasted like squashed rubber as she applied herself and her red marking pen to the same report she had picked up hours ago. By twelve thirty her hand was cramped. She was clenching and unclenching it when Peter Cummings walked through her door. He closed it behind him, plunked himself down in front of her desk and growled,

"We need to talk."

"I have absolutely nothing to talk to you about." She reached for her phone but his big hand clamped over hers.

"Alone." His lips curled in a smirk as he made himself comfortable in the chair and said, "We'll start with the golf game where you dumped me into that dirty slough."

She took a deep breath, "You know perfectly well it was your fault the cart tipped."

Shaking his head he unbuttoned his stylish three-quarter length camel hair coat, and unwound the white silk scarf around his neck letting it fall loosely down his still massive chest. He placed his matching camel hair peaked hat on the corner of her desk, and she noticed the toll his diet had taken. His jowls were now loose and flaccid, the lines on his pale, almost grey, face more pronounced. His eyes were sunken into his skull under thick grey--black eyebrows.

"Let's cut to the chase." He pulled his chair closer knocking his knees against the front of her desk.

She waited calmly, hoping at least one of the staff would get back from lunch early. Where was everyone? She prayed for someone, anyone, to walk into the outer office.

"Here's my proposition," he announced in his gravelly voice. "I will not process assault charges against you for kicking me in the balls if you produce Jeanie. Without the kid, Troy."

"Produce Jeanie?" She repeated in disbelief.

"Yeah. My wife, Jeanie." He leaned forward to peer at her. His recessed eyes looked like two bullet holes in a sheet of grey metal. "Surely that's not too much to ask. For a husband to see his wife?"

"Jeanie will never agree to see you. Surely you know that." She glanced surreptitiously at her watch, but he noticed. Of course he noticed, as he slouched back in the chair and drawled,

"We've got lots of time, sweetheart. Your boyfriends and that dyke think I'm at my ranch in Arizona. Davey boy took me to the airport, stood with me when I bought a one-way ticket. But he couldn't come into the departures lounge and I got away. Even cashed in my ticket behind his back." He huffed a terse laugh. "Now. Where is Jeanie?"

"You're crazy as a coot and--"

"Carrie?" Jim's voice reached them from the outer office.

"Shit!" Pete jumped up, grabbed her wrist and twisted. A bone cracked, Carrie screamed, and he whispered, "Tit for tat, sweetheart." He hurried to the door and yelled, "Get her for me, bitch!"

He collided with a desk, but quickly recovered. Jim held out his hand and tried to block the door of the outer office to the hall. But Pete shoved his shoulder into Jim's midriff sending him flailing against the opposite wall with a loud smack. Jim slid down the wall, still grasping Pete's white scarf in his hand. He squatted and using the wall as a brace he sidled up. He glanced at Pete's receding back, then at a pale Carrie. His indecision prompted her to yell,

"Go after him! Don't let him get away! I'm okay."

But she wasn't "okay". She supported her left wrist in her right arm and saw that a bump had appeared on the back of her left hand. Why? It was her wrist that was dangling and hurting. She heard the elevator ding as Jim prevaricated and knew that Pete was long gone. Again. She turned away in despair. Now they would never get Cummings to trial. He would just disappear, Jeanie or no Jeanie.

Jim dialed 911. She wandered to the window nursing her wrist and gazed absently onto the street below. Jim came to stand beside her. They had a bird's eye view of the intersection from the fourth floor window.

"He said 'tit for tat', Carrie murmured.

"What?" Jim asked as he put his arm around her.

"My wrist." She leaned the back of her head on his shoulder. "Probably because I stomped on his wrist to get his gun. In the playground."

He finally noticed her wrist. "Jesus, Carrie. It looks broken."

"There he goes!" She leaned forward to watch Pete emerge from her building, turn right and run between the crowd of office workers returning from lunch.

"The bastard is getting away." Jim said in frustration. "And you need a doctor."

But they both remained glued to the window, following Pete's movements.

Hatless and with his open coat flapping behind him, he had reached the intersection and was about to cross with the light when he looked back. Possibly to check if anyone was behind him. He froze.

"Oh, no!" Carrie cried when her eyes tracked his.

He was staring at Jeanie and Troy on the other corner. They were waiting for the light to change, laughing, huddled close, looking into each other's eyes and completely oblivious to the menace across from them.

Pete whirled, pushed aside a couple of older women and jumped down the curb with his head up and his eyes focused only on Jeanie.

Screams, honking horns and squealing brakes reached Carrie and Jim through the glass. The front end of a Ford half-ton had picked up Pete as he slipped on the snow-covered asphalt. It was difficult to say whether he slid into the truck or whether the truck hit him squarely. In any case, his open coat caught on the grill's blue oval crest, Ford's signature symbol. Carrie sucked in her breath as Pete hung there for a second before the momentum of the truck propelled him off. The double tires of the half-ton bumped over the top half of Peter Cummings before the driver was able bring the truck to a screeching halt.

Carrie and Jim had a good view of the stricken body. Blood seeped from under the truck's tires onto the snow and ice in the gutter. She shook uncontrollably and still supporting her lower left arm, she buried her head in Jim's chest. His arms went around her carefully as he continued to watch the scene below. The strident sounds of multiple sirens brought his attention back to Carrie. He released her, stood back and looked at her swollen hand and wrist.

"Is it broken?" Carrie whispered as the pain registered.

"I think it probably is. Here, I can at least put it in a sling." He gently slipped Pete's scarf under her forearm and tied it at her neck. He kissed her quickly and said, "Let's get you to emergency."

"We'll never get through that…" She gestured to the window with her chin.

But Jim was talking to 911 again, explaining the situation. He pocketed his cell phone, plucked her coat off the wall hook and draped it over her shoulders.

"Come on, you brave old girl. My Spartan. My beloved. We'll meet your ambulance at the back door."

Chapter 41

Susan's breath whistled out in an exasperated sigh, "Wait another week. At least until your wrist is healed completely and the cast is off. Wait until all the details of this Cummings' mess are sorted out once and for all."

That's what I have a lawyer for," Carrie retorted. Using her right hand, she tucked her bathing suit along the side of her full suitcase. Charlie, lying with his head on his forepaws, watched her every move with baleful eyes. "Thanks for looking after Charlie. He should cheer up in a few days." She picked up her glass of wine and sat on the bed.

"Yeah, maybe." Susan sounded doubtful as she fiddled with the dog leash. "Will you be safe by yourself at this island retreat?"

Carrie smiled. "Of course. Dad..." She sucked in her breath. Why couldn't she say his name without getting teary? She started again, "My father's estate employs a local couple, year round. Mateo and Sofia--they live in one of the guest cottages and they're meeting me at the Port au Prince airport. I've known them forever. They taught me Spanish, which I've mostly forgotten now."

"What will you do all day?" Susan asked, still skeptical.

"Swim, walk, read, refresh my Spanish. Veg out," Carrie set her glass down.

"And worry about what's happening here," Susan picked up a pair of socks from the floor and handed it to her.

"No, that's what I have you for," Carrie said as she tried to close the case. "Damn. I'll have to take out the book Jim loaned me." She rummaged through her folded clothes, found the book, but dislodged a plastic bag which Susan picked up and asked,

"What the hell is this?"

Carrie removed it from the bag and held it up, "This is a hood ornament with my name replacing "Lagonda" on the emblem. From Alvena's Aston Martin." She put the shining feather pendant around her neck and beamed at her friend, "You like?"

Susan shaded her eyes against its silver glitter and nodded her approval, "Well, it's certainly unusual. Which one of those jocks gave it to you? Don't answer that--give me one solid reason for your leaving right now."

"I have had it up to here," She reached to the ceiling. "With dude-dominated boards who speak the environmental talk while they blithely flout the laws. While their governments look the other way. They toss me off as a "zealot" while their money and power scorns morality." She drained her wine glass and held it out for more.

"Come on, Carrie." Susan filled the extended glass to the brim. "You know these rich Albertans who serve on boards are conditioned from birth to believe that Liberal federal governments are out to screw them. So why not ignore their laws and regulatory restrictions?"

Carrie cradled her full glass thoughtfully before taking a few sips. Her cast clicked against the glass' stem, but the wine fueled the manic energy that pulsed through her body as she tackled her favorite topic. "These emission credits the government has introduced are arbitrary. They make companies look as though they're advancing to net zero, but in reality, the carbon intensity of their emissions remains high. Those credits are just permits to contaminate the air and water around us." She paused, "Haven't we discussed this before?" She drank more wine and continued her exhortation, "Humans have no business trying to save the planet. Earth preceded us and will survive us. Instead, the race to tackle pollution is about saving ourselves, by preserving an environment that keeps the planet habitable for our descendants."

"Carrie..." Susan tried to interrupt.

"This is exactly what I'm running away from; companies that are putting too much emphasis on the 'net' and not on the 'zero'; companies who are protecting the business interests of prominent Liberals; people who sink to even lower levels when real money is involved; those misogynic pricks whose rhetoric on the need to get off fossil fuels is so completely false and phony; the political money junkies out for every dollar they can be bribed with." She looked out the frost rimmed window. "And to get away from this lung piercing cold."

Susan shook her head in admiration, "You are so eloquent when you're drunk but I don't think 'misogynic' is a word."

Carrie took off her necklace, holding it up to the light again before sliding it back into the bag. She tucked her treasure into a side pocket and closed her case. "Let's get something to eat before the taxi comes." She bent to pat her wagging dog. "I need this trip right now, Sue."

"I know you do," Susan agreed. "The purple shadows under your eyes can attest to that."

....

Two weeks later, Carrie rose from the king-size bed, yawned and checked the clock. She had slept almost twenty hours. She showered and checked the fridge. As expected, Mario and Sofia had filled it with local fresh fruit and vegetables, complete with sweet rolls from Sofia's oven. The electric coffeemaker needed only a poke of her finger. She piled a plate leaving an empty space for her dad's favorite mug. When the coffee was ready, she went out to the porch and sat in a reclining chair. The melodies of tanagers and motnots mingled in a lovely bird chorus. A single scarlet ibis jerked his long bill down into the ocean shore searching for his breakfast.

Feeling replete with good, healthy food she wandered down to stand in the shallows of the Gulf of Paria. The waves quietly whished, ebbing and flowing over her feet and the sand. She peered through the light mist trying in vain to make out the coast of Venezuela. Keeping her cast high, she sank down in the sand and let the cool, saltwater wash over her lower body.

"Hey, the tide's coming in! Don't get that cast wet." Mateo, his eyes crinkled with worry, hovered over her. He bent down, helped her up and wished her a Merry Christmas in Spanish.

"Feliz Navidad to you too. What time is it?" Carrie smiled her thanks.

"Almost drink time." He pointed out a passing boat and waved.

The boat sat low in the water and familiar Christmas melodies lifted across the waves over the sound of the motor and the wind. Mateo shook out her towel and walked with her to the showers.

She washed off the sand and salt water under the outdoor shower, and on her way past Sofia and Mateo's cottage she called through their open window to request a later dinner. They called "Feliz Navidad", and Carrie wondered why Sofia giggled behind her hand. "Must be my Spanish", Carrie thought as she wrapped the towel more securely around her middle-aged body. She went directly into the bathroom to wash her hair with one hand and stayed under the shower until the water ran cold. Shivering, she dried her back and front awkwardly and gave her legs a quick once-over. She emerged from the bathroom bending her head to wrap the towel turban-like around her hair as she bumped the door closed with her hip.

"Merry Christmas!" Jim and Dave called from their perches against the headboard of the king bed. They raised their champagne glasses and patted the space between them.

Carrie dropped the towel and, protecting her wrist, took a flying leap into their arms.